Praise for SWEET REVENGE

"*Sweet Revenge* is an intense, fast-paced read. A strong plot, memorable characters, genuine emotions—not to mention plenty of heat. What more can a reader want?"
—Sherry Thomas, author of *Tempting the Bride*

"*Sweet Revenge* is a sexy, action-packed romance with a to-die-for hero and a true love that will make you swoon."
—*New York Times* bestselling author Courtney Milan

"A dark, riveting tale from beginning to end. Zoë Archer's books are not to be missed!"
—*USA Today* bestselling author Alexandra Hawkins

SWEET
Revenge

ZOË ARCHER

St. Martin's Paperbacks

This is a work of fiction. All of the characters, organizations, and events portrayed in this novel are either products of the author's imagination or are used fictitiously.

SWEET REVENGE

Copyright © 2013 by Zoë Archer.
Excerpt from *Dangerous Seduction* copyright © 2013 by Zoë Archer.

All rights reserved.

For information address St. Martin's Press, 175 Fifth Avenue, New York, NY 10010.

ISBN: 978-1-250-01559-4

Printed in the United States of America

St. Martin's Paperbacks edition / June 2013

St. Martin's Paperbacks are published by St. Martin's Press, 175 Fifth Avenue, New York, NY 10010.

10 9 8 7 6 5 4 3 2 1

To Zack, for his unwavering strength and love

ACKNOWLEDGMENTS

I'd like to thank my unbelievably awesome editor, Holly Blanck, who loves the world of Nemesis, Unlimited, as much as I do. Thanks also to my agent, Kevan Lyon, for her continued kickassery. I'd also like to thank Danielle Fiorella for giving me such a gorgeous, pitch-perfect cover, and Elizabeth Wildman for her excellent copy. And last, but most assuredly not least, I want to thank the women of The Loop That Shall Not Be Named, because, in addition to being incredibly smart, funny, and filthy, they have been a source of sanity and fellowship in times when I have desperately needed both.

CHAPTER ONE

Yorkshire, England, 1886

Most prison escapes took months, sometimes years, of planning. Jack Dalton had one day.

He stood in the rock-breaking yard of Dunmoor Prison, hammer in hand, waiting for the warder to secure a shackle around his ankle, chaining him to the other convicts. Unrelenting afternoon sun beat down on him and the two dozen men. Squinting, Jack stared up at the sky.

Bloody perfect. The only sodding day it's clear on the moors, and it's the day I have to break out of this shithole.

It didn't matter if ten thousand suns shone in the sky. He had to get out today.

Lynch, the warder, moved from convict to convict, fastening iron bands around each man's ankle, and the band attached to a chain that stretched between the prisoners, who stood in two parallel rows. The chain rattled whenever someone moved. A scar encircled Jack's ankle, a thick ridge of skin he had developed after five years of hard labor. The first few months had been rough. The shackle had dug into his requisition striped worsted stockings, gouging into the flesh beneath until he'd bled.

The wound had gone putrid, a fever had burned through him, and he had almost lost not just the leg but his life. Yet Jack was a tough bastard. Always had been. Hatred kept a bloke tough. He lived, kept the leg, and got stronger.

Today he would need all of his strength. Impatience stung like hornets beneath his skin. Lynch was almost done with the first row of convicts. In another minute, the warder would start moving down Jack's line, and then the window of opportunity would slam shut. Already, Jack's gaze moved through the yard, looking toward the thirty-foot-high wall that kept the convicts of Dunmoor from the miles of rolling country, and the freedom that lay beyond.

"D.3.7., eyes straight ahead!"

Jack's gaze snapped back to a blank stare, retreating behind the false front of apathy. No one had called him by his name in over five years. Sometimes he forgot he had a name, just a letter and a number. Once, he'd been Diamond Dalton—not because he favored diamonds. Hell, he had never owned a single diamond, and had seen a real one only a handful of times. No, they called him Diamond because he'd been formed by crushing pressure into the hardest thing to walk the streets of London.

Only Edith had called him Jack. Sometimes, when she was feeling nostalgic for their childhood, she had called him Jackie.

"Jackie," she had whispered, reaching up to him with a blood-spattered hand. "Jackie, take me home." And then she had died.

Even after all this time, the memory scoured Jack. The burn of rage pulsed through him. He knew it better than his own heartbeat. It was more important than the beat of his heart, for anger remained the only thing that kept him alive. Anger, and the need for vengeance. He would have his revenge soon.

Lynch reached Jack's row. It had to be now.

"Oi," Jack whispered to the convict standing next to him. "Stokes!"

The thick-jawed man flicked his gaze toward Jack, then straight ahead. "Shut it, idiot!" The punishment for talking could be the lash, or if the governor was feeling particularly brutal, time in the dark cell, deprived of light and all human interaction. Sometimes for weeks. Men went mad in the dark cell. God knows Jack almost did.

He didn't fear punishment now. The only thing that scared him was not making his escape in time.

"You hear Mullens is getting out next week?"

"So what? I ain't gettin' out for eight months."

Jack's sentence had been much longer, thanks to the manipulation of the justice system. If he didn't try this breakout, he would be stuck in Dunmoor for thirty-seven more years. Making him seventy-three years old by the time he tottered out the front gate—if he survived that long.

He would likely die today. So long as he took care of his business beforehand, he didn't much care about dying afterward. It wasn't as though his life merited clinging to.

"I heard . . ." Jack glanced quickly at Mullens, who stood in the row in front of them, and then at Lynch, moving closer. "When he gets out, he's going straight to your mollisher."

Stokes frowned at the mention of his woman. "Lizzie? But he ain't even met her."

Jack shrugged. "Maybe he heard you talking about her so nice, he had to see for himself. Said he'd give it to her right good. And she'd want it, too, not having a man around all this time." He clapped his mouth shut as Lynch approached.

The warder glowered at Jack. "Better not be talking, D.3.7. The governor got a new flogging pillory, and he's keen to try it." Lynch's eyes gleamed with eagerness.

"No, sir."

"What's that?" Lynch leaned closer. "Sounded like talking."

Jack shook his head, hating the bastard. Some of the warders were decent enough, just trying to do a job for rubbish pay, but other screws, like Lynch, enjoyed their power and spent their time thinking up new ways to bully and harass the prisoners. Lynch particularly liked making up perceived infractions.

With a smirk, Lynch bent down and secured the shackle around Jack's ankle. *Damn it.* He'd been hoping to goad Stokes enough before the shackle was clapped on, but Lynch had put an end to that plan.

It took everything Jack had not to smash his sledge-hammer down onto Lynch's head, knocking off the warder's blue shako hat and spilling his brains all over the rock-breaking yard.

Stay fixed on your goal, Dalton. Killing Lynch might be satisfying, but it also meant he'd be taken down by the other warders, locked in the dark cell for months, and then dragged out only to be hanged.

So he let Lynch finish fastening the shackle and move on, keeping the bastard warder's brains inside his skull.

"Next week," Jack hissed at Stokes. "Mullens goes for Lizzie."

Stokes wasn't known for having a long fuse. He exploded like a burning arsenal at the smallest hint of provocation.

"I'll beat your damned face in," Stokes snarled. The

convict broke rank, lunging for Mullens. Everyone in the row stumbled forward, pulled by the connecting chain.

Startled, Mullens barely had time to turn around before Stokes tackled him. Convicts fell, shouting out in anger and confusion. Others cheered Stokes on as he rained punches down on Mullens. More yelling filled the yard as warders came running. Chaos filled the enclosure, a blur of the dark blue warders' uniforms and the pale, coarse uniforms of the convicts. Fists were thrown. Some of the warders had clubs, beating down the prisoners whether they fought or no. Jack grunted when he caught the back of a club across his shoulder, but he didn't fall.

Bedlam, everywhere.

Now.

Hefting his hammer, Jack brought it down hard onto the chain binding him to the other convicts. The thick links shuddered, but stayed intact. He slammed the hammer down again, and again. The vibrations carried all the way up into his leg, jarring him until his teeth rattled. The weight of the hammer felt like nothing. He'd been swinging it for five years. When he had been tried and convicted of attempted murder, he'd already been strong. Now, years of hard labor had transformed him, and the heavy hammer felt like a bird's hollow bone.

He kept on pounding until, at last, the chain broke.

He ran from the yard. Sounds of fighting and confusion echoed behind him. No one noticed him amid the chaos.

His thoughts spun out of control, his heart racing like a locomotive, but he forced himself to be cold, logical. In his mind, he pictured the layout of the prison. Six main buildings radiated out like spokes, with narrow walls leading straight out from three of those buildings toward the huge double walls that encircled the whole prison. He'd never be able to climb the outer wall, not without a ladder, and those were in short supply in the clink. Instead of heading straight to the wall, Jack ran toward one of the smaller, two-story buildings that served as a dormitory for the unmarried warders who lived on prison grounds.

Pressing himself back against a low outbuilding, Jack watched as warders streamed out of the dormitory, all of them speeding toward the yard. Too focused on the riot, none of them saw him.

Once he felt certain the warder house had cleared, he sprinted to it. He tried the door. Locked. Jack swung his hammer again. It pounded against the lock, splintering the edge of the door. Finally, the door flew open.

Jack quickly took in the rows of tables covered with the remains of half-finished tea, the potbellied stove in the corner, photographic prints of the queen and the royal family. Nothing here would help him. He ran the stairs two at a time, the wooden steps shaking beneath his heavy boots.

Upstairs, beds formed two orderly lines. Unlike the convicts, who had to roll their straw mattresses up every morning for inspection, these beds were all made, tight as a parson's arse. Jack wondered what it would be like to sleep on actual horsehair, or even feathers. He couldn't remember if he ever had. What would it matter? His next sleep would be his last.

He ran between the rows of beds, until he reached the window at the far end of the room. Setting the hammer down, he pushed the window open. Unfortunately, he needed both hands for this next stage, so the hammer had to stay behind. Having a weapon was added insurance, but his fists could inflict plenty of damage. He planned on using them later, beating Lord Rockley into pulp, and then wrapping his fingers around the murderer's throat until his breathing stopped.

Jack smiled grimly to himself. He couldn't wait.

Climbing from the window, Jack hauled himself out, grabbed hold of the roof's edge and pulled himself up onto the roof.

Jack crouched down. From his vantage, he could see the continued commotion in the yard, convicts and warders brawling. He turned his gaze from the riot to the rest of the prison. Never had he seen it from so far up. The windows in the cells were tiny notches set high in the wall, and the only way to look out of them would be to stand on a bucket or a stool. But that was a punishable offense, so he seldom tried it.

He didn't care about the prison anymore. All that mattered was the rolling heath that surrounded the prison, stretching out for miles. That's what he had to reach. The next stage of his escape.

Still crouched low, Jack moved along the roof, until he positioned himself directly above a brick wall that stood about fifteen feet high. This wall ran straight toward the circular stone walls that surrounded the prison, the last obstacles between him and freedom.

He leaped down onto the brick wall. It was narrow, and he struggled for balance. He felt himself start to slip. Boots dug in for stability, he righted himself, then ran lightly along the top, heading toward the first stone wall. The two walls were the same height, and they intersected. He continued on the brick wall toward the final border at the edge of the prison, looming ahead. Below him was the barren outer yard. No one ever walked among the patches of dead earth and dying weeds. It served as a space for attempted escapees to be caught before they reached the outside world. Sometimes, Jack had heard gunfire, and the shouts of guards.

Sometimes, but not often. Few tried to escape, and even fewer made it.

"But I will," he muttered to himself.

It looked like he would, too. So far, no one had noticed him, too busy beating down the riot in the stone yard.

Jack sprinted the last stretch of the brick wall. The outer wall rose up taller than the one on which he ran, looming high and daunting. He shoved past uneasiness and kept on running, gaining momentum. Though his heavy boots wanted to drag him down, he leaped, scrabbling for a hold on the outer wall. His fingers clutched at the top edge, hands burning as they took the full brunt of his substantial weight.

As he hung there, someone at a distance shouted. "Oi! Escaping prisoner!"

Fuck. Jack did not waste time seeing which warder had spotted him. He pulled, hauling himself up.

"Stop immediately," the warder yelled, "or I'll be forced to shoot!"

Ignoring him, Jack continued to draw himself higher, muscles clenching with effort.

A whine, and then chips of granite exploded around him. Jack cursed. The warder had fired on him. Then did so again.

Jack didn't want to attempt crossing the moors leaking blood. He would lose precious energy, and he needed it to end Rockley's miserable life.

With a burst of strength, he heaved himself up, then over. Still dangling by his fingers, the ground spun thirty feet below. Here was another hazard. If he landed wrong, he'd break a leg, maybe his back. He couldn't hesitate, though. The screws and governor would be alerted to his escape, and he didn't have much time before they massed in pursuit.

Jack drew a breath, forcing himself to relax, then let go.

The ground rushed up to meet him, and he bent his knees in preparation for the landing. He hit the earth boots first, keeping on the balls of his feet. The impact jarred through him, and he quickly tucked his head against his chest and rolled.

Rocks dug into him as he tumbled. He fought to keep his wind and his stability. Finally, he slowed, and straightened to stand.

He staggered for a moment, balance thrown by the impact and roll. As the world settled from its mad spin, he saw the stretches of scrub-covered moor, the merciless blue sky. No walls, save for the ones behind him.

"Freedom," he said roughly.

But it wasn't true freedom. He had a responsibility to carry out, an obligation driving him to run toward certain death in pursuit of vengeance.

Voices rose up from the other side of the wall, warders assembling to go after him. He'd come down far from the main gate, though, and it would take the screws a few minutes to reach him.

With his head still reeling, he took off at a run, determined to lose himself in the moors.

Jack threw himself down beneath a thicket of gorse. Thorns scraped his face and tore his uniform, but his attention remained pinned on the sounds of shouting men and baying dogs. His lungs burned and his legs ached. For hours he'd been running across the heath, always staying just a few steps ahead of his pursuers. Mud spattered his clothes and face, blisters burned on his feet inside his heavy boots, and he felt himself more hunted animal than man.

But he was getting close. So close.

He waited, panting, listening.

"Seen him?"

"Think he went this way."

"We got to round him up soon. Night's falling."

"I got some tracks over here! And here's his jacket."

Jack held his breath. The screws' voices faded, and he allowed himself a small exhale. The dummy trail seemed to be working, but he wouldn't chance a dash until he was well sure the warders were gone.

He wanted to run, feeling time slip away like a slackening noose. His prey was near, and the predator in him wanted nothing more than to make the kill. But he had to be smart.

His mouth quirked in a bitter smile. No one had ever hired him for his brains. *Don't think, Diamond,* Fowler used to say. *You're a big, mean bastard. You're what keeps the riffraff from getting to his lordship.*

Fowler might be there tonight. Him, and Curtis. Maybe Voss. But Jack couldn't count on their friendship. Rockley paid them to do a job, and friendship didn't buy pints. So when Jack came for Rockley, he'd have to take the others out. Suited him just fine.

Jack's conscience was a mean thing, no bigger than a pebble. He'd mow down any obstacle to get what he was after, even men he once considered friends. His conscience had room for only two regrets: the first, that he hadn't protected Edith. And the second, that he'd failed the first time he had tried to kill Rockley.

This time, he'd get the job done.

He listened to the fading voices of the warders as twilight fell in heavy waves. His throat burned with thirst, his lips were cracked. He almost longed for the weak, piss-flavored beer they doled out at mealtimes in the prison.

The warders' chatter finally stopped. His false trail wouldn't distract them for long, though. Time to get moving again.

He scrambled out from beneath the gorse and studied the sky to get his bearings. The village of Cambrey was situated some four miles to the northeast of Dunmoor Prison, and that's where he would find the Queen's Consort Inn. The same inn where Rockley now stayed.

Keeping low to the ground, Jack ran.

It had been damned lucky, if a man like Jack could ever consider himself lucky. Only that very morning, he'd finished cleaning his cell. Usually, prisoners waited outside their cells during inspection, but as he was stepping out into the corridor, the inspecting warder had stopped him.

"Nice bit of news, eh, D.3.7.?"

Knowing he could not speak, Jack had only looked at the warder.

"That toff you tried to kill, Rockwell, Rockburn? Heard he's out at Cambrey, lodging at the inn. Guess he's here to hunt. Can't think of another reason why some la-di-da gent would come out to Satan's arsehole." The warder had laughed. "Ain't that a pretty business?"

No time to be surprised by the news. He'd had to act on the opportunity given to him. Jack had spent the hours between inspection and afternoon work fixing a plan for escape. Having Rockley so close, when he spent most of his time in London, had been chance, or fate, or, as the chaplain said, providence. And Jack wouldn't waste this rare opportunity.

Night fell in a thick black shroud. But distant lights served as his direction. He stumbled on, keeping that glimmering in his sight. It had to be the village of Cambrey. The final step of his journey to hell.

He kept well away from the rutted road leading into town, even though he spotted only one cart jouncing down the lane.

As he jogged nearer, the shapes of the village buildings turned solid and defined. Merchant shops, a church, a few houses lining the high street. The only building that snagged his attention, though, was the inn. It stood at one end of the high street, a two-story structure with a yard and a stable. Light poured from the windows, pushing back the darkness, and the sounds of a piano and cheerful talk tumbled out. Beyond the tuneless, cheerless hymns they sang in chapel, he hadn't heard music since before his imprisonment. He wanted to soak it in, the sounds of normal life. Music, gossip, and petty grievances that might result in sore feelings but not death.

It seemed everything in Jack's life resulted in death. Including his own.

Crouching behind a low stone wall, he assessed the inn. Lights shone in the second story. Some of the rooms looked small, cramped. Rockley wouldn't stay in any of those.

The room at the end, though, looked promising. It appeared larger than the other rooms, with a canopied bed and its own fireplace. The finest accommodations the inn had to offer. Rockley had always flaunted his wealth and rank, and it made sense that if he stayed at this inn, he'd take the best room in the place.

Jack's gut clenched when a man's silhouette appeared at the window. With the light behind him, it was impossible to make out details of the man's face, but he definitely had the size and form of Rockley. Tall, wide shoulders of a sportsman, and upright, proud posture that screamed out privilege and noble blood. The kind that literally got away with murder.

Hatred darkened Jack's vision, and he choked on bile. He spat on the ground.

Rockley moved away from the window, but he didn't appear to leave the room. Perfect.

Prowling through the shadows, Jack closed the distance to the inn, until he stood at the base of the inn's wall. Rockley likely had men in the taproom, if not outside his door. Jack had been one of those men once. He knew where they would be, and that they'd use fists and pistols to keep anyone from getting to his lordship.

Wiping his damp hands on his thighs, he stared up at the second story. Exhausted and thirsty, dizziness swamped him. *So bloody close.*

He shook his head, forcing it to clear, then began to climb. He grappled for hold into the masonry's gaps, pushing his fingers into the worn mortar. Biting back curses, he climbed higher, trying to go as quietly as possible. If he got caught now, with Rockley only twenty feet away, he'd lose his sodding mind.

Nearer, nearer. The window to Rockley's room drew closer. And as it did, Jack's pulse hammered violently, rage growing with each handhold, each inch higher.

Finally, his fingers closed around the windowsill. Thank the devil the night was a mild one, and Rockley had left the window open. No shattering glass to alert the men stationed in the corridor or downstairs. With a final heave, Jack pulled himself up and through the window, and then he stood in the room.

He'd almost reached his goal, and now he was ready to kill. But he froze before taking a single step.

He faced the most beautiful woman he'd ever seen. Trim and tall, blond hair, sherry-brown eyes. Angular jaw and unsmiling mouth. Clothing smart but not fancy. And she pointed a revolver at his head.

* * *

Evangeline Warrick stared at the man at the other end of her Webley .450. Though calling him a man seemed inapt. The term *brute* had been coined to describe such a . . . male.

Dark eyes, wild as an animal's, burned into her. He took a step toward her.

"Hands, Mr. Dalton." Eva was careful to keep her voice steady, calm. "Let me see them."

"Easy, love." He spoke as though calming a startled horse. "Not here to hurt you." He took another step closer.

Eva cocked her gun, her aim holding. "Put up your hands, Mr. Dalton. And do not take another step."

His hands came up, and dear God, were they big. Just like the rest of him.

"I just want Rockley," he said. His accent was rough, his voice deep.

"You aren't going to get him."

Dalton raised a brow. Or she *thought* he did. In truth, grime coated the convict so thoroughly, she could barely make out the details of his face. Mostly, she saw those eyes, keen and hard. She had seen the gazes of desperate men before, men driven to the very edge, but none of them sent a thrill of caution down her spine the way Jack Dalton's eyes did.

"Now he's using women as bullies?" His mouth curled into a sneer. "Gun or no, you'd be wise to be careful around Rockley. Better yet, put a bullet in *his* brain, not mine."

"That isn't how we work," she answered.

"We?"

"We," answered Simon, stepping from the shadows in the corner. Marco came forward, as well. Neither of them had their weapons out, though they were both armed. They knew she could handle herself with a gun, and trusted her to keep Dalton reasonably controlled. She knew precisely where to shoot a man to incapacitate him.

Dalton snarled, his gaze darting back and forth between Simon and Marco. Then back to her. "Where's Rockley?"

"Not here," she replied.

"Tell me where he is." Menace poured from Dalton in waves, and Eva wondered if she truly was going to use her revolver. She didn't want to. Shooting a man could be loud and messy, and complicate things unnecessarily.

"In London, I presume."

"I was told—"

"That Lord Rockley was staying here," Marco supplied. "It's what is known as *baiting the trap*."

Dalton moved far more quickly than his size would suggest, and too quickly for even an experienced shot like Eva to fire. One moment, he stood near the window, hands upraised. The next, he had Marco on the floor, one hand around Marco's throat. Marco fought against him, but Dalton's sheer size and brawn rendered Marco's training almost useless.

Simon got himself behind Dalton and looped his arm around Dalton's neck. He grasped his wrist to capture Dalton in a headlock.

Stepping close, Eva placed the muzzle of her Webley against Dalton's temple, making sure that, if she had to fire, she wouldn't hit her colleagues.

"If you want your chance at vengeance," she said, low and quick, "release Marco immediately."

Slowly, Dalton's hand uncurled from around Marco's throat. The only sound in the room came from Marco, dragging air back into his lungs and coughing. Simon kept his arm tight around Dalton's neck, slightly loosening the pressure so the convict would not asphyxiate.

"Go sit on the bed, Mr. Dalton," Eva commanded. "And I ought to warn you, this gun of mine has been complaining for weeks that it hasn't had a drop of blood. Do not give me a reason to satisfy its thirst."

Dalton stared at her from the corner of his eye. This close, she could see that his eyes were the color of darkest coffee, verging on black. A feral intelligence shone in his gaze, like a wolf learning the ways of man in order to stalk and kill human prey.

He had enough astuteness to recognize that he had to comply. He nodded tightly.

Simon released his hold on Dalton and stepped away. With that peculiar savage grace of his, Dalton rose up. Marco scrambled to his feet, rubbing at his throat and scowling.

Eva edged back, not wanting to be within striking distance of Dalton. And his size made her distinctly uncomfortable. She was not a small woman, nor especially delicate, but she knew with absolute clarity that Dalton could snap her into matchsticks.

He sent her a glare, then walked toward the bed. As lightly as he moved, his boots still shook the floorboards. She had heard that the boots of prisoners were especially heavy, weighing as much as fourteen pounds, as if trying to pin them to the ground. Yet the sheer muscle mass of Dalton seemed to rattle the whole inn. Did the governors of prisons realize that hard labor turned rough men into weapons? Dalton's arms appeared to be as thick and tough as coiled rope.

Approaching the canopied bed, he eyed it warily.

"Sit," she ordered.

Teeth gritted, he did so. Strange—he looked almost

uncomfortable. Eva had sat upon the bed earlier and
felt its plush softness. One could have a very good sleep
there. Or a very pleasant night with the right company.

Realization struck her. For the past five years, Dalton
knew only his crude bed in Dunmoor Prison. At best,
that meant a straw mattress on an iron-slatted frame,
with coarse woolen blankets for warmth. Such luxury
as this feather mattress and the fine-combed cotton bed-
clothes must feel alien to him, or worse, a taste of comfort he had not experienced in a long time—if ever.

She shook her head. Dalton was a means to an end.
Likely he would crush the life out of her without a
moment's hesitation. She could not afford to feel sympathy for him, or endow him with a sentiment he probably didn't feel.

In his filthy and torn prison uniform, radiating animal energy, he presented a strange picture as he sat
upon the rosewood bed, lacy fabric hanging from the
canopy. Everything looked impossibly fragile in comparison.

"Talk," Dalton growled. "Tell me who you lot are,
and how you know my name."

She almost smiled at this. The gun was in *her* hands,
and yet he had the boldness to issue a command.

"We know all about you," she replied.

"There's a file at headquarters," added Simon. He
held his fingers an inch apart. "This thick."

Eva had studied the file thoroughly, including the
photograph from Dalton's admission into prison.
Sometimes, prisoners fought against having their pictures taken, since it meant having their face on record.
More than a few photographs showed prisoners contort-
ing their faces to disguise their features, or being held
down by force. Not Dalton.

He had stared at the camera boldly, defiantly. *Take a good look,* his expression seemed to challenge. The countenance of a man who had nothing left to lose.

But he *did* have something to lose. Eva and her colleagues counted on it.

"Headquarters." Suspicion sharpened Dalton's gaze. "You're coppers?"

"Strictly a private organization," she said. "We operate entirely outside of official channels. No one in the CID or government knows we exist."

"Which is precisely how we want it," Marco added.

"Mercenaries," Dalton surmised.

Eva smiled a little at that. "Of a sort."

"So, Rockley hired you to lure me out of Dunmoor." He snorted. "Couldn't kill me behind bars, so he finds a way to kill me on the other side of the wall."

"We do *not* work for Rockley," she insisted, voice tight. The very idea that they would work with someone like the baron filled her with a toxic sickness.

"Then who *do* you work for?"

"A girl. You wouldn't know her." She kept her gun pointed at him. He would be waiting for her to drop her guard, but that was not going to happen. "About a month ago, this young woman, whom I'll call Miss Jones, was mostly wickedly seduced and abandoned. Her reputation was destroyed. Now she and her parents seek restitution, which we will help obtain."

"Some gentry mort falls for a line, winds up on her back, and I'm supposed to care?"

"The ruin of any woman isn't to be taken lightly." Simon spoke through gritted teeth. "And she isn't gentry. Just a merchant's daughter."

"Little difference." Dalton shrugged. "Girl gets charmed into opening her legs, winds up with a bastard child or nothing at all. And the gent goes about his merry business. Not saying it's right, but it's an old story."

"This time," said Eva, "the story will have a different ending."

"Cheers if you can make the cove pay." Cynicism dripped from Dalton's voice. "But what happened to the girl ain't my business."

"It will be," she answered.

He crossed his arms over his chest, and the coarse fabric of his shirt pulled against his muscles. Both Marco and Simon were exceptionally fit men—their work demanded it. But Dalton possessed an animal strength, brutal and uncivilized. Simon, Marco, and her other male colleagues were trained warriors. Dalton was a beast.

"Love," he rumbled, "I've got the screws hot on my tail. They'll be here in an hour—"

"Less," Marco said.

Dalton shot Marco a glare before returning his gaze to Eva. His words had been terse and impatient, but the way he stared at her made her think he hadn't seen a woman in a very long time.

"So either speak plain or shoot me," he continued, "'coz I don't plan on lingering."

She drew a breath. "The man who seduced Miss Jones is Lord Rockley."

Dalton's arms uncrossed as if readying for battle. His smirk fell away, replaced by cold, brutal hatred. Even knowing the details of Dalton's history, she had not fully anticipated seeing such naked enmity, devoid of all pity. A shiver struggled to work its way through her body, but she ruthlessly suppressed it. Dalton was the sort of man to exploit any weakness. She could show none.

"We're going to make Rockley pay." She made certain

to keep her voice level, as though the slightest hint of emotion would tip Dalton into crazed fury. "And you, Mr. Dalton, are going to help us. If you do not agree to do so, we'll keep you here until the warders arrive. Escaping from prison is a serious crime. One that will see you well punished." She stared coolly at him. "Time is running out, Mr. Dalton. A decision has to be made."

For a moment, he did not move, did not speak. Then, "Who the hell *are* you people?"

She spoke before Marco or Simon could answer. "Nemesis, Unlimited."

CHAPTER TWO

Stay and dance at the whim of this passel of bedlamites, or knock them all out and take his chances on the moors, with the screws closing in. Jack didn't like either choice. Still, it had been so long since he'd had any choice at all, even deciding between two bad options was a luxury.

"Don't plod over your decision," the woman said, cold as a knife between the ribs. "We'll need enough time to get out before the warders arrive."

Jack stared at her. Such a pretty piece, but full of poison. He'd known women like her, except they didn't have a gentry mort's fine words and manners to disguise their ruthlessness.

She stared back in challenge. Maybe it was on account of him not seeing a woman besides the prison laundresses for the past five years. Maybe he was a sick bastard who'd gotten even sicker during his incarceration. But something about the way this woman looked and spoke, with her unyielding spine and amber eyes, stirred him up.

For fuck's sake, she's got a gun on me.

"They're here." This from the blond toff, standing at the window. Voices from outside drifted up, the shouts of the warders as they roused the villagers.

"The critical moment is upon us, Mr. Dalton," the woman said. "Make your choice."

He stood, and noted with some satisfaction that the woman took a step back, putting more distance between them. "You've got a plan for getting out of this place?"

She tipped her chin up. "We always have plans."

"Then we go."

The two men and the woman shared a glance, a silent exchange that made Jack edgy. At least none of them looked nervous at the idea of getting away from the warders. When people were panicked, they made bad decisions.

Jack wasn't panicked, just determined.

The woman tucked her gun into a reticule as calmly as if she were stashing away a tin of comfits. "Do everything they tell you to," she said to him.

"If you wanted a dog," he answered, "you should've gone to the wharf."

"And if you want to stay out of prison, you'll do what you're told." She opened the door and walked out, her stride direct and purposeful. The warders' voices barked on the ground floor. Jack recognized the sound of Warder Lynch. Likely the bastard was eager to do Jack some violence.

The dark-haired gent shut and locked the door behind the woman, muting the sounds from below.

"Where's she going?" Jack demanded.

"Eva is buying us time," the darker man replied. "Which we're losing by hazing about up here."

Jack wondered if *buying time* meant that the woman—Eva—might use that revolver of hers on the warders. Trading bullets with the screws would be dangerous and messy, and she'd already proven that while she was dangerous, she wasn't messy. No, she was a tidy morsel, from the top of her pinned curls to the hem of her dress, with a lot of mettle in between.

"How are we looking out there, Simon?" the dark-haired man asked the blond.

"Damn warders are a bunch of low-pay amateurs," Simon muttered. "They've got no one patrolling the perimeter."

"Let's be grateful for a badly trained workforce." The dark man reached for Jack, but pulled his hand away when Jack reared back.

He didn't want anyone touching him. Nobody did before he went to prison, and he hated it when the screws shoved him around on his way to chapel or to the rock yards. They wouldn't touch him ever again.

Turning from the darker gent, he saw the blond one, Simon, straddling the open window.

"Going to assume you can climb down as well as up," he said, then disappeared as he eased out the window. Jack had to admit that the toff moved as slick as any second-story man leaving a burglary.

"That's Simon, incidentally. I'm Marco."

"I don't give a buggering damn."

"You ought, since we're all that's keeping your neck from being stretched." After shouldering a pack, Marco waved him toward the window. "Now climb."

Jack bit back a mouthful of curses. For now, he had to play the puppet. When the time came, however, he'd cut the damn strings, and maybe some throats, too.

After giving Marco a glare, Jack moved quickly to the window and climbed out. Cold air bit through his damp, thin uniform and the moors stretched out dark and empty beneath a sky just as barren. This time of year, he wouldn't last the night on the heath. Without shelter, he'd be nothing but frozen meat by morning.

These damned Nemesis people better have something lined up, or we'll all be freezing our arses off.

He balanced himself on the worn brick, then clambered down the wall. Glancing up, he saw Marco watching him from the window. Likely making sure he didn't cut and run.

Once the ground was near enough, he jumped the rest of the way down, landing in a crouch. Simon waited nearby, his gaze never resting, body poised for movement. The bloke looked like a toff, but he didn't carry himself like one. More like a soldier, or a thief.

Jack, too, kept his every sense alert, tense as piano wire. The screws were just inside—he could hear them questioning men in the taproom of the inn. Just hearing the scrape of Lynch's voice sent hot fury through Jack's muscles.

"I ain't going back," he muttered.

"You won't." Simon's words were clipped. "So long as you keep to the terms of our arrangement."

Before Jack could ask just what the hell that arrangement might be, Marco dropped down from the window, quiet as a serpent.

Whoever these people were, they had impressive skills. But it wasn't the two men Jack thought of. He could hear Eva inside, the low, clear notes of her voice plucking along the back of his neck.

"Time to run," Marco said. He nodded toward the west, a long stretch of open moorland that led to nothing. Nothing that Jack could see, at any rate.

"You can't just leave her in there." He wasn't about to carve Eva's name into his arm, but it didn't feel right abandoning her to the warders. There had to be at least eight screws in there. She was only one woman. Bad odds.

"Eva can take care of herself," Simon answered.

Jack looked back and forth between the two men. They held fast to the shadows, but he could see enough of their faces to read complete confidence there. Confidence in Eva.

He shrugged. She wasn't his woman. Never would be. If these blokes thought nothing of leaving her with a pack of edgy warders, he wouldn't stop them.

"My legs itch," he said. "Only thing that cures 'em is a run."

Simon nodded once and darted off. With Marco right on his heels, Jack followed, plunging into the darkness. It felt good to move again, despite his exhaustion. Too long inside prison walls had given him a permanent hunger for action, the need to feel his lungs and muscles burn from use.

Yet as he sped into the night, he couldn't stop himself from thinking of Eva, all alone, facing down a gang of warders on the hunt.

Hope she's as strong and clever as these blokes seem to think. She has to be.

Eva made her way down the stairs, careful to keep her pace brisk but unhurried. She was just a guest drawn from her room by the fuss downstairs. Her time constraints were narrow, needing to give the others a decent head start, but not so much that she'd have trouble catching up with them.

Her hand glided along the wooden rail worn smooth by generations of guests walking up and down these same stairs. The wood felt as solid as Dalton looked. He had the immovable will of an ancient oak, too. She could only hope he was following Simon and Marco's orders, and hadn't tried something stupid or obstinate, such as attempting to escape.

She reached the ground floor and, following the

sounds of commotion, headed toward the taproom. Fixing a curious but vacant expression on her face, she entered the large room. A group of warders were gathered there, their dark blue uniforms incongruous in the cheerful taproom. She recognized the hard eyes of professional guards, almost as dangerous as the clubs most of them carried.

Two of the warders were armed with shotguns, and the men in the taproom eyed the weapons nervously. These were firearms meant for hunting men, not grouse.

One of the armed warders stood close to the innkeeper. He twisted his hands in his apron as the warder interrogated him.

"He was heading in this direction. Got two eyewitnesses who spotted him making toward this inn."

"I've been down here in the taproom the last hour, and I haven't seen anyone."

The warder turned toward the other guards. "We split up and search the place. Inside and out."

She stepped into the doorway, effectively blocking it. "My goodness, what a to-do!" Inwardly, she shuddered at her breathy, vapid tone, but being part of Nemesis meant she had to do many things she found unpleasant. Including playacting the part of a featherbrained woman.

"What is all this ruckus about?" She stared with wide eyes at the warders. The guards removed their caps, deference at odds with the brutal bludgeons they carried.

The one guard who had been grilling the innkeeper spoke. "Are you a guest at this inn, ma'am?"

"I am, Mr. . . ." She glanced at the patch on his jacket. "Lynch. Goodness, you gentlemen look like soldiers in your ensembles. I wasn't aware there were any troops stationed nearby."

"We're warders, ma'am, from Dunmoor Prison. A very dangerous convict escaped today, but don't worry, we'll get him back. Alive or dead." He spoke this last word with particular enjoyment, as though looking forward to the prospect of killing Dalton.

"Convict?" Her hand came up to flutter at her throat. "You mean, a criminal is on the loose this very moment? But how very dreadful! Like something out of the penny papers."

The group of warders tried to edge past her, but she impeded them with a light sidestep.

"Have you seen any suspicious characters?" Lynch asked. "The man we're looking for is a big bast—uh, a big man. Dark hair, dark eyes. Answers to Dalton, but he might be using an alias."

"I have been alone in my room all evening and saw nothing. Surely if such a large villain had passed this way, I would have noticed something. And anyway, I thought this part of the country was supposed to be safe. Convicts escaping from prison! Never would I have dreamed up such a lurid tale."

As she spoke, she moved from side to side, as if thoughts of a fugitive made her restless and frightened. It also had the effect of preventing the warders from leaving the building or getting upstairs. She made certain her accent held the polished notes of a woman of quality, and for once she was grateful for the rigid code of social mores that kept the warders respectfully trapped. They wouldn't push a lady aside.

Apparently, though, even this code could reach its breaking point. One of the warders looked back at Lynch, unable to hide his frustration. "Sir?"

Lynch came closer. "Ma'am, if you'd step to the side—"

"Come to think of it," she said, "I may have seen someone. I was standing at my window, thinking about how very dark it is here compared to London. Not a streetlight to be seen. Even when the fog rolls in, you know, it's so terrifically bright. Why, without my heavy curtains, I might never get a wink of sleep."

"You say you saw something," Lynch said through gritted teeth. "Ma'am," he added.

"Oh, yes. I was standing at my window, and I saw a figure outside. Exceptionally big, as you say." She remembered how Dalton had loomed over her, and how he made even the simple act of breathing seem dangerous. "I thought perhaps it was a farmer, out milking his cows or some such rustic endeavor. But cows aren't milked at night, are they?"

Lynch's patience continued to fray. "Did you get a good look at him?"

"As I said, it is *exceptionally* dark out here, but, thinking on it now, he might have caught a little light from the inn. And I remember clearly now how strange I thought his clothing. All covered with these peculiar arrow markings. I assumed it was some eccentric local dress."

Snapping even more alert, Lynch said, "That's our man. Where was he heading?"

"Somewhere over there." She waved her hand toward the east, precisely the direction opposite from which she knew Simon, Marco, and Dalton to be heading.

The warders did not waste further time. With murmured apologies, they stepped around her and exited the inn. Lynch remained long enough to mutter, "Obliged, ma'am."

She decided against using more ridiculous chatter to detain him longer. Any further delays, and he'd grow suspicious. With a nod, she let him pass. Hopefully, she'd bought the others enough time to make decent progress toward their rendezvous point.

"This is exceedingly distressing," she announced to the men in the taproom.

The innkeeper came forward, wreathed in a strained smile. "I can assure you, madam, that such occurrences are quite rare, and that the warders will have that blackguard caught very soon."

"Just the same, I believe I'll retire to my room for the rest of the evening. And I will be sure to lock the door."

"Excellent plan, madam."

With a sniff, she left the taproom and made sure that her footsteps on the stairs could be heard. Once at the top of the stairs, she waited a moment to see if anyone followed or left the taproom. Everyone remained within, discussing the shocking turn of events.

Silently, she crept back downstairs, then turned quickly into a hallway not visible from the taproom. There had to be a back or side door she might use. The option remained of returning to her room and going out the window, but likely Marco had locked the door. Picking the lock would be the work of less than a minute, yet she didn't relish the prospect of climbing down whilst wearing skirts. They had an unfortunate tendency to tangle in her legs.

Moving noiselessly through the hallway, she tried a door which proved to be a linen closet, and then came upon the kitchen. Peering inside, she found the room empty of everything but pots, pans, a sink with running water, and a huge iron stove. A basket waited by the back door.

She was outside in a moment, and shut the door behind her. Slipping through a rather barren kitchen garden, she reached a low fence and swung over it, then took a moment to get her bearings. She stood in a narrow lane that ran alongside the inn, and just on the other side of the lane stretched the moorland into which Simon, Marco, and Dalton should have fled. They'd wait for her, but not forever. Right now, Dalton was their most important resource, and they'd get him to safety as soon as possible. Simon and Marco trusted her to take care of herself if they became separated.

If she could avoid sleeping in a frigid barn, she'd do so. And she wanted to be in London for the planning of their operation against Rockley.

Quickly, she crossed the lane and headed into the sweep of moor rolling beyond. The voices of the warders came far too close for her liking, but she judged them to be on the other side of the inn, following her false lead.

She set up a brisk trot as she moved farther into the darkness. It would be a clean getaway.

A warder's boots crunched on the rocky ground. *Hell*. She had to keep going.

"Oi, ma'am, you oughtn't go out there!"

Without turning around, she gave him a little wave and kept going.

"Ma'am! You'd best come back now! Ma'am!"

Suddenly, there was Dalton, right in her path. He seemed a myth conjured from the darkness, an Iron Age warrior pulled forward in time.

"You should've stayed with the others," she hissed.

"And you were taking too long." He gripped her wrist, and, despite their circumstances, the feel of his rough hand against her skin made her pulse stutter.

The warder let out a shout. "I see 'im! It's Dalton!" He blew the whistle that hung around his neck.

With her free hand, she gathered up her skirts. "Run," she said.

They ran.

* * *

Jack had more important things to think about besides Eva's fine-boned wrist beneath his palm. The screws were coming, including Lynch, chasing after them, their whistles and shouts stabbing the quiet. He'd be lucky if all they did was capture him and drag him back to Dunmoor.

As he and Eva ran across the moor, he kept his mind and body focused on speed. But he couldn't shake his awareness of touching her. The strength in her came as an eye-opener, and not a surprise. He ought to know that if a woman looked comfortable holding a revolver, she probably didn't have fragile doll limbs.

Those legs of hers had a hell of a lot of speed, too. Despite her skirts, she kept pace with him, running like she was born to it.

A shotgun blast tore through the air. He pulled them both into a crouch.

"Keep going." Her words were tight but steady. "They won't fire directly if I'm with you."

Made sense. Likely they thought her his hostage, not the woman who blackmailed him into collaboration.

He and Eva kept running. The shapes of Marco and Simon emerged ahead.

"The hell, Dalton?" That was Simon. Jack was beginning to know the toff's smooth, fancy-bred voice even in the dark.

"Sounded like a screw was going after her. Don't know about you nobs, but I don't leave nobody behind. How long would it take them to figure out where we were headed once they had her?" It had been a rule drilled into him by Catton, taught to him when he was no bigger than a keg. His years as a housebreaker were behind him, but the lessons remained gouged into his brain.

"Your help wasn't necessary," she said.

"I'm choking on your gratitude."

The four of them sped on, the warders in full pursuit. Another shotgun blast was fired into the air. It wouldn't be long before Lynch got tired of warning shots and took direct aim.

"Wherever the hell we're going," he panted, "it better not be far."

"Don't look," said Marco.

"What?"

Eva snapped, "Cover your eyes."

He was about to ask why, when Marco suddenly turned and pulled something from the pack slung across his shoulders. Marco lobbed the object toward the warders, turning away as he did so.

There was a small concussion, followed by a huge flash of light. The screws fell back, and then Jack had no idea what followed because he couldn't see a damn thing.

"What was that?"

"Phosphorous and a quick-burning accelerant," Marco answered.

Meaningless words. "You sodding blinded me."

"Told you to cover your eyes." There was no sympathy in Eva's voice. "It's short-term, anyway. Lasts long enough for us to temporarily hold back the warders." Now it was her hand around his wrist, pulling him forward. He could only stumble on in her wake as she led him. What lay ahead, he didn't know. All he could do was trust her—and he trusted no one. Especially not a woman with strong hands, clever eyes, and a revolver in her reticule.

Though the warders had retreated, Eva couldn't be easy. Not until they were safe at headquarters. The guards weren't the only threat. Blinded and angry as a bull,

Dalton stumbled behind her. She suspected the only rea-
son he wasn't swearing like a fishmonger was to make
sure the warders could not follow the sound of his voice.
No doubt he thought any number of vile things, however.
She could practically hear him cursing her, Simon, and
Marco. Yet he let her lead him.

Only to save himself. Without her guidance, he'd
stumble around the moors and right into the hands of
the pursuing warders. If given the opportunity, Dalton
would break their necks.

It was like leading a lit cask of gunpowder. The only
thing to wonder was when he'd explode.

Finally, the outline of a carriage appeared on the crest
of a hill. Dalton slowed, his muscles tensing.

"I hear horses," he said, low.

"Our means of escape." She and the others approached slowly.

"Come any nearer and I'll use my whip to give you
a shave!" The driver lifted his arm.

"It's us, Walters," answered Simon.

"Oh, Mr. Addison-Shawe! Nearly stopped my heart,
you did." He peered down at them. "Get your man?"

"We did."

"Hop in, then."

Marco climbed into the carriage, and she started to
do the same, tugging Dalton behind her. But he easily
broke her hold on him, pulling away. He must have
gotten his sight back, because he glared at the carriage
and the driver.

"I'm not getting in there until you tell me who this
bloke is and where you're taking me."

"I'm a friend, I am. Nemesis did me a good turn,"
Walters said before she could answer. "Got me my farm
back when the law wouldn't help. If they need me, I'm
theirs."

Dalton raised his brows at this, but still did not get into the carriage.

Casting a concerned glance over her shoulder, she strained for signs of the pursuing warders. "We don't have time for your suspicions."

"A lady who travels with a gun in her pocketbook, a man who carries exploding bombs, and a toff who acts like a crack thief. Trustworthy lot."

She exhaled, frustrated. "Walters is taking us to the nearest train station. We'll catch the express to London, where we're headquartered."

"And then?" he demanded.

"And then we'll talk."

He snorted at that. But whatever his reservations, the prospect of waiting around for the warders seemed less appealing. Muttering, he stepped into the carriage, and it tilted until he found his seat. Good God, was the man made entirely of muscle?

She turned to Simon. "My doubts still stand," she whispered.

"He's a brute and a criminal," Simon answered low, "but he's our best weapon against Rockley. The plan moves forward."

There was nothing she could do. Not standing out on the moors in the middle of the night, with a gang of armed warders hunting them. She checked the contents of her reticule—money, Webley, keys, handkerchief, chloroform. She hoped they wouldn't need to use the chloroform on Dalton. Carrying him would be like lifting a mountain.

Satisfied that everything was in place, she climbed into the carriage, seating herself opposite Dalton. He stared at her, eyes gleaming like jet, as Simon took his seat next to her.

Marco rapped on the roof, and the carriage was in

motion. Before long, they sped through the moors, rocking over the rolling heath.

"He's got no lights out there," Dalton rumbled. "Going to crash us for certain."

She turned her attention away from the windows. "Walters knows this countryside better than a man knows—"

"His wife's arse," he supplied.

"The back of his hand." Her mouth curled. "Really, Mr. Dalton, my threshold for being shocked is extremely high. You'll have to do better than that."

"I'd like to try."

If her cheeks felt warm, it was only because she had been running across the moors. Certainly not from the husky rasp of his voice in the small confines of the carriage, or the erotic challenge of his words.

Simon cleared his throat. He grabbed a cloth-wrapped bundle next to him and tossed it to Dalton. The convict nimbly caught the package.

"A change of clothes." Simon eyed Dalton's filthy prison uniform. "Charming as those garments are, they're not suitable for traveling on a public train."

"They're not suitable for a dog to wear, neither."

"That's a considerable amount of hatred for an inanimate object," she noted.

Staring down at his knee-length breeches, Dalton made a sound of disgust. "Never want to see this bloody crow's foot again. One of the first things they do when you get to prison is take away your clothing and give you a uniform. You don't think you'll care, until you see hundreds of men dressed just like you. No one's got a name, just a number. And this sodding mark, all over your clothes. It's like you're nobody."

Stunned into silence, she could only nod. Up to this point, Dalton hadn't spoken at such length. More than the extent of his speech, however, she was shocked by how powerfully he'd been affected by the dehumanizing conditions within the prison. Easier for her to believe that he was an unfeeling beast, driven only by an animal need for revenge. The bleakness in his voice belied this.

"Then you'll find the garments we've provided more to your liking." Her words were flippant, her thoughts anything but.

"Pull over," he said.

"Carriage sick?" asked Marco.

"I'm supposed to change, ain't I? So pull over and I'll change."

But Simon shook his head. "We'll lose time if we stop. You'll have to do it in the carriage."

Dalton shot her a glance.

"The bodies of men are no mystery to me, Mr. Dalton," she said. "I won't fall unconscious at the sight of yours."

"I'd wager not much would make you faint."

"She can pull a bullet out of a man without the bat of an eyelash," Marco said cheerfully. "Took one out of my thigh, calm as a lake. And I've got a pretty little scar for a souvenir."

Dalton chuckled, and the unexpected sound tumbled over her skin like rough velvet. "The bullyboys of the East End would find you damn useful."

"Sadly for them," she replied, "I already have employment. Perhaps it's *your* delicate sensibilities that are disturbed, Mr. Dalton, by the thought of undressing in my presence."

A corner of his mouth turned up. "Never dare me, love."

She most assuredly didn't like him calling her love,

but she merely folded her arms over her chest and waited.

Dalton sent glances toward Simon and Marco. "If she becomes lust crazed by the sight of me in the altogether . . ."

Simon snorted. "We'll protect your honor should she assault you."

Dalton grinned, a flash of white teeth in the darkness. "Don't."

"Oh, get on with it!" She cursed the short temper that allowed her to be so easily baited.

He shrugged his wide shoulders. Then grabbed the hem of his smocklike shirt and pulled it over his head.

Forcibly, she kept her lips pressed together, refusing to make even a single sound of shock or amazement. But, *good Lord*. The man was . . . astonishing. Every muscle in his arms and on his torso was sharply defined, as though the primal essence of masculinity had been pared to its elemental state. Oh, she'd seen many bare-chested men, including Simon and Marco, but they were lean where Dalton was broad, men shaped by training, whereas hard labor had formed Dalton into unfettered strength.

Not a dram of extra flesh. He seemed forged from iron, like a brutal but effective weapon.

Against the shrill warnings of her better judgment, her gaze moved across the breadth of his chest, noting the dark hair dusting his pectorals and trailing down in a line along his ridged abdomen. And lower.

"Careful, love." His deep voice dragged her attention back up to his face. "You'll set the carriage to blazing."

She forced herself to turn to Marco. "Hand me your pack."

He did so, and she rifled through it until she found

what she sought. Pulling out a canteen, she gave it an experimental shake. It sloshed, revealing that it was full. Little surprise, as all Nemesis operatives kept themselves in a continual state of preparedness. "Water?" she asked.

"Grappa's in the flask," he answered.

She would definitely want that. Later. Right now, water suited her needs.

Tossing the canteen and a handkerchief from her reticule to Dalton, she said, "Doesn't matter how you're dressed if your face is filthy." Since neither she nor Marco and Simon were disguised as laborers, Dalton's grimy appearance would certainly attract attention on the train.

The little scrap of fabric looked like an elf's frippery in Dalton's large hand, its snowy white cotton contrasting with his brown hands. He eyed it warily.

"It's just a handkerchief," she said impatiently.

"Don't have a lot of experience handling women's dainties." He held it out, pinching it between thumb and forefinger. "If I use this, it'll be ruined."

She shrugged. "I have dozens more." Then she started as Dalton sniffed the handkerchief.

"Smells like lemons and . . . some kind of flower."

"Verbena." She felt strangely uncomfortable, as if he had discovered a closely guarded secret. But there was nothing secret about the type of perfumed soap she preferred, purchased from a shop just down the street from her lodgings.

"Pretty," he rumbled, and that strange sensation intensified. "But I don't want to smell like a lady."

"For God's sake." Simon clenched his hands. "Better you reek of perfume than peat and bog."

Muttering something about blokes who smell like flowers, Dalton unscrewed the cap on the canteen and wet the handkerchief. He scrubbed at his face, stripping off layers of grime. Forehead, nose, cheeks, chin. Even behind his ears and along his neck. The motion brought the muscles of his arms into high relief as they flexed and released.

Finally, he was done. He gazed at the handkerchief. It was, indeed, ruined, streaked with so much dirt that a laundress would weep in despair. "Guess I'll keep this."

"Burning it would be a better option." Yet her offhand words belied her keen interest. For the first time tonight, she looked upon the face of Jack Dalton.

She had seen his photograph in the file. It had been taken before he'd been incarcerated, before prison regulations had demanded he shave his generous mustache. She had thought that he might be passably attractive, if one was attracted to hard-eyed ruffians. Now he was clean-shaven. Though shadows filled the carriage, enough light remained that she had a good sense of his face.

He wasn't handsome, not in Simon's aristocratic fashion, nor did he possess the Continental charm of Marco's half-Italian lineage. In fact, of the three men, both Marco and Simon would be considered better looking. Yet Dalton had a rough, raw masculinity, his jaw square, his mouth wide. He had a pugilist's nose, slightly crooked with a distinct bump on the bridge. A scar bisected his right eyebrow, and there was another just over his top lip, on the left. The face of a man who had lived hard, who expected little and was often not surprised when little was given.

Assuredly, she had seen more handsome men, but none of them were as striking as Dalton. Not a one had his compelling, dark gaze. A gaze that was fixed directly on her.

She lifted her chin. It was ridiculous to pretend she wasn't staring.

"An improvement," she said. "No one will give you a second look at the train station." That was a lie. Gazes would be drawn to him, for he possessed a shadowed magnetism. It would be deuced difficult to hide him anywhere—another point against him. She would bring that up once they reached headquarters.

He tucked the handkerchief into his discarded shirt, then bent to untie his boots. The movement brought him very close to her, so close that if she leaned forward a few inches, she could put her hands on his shoulders, her lips on the back of his head.

Heat radiated from him, pressing close around her. She caught a trace of her own soap's fragrance on him, as if they had been in a tight embrace and the scent of her skin had transferred to him.

He looked up through his spiky lashes, and their gazes tangled. For a long, breathless moment, they simply stared at one another, suspended, ensnared.

"Hurry up, Dalton." Simon's voice was clipped. "We'll be at the station soon."

His words severed the threads binding her and Dalton. A wry smile curled at the corner of Dalton's mouth, and he finished unlacing his boots. His striped wool stockings followed, revealing calves dusted with more dark hair. The sight of his large bare feet was primal, her own not unsubstantial feet appearing tiny beside his.

After a quick gaze in her direction, he moved to the fastening of his knee-length breeches.

She didn't *want* to watch his fingers undoing the buttons, but the sight riveted her. The deftness with which his large hands moved came as a surprise. He tilted his hips to gain enough room to remove his breeches. She forced her gaze back up the length of his chest, fighting to maintain a disinterested expression. Only a few minutes earlier, she'd claimed to be hard to shock. Now she had to prove it.

Though the carriage creaked and jounced noisily across the moors, she was acutely aware of the sound of fabric sliding down Dalton's hips, then lower. She kept her focus trained on the hollow of his throat, but her mind filled in the details, coaxing her to envision his thighs, roped and hewn. And—there was no helping it— she imagined his cock, nestled in thick dark hair.

Don't look. For the love of your pride, do not look.

His voice rumbled out of the darkness. "Doesn't cost anything to have yourself a peek, love."

"Dalton!" Marco snapped. "Treat Miss Warrick with respect, or I'll polish your teeth with a bullet."

She waved a hand. "It's a small matter if Mr. Dalton encourages me to contemplate his shortcomings." Then, deliberately, she let her gaze fall to his groin. "My jacket must be extremely warm, for I had no idea the night was so cold. That *is* the explanation, isn't it, Mr. Dalton?"

He made a sound midway between indignation and amusement.

Satisfied with his response, she moved her gaze to his face. He might be able to see the heat staining her cheeks, yet there was nothing she could do about her body's unwanted response. Truly, she had seen men in all states of dress and undress, knew exactly how their bodies looked, and even how they felt. There was no mystery to the male physique. So why was she so affected by the sight of a naked Jack Dalton?

It was purely logical. After all, they had met only

hours earlier. He was a stranger, and a dangerous one, at that. No wonder her pulse accelerated when she looked at his penis, the most intimate part of a man's body.

Despite her belittling claim, she finally had the answer to the question about men with large feet and large hands. They were . . . proportional.

Consider the spirit of scientific inquiry fulfilled, she thought with an inward smile.

"If you're quite finished attempting to incite Miss Warrick to a lust-crazed frenzy," drawled Simon, "get dressed."

Fortunately, Dalton didn't complain about Simon's command. He clearly saw the value of arriving at the train station clothed rather than nude. After undoing the bundle, he removed a shirt, trousers, waistcoat, jacket, and boots.

"None of this is going to fit," he said. "Not even the boots."

"We went off your vital statistics from your file," Marco answered.

"That was before I did five years of hard labor. Gotten bigger since then. My feet spread, too."

"Stopping at the high street shops is impossible," she said. "So you'll have to squeeze into what we've got."

He shrugged, and went about the awkward task of dressing in a moving carriage shared with three other people. She would never admit to anyone her small, internal sigh of relief when he dragged on the trousers. The waist fit him well enough, with actual room to spare, but his thighs strained against the material. He could barely pull his arms through the shirtsleeves. The shirt actually tore a little on the shoulder seams, and he grimaced.

"The waistcoat and jacket will hide that," she said, brisk.

Except he couldn't button the waistcoat, and the jacket was taut across his shoulders, its cuffs inches above his wrists.

Marco tried to fasten the collar to Dalton's shirt. "It's like dressing a lion as Little Lord Fauntleroy."

"You're sodding choking me," Dalton rasped.

Frustrated, Marco flung the collar to the ground. "Unless we have a spare wheel rim, nothing's going to work."

"Just tie the neck cloth around him." She waved the long piece of silk foulard at Marco, but Dalton snatched it from her hand.

"Can tie my own damned neck cloth." And he did, though Simon rolled his eyes at the inelegant knot. "There," Dalton said with a growl. "Now I look like the bloody Prince of Wales."

"If His Royal Highness were ten inches taller, three stone heavier, and had spent his formative years in a bull-baiting ring," she said, "you would be his perfect likeness."

Dalton opened his mouth, but before he could speak, the carriage slowed. "Train station," Walters called down.

Everyone within the carriage stilled. Their gazes met in silent acknowledgment. Even Dalton understood. They had completed only the first stage of their plan, and the danger was far from over.

CHAPTER THREE

Jack waited inside the carriage as the others got out and made a quick survey of the train station. The screws might be here, lurking just inside so he could tumble right into their trap. He doubted they'd be able to reach the station so quickly, especially on foot, but he couldn't shake his fear that they were here. He couldn't let himself get this far only to be dragged back to Dunmoor. With this brief taste of freedom, only one path remained for him: kill Rockley.

His fists clenched in anticipation. He'd run, he'd hide, he'd do whatever he must for as long as necessary. If Rockley met death at his hands, it would all be worth it.

First, he needed to put as much distance as possible between himself and Dunmoor. Then . . . he'd figure the rest out. He would have to lose these Nemesis people. Or take advantage of them and their wickedly clever schemes until they were no longer useful.

Eva appeared in the door of the carriage. With the lights from the station behind her, he could only see her outline and the shadowy suggestion of her face. She might have been any slim woman. Except he knew her shape now, her scent. The way her breath sped when something stirred her up.

His cock gave an interested throb.

Don't be a sodding idiot. Got the screws on my tail and a gang of lunatics holding the reins. And she's *one of the lunatics.*

"We're clear," she said.

He moved forward to get out, and she edged quickly back. Keeping more distance between them.

Stepping down onto the gravel outside the station, he squinted toward the lights. Simon stood at the ticket booth, and Marco struck a casual pose nearby, looking for all the world as if he didn't have an escaped convict's uniform and boots in his pack. A few other people milled about the platform—some working blokes, a gent in a banker's suit and with an air of respectability, a woman with two small children—but no sign of the warders or even the local constabulary.

"Stay close to me," Eva said under her breath. "And try to look inconspicuous, though"—she eyed him—"that's a rather tall order."

"I look like an organ grinder's monkey," he muttered, fighting the urge to tug on his tight clothes. His boots pinched, too, but the Nemesis gang had been clever in bringing him a change of shoes. The soles of prison-issued boots bore the crow's foot mark, too. Anyone with half a brain in their head would see his footprints in the dust.

"Trust me, Mr. Dalton, no one would ever confuse you with a playful little monkey. Perhaps one of those terrifying gorillas at the zoo. The ones that beat their chests and roar."

He held up the back of his hands. "Got less hair."

"Not in certain places, you don't."

Heat settled low in his groin. "Going to put that in my file, too?"

"I'll save that for my own personal records."

God, she was a saucy one! And damn him if it didn't make his mouth water.

She moved toward the driver of the carriage. "What do we owe you, Mr. Walters?"

"The bill's been settled, miss. You got me my farm back. A little jaunt through the heath ain't nothing." The older man glanced at Jack. "Mind you, stay sharp around this 'un. Got a bad look about 'im."

Jack had heard far worse about himself on a daily basis. He just stared right back at Walters until the driver looked away.

"I promise to be as sharp as a razor," she answered.

"As if you could be anything less." Walters chuckled, then, with a tip of his hat and snap of the ribbons, the carriage drove away.

Jack eyed the brightly lit station, the urge to break and run screaming through his body. A film of sweat clung to his back.

"It's safe." Eva's soft murmur startled him. Even more startling was her hand on his sleeve, almost gentlelike.

"Looks so damn normal. I haven't been around normal in five years." It was an ordinary country train station, with a waiting room and ticket booth and a single, open-air platform. A farmer nodded in sleep as he sat on a crate, his arms folded over his chest, and a big orange tabby groomed himself near the porters' stove.

"The inn didn't seem to bother you."

He shrugged, the movement cut short by the snug coat. "Had other things on my mind."

"Like killing Rockley." She tipped her head toward the station, where Simon and Marco waited. "You'll get your chance at him soon enough. But we have to get to London first."

"Right. Yeah." He exhaled, the sound jagged, then nodded.

When she took her hand from his sleeve, he felt oddly sorry, and they both headed for the station. Marco and Simon watched him, wary as cats, as he approached. Though his boots squeezed his feet, they were a damn sight lighter than those millstones he'd had to wear. He might even float away. Except one of these Nemesis lunatics might shoot him out of the sky. He wouldn't ask what their plans for him were. Not here, where anyone might be listening.

"Next train to London is coming in twenty minutes." Simon consulted his pocket watch. A nice bit of gold, that. Could fetch a pretty sum at one of the shops.

Simon caught Jack's assessing look and glowered. As if he didn't know what it was to be hungry and see every ring and bauble as a meal. Jack had been hungry. He was born hungry. Exactly what Rockley preyed upon, exploited. A man who wanted to eat was a man easily controlled.

But even a starving man reaches a breaking point.

Jack stared at Simon, then turned away to watch the train tracks. No one in their group spoke, except a low exchange every few minutes among the other three. They didn't try to make him talk. He didn't know whether it was to protect him or just because they hadn't a desire to hear his voice. Either way, he didn't care. Nobody ever said he was witty like the music hall patter boys. Nobody wanted him for conversation.

To keep from looking around and acting suspicious, he made himself count the slats between the train tracks. There weren't many visible beyond the gas lamps of the station, so he did it over and over. All the while he thought he felt dozens of eyes on him, thought he heard

the warders charging near, thought a hundred things—
none of them peaceful.

Eva drifted closer to him. Like the two men, she was
calm, giving not a hint of anxiety. In fact, she looked
slightly bored, just as a woman might when waiting for
a train to take her out of the quiet of the countryside.
She didn't speak, but gave him a small nod. The
damnedest thing—that tiny crumb of assurance actually made him feel a little bit better. This, from the
woman who'd stuck a gun in his face.

*Maybe my time in Dunmoor drove me mad. It's
happened to other men.*

Much as he tried to mirror the calm of his three co-
horts, he nearly jumped out of his tight boots when a
train whistle pierced the air. The train itself sounded
awful loud as it chugged into the station. Five years
since he'd heard a steam engine or the squeal of the
brakes.

The stationmaster stepped out onto the platform.
"Ten-fifteen to London, with stops in Doncaster,
Grantham, and Peterborough!"

Jack didn't allow himself to breathe any easier,
not when he followed the other three onto the train, not
when they seated themselves in a first-class compartment. Jack sat next to Marco, with Eva and Simon taking the facing seats. Only when the train pulled from
the station did he exhale. But the screws could still
telegraph ahead to other stations, and he'd be met by a
mob of the local coppers.

A few minutes passed, silent except for the rhythmic
clacking of the train. It didn't seem as though anyone
planned on joining him and the others in their compartment.

"The lot of you, spill." He fixed his gaze on each of
them in turn: blond toff Simon; swarthy, cunning Marco;

and *her.* "You've got some scheme for me, and I want to know what it is."

All of them traded looks, turning his simmer to a full boil.

He jerked his head toward Simon. "You bloody tell me, or I'll beat that one's face to a stain on the upholstery."

"That assumes you'd be able to beat me to a stain," drawled Simon.

Jack grinned, eager for blood. "Oh, I can. These hands have broken rocks. Your skull is a lot softer than granite."

"Only one way to find out."

"The bell has been rung, gentlemen," Eva snapped. "The round is over, so back to your corners."

"May as well let him in on the plan." Marco glanced back and forth between his comrades. "Sooner or later he's got to know."

"I ain't a damn halfwit," Jack snarled. "I'm sitting right here, so you talk *to* me, lad, or don't talk at all." Prison had glutted him on being talked of like a thing, not a man.

Finally, Eva spoke. "Remember that girl we mentioned, the one who had been ruined by Rockley?" At his tense nod, she continued. "Her father's just a merchant. He doesn't have any power, any pull. When he made his complaint to Rockley, demanding either marriage or some kind of restitution, Rockley ignored him."

"And the courts weren't helpful, I'm guessing," Jack said.

"You said it yourself, a girl gets seduced and the man responsible walks away with no harm. Especially if the man in question happens to be a powerful aristocrat like Lord Rockley." She spat his name as if clearing poison from her mouth. "You know that better than anyone."

"Aye," he said bitterly.

"The titled and wealthy hold all the power," said Marco, "and their wrongdoings often go unpunished. For many, justice is hard to come by, if not completely out of reach. The downtrodden and voiceless need redress, but they've nowhere to get it."

He'd seen that plenty in the streets of London. So many times. Hell, that's why he'd been thrown into prison.

Eva's eyes were hard. "That is where Nemesis gets involved."

He frowned. "Doing what?"

"We're in the business of vengeance." Simon smiled, cold as frost.

"Justice," said Eva, "by any means necessary."

"Nemesis was formed four years ago," Simon explained. "Back then, it was just me, Marco, and a man you'll meet later called Lazarus. We didn't have a name, or a plan. Only a common purpose—to correct the imbalances in our society. Marco used to work for the government, and both Lazarus and I were soldiers. But we realized that there was something rotten at the heart of the country we fought for."

"You mean, the rich got all the power," Jack said, "and everyone else twists in the wind."

Marco nodded. "Exactly. The three of us met by chance in a tavern. It was the day that William Vale was hanged for killing the landlord who'd been squeezing him for more and more rent, until Vale's family was thrown out into the streets in the dead of winter. His wife and infant son took sick and died. But there was no one Vale could complain to, no way to seek justice. Except to get it for himself."

Being in prison at the time, Jack hadn't heard of the case, but the particulars didn't surprise him. The world was full of stories just like Vale's.

"Wasn't right that an honest man had to lose his family, and his life, because of someone else's greed," Simon continued. "That's what Marco, Lazarus, and I found ourselves railing against in that tavern. We didn't know each other then, but we all swore that we'd try to make a difference. No matter what it took."

Jack knew liars, cheats, swindlers. They all thought themselves expert at bending the truth, spinning yarns so finely that even the cleverest bloke got himself tangled up and hanged. Not once did they fool him. Jack wasn't clever, but he'd been born with an instinct that let him spot a lie.

He didn't know how or why he had that sense, only that it had saved his arse dozens of times, including when Catton had told him to just go down that alley. The contact would meet him there, and the goods would change hands. Catton had said all this smooth as treacle, no different than when he'd told Jack about other swaps. But Jack had known, and when the knife came out, intending to slit his belly open, he'd been ready. Had a good scar from that fight, but he lived. And Catton wound up dead at the hands of one of his crew years later.

So he knew when someone wasn't being on the level, or veering from the facts. And this Nemesis crew was telling the truth.

He didn't like it one damn bit.

"You want me to kill Rockley," he said.

Eva looked angry. "Assassinations and murder are *not* part of our ethos. That's one way we keep below the government's notice."

"Don't worry, love, I'm right eager to kill him."

"We don't do that," she said through clenched teeth.

"Painting yourself with a noble brush." He snorted. "But you plant false information to make a man break out of prison, hold a gun on him, and threaten him if he doesn't do what you say. Regular heroes, you are."

Not a one of them looked particularly shamefaced by their actions.

"Justice by any means necessary," repeated Simon.

Jack leaned forward. "If you don't want Rockley dead, then you got the wrong man to break out of prison. There's a file on me at your headquarters. You know why I want to kill him."

"It's alleged that he killed your sister, Edith," Simon noted.

Surging to his feet, Jack snarled, "The fucking bastard murdered her! No *alleged* about it."

Eva rose, and so did the other men. Stepping close, she planted her hand on the center of his chest. "Keep your voice down and watch your damn language," she hissed. She sent a meaningful glance toward the door of the compartment, where a chalk-faced conductor peered inside.

"Problem, miss?"

With a smile that any actress would've been proud to claim, she shook her head. "My cousin . . . he forgets sometimes that he isn't fighting Boers anymore." She smoothed her hand down his chest as if tidying his wrinkled shirt, patting and stroking him.

His mind fogged.

"Apologize, Henry."

The fog broke apart, leaving him aware of exactly where he was and why he had to play along. "Sorry," he gritted.

The conductor sniffed. "Mind, this is a respectable train. Vulgarity is not tolerated, even from veterans."

"We shall do our utmost to preserve the decorum of this conveyance." By God, she could make herself sound sweet and meek! Jack hardly recognized her, until she turned her gaze back to him, and there was nothing sweet or meek about her. Just determined.

As he stood toe-to-toe with her, she looked so much smaller than him, yet he'd be a fool to underestimate this woman. He might have more bodily strength, but she was clever as hell and more resolute than a prizefighter. Dangerous qualities on their own. Together, they were lethal.

Wrap all that in a lovely package like Eva, and a man had to watch where he stepped, or else he'd go plunging to his death.

Quickly, the conductor entered, took their tickets, and scurried off.

She narrowed her eyes. "Do you think you can control yourself?"

"No," he said.

Her lips quirked, and he realized with a start she was holding back a real smile. "Well, you're honest. There's some credit in that." She nodded toward his seat. "Sit, Mr. Dalton."

"Ask."

"I will not—"

"Five years I had men telling me where to go, what to do, how to think. Nobody asked me anything. Just ordered. But I ain't in prison anymore. So if you want me to do something, you better ask."

She must have seen that he meant every word, because at last she said, "Please, Mr. Dalton. Please sit."

"You first." He flashed his teeth. "They say it's rude to sit before a lady."

She made a very unladylike sound at that, but she did take her seat. With cagey glances, the two men did the same. Finally, Jack also sat down. They all stared at one another as if holding lit sticks of dynamite.

"You lot say you're seeking vengeance for the, what did you call it? Downtrodden and voiceless." His words felt like acid. "Where were you five years ago when Edith lay dying? She needed you then."

"As we said, Nemesis didn't exist five years ago," said Marco.

"But if it had," Simon added, "we would have done everything we could to help her."

Jack sneered. "That's the prettiest thing I've ever heard. Easy to make promises when they don't have to be kept."

Spreading her hands, Eva said, "Unfortunately, your sister is dead. Nothing you or I can do can change that. But what we *can* change is whether Rockley will ever harm another woman. When Miss Jones's father came to us, we did some investigating into Rockley's history. He's done this kind of thing before—hurt women. Your sister, Miss Jones, and others. Yet his rank and power make him virtually untouchable."

"He can't hurt anyone if he's dead."

"That isn't an option," she said.

"Cut off his cock, then."

Both Marco and Simon winced.

"Tempting as that prospect might be," she murmured, "there are other ways we can harm Rockley, and get a measure of retribution for his latest victim. And that, Mr. Dalton, is where you come into play."

Dalton was all calculation as he stared at her. She had familiarized herself with his file, knew the general details of his life. But for a former street rat turned boxer turned bodyguard, he possessed far more intellect than she had expected. That made him all the more treacherous. Underestimating someone was a short journey to catastrophe.

Bitter experience had taught her this valuable lesson. She had the scars to prove it.

"Lay it out for me," Dalton said.

"Rockley will pay for what he's done. To Edith, to Miss Jones. The dozen other women he's hurt. Do you know how he seduced Miss Jones? He saw her behind the counter at one of her father's shops. Wooed her. Made promises of marriage, promises that he'd help promote her father's business to his genteel friends."

"He didn't make good on those promises," Dalton surmised.

"As soon as she slept with him, he abandoned her. All her letters went unanswered. Her calls were turned away. And she realized she'd ruined not just herself, but if word ever got out about what happened between her and Rockley, her father's business would suffer. Such is the nature of our *moral* world." She drew a breath. "So, you see, we *will* bring Rockley down, make sure he is utterly ruined. But it must be done from the inside. Chip away at his foundations until he collapses."

"And you plan on doing that, how?"

Marco planted his hands on his knees. "We find out everything we can about Rockley. His associations, his movements. He's too well guarded for us to get close enough to learn more, but we do know that, on top of some suspicious connections, he's involved with illegal enterprises. Somewhere in all that is the key to taking Rockley down."

"That is why we need you." Eva kept her attention entirely on Dalton, watching the minute shifting expressions that crossed his face. No, he was far from stupid. There was a fatal, gleaming intelligence beneath the abundance of muscle, and she feared it as much as it drew her in.

He made a sound that was part growl, part laugh. "Him and me weren't chums. We didn't unload the secrets of our hearts over pints of bitter. All I did was watch Rockley's back when he'd go jaunting about town."

"Exactly." Warming to the subject, Simon leaned forward. "You've got intimate knowledge of Rockley's habits, his movements and vulnerabilities. Information available nowhere else."

"He's got plenty of other blokes working for him."

"But *you* are the only man who has ever left his employ and lived." Eva had researched the subject exhaustively. From the beginning, she'd been leery of using Dalton. Nemesis was only as strong as its people, and reading his file had convinced her that he was too vicious, too undisciplined, his connection to Rockley too personal to handle the mission.

She was still wary of him, but not quite for the same reasons.

"So I'm going to be the one who draws up the map." He drew an *X* in the air. "Ten paces then dig here for the treasure."

"The treasure in this case being Rockley's weaknesses."

He considered this, looking out the window at the dark countryside speeding past. She had to give Dalton credit. He played this game close, revealing almost nothing. She was well trained in the art of deciphering people. Being experienced with deception, she could see its painted surfaces everywhere. Whatever Dalton thought, he kept those thoughts deliberately obscured.

"Supposing I don't help you," he said at last, turning back to face her. "Supposing I tell the lot of you to go bugger yourselves and I find Rockley and kill him."

"You wouldn't get that far," Marco said, "before we stopped you."

Dalton smirked. "Think you could?"

"Consider everything we've done tonight," she said. "What we're capable of."

His nostrils widened, his lips compressing. Yes, he understood exactly how Nemesis operated. They had him well and truly trapped. And he didn't like it.

She couldn't blame him. Her own life had followed a course of her own choosing for that very reason. Freedom was a rare delicacy for most women. Sacrifices had to be made in order for her to taste that delicacy. She never regretted those sacrifices, for the end result was infinitely better.

Dalton had been imprisoned, and now Nemesis had him caught once more. No one would care for the circumstances, and a man such as him would chafe like a wild bull beneath the yoke.

"Say all this works, say we do bring Rockley down, I'd better get something in return."

"You're in no position to make threats, Dalton," Simon clipped.

Hostility snapped between the two men like a whip.

Though she seldom played the role of peacemaker, she had to diffuse the tension before Simon and Dalton began to throw punches. "You might get a chance to start over." She added quietly, "And justice for Edith."

Dalton became as mute and still as a mountain. As forbidding as one, too. How would they ever control him? He had broken himself out of prison for the chance to kill Rockley, a feat few could achieve. The irony almost made her laugh. By proving he was exactly the man Nemesis needed, he had also proven he would not easily submit.

The train began to slow, and the conductor walked past, calling the name of the stop.

As the station slid into view, she and the others eyed the platform, searching for waiting police. The only people standing on the platform were a few weary travelers and an old woman with a battered pram. Instead of a baby, however, the pram held paper-wrapped bundles. Pies. Passengers stepped out of the stopped train to buy pies from her, tearing into them before they even got back onto the train. Not everyone could afford the dining car, and it was likely closed at this hour.

Eva pulled a handful of coins from her reticule and handed them to Simon. "I think we could all use something to eat." She nodded toward the old woman.

He stood, but not before grumbling and giving her a sour look. Marco chuckled as Simon hopped off the train.

Dalton drummed his fingers on his knee, his gaze vigilant.

When Simon returned, he carried an armful of pies, all but throwing them into everyone's laps. "Hope everyone likes mutton. If you don't, too bloody bad."

"What excellent service," said Marco.

"And so courteous," she added.

Still scowling, Simon unwrapped his meal and took a bite. "Sod off," he said deliberately through his food. He accompanied this charming request with a spray of crumbs.

After the stationmaster made a final announcement, the train pulled from the station.

Marco dug into his food, and she pulled open the paper to break off pieces of savory pastry. As she nib-bled, her gaze kept straying to Dalton. The pie looked like a fairy cake in his large hands, and he stared at it.

Longing gleamed in his eyes.

Prison diets didn't include mutton pies. At best, a convict could hope for a few ounces of boiled meat thrice a week, maybe a bit of cheese. The rest of their food was gruel, tough bread, and potatoes. With a diet so austere, a mutton pie would look like a dish straight from the queen's own table.

So why wasn't he eating it?

His gaze kept darting to Marco and Simon. Not precisely as if he were afraid they'd take his food, but distinctly uncomfortable with their presence. Oddly, he didn't look at her. Just the other men.

She sifted through her memory for some clue as to why Dalton couldn't allow himself to eat, no matter how much he wanted to.

And then she understood why.

Slowly, she slid her foot across the floor, then nudged Marco's boot. He frowned at her. In response, she flicked her gaze toward Dalton, back to Marco, then to the door of the compartment.

He raised a brow. *Are you sure?*

She nodded.

With a shrug, he stood. Herein lay one of the many benefits of working closely with the same people for several years. Words were often unnecessary.

Marco gave Simon a speaking glance. Another silent exchange, this time between the two men. Dalton watched it all, but said nothing. At last, Simon relented, and also got to his feet. He followed Marco out of the compartment, but not without sending Eva a look weighted with significance.

Poor Simon. He'd been brought up to think women

were delicate, fragile creatures that had to be sheltered and protected like so much china bric-a-brac. Decades later, with ample evidence to the contrary, he still struggled.

Simon and Marco drifted down the passageway, carrying their dinners. They had left the door to the compartment open.

Dalton stared at her. "How'd you know?"

"I read reports about prisons. Before we—"

"Baited me to break out."

That was the truth, and she didn't feel the smallest twinge of embarrassment. "If Nemesis planned on employing you, we needed to get a sense of where you'd been, how you've been living." She glanced down at the wrapped pie. "Convicts eat alone in their cells."

Five years had passed since he had eaten in anyone's presence. It would take more than a few hours to break him of the habit.

"I can't leave you here alone, though," she said. He could try to escape.

He shook his head. "It's different with a woman."

She couldn't help but smile. "I should hope so."

Slowly, as if uncovering a forgotten treasure, he unwrapped the pie. His fingers stilled. Without looking up, he muttered, "Thanks."

A single word, reluctantly given. Yet her heart contracted sharply. She tried to push away sentiment, for she had a job to do, and she'd do it well. She always did. His simple, unadorned gratitude touched her, though.

Working with Dalton was going to be far more challenging than she'd planned.

He moved to take a bite, but his gaze flicked back to her. She noticeably looked away, staring out the window. Yet the darkness outside and brightly lit interior made the window a mirror, and she watched him eat his first meal outside of prison.

With the first bite, his eyes closed. A groan echoed in his chest. A sound of deep, sensuous rapture.

Unexpected heat uncurled in her belly, settling between her legs. If she wasn't watching him eat, she would have believed him in the throes of sexual ecstasy. The window's surface reflected Simon's concerned face as he peered into the compartment from the open door—and no wonder. Likely both he and Marco thought Dalton had her pinned beneath him, making up for five years of enforced celibacy.

But no, Dalton merely ate. Simon disappeared to allow him privacy, and Eva almost joined him. Yet she couldn't move, couldn't look away, her pulse a thick beat through her body.

She expected him to devour his food in a few quick gulps. Instead, he took his time with it, breaking off pieces of pastry as if to feel its texture, and licking his fingers slowly. Impossible for her to watch his tongue and lips without thinking of them on *her*.

Damn him, why couldn't he behave only as a beast? Why did he have to reveal unforeseen depth of feeling and sensuality? How was she to deal with him, when he refused to conform to her fixed beliefs?

Despite his slow consuming of his meal, it was only one mutton pie, and he finished it with obvious reluctance. Before he could lick the paper, she said, "Have the rest of mine."

He gazed at her, offended. "I'll not grab food out of a woman's hands."

"The woman in question isn't very hungry, and her food would go to waste otherwise."

Though he had to still be ravenous, he didn't move to take the offered pastry.

"Don't be a prideful ass." She held her food out to him. "Considering how we've got you over a barrel, this can be some compensation."

"A pie doesn't make up for you lot blackmailing me."

"It's a start."

He continued to stare at her until, finally, he took the food. Their fingers brushed as he did so. They had touched before, yet each new contact seemed to create new pathways of sensation, expanding farther and farther through her body.

She pulled back, her hands folding in her lap, and she fixedly stared out the window. This time, she did not watch him eat, but tried to pick out details from the night-swathed landscape rolling past the window.

"The canteen is still in Marco's pack." Were they close to Grantham yet? She hoped they were. Everything would become secure and orderly once they returned to headquarters.

She couldn't stop herself from watching him drink. A few droplets of water ran down his chin and along his throat to disappear beneath the knotted neck cloth.

He replaced the canteen, but found the flask. His eyes met hers in the glass. The flash of his grin made heat move through her all over again—brutal thugs didn't grin like scoundrels, full of wicked intent. This one did.

He took a pull from the flask and gave an expressive shudder. "Even on Rockley's penny, I never had liquor like this."

"Marco enjoys fine spirits."

"Here's to Marco, then." He raised the flask before taking another drink. Then he capped the flask and returned it to the pack. She had expected him to down the whole thing.

"Without offering a drink to the lady?" She gazed at him severely.

His eyebrows rose. "Didn't think ladies liked spirits."

"*This* lady does." She held out a hand.

He passed her the flask, and watched with naked fascination as she uncapped it and took a good, long swallow. She couldn't remember appreciating a drink more. The grappa burned like redemption.

"I'll be sure to remember Marco in my evening prayers." He purchased grappa regularly from an importer, claiming that his Italian blood couldn't tolerate coarse English whiskey. Ridiculous, particularly since she had witnessed him drain more than a few glasses of whiskey at the end of an especially difficult assignment.

After taking one more sip, she gave the flask back to Dalton.

At that moment, Marco and Simon returned to the compartment, closing the door behind them. Spotting his flask in Dalton's hand, Marco scowled and snatched it away. It seemed to be a measure of Dalton's improved humor that he didn't plant his fist in Marco's face.

"How does this Nemesis operation work?" he asked. "You run adverts in the paper: '*Downtrodden? Want justice? Nemesis, Unlimited has all your vengeance needs. Find us at the corner of Dean Street and Fetter Lane.*'"

Marco rolled his eyes. "Don't be ridiculous. We started finding clients just by keeping our ears to the ground, using our sundry connections to find out when someone was being wronged. After our first few cases, word spread. Former clients bring us new cases, and we still use our connections to find those in need of help. No advertising necessary."

"Ever turn anyone down?"

"All the time," Eva said. "Some people think Nemesis is their own personal bully squad. They want us to collect debts or throw acid in a rival's face. But we work to obtain justice for those who have been truly wronged, we don't deal out thuggery. Yet there's always legitimate work for us, and we usually take on several cases at once."

"Can't imagine that these clients of yours pay handsomely."

"We take small remuneration for our services," she said, "but Nemesis is funded out of our own pockets."

Dalton snorted. "Bad business model."

"It's not about the money." Simon's lip curled. "It never has been."

Dalton looked patently skeptical. "Tell me what happens when we get to London."

"We review options, devise strategies." Simon neatly flicked back the tails of his coat as he took his seat. "Plan our course of attack."

"Based on information that *I* give you. And then?"

"And then . . . Nemesis will do its job."

"After that?" Dalton demanded.

"We can't think beyond our immediate goals," she said. "Otherwise, we lose focus."

Dalton's mouth curled. "No need for you lot to worry about the future. You don't have the warders biting at your heels."

"Earlier this evening," she noted, "you seemed willing to die to get vengeance on Rockley. A few weeks of uncertainty is nothing by comparison."

He crossed his arms over his chest and scowled. "This is why I don't like mixing with clever people. They twist you around so much you don't know your nose from your arsehole."

"What an enchanting image."

Silence pressed down in the compartment. They all seemed to run out of words, as though a tap had been opened and everything worth saying drained away.

She burned with impatience to reach headquarters so they might begin the next stage of their plan. The others must have felt the same way, all of them restive, legs crossing and uncrossing, knuckles cracking, fingers drumming on kneecaps or any available surface—the dozens of small yet irritating ways men channeled their pent-up energy.

Dalton seemed torn between restlessness and exhaustion. With his arms still folded over his chest, he kept glancing around as if anticipating an ambush. But then his eyes drooped shut. An instant later, he snapped them open, fighting sleep. Yet escaping from prison and a long chase across the moors had taken their toll. No matter how he struggled, sleep dragged on him.

At last, he could fight no more. His head tipped back, leaning against the seat. Dreams began at once, his dark eyelashes quivering. What did he dream of? Murdering Rockley, most likely. Or maybe he dreamt of his sister. The file contained only the most basic information: Dalton and his sister had different fathers, and their mother had died some time shortly after Edith's birth. They had grown up in East London. At an unknown point, Edith had become a prostitute, Dalton a thief and then a bare-knuckle boxer in underground fights before finally being hired as a bodyguard by Rockley. Whether the siblings were close wasn't covered in the report. Edith meant enough to her brother to warrant attempted murder.

Or maybe Dalton dreamt of someone else. A sweetheart, perhaps. He hadn't said anything about a woman waiting for him, but that possibility couldn't be ruled out. A man like Dalton wouldn't want for female company. He'd be irresistible to any woman with a taste for danger. Almost every woman craved a dangerous man.

Not me. I've enough of it in my work. Don't need it in my lovers.

Yet she watched him sleep, watched the softening of his face, and how, when he wasn't scowling or cursing, his mouth verged on sybaritic.

A sharp jab in her side pulled her attention away from Dalton. Simon frowned at her.

"Be on your guard," he whispered, throwing a significant glance toward Dalton.

"I'm always careful," she whispered back.

"There's a first time for everything."

She made a hand gesture learned on the London docks. Yet the warning was a good one. If this mission failed, everyone in Nemesis would wind up either in prison or dead. The stakes were far too high to rely on something as fallible and easily fooled as the human heart.

CHAPTER FOUR

He didn't trust anyone, least of all her. Jack watched Eva's face as the train slowed, looking for any hint of what she might be thinking. She kept her expression so damn cool, though. She could be planning his murder or an afternoon tea. Either was a possibility. Her gaze stayed on the windows as the platform at King's Cross Station slid into view. She and the two blokes kept themselves alert, wary. Jack did the same.

The bits of sleep he'd had on the ride had revived him. He no longer felt like his eyes were full of sand. So he stopped looking at Eva and stared out the window, too. Despite the lateness of the hour, people milled on the platform, waiting for the train. No gang of coppers there to arrest him. He stayed cagey. The police could be lying in wait. If they thought he'd go down without a fight, they'd soon learn their mistake.

"Keep yourself easy." Eva reached across the compartment and laid her hand atop his, startling him. Her fingers tried to pry his fist open. They couldn't. "Act like an escaped convict, and that's precisely what everyone will see."

"Think I don't know that?" he growled back. But he relaxed his hands. He felt a stab of disappointment when she took her hand away and smoothed it down the front of her skirts, as if to wipe away the feel of his skin.

The train stopped with a hiss. Marco, Simon, and Eva stood. Drawing a breath, Jack stood, as well. Simon moved out into the passageway and opened the door. He glanced up and down the platform, illuminated by hundreds of gaslights.

"We're clear." Simon placed his hand on his pocket and stared at Jack. "Make a break for it, and I'll unload my gun into your back."

"Keep threatening me," Jack answered, "and I'll feed you your goddamn gun through your arse."

Scowling, Eva stepped between them. "The both of you, enough chest-beating. Our cab's waiting." She shouldered past Simon and stepped out onto the platform. Jack followed, giving Simon a glare and an extra shove with his arm as he moved past the blond toff. Jack had to give the bloke some credit, though. He didn't move an inch when Jack shoved him, and Jack hadn't been gentle. Strong, that one. Couldn't trust a man like that.

The clock in the station declared it to be half past two in the morning. Only a few dozen people moved around the platform instead of the usual mobs waiting for trains to take them north. He'd been to King's Cross a dozen times, maybe more. Even so, he hadn't been in a huge train station in years. Unease gnawed on the back of his neck. The very size of the place made him edgy, with its massive vaulted ceiling. His too tight suit already made him feel squeezed. This made it worse, his heart pounding as if trying to force its way out of his chest.

"Let's go." Eva led the way down the platform, with Simon and Marco staying close at Jack's heels.

He could do it. Now. Break away from these Nemesis madmen and track Rockley down on his own. There were dozens of places in the station he could lose himself if he ran fast. Behind the colonnades. Across the tracks and into the goods or coal depot.

"I wouldn't." Eva spoke over her shoulder. "Simon's a crack shot. He's got a shelf of trophies from Eton."

"Harrow," said Simon.

She waved a slim hand. "Those distinctions only matter to you. Either way, Dalton, you better not risk it."

"Don't like being threatened," he growled.

She turned and faced him so abruptly, he nearly collided with her. "Don't give us a reason to threaten you." A man in a wrinkled tweed suit gave them a curious look, so she pasted a bright smile on her face. "Come, Cousin Henry, Mama has made up a room for you and I'd wager she's keeping herself awake for your arrival."

The man in the tweed suit moved on.

"She better have a drink waiting for me," Jack said. He surely needed one.

"One of her famous cordials, no doubt." She tipped her head toward the arches that led to the booking office and the exit. "Do hurry along, cousin. We don't want to be discourteous to Mama."

He thought of a dozen rude things to say, but didn't want to attract any more attention. It seemed the smarter course of action to just follow along with these Nemesis lunatics and consider a plan of escape as he went.

The four of them walked quickly through the station, passing the ticket office, and then out onto the street. Several cabs lined up on St. Pancras Road, the heads of both drivers and horses drooping as they dozed. Only one driver looked awake, and he waved at them as they emerged from the station. Another one of their "friends," Jack assumed. The others hastened toward the waiting cab.

"Come on, Dalton," Eva said when Jack remained on the curb.

"Give me a bloody minute." He drew in a deep lungful of air. It was heavy with the scents of coal smoke, horse dung, mud. Not a trace of rock dust or bitter Yorkshire wind. Thank God.

He was back. Back in London. He never thought to be here again.

"Now, Dalton," Eva said, yet her voice was far gentler than her words.

He didn't want to stand out here, waiting for some copper to stroll by on patrol, so he got into the cab with the others. As soon as the door closed, they were off, clattering away from King's Cross Station.

London. London. The name beat through him like another pulse as he stared out the cab window and the passing streets. He'd been born here, and his earliest memories involved him running barefoot and filthy through the city's knotted streets. A wretched, glittering trollop of a city. Christ, how he loved it. Missed it. As the cab drove into the night, he kept his starved gaze on the city, past churches and squares and grimy streets. Though most of London's citizens were tucked in their beds, the lanes quiet and still, there were still others out on their particular nighttime business, scuttling like roaches beneath the street lamps.

Eva and the two men spoke to one another in low voices, but Jack barely heard them. Somewhere out there was Rockley. Somewhere in London that son of a bitch drank and fucked, little knowing that his miserable life was soon to end.

The cab turned into a narrow lane lined with darkened shops. The lane itself looked empty, and the lodgings above the shops had their shutters and curtains drawn. Once the hired carriage stopped, Marco hopped out, with Simon following. Eva remained in the carriage as Jack peered curiously through the cab's open door.

Of all the places he thought Nemesis would take him, he wasn't figuring on Clerkenwell, a place more suited to shabby paper shufflers and Italian immigrants than secret organizations bent on vengeance.

"Expecting a fortified palace, perhaps?" Eva's voice was arch in the dark confines of the carriage.

"Some gun towers, at the least."

"Not very discreet, gun towers." She waved toward the carriage door. "Let's not stand on custom, Mr. Dalton. After you."

He clambered from the cab, frowning when he saw Marco standing at the door to a chemist's shop. "Got a case of clap, gov?"

Marco scowled, but Jack heard Eva's soft snort of laughter behind him as she got out of the carriage. Marco unlocked the door to the chemist's.

Following everyone inside, Jack decided not to voice his questions. He'd just wait to see how everything played out. Keep his eyes and ears sharp. That was always the best way to learn something. Talk too much, ask too many questions, and people start to get suspicious. The Nemesis crew was already chary enough. No need to give them further fuel.

The shop itself was silent and still. Bottles lined up like informants along built-in shelves, with premade tonics keeping company beside faded advertisements touting a return to health and vigor. A brass scale sat ready to dole out judgment from atop a glass-topped counter. The faint acrid smell of chemicals hung in the air.

Stepping behind the counter, Eva ran her fingers beneath its overhang. She appeared to grasp something, and pulled. There was a quiet unlatching sound. One of the built-in cabinets swung open, revealing a steep wooden staircase heading upward.

Jack raised his brows. Nemesis liked to keep its tracks hidden.

He had little option other than to follow Eva as she headed up the stairs. She didn't bother turning on the gas lamp, but walked up through the darkness in perfect comfort—as though she spent every night skulking about in the shadows. Not an unreasonable assumption.

She kept glancing behind her, as if making sure he was still there.

The narrow stairwell pressed in on all sides, the stairs creaking beneath him. Compared to her light tread, he felt huge and ungainly. Even Marco and Simon trailing after him seemed to have cats' feet as they all ascended the stairs.

It had been decades since he'd been a housebreaker. He'd lost his touch for subtlety and surprise. That wasn't how he'd earned his bread. As a brawler and then a bodyguard, his job had been to make sure everyone had seen and heard him coming. Maybe that's why his attempt to kill Rockley had gone so spectacularly badly. He should have fallen back on old habits, gone for a carefully planned and secret attack. Instead, he'd just barged right into Rockley's place and wrapped his hands around the bastard's neck. One of the other bodyguards on duty had come up behind Jack and knocked him out. By the time Jack had woken up, he'd been lying on the floor of a Black Maria, his hands in manacles, on his way to the station.

That's what lack of finesse had gotten him—imprisonment, without even the benefit of getting revenge.

Another door stood at the top of the stairwell. Eva knocked—three short taps, a pause, and then another tap. Locks clicked as they were unbolted. The door opened.

A dark-haired woman stood on the other side of the door. Gas lamps burned behind her, throwing her into shadow.

"Everything went as planned?" the woman asked Eva. "No difficulties?"

Eva said, "You sound almost sorry, Harriet."

"Always looking for an excuse to practice my surgical skills." She gazed past Eva to Jack. "That him, then?"

"Silly us," said Simon, "we brought back the wrong convict."

Harriet clicked her tongue, then stepped back, allowing them inside.

As Jack crossed the threshold, he took in the details of the room. Maybe he *had* been expecting something a little . . . grander. Not this ordinary parlor, with a plain round table in the middle, surrounded by battered bentwood chairs. Two upholstered chairs were shoved against the walls, which were covered with striped wallpaper that peeled up along the seams. A framed print of the Lincoln's Inn Gate House hung on the wall.

Beyond the parlor, Jack could just make out a kitchen with a closed range stove and another set of stairs that presumably led to more rooms.

"The hell is this place?" Jack demanded.

"Nemesis's headquarters." Eva set her reticule down on the table. As she did, Simon and Marco set their gear down, as well. They all seemed to exhale, their faces looking tight and drawn in the artificial light.

"Looks like a clerk's lodgings. A badly paid clerk."

"We save our funds for things of importance," Simon

said, curt. He shut the door and did up the numerous locks, including sliding a thick bolt into place. "Explosives. Train tickets for escaped convicts."

"Tea for returning operatives." This was spoken by a man with a salt-and-pepper beard, coming into the parlor with a tray holding several chipped china cups and a teapot covered in painted flowers. He glanced at Jack inquisitively, but only put the tray on the table. He poured out four cups, added cubes of sugar and milk from a small pitcher, then handed them around, even giving one to Jack.

"Cheers," Jack said, guarded. The cup was tiny in his hand, but he held it up and sniffed at the tea.

Eva, holding his gaze, sipped at her tea. "There's a disappointing lack of opium in it."

He waited until she and everyone else looked away, then took a drink, his first real cup of tea in half a decade. Maybe gentry folk drank better brews than this, but he wouldn't know the difference. As it was, the tea was strong and wonderful. Barely, he resisted the impulse to close his eyes and groan in delight. Jaysus, but he missed this.

"I'm Lazarus," the older man said. He might have been on the far side of fifty, and not especially tall, but he looked fit and he carried himself like a man who once had earned his coin through Her Majesty's Army. Which confirmed what the others had told Jack on the train. Lazarus tilted his head toward the woman who'd opened the door. "You already met Harridan Badly."

"It's Harriet, you ass," she snapped. "Harriet Bradley." Now that Jack could see her better, he realized that Harriet wasn't young, either, somewhere in her middle forties, but still slim and handsome. Her skin was the color of tea with cream, her features were slightly

African, her hair thickly textured. A woman of mixed blood.

Dislike and something else crackled between her and Lazarus as they glared at each other across the parlor.

"Desmond and Riza are out in the field right now," Eva said. "And now you've met everyone in Nemesis."

"Good to sodding meet you." Jack threw back the last of his tea, not caring that it burned his mouth, and slammed his cup down on the table. It broke apart, bits of cheap porcelain scattering over the wood. "I'm leaving. Got a murderer to kill." He swung back toward the door.

Marco and Simon were on him in an instant, gripping his arms, struggling to restrain him.

He snarled out a laugh. "You think you can hold me?"

"Either you stay here and do what we say," Marco said through gritted teeth, "or we hand you to the authorities."

Anger boiled through Jack. "I broke out of Dunmoor but wound up in another prison." He shook Marco off. The dark man stumbled against one of the upholstered chairs, then righted himself quickly, agile as a liar.

Before Jack could shove Simon, Eva stepped in front of him. "By now, Rockley's been informed that you've escaped," she said. "Security around him is going to be impenetrable. You wouldn't be able to get to him, even if we let you go." She took a step closer. "All you would be doing is running straight toward your own death. Without even the satisfaction of vengeance. If that's what you want"—she moved aside and undid all the locks on the door, even the bolt—"then go."

His gaze moved back and forth between her and the

door. Was she speaking the truth? Jack had escaped
from prison that very day, and the prison wouldn't want
to make public the fact that one of their convicts had
gotten free. And Dunmoor was hundreds of miles from
London. At most, there might be a notice in the York
papers. No one in London would know.

But . . . Rockley had always kept his claws out for
any bit of information relevant to himself. He lined the
pockets of bureaucrats and informants all over the
country. Official word wouldn't get out about Jack's
escape, but doubtless one of the warders—if not the
prison governor himself—had been kept on retainer.
Jack had tried to kill Rockley and survived. Without
question Rockley would have kept an eye on him. A
telegraph had surely been sent, informing that piece of
garbage that Jack was at large. Rockley's edginess had
probably gotten even worse since Jack had tried to
murder him. Which meant he would have doubled or
even tripled his usual number of bodyguards. Jack had
once been one of those bodyguards. They were rough,
mean men, just like him. And just like him, they'd stop
at nothing to keep anyone and everyone from getting to
Rockley.

Eva was right. If Jack so much as belched in Rockley's direction, he'd be taken down. There'd be no justice for Edith. Only her brother's cold, rotting body
lying in the street.

He swore, using the filthiest words he knew.

"Curb your language," Simon hissed.

"I'll say whatever I bloody want. Get off me." Jack
rammed his elbow into Simon's flat stomach. The toff
only grunted softly, but didn't let go.

She peered at Jack. "Mr. Dalton appears to have
grasped some logic. He won't be leaving us. Will you,
Mr. Dalton?"

He glowered at her. "I'll stay. For now."

"How gracious." She nodded when Simon finally let go of Jack's arm, though the blond gent looked sour to do so. Quickly, she fastened all the locks. The bolt made a solid thunk as it slid into place. They didn't mess about, these Nemesis folks, not when it came to watching their arses. "Consider this place your refuge from a hostile world."

Jack paced around the parlor, noting with a dark satisfaction that everything in the room rattled when he walked, the crockery and bits of bric-a-brac clattering like bones. "'Cept you lot are just as hostile as a gang of cutthroats."

"There are certain throats that need to be cut," she answered, turning back to him. "Metaphorically. And you are going to be the blade that cuts Rockley's."

"Metaphorically," he said snidely, "on account that you don't work that way."

"Nemesis doesn't murder," Lazarus said. "Not in cold blood."

"That's so damn pretty I should tattoo it on my chest," Jack fired back.

Lazarus paced over to him. The older man shoved up the sleeve of his jacket, revealing a burly tanned forearm dusted with silvery hair. But there was ink there, too, faded and smoky. Hard to tell what the pictures had been when they were fresh decades ago, but they looked like they once had been knives. Seven of them in neat succession running up Lazarus's forearm.

"These are for the men who died at Lucknow," Lazarus snarled. "My friends. And I killed God knows how many rebels during those sieges. Got me a Victoria Cross for my efforts, but it didn't matter. There's too much blood that gets spilled, oceans of it, and I've been the one spilling it. But we've all left that behind." He looked pointedly at each of the Nemesis crew in turn, including Harriet and Eva.

"No one's got my respect more than soldiers," Jack said. "They go to war knowing they're going to kill. They know they could die, too. But Edith never thought she'd take a knife to the belly. Rockley's knife. You've seen how long it takes to die from a hole in your gut, Lazarus. She had plenty of time to feel pain and be afraid."

His words burned like acid as he spoke, and his mind choked with pictures of Edith as she lay in a growing pool of her blood on the floor of the brothel, and him unable to do a damn thing to help.

"So don't tell me what you did and what I have to do are the same thing," he rumbled. " 'Cause they ain't."

Silence fell, heavy as a corpse.

"Once a man dies, his suffering is over," Eva said quietly from the other side of the parlor. "But ruination can last a lifetime."

He stared at her, barely aware of the others in the shabby little room. "Just picture it: the only family you got in the whole world, stretched out at your feet, dying too slow to be merciful but too fast to get a doctor. Picture that"—he pointed a finger at her—"and then tell me you'd be satisfied with *ruination*."

Her cheeks whitened, and she pressed her lips into a thin line. Finally, she spoke. "We aren't murderers. And as long as we need you, you aren't a murderer, either." Before he could shoot back a response, she held up her hand. "One thing we *all* are is exhausted. Time for us to get some rest, and then we resume our discussion in the morning."

"I want Rockley dead, and you lot say I can't kill him," Jack said. "Soon as I get my chance, I'm going to end his goddamn life. End of discussion." He stepped close to her, deliberately trying to intimidate her. Yet drawing near her, he found himself oddly intrigued by the soft strands of golden hair that had come loose from their pins and teased over the back of her neck. What would those little wisps feel like against his fingers? And why did he have the need to know?

She crossed her arms over her chest, but the movement was more combative than self-protecting. He almost admired her refusal to back down. Except she wasn't backing down from *him;* that, he didn't like one bit.

"The conversation's far from over," she said. "And I'm not going to say another damn word about it until I get some sleep."

But her words had a strange kind of power to them, for as soon as she said that word *sleep,* he felt as though his bones were made of lead. The snooze he'd caught on the train had fueled him for a small while. He'd burned through that fuel, however, and his whole body ached with weariness. Pain crept behind his eyes. His jaw throbbed with the force it took to keep from yawning wide as a crocodile.

Even if he headed outside, he wouldn't make it far before keeling over. Damn prison life getting him used to regular sleep. When he'd been on the streets, he could go days with nothing more than a quick doze leaning up against a wall.

"Going to put me up at Claridge's?"

Marco grunted. "Delusional. Come on, then." He walked through the kitchen and up the stairs.

Seeing that he was supposed to follow, and given that he'd tip over from exhaustion at any moment, Jack decided to go along. He climbed the stairs, hearing Eva's lighter step behind him. At the top of the stairs was a cramped hallway, a threadbare hooked carpet

partially covering the scuffed floorboards. Two doors
faced each other. Marco opened the door on the right.

Glancing inside, Jack found a narrow bed covered
with a faded calico quilt. A dresser, desk, and wash-
stand with a basin made up the rest of the furnishings.
The braided rag rug looked as though it had been present for the queen's coronation. Yellowed lace covered
the single window. No gaslights, just an oil lamp set up
on the dresser and a squat coal stove crouched in the
corner.

"Until we're done with you," Eva said, walking into
the room, "this is your home."

"Claridge's has nothing on this palace." In truth, the
plain little room *did* look like a palace to him after his
bare cell. No bars on the window, no slot in the door
through which he could be seen by patrolling warders.
Jack took a step inside, examining every detail, from
the web of cracks in the plastered ceiling to the book
lying on the desk. *The Return of the Native.* Sounded
like an adventure story.

"I'm in ecstasy from your approval," drawled Marco.
"The privy's in the backyard. Only the kitchen's got
running water. If you'll want a wash, you'll have to
fetch and heat the water yourself." With that, he stalked
back down the hallway and down the stairs.

Leaving Jack with Eva. They hadn't been alone together since the train, when she'd given the other gents
the boot so he could eat comfortably. He became aware
suddenly of the smallness of the room, and her presence within it. Though he ached with tiredness, a fine
electric tension threaded itself over his skin. Hard to
say in the lamplight, but her cheeks looked a little
pinker than they had when Marco had been around.

They stared at each other warily, and he noticed
how she kept herself out of striking distance.

Baffling, that's what she was. Tough and hard as a bruiser, but she showed small moments where she seemed almost . . . kind. Like when she let him take his first long, deep breath of London air.

And there was something else between them. Something that wasn't kindness at all. She looked at him not as a pawn in Nemesis's game, and not as a subject of pity. But with the kind of sexual awareness a woman had for a man. She didn't want to, he could tell. Yet it was there, anyway.

Maybe he could make use of that, somehow. Work his way free of Nemesis by exploiting her interest in him.

He almost laughed at that. Him? Play the seduction angle? That was for pretty lads and confidence men. He was a sledgehammer, not an artist's chisel. As he watched her move through the little room, making tiny adjustments to the quilt and the furniture, he knew he couldn't trap her using seduction, not without getting trapped himself.

Better to think of her as just another Nemesis obstacle than a woman.

Better . . . but not possible. He still smelled of her, that pretty citrus and flower smell.

"This has to be better than Dunmoor," she said.

He didn't want her to think that he was in any way grateful, so he just shrugged. "It'll do. Isn't permanent, is it?"

"Once we bring Rockley down and get some restitution for the wronged girl, you'll be free to lie in any gutter you please."

He scowled at the mention of the bastard. "Haven't slept in a gutter since I was a tyke. And I didn't for long. You can get gnawed on by rats for only a short while before you think of other places you'd rather be."

A troubled frown crossed her face, brief as mercy. "Thousands of others in London have the same story."

"But not you." He gave her a thorough stare, from the top of her slightly mussed blond curls to the hem of her skirts. A stripe of mud edged the fabric, a souvenir from her sprint across the moors, but the quality of her clothes was good. No secondhand dresses and petticoats for her. And her underwear was probably snowy white.

A picture of her in nothing but her chemise, drawers, and corset popped into his mind, as vivid as if he'd taken a photograph. It was a damned pleasant image.

"Not me," she said, a nice bit of huskiness in her voice. She cleared her throat. "It's late, and I'm starting to see double. We'll work out our strategy in the morning." A clock somewhere in the flat chimed three. "*Later* in the morning."

He might not be able to work the seduction angle, but it wouldn't hurt to keep her as off balance as he was. "Which room is yours? I might get a night terror and need soothing."

"Somehow I feel that nightmares would be more afraid of *you*. And you'd look rather ridiculous wandering the streets of Brompton in your nightshirt."

"Before I went into the clink," Jack said, folding his arms over his chest, "I slept naked, so I'd be running around Brompton with my tackle knocking against my knees."

She gave a low, worldly chuckle. "I've seen your *tackle,* Mr. Dalton, so you can't paint yourself in such a flattering light."

"Against my thigh, then." But neither he nor his cock had forgotten she'd had a look back in that carriage on the moors. And they were both interested. "But we're in Clerkenwell, not Brompton."

"Your knowledge of London geography hasn't vanished during your incarceration."

"So you don't live here."

Her brows rose. "God, no. Is that what you imagined? That all the Nemesis operatives dwelt under one roof?"

He didn't much care for her tone, as if he were some snot-nosed kid who didn't know the first thing about life. "Gangs of thieves do it all the time."

"Thieves don't have other identities to protect."

"But you do. An identity that lives in Brompton." He wondered who that other Eva was, how she might be different from the one who helped convicts escape and then blackmailed them into collaboration.

"All of us have lives and homes elsewhere. And jobs, too. That's how we keep Nemesis funded." A neat dodge on her part, telling him nothing about herself.

"I'm right sorry we won't be sleeping under the same roof." Which was the truth. Of all the Nemesis crew, she was the only one he liked talking with, and he found himself looking forward to those quick flashes of wicked humor in those sherry eyes of hers.

"Given that I'm certain you snore, I'm not sorry." She added, "You aren't going to have the run of the place, though. Lazarus will be staying here while you're our—"

"Prisoner," he said.

"Guest," she countered.

"Pawn."

"Temporary operative."

This time, it was he who laughed, a quick bark of laughter that caught him off guard. "A pretty way with words, you've got. Precise and nimble. Like one of them sailors' carvings on ivory."

"Scrimshaw." Her mouth curved. "I rather like that

image. Perhaps you've a bit of the poet in you, as well, Dalton."

"This is my pen." He held up a fist. "I use it to write sonnets across blokes' faces. That's the only poetry I know." Lowering his hand, he said, "Describe me however you want—we both know Nemesis has got me by the baubles."

She pursed her lips. "Not forever."

"When you've got a man by his baubles, love, even a minute feels like a lifetime."

"Having none of my own, I'll have to take your word for it."

Goddamn, she was a brazen one. And goddamn if she didn't intrigue him, this woman who talked in a posh accent about a man's goolies and led two lives. A woman like her couldn't be trusted.

He didn't trust her, not by a mile, but he was fascinated by her.

"Eva!" Simon shouted up the stairwell. "Everything all right up there?"

Jack wanted to yell down to the toff that he could go bugger himself, but Eva called over her shoulder, "My virtue's intact, Simon."

"What's left of it," hooted Marco.

"Spoken by the biggest trollop this side of the Thames," Eva answered. She walked to the bedroom door and leaned out into the hallway. "And stop shouting up the stairs. This isn't the dockyards." Turning back to Jack, she said, "On that charming note, I'm leaving. We've a lot of ground to cover in the morning, so I suggest you get some rest."

"Don't know how I'm supposed to," Jack growled, "with that murdering son of a bitch out there and me shackled to a bunch of bedlamites."

She didn't look insulted. "It's because we're all

somewhat insane that the success of our missions is ensured. And, believe me, Mr. Dalton"—her gaze held his—"we *will* succeed in this operation against Lord Rockley. He'll pay for what he did to Miss Jones, and to Edith."

Staring into her eyes, he felt more than her presence as a woman. He'd been around some of the toughest, meanest bastards—he *was* one—and none of them had half her resolve. The truth gleamed in her gaze: she truly believed that she and her crew would take Rockley down.

"In my experience," he said, "no one's more dangerous than a man who believes he can't fail. His confidence makes him sloppy and reckless."

"I'm not a man," she pointed out. As if he didn't know.

"A woman who has faith in herself is like a gun that shoots fire. She'll burn everything down just to hit a single target."

She tilted her head, studying him. He wondered what she saw.

I don't give a good goddamn.

Still, he liked seeing her try to puzzle him out. Maybe he wasn't entirely what she had expected him to be. Good. Let her ponder and stew and fret. Only fair.

"Good night, Mr. Dalton. Welcome to Nemesis."

"You're wrong about something, Miss Warrick." He planted his hands on his hips. "I don't snore."

"How do you know that for certain?"

His smile was a leisurely one. "None of the women who shared my bed ever complained."

She shook her head, then turned and left.

He listened to her footsteps as she walked down the hall, and down the stairs. The room in which he stood wasn't pretty, but it turned far more dingy as soon as she left. There were murmured exchanges down below—he didn't quite catch all the words, but it was clear that Lazarus was being warned to stay on his guard around Jack. After some more words, people filed out of the flat. Marco, Simon, Harriet. And Eva.

The past five years he'd spent making sense out of quiet nighttime sounds. Lights out in prison didn't necessarily mean falling asleep right away. He learned to tell guards apart by the rhythm of their walks. He knew that the man two cells down from him whimpered the name Cathleen every hour. He figured out who was a restless sleeper and who liked to give himself a wank before nodding off and who ran into the arms of forgetful sleep as fast as he could.

As for Jack himself, he hadn't thought of pretty girls or foods he missed, or even about how rough life was within the walls of Dunmoor. No, he'd lie awake, staring at the stone ceiling, and think about killing Rockley.

He'd do the same this night, even though he wasn't in prison any longer.

Two strides took Jack to the grimy window. Holding back the curtain, he stared out at the little courtyard behind the house. There wasn't a lot in the yard. Just a bench, a bucket lying on its side, and the previously mentioned jakes. Hard to tell in the dark, but not much grew out there except some weeds poking up through brick pavers. Beyond the yard were more houses, all of them dark and shuttered.

He'd never been able to look out his cell window. A view like this would've been prized. But suddenly, it wasn't enough.

"Where the hell are you going?" Lazarus demanded as Jack shouldered past him in the hall.

"Can't go out," Jack growled, "so I'm going up. This place got a roof, don't it?"

For a moment, the older man just stared at him. Then, "This way."

Jack followed Lazarus through a narrow door—he barely fit through the thing, turning sideways and ducking his head—and up another, even tighter staircase. They emerged onto a slate-shingled roof that fell away sharply on all four sides. The flat part of the roof wasn't sizable, only three good strides in any direction, and the chimney took up a decent section of it. Grime and soot coated everything. Bitter cold poked chilled fingers through the gaps in his clothing.

But Jack didn't care. He walked to the edge of the flat part of the roof. Stared up at the sky, the London sky, the one under which he'd been born. It was such a damn luxury to have the night surrounding him, when he'd been herded indoors at the first sign of darkness for five years.

"You won't see any stars," Lazarus said. "Not with the smoke and fog."

"I'm not here for stargazing." When he'd been on the lam, after his escape from Dunmoor, he hadn't been able to appreciate being outside. But here he was now. With London spread all around him—Bethnal Green and Whitechapel to the east, Smithfield Market and St. Paul's Cathedral to the south. And off to the west, in the posh neighborhoods of Mayfair and St. James's, that's where he'd find Rockley.

Eva was out there, too. Heading toward her other life in Brompton as a . . . a what? She said they all had jobs to keep Nemesis afloat, so what did she do? Was she some gent's fancy piece? She couldn't be a factory girl like the ones Jack knew. A shopgirl? Maybe she was one of those "modern" women who worked as a clerk and could use a fancy typing machine. None of it seemed right, though.

He could ask Lazarus, but it wouldn't do to have the old soldier know how much she interested him. He'd give none of these Nemesis lot anything that could be used as a weapon. They were the sort who hoarded knowledge and used it against people. Maybe Rockley. Certainly Jack. Ruthless bastards.

And he'd delivered himself to them. Right on a fucking platter.

"It's colder than a Frenchwoman's cunt out here," Lazarus grumbled. "Time to go back inside. You'll be no good to us if you catch the pleurisy and die."

"I never get sick," Jack said.

"And tonight won't be the first time, not while I'm on watch." The older man nodded toward the door. "Down you go."

"Or what?" Jack rumbled.

"Or I summon the coppers and you don't get to look at this fine night sky ever again."

Anger churned in Jack like bad gin. If he could, he'd sleep on this roof, no matter how blasted cold it was. But it was clear from the set of Lazarus's jaw that he'd make good on his threat if Jack didn't do as he was told.

Cursing foully, Jack ducked through the door and trundled down the staircase. Each step back toward his little room felt like more weights being added to his invisible shackles. He'd broken out of prison, yet he still wasn't free.

A voice whispered in his mind, *Have I ever been?*

CHAPTER FIVE

"You shouldn't be alone with him," said Simon.

Eva glanced over at him as the hansom cab rattled toward her lodgings. That they'd been able to find any cab at this hour—and a sober driver—had been something of a miracle. She'd been fully prepared to make the long trek on foot. But in that inimitable way of his, Simon had simply walked out onto the corner, and a hansom had rolled up, asking their direction.

Things came so easily to a man like Simon. Cabs included. He had everything—birth, wealth, position, aristocratic blond good looks that made women instinctively pat their hair and widen their eyes like fawns eagerly awaiting a wolf. Of all the Nemesis operatives, Simon seemed the least likely to involve himself in their work. Why should he? He'd never been on the wrong end of justice before. He served as Nemesis's de facto leader, but he never made unilateral decisions. Everything was discussed among the operatives.

Simon's time in the army had shown him hard lessons. And, like a few other men of his class, he had a strong belief in morals and ethics. Not so strong that he wouldn't make use of a man like Jack Dalton, however.

"We've utilized men such as him before," she pointed out.

"They were easily manipulated. Too afraid of the consequences of defying us to be a threat. But him . . ." Simon exhaled roughly. "He's got nothing to lose."

"Except vengeance." She and the others of Nemesis had counted on Dalton's need for revenge as a key element of their plan. What none of them had anticipated, she especially, was the depth of his feeling. It was far more than the animal desire for retaliation.

The pain in Dalton's eyes when he spoke of his sister dying . . . beyond loss, there was self-recrimination. Somehow, Dalton held himself responsible for Edith's death. Having read the file, Eva knew that Dalton had had nothing to do with Rockley's going to the brothel where Edith had worked. Dalton hadn't been anywhere near Rockley that night—his bodyguards received one day off a week, and that day had been Dalton's. Somehow, Dalton had learned of Edith's death that same night, and had unsuccessfully tried to avenge her in the early hours of the morning. Yet he still felt culpable. Eva had seen it in the glaze of rage and anguish in his dark eyes.

Killing Rockley wouldn't bring Edith Dalton back from the dead, but to her brother, it had to mean some measure of absolution. A man would do almost anything to achieve forgiveness.

"He's going to be trickier to handle than the others," Simon insisted. "Remember Fetcham? He was a bruiser, too, but when it came right down to it, he fell in line. Dalton's far more dangerous."

"I can handle him," said Eva. "Thumbs to the eyes, a knee to the groin. He might be big and strong as a bull, but every man has vulnerable places."

Passing lamplight glanced off the pristine planes of Simon's face as he frowned his displeasure. He verged on being too handsome, if such a thing were possible, almost uncomfortable to look upon. To her, however, he was merely Simon, her colleague, the architecture of his face admirable but not stirring.

Not like Dalton. He wasn't handsome, not in the known sense of it, anyway. Yet she couldn't banish his face from her mind, its rough contours and hard lines. If Simon was a mathematically perfect temple, its columns placed precisely, the proportions expertly rendered, Dalton was a granite mountain, all crags and peril, alluring because it was hazardous. Both drew the eye, but for very different reasons.

"It's not Dalton's size or strength that has me concerned," said Simon.

"A little credit, if you please." Eva fixed him with a wry look. "I'm hardly the sort to be led astray by a suggestive remark or carnal glance."

"No, you aren't."

At least there was no recrimination in Simon's tone. Once, years ago, he'd intimated that he would like to take their relationship beyond the professional. She'd immediately quashed that idea. There had been some wounded feelings right after her refusal, but Simon's speedy recovery had proven to her that, at most, he'd been mildly curious. Not enthralled. Not even enamored. She hadn't been hurt by his quick rallying. If anything, it proved what she already knew—she was better off on her own, free of entanglements.

"Just . . . be wary around Dalton," Simon pressed. "He's got a way of looking at you."

Her heart gave a strange, small leap. "The man's been in prison for five years. He'd look at a toothless crone the same way."

This time it was Simon who was wry. "Believe it or not, but even in the depths of a man's lust, he knows the difference between a beldam and a beauty."

"How encouraging."

Simon continued, "Dalton assuredly knows what he sees when he looks at you."

The woman who's got his baubles in her hand. Or is it more than that?

It didn't matter. She was a dedicated operative. Dalton might be different from what she had anticipated, but she had a responsibility to Nemesis's client and the greater good. He was simply another cog in the larger machine, a machine she was determined to run with the same capable skill she'd shown throughout her years with Nemesis.

The cab rolled to a stop outside the door to her lodgings. It was a perfectly respectable building in a perfectly respectable neighborhood; so respectable, in fact, that no one was awake to note that she wasn't married to the man riding with her in the hansom. After bidding Simon good night, Eva climbed the front steps, then let herself in.

She walked up the two flights of stairs leading to her rooms. The ground floor was where her landlady, Mrs. Petworth, lived, along with Mrs. Petworth's daughter. Miss Axford resided on the next story, a soft-spoken girl who worked at a stationer's shop, as well as the Ratley cousins, both women employed as transcribing clerks at the same firm.

Reaching the door of her rooms, Eva saw light filtering out from beneath the door of the woman who lived across from her. Miss Siles was a writer, and kept appalling hours as she struggled to become the next George Eliot. As Eva fitted her key into the lock of her door, she heard the creak of the floor in Miss Siles's rooms. Pacing. Again. She paced far more than she actually wrote. Thankfully, she was also much too absorbed in her creative process to notice that the woman who lived across the hall was coming home at three-thirty in the morning. Hardly the hours a respectable tutor kept.

Mrs. Petworth often reminded Eva that she rented only to decent women of good repute.

A smile touched Eva's lips as she wondered what Dalton might think of that policy. He'd likely have something to say about her reputation, and it wouldn't be good.

She stepped inside her rooms and shut the door behind her, then turned the lamp on low. Soft light filled the snug but comfortable space, illuminating the table at which she conducted her lessons, the armchair by the fireplace and the books gathered around the chair's feet, and the painted folding screen which concealed her bed. Watercolors painted by her students hung upon the walls. What they lacked in skill they made up for in enthusiasm.

She gave a quick but thorough scan of the chambers, checking for indications that anyone had been there. Everything was just as she'd left it earlier. Not even the single hair she'd left on her bed had been disturbed. Searches almost always began with the bed.

She tried to picture Dalton in her rooms. He'd seem as out of place as an ironclad in a duck pond.

Papers and lesson plans were scattered upon her table, and as she gathered them up, she considered then rejected the idea of making herself a cup of tea. Far too late for that. What she really needed was to take her own advice to Dalton and get some sleep. It had been a phenomenally long day. She'd been awake for over twenty-one hours. At the least, she didn't have any students scheduled for tomorrow. Checking her calendar, she noted that her next appointment was for the day following next. The Hallow children. Both girls were making decent progress with their French, but they couldn't retain historical dates for love or money.

Mr. Hallow didn't care if his daughters knew the date of the Treaty of Windsor. He only wanted them to speak French passably, to paint with a fair degree of skill, and to have enough general knowledge to successfully converse at the dinner table. In short, he wanted them to be like the daughters of the aristocracy, even though Mr. Hallow was a grocer who owned two shops. Like most everyone in London, he had aspirations. For himself. For his children.

Eva stacked her papers up into neat piles. She needed to keep everything tidy. Her students all came to her rooms for their lessons. Her clients didn't have enough money to have governesses, nor to send their daughters away to school. Eva was there to give the girls a bit of polish—and, unbeknownst to their parents, some actual useful skills, such as mathematics, geography, and history.

None of her students nor their parents knew the truth about Eva. Even Eva's own parents believed she was just a tutor, and nothing more.

As a gentleman, Simon had no need of *work,* per se, but he managed his investments and estates with none of his aristocratic friends or colleagues aware of his other work. Marco continued to serve as a consultant to the government in matters of foreign policy. Lazarus had a military pension, but would take occasional construction jobs. And no one at the accountancy firm where Harriet clerked had the vaguest inkling that she did anything other than sort through financial records.

Eva rather liked having dual selves. A secret belonging only to a select few. And while Simon, Marco, and the others knew she taught, none of them had ever been inside her rooms, nor seen her at work. The only person who knew everything about the two Evas was Eva herself.

Satisfied everything was in order, she checked the locks on her door one last time, then began to undress. Undoing the hooks running along the front of her bodice was a relief. She did the same with her corset cover and corset. Nearly twenty-four hours had passed since she'd dressed in the predawn darkness, preparing for her journey out to Yorkshire. Now her clothes felt limp and stale.

What must it be like to have a maid, dressing and undressing you? All of her garments fastened in the front. Wealth was never a possibility when tutoring the children of shopkeepers. She might have made more as a governess, or teaching at a day or boarding school—but that meant her time wouldn't be her own, time she needed for Nemesis.

It wasn't about the money. It never was.

Girls like the Hallow daughters were precisely the sort that Lord Rockley preyed upon. Without the benefit of wealth or status, Miss Jones had nowhere to turn. Neither would the Hallow girls. As Dalton had said, it was an old story. Rich man, vulnerable girl. But Eva was determined that no female would ever suffer again because of Rockley.

Standing in her chemise and drawers, she shivered. The fire hadn't been lit. A lingering chill seeped through the windows that faced the street, and weariness robbed her of heat.

This wasn't a kind world to women. It never would be. She couldn't simply accept it, however.

She stripped out of her chemise and drawers and put her clothing away into the somewhat battered oak wardrobe, then donned her nightgown. There were finer nightgowns, to be sure, confections of silk and lace, but no one ever saw Eva in her nightclothes. The little blue ribbons trimming the neckline and cuffs were for herself alone.

She recalled the flash of heat in Dalton's eyes, and Simon's words about how Dalton looked at her. How might he look at her as she stood by her bed in her simple nightgown? Would his gaze go shadowed with desire? And why should that image make her own heart beat faster?

Broken hearts and dashed promises littered the Nemesis case files like so many carcasses in the morgue. Even Miss Jones had been led astray by promises that would never come to pass. What was love but another means of calamity? She'd not allow herself that kind of weakness.

Besides, she needed to protect her work within Nemesis. Which severely limited her options. And she wouldn't make the mistake of becoming romantically involved with any of her colleagues.

Which meant nights alone. No one to truly confide in. A deliberately solitary existence.

It's worth it. She needed to believe that.

She extinguished the light and climbed into bed. Nearly a whole day without sleep. Yet her thoughts wouldn't quiet, circling her on their raven wings and cawing.

They'd find some way to ruin Rockley. It hadn't become clear yet, but everyone within Nemesis possessed the same tenacity. All that was left was to discover the how of it.

Dalton was the key. From the beginning, when the initial plan had been hatched, she'd protested his involvement. A thug, a brute. More a liability than an asset. But she'd been wrong. He was far more than muscles controlled by a rudimentary brain. He had thoughts of his own, needs, emotions.

What troubled her the most, what chased her down dream-lit corridors as she finally succumbed to sleep, was the interest and hunger that gleamed in his dark eyes when he looked at her. More troubling was the answering awareness she felt within herself.

Eva heard the shouting through the ceiling of the chemist's shop. The few customers kept glancing up from their examination of tonics, worried frowns pinching their brows.

"How long?" she asked Mr. Byrne.

"Started up 'bout an hour ago," the chemist answered. Like the customers, Mr. Byrne looked uneasy from the sounds. "As soon as Mr. Addison-Shawe and Mr. Spencer gone up. Don't recognize who 'tis they're yelling with, though."

"Someone new." Bottles rattled as heavy footsteps thumped overhead. "He won't be staying."

"Hope not." The chemist looked balefully at the door as his would-be patrons hurried out, the bell jingling behind them in cheery counterpoint to the angry male voices from above.

Mr. Byrne was quite aware of Nemesis's activities. As someone who'd grown up in reduced circumstances and had seen firsthand the lack of parity between rich and poor, he approved of their work. Which was fortunate, because as their landlord, he kept their rent accommodatingly low.

Eva unlatched the secret door and stepped into the stairwell leading up to the Nemesis rooms. Mr. Byrne shut the door behind her. As she walked up the stairs, the voices grew louder, crashing together like battleships. With her hand on the doorknob, she took a deep breath. The day had hardly begun, and it already promised to be an upward climb.

Entering the parlor, she removed her hat, coat, and gloves and found Simon and Dalton standing nearly chest to chest, their faces dark with anger. No one noticed her. Marco struggled in vain to separate the two men, trying to shove them apart. Lazarus and Harriet stood off to the side, bemused. Amazement struck her all over again, seeing Dalton's massiveness, how he seemed to fill the room with not merely his size but his presence. Simon—lean, strong Simon—looked like a sapling beside a giant oak.

"How many times do I got to tell you?" Dalton snarled. "I don't know a sodding thing about Rockley's business, so stop bloody asking me."

"Are you deliberately being obtuse?" Simon fired back. "The more you fight us, the tougher it's going to be and the longer it's going to take."

"And I don't give a damn. I just want Rockley."

"*This* is how we're going to bring him down. If you'd just—"

"Here I thought we specialized in *covert* missions," Eva said dryly.

Both men turned the force of their glares on her. Had she not been experienced in dealing with large, angry men, she might have been afraid. As it was, she simply folded her arms over her chest and stared back at them coolly.

They spoke over each other.

"This oaf was—"

"Been trying to tell Lord Cuntshire here that I—"

She ignored them, walking past the two shouting men and into the kitchen. There, she calmly made herself a cup of tea. From one of the cupboards, she produced a bottle of whisky, and added a generous dash of it to her brew. As she did this, the yelling in the parlor died away. She glanced up from attending to her drink and found both Simon and Dalton staring at her from the doorway to the kitchen.

She took a sip of her tea, enjoying its heat and burn. "Quite done?"

"You were right," Simon clipped. "Using Dalton is a mistake. He can't help us at all."

The glower on Dalton's face deepened as he looked at her. "You thought bringing me on was a mistake?"

"I thought so, yes," she answered mildly, then took another sip. "Opinions can change, however."

Dalton stalked into the parlor, and, after sending Simon a warning glance, Eva followed. Marco, Lazarus, and Harriet all sat warily at the table.

"Got it right the first time," Dalton said, pacing around the room. "If you want someone beaten to a stain on the carpet, I'm your man. Otherwise, you'd have been better off leaving me to rot in Dunmoor."

"Let's agree to disagree on that matter. Right now, we need to go over the points of what we do know about Rockley's disreputable activities and formulate a strategy from there. Please sit." She waved toward one of the upholstered chairs.

He shook his head. "Feels like I'd explode like dynamite if I sat still too long."

She understood. He'd been confined for years, and now he had freedom—or a small measure of it—with the one man he wanted dead traipsing around London. No wonder restless energy poured from Dalton. It seeped into her own body, until she felt ablaze as a theater marquee. But she needed her poise and equanimity. She couldn't let him rouse her, and she couldn't cede power.

So she stood near the fireplace and took measured sips of her tea, watching him pace. "This is what we know: among his other business ventures, Rockley has a government contract for the manufacture of cartridges. The contract has been making him a considerable amount of money, but not merely from the sale of the cartridges. That much is public knowledge." She set her teacup down on the mantel, and made certain she had Dalton's attention. When he halted in his pacing, she continued. "Yet what isn't public knowledge is that he's been embezzling."

Dalton frowned. "Skimming the profits?"

"He's billing the army for the full cost of the cartridges," said Marco, "but Rockley's using third-rate materials for their manufacture, which means he has to be pocketing the difference."

"Cheap alloys instead of copper for the jackets," Eva explained. "Even worse for the primers."

Lurking moodily at the door leading to the kitchen, Simon growled. "This is how we found out about the embezzling in the first place. I still have contacts in the army, and they've told me that the cartridges being made by Rockley are inferior in quality, certainly not worth the money being paid for them. He's got to be pocketing the difference. " He turned his gaze toward the window, a frown deep between his brows. "It's possible that Rockley's shoddy cartridges helped bring about the fall of Khartoum. Old army friends told me about what happened there. A damn massacre, and not just because Gladstone dragged his heels sending the relief force."

Dalton muttered a curse. Even cut off from the world as he'd been, he must have heard about the death of General Gordon and his troops at the hands of the Mahdists in the Sudan. The event had become a national rallying point, with the public crying for retribution.

"Could be that bad cartridges had nothing to do with Khartoum," Dalton said.

"Had those men been given working, reliable bullets," Simon answered, fury edging his voice, "they could've held out longer, those two days until Beresford and his gunboats arrived."

Dalton said, "If you've got Rockley pinned with this government contract business, then it's all settled. You can deliver him to the government on a tray, all nice like."

"There's the rub," Eva said. "Nemesis has been stonewalled. All our attempts to go further in our investigation reach dead ends. Rockley's put up too many impediments." She gazed at him, full of meaning.

"You lot think I can tell you anything about it?" Dalton's laugh wasn't particularly agreeable. "Come put your hands around my arm, right here." He pointed to his bicep.

"Why?" Marco demanded.

But Eva had already crossed the parlor and stood beside Dalton. She did so warily, still not trusting him not to lash out. Unlike Marco and Simon, Dalton was in his shirtsleeves, the cuffs rolled back to reveal thick forearms. Someone had obtained a slightly better-fitting set of clothing for him, for it looked as though he was not about to burst out of his garments with the next breath. Yet he still strained against the fabric of his shirt, shoulders pulling the woven cotton tight. It would take some exceptional tailoring to contain him.

As though something as quotidian as a suit could contain Jack Dalton.

He held out his arm, and, having already decided to oblige him, Eva cautiously attempted to encircle his bicep with her hands. An impossible task. She would have needed at least one more hand to fully surround his upper arm. Heat radiated up from his skin, and he felt hard and solid as forged steel.

I'll never underestimate him, she thought.

Their gazes met.

"That there is all Rockley ever wanted from me," Dalton said, his voice a low rumble. "I didn't keep a ledger of his money dealings. We didn't gab over cigars and brandy about the stock market. The bastard barely ever *talked* to me. He kept me around for one reason, and you've got your hands around it."

Eva released her grip on him, though the feel of his hard flesh seemed branded into her palms and along her fingers. She stepped away quickly.

"There are men with more information about Rockley's business transactions," she said. "Every last one of them is either in his pocket or dead. You are the *only* man who's been that close to him."

"The only one who's left his employ," added Lazarus, "and still draws breath."

"He tried, though," Dalton noted. "Wanted me hanged instead of imprisoned."

"Because he knew you could be a threat to him."

Yet Dalton shook his head. "Bloodthirsty and proud, that's all. It'd be an insult to him if the bloke who tried to murder him wasn't killed somehow."

"It was more than pride and a hunger for blood that motivated Rockley. He wanted to bury you and the information you possessed." She stared up at him. "Just think. Think about what you know of Rockley. The answer's in there somewhere."

Dalton growled in frustration. "Even if I knew something, which I don't, I'm no good at this *thinking* business. Never done it before."

"That's patently untrue." She put her hands on her hips. "Nemesis planted the story that Rockley was near Dunmoor, but *you* thought your way out of that prison. None of us told you how to escape. That was all your doing. And you came up with a plan in less than a day. Sounds suspiciously like *thinking* to me." More quietly, she said, "It's in you, Dalton. Have more faith in yourself."

For several moments, he was silent as he studied her face. Looking for the truth of her words. Uncertainty lurked just beneath his gaze—this close, she saw that there was a faint corona of gold around his pupils, a gleam of brightness within the shadows. It stunned her, that this primal force of a man could have any reason to doubt himself. That he viewed himself merely as a mindless thug. Yet that must have been what he'd been told his whole life. What could that be like? To be told you have only one value, and that value was definitely not your ability to think?

It had been that way for women in Britain. Only lately had these ideas begun to change.

But not for Dalton. Low, so low that his voice was more of a bass rumble than words, he said, "No one's ever thought of me as anything more than hired muscle. No one, except you." He narrowed his eyes. "Only because you want something from me."

"My purpose is entirely mercenary." She wouldn't insult him with anything less than candor. "But that doesn't negate what I said. It only strengthens it."

Again, silence from him. Then he said in a low, gruff voice, "Thanks."

She didn't want to be moved. She didn't want to feel anything at all for him. Intentions, however, have a way of dissolving just when they are needed the most, leaving us exposed. Her carefully cultivated resolve flaked away, the very smallest piece of it, uncovering a tiny, undefended bit of heart. A simultaneously cold and warm sensation.

Because of him. This *convict.*

She turned away. For want of something to do, to erase the feel of him beneath her hand and collect the loosened pleats of her composure, she picked up her tea. It had gone cold, but she drank down the remains of it anyway, swallowing past the whiskey burn.

A mirror hung over the mantel, and she stared at the reflected room, everything and everyone within it reversed. Simon and Harriet gazed at Eva with looks of concern, and Dalton kept his attention on some distant point outside the window. She realized that she hadn't seen him in full daylight before. Without the night's shadows, he looked only slightly less sinister, but just as forbidding.

"We need," she began, then cleared her throat, "we need to detail Rockley's habits, how he spends his days. It should help us find areas that can be investigated and exploited further."

He frowned. "You haven't already tailed him?"

"Tried to."

A not particularly nice smile curled Dalton's mouth. "Got away from you, did he? Thought you lot were supposed to be good at this kind of skullduggery."

"We are," Marco answered hotly. "But Rockley's a slippery one. We can't keep a bead on him when he goes out."

"His coachmen get training," Dalton said. "Never take the same route twice, never go straight to a destination. In case anyone—like you folk—tries to follow him."

"This is precisely why you'll come into play, Dalton." Harriet stood and pulled out several pieces of paper, as well as ink and a pen, from a side table. She held them out to him. "Write down everything you know about Rockley's daily schedule."

He stared at the paper and writing implements.

"Ah," said Harriet, lowering her hands. "You can't."

Dalton's look was thunderous. "'Course I can read and write. We had ragged schools in Bethnal Green."

"Then . . ." Harriet waved the paper and pen at Dalton.

Still, he didn't take the writing materials. He might be literate, yet Eva suspected he wasn't entirely comfortable with the process of writing. Likely his education stopped at an early age. Time spent in the schoolroom meant less time earning money. Even very small children could weave baskets or put matches in boxes.

As the awkward moment stretched on, she stepped forward and took the pen and paper. Making herself brusque and businesslike, she sat at the table. "It's always faster if someone else serves as amanuensis. Besides, most men have appalling handwriting."

Without looking at him, she arranged the paper, opened the bottle of ink and dipped the pen nib in. Finally, she glanced up, and caught his brief look of gratitude. It couldn't be easy, admitting to a room of strangers that you didn't possess a skill everyone else had.

"Right, then," she continued, "we'll need Rockley's full schedule. Starting with the time he wakes up. Every hour needs to be accounted for."

Using his heel, Lazarus pushed out a chair for Dalton. Dalton eyed the seat warily. Gingerly, he lowered himself into it, filling the small chair, and it creaked beneath his weight. He looked as comfortable as if it had been upholstered with broken glass.

"Um . . . yeah . . . let's see." He shifted and the chair gave another squeak of protest. "Rockley . . . uh . . . wakes up . . . wakes up at . . . uh . . ." He dragged his hands through his hair, tugged at his unbuttoned collar, and readjusted his position in the chair.

He looked more uneasy than her students when she surprised them with a quiz.

"Come on, Dalton," Marco said impatiently. "You've been thinking about killing Rockley for five years, and you worked for him for seven. Don't tell us you don't remember the blighter's schedule."

"I remember it fine," Dalton snarled. He looked both furious and embarrassed. "It's just that . . . this sitting around and *thinking* business don't come naturally to me."

"You're more physical than intellectual," said Harriet.

He seized on this word. "Physical. That's me. Don't spend much time pondering mysteries."

"Simon," Eva said, "can we find something, ah, physical for Mr. Dalton to do?"

Half expecting Simon to object or say something snide, she was surprised when he left the parlor and climbed the stairs to the next story. Sounds of him moving around upstairs thumped through the parlor.

"It can help to give the body something to do while the mind works," Eva explained to a curious Dalton.

"A distraction," he said.

"But it can assist in channeling thoughts rather than divert them." She'd actually used the technique a time or two on some of her more energetic students, giving them a jumping rope as they recited their French conjugations. Her downstairs neighbors never appreciated the method, however.

She hadn't brought her jumping rope with her today, and it would look like a tiny piece of string in Dalton's hands. Hopefully, Simon would come up with a good solution.

A minute later, he appeared in the parlor, holding what appeared to be a pillowcase stuffed with rags. In his other hand, he carried a hammer and nails. Simon gathered the open edge of the pillowcase together, then held it to the top of the door frame leading to the kitchen. He then hammered the pillowcase to the door frame.

Standing back to admire his handiwork, he said, "A makeshift punching bag. Not precisely what you'd find at the West London Boxing Club, but it should suffice." He turned to Dalton. "Using those hamfists of yours ought to provide enough distraction."

"That it might." Dalton rose up quickly from his chair and examined the improvised punching bag. "All I have to do is picture your pretty face and my punches won't go wide."

Lazarus and Marco snorted, and Harriet concealed her laugh behind a discreetly cupped hand.

"Let's begin." Eva wanted to make certain that a spontaneous round of pugilism didn't break out between Simon and Dalton. She waved toward the punching bag. "Go ahead, Mr. Dalton."

An eager fire in his gaze, Dalton positioned himself in front of the punching bag. Raised his big fists. Struck the bag. Again. And again.

A grin spread across his face.

She didn't know what stunned her more. The brutal, deft skill he had with throwing punches, his body perfectly tuned, his movements precise as a surgeon's. Or the real smile he wore, warming the hard angles of his face with genuine pleasure. A strange duality that he inhabited simultaneously. And one that caused flutters of interest low in her belly.

For God's sake, you're not a tigress searching out the biggest, fiercest male. It was too primitive. Too primal.

Yet she couldn't look away as Dalton rained blows down upon the punching bag. He fell into a natural cadence, moving himself this way and that in small, exact increments. He had a good sense of rhythm. Made a woman think of other kinds of activities that required rhythm.

She rolled her eyes at herself. One would think she was a girl just discovering men for the first time. She was a woman grown, a woman who'd had her share of lovers and was no neophyte where men were concerned. She needed her focus.

Yet she caught Harriet's eye, and both women exchanged knowing glances. Eva had the absurd urge to giggle. She never giggled.

"Decent technique, Dalton." Simon's words sounded begrudging.

"Trained at Potato Maclaren's," Dalton answered without breaking pace. "And on the streets. Won thirty-three bare-knuckle fights before I signed on to guard Rockley."

His file said as much. Yet it was entirely different to see a man in action than simply reading about it.

"Whenever you're ready," she said to Dalton. Her pen was poised above the paper.

He spoke without hesitation. "Rockley's up every morning by eleven-thirty. Takes coffee at home. He's particular about his dress, so it takes him a while to pick his clothes for the day. Out the door by one. Goes to his man of business's offices in Lincoln's Inn Fields."

"We know that much," Marco said. "But after that, we lose him."

"Ain't always the same with him from day to day," Dalton answered. "If he's with Mitchell, his man of business, for fifteen minutes, then it's a regular day and he goes to the Carlton Club."

"Not the Reform Club." Lazarus scoffed. "Figures."

Eva's pen didn't stop, the nib scratching across the paper as she transcribed everything Dalton listed.

Ignoring Lazarus, Dalton continued. "But if he's only with Mitchell for ten minutes, then the news is very good, and he'll wind up at Rotten Row to watch the pretty ladies in their carriages or taking a turn on horseback. If he chats with a fine-looking piece, he'll go to luncheon afterward. If he doesn't meet any pretty girls, he goes to the gymnasium. A private one near Pall Mall."

"And this is his standard routine?"

Dalton sneered at the punching bag. "He don't even know he does it. Probably thinks he's being—what's the word?—spontaneous. But working seven years for Rockley taught me things about him he don't even know about himself."

As Dalton continued to throw punches, Eva studied him. Did he even know how perceptive he was? He seemed so quick to dismiss himself as nothing more than muscle.

"Then he usually goes home to bathe," Dalton continued, unaware of her speculation. "His nights aren't always the same. Dinners, the theater. One of them fancy balls during the Season." He cast Eva a quick glance. "Brothels."

As if the mention of that word could send Eva into a fit of hysterics. She wrote it in neat letters. "One brothel in particular, or did he frequent several?"

He paused only slightly, realizing he wasn't going to shock her, then said, "He had about four he liked especially. Mrs. Arram's House of Leisure. The Golden Lily. The Songbird. And Madame Bernadine's Parlor."

"Excellent." She wrote the names next to the word *brothels*. "And that constituted the whole of his day?"

"Far as I can remember."

Eva sat back and studied what she had written. The other Nemesis operatives gathered around her, reading over her shoulders. It looked like a tree, with points branching off certain locations, leading to more possibilities as to where Rockley would spend his time. Between Rockley's drivers deliberately using obfuscation in their routes and the seemingly random decisions the nobleman made throughout his day, it was no wonder Nemesis hadn't been able to track him.

Dalton, meanwhile, continued to shower the punching bag with hits.

"Maybe the man of business is the link," Marco offered. "The evidence could be with him."

"Too readily accessible," said Harriet. "If I was looking for proof of Rockley's dubious business dealings, that would be the first place I'd try. He'd know that, too."

"The Carlton Club?" suggested Lazarus.

"Possibly," Eva said. "Yet it's such a fortress of conservative politics, I wonder if he'd dare keep evidence of his treason there."

"Damn it." Simon growled in frustration, and the other Nemesis operatives looked equally frustrated. "We're not making any progress."

Eva glanced back and forth between the diagram of Rockley's activities and Dalton, her mind furiously working. She understood then what had to be done. It would be dangerous, for many reasons. But she never shied away from danger, not when it came to seeing justice done.

"Rockley needs to be followed again," she said, pushing back from the table. "But this time, by Mr. Dalton." She planted her hands on her hips. "With me accompanying him, of course."

CHAPTER SIX

Jack stopped punching the bag and watched Nemesis split apart.

"Absolutely not," the blond toff said.

"Don't be irrational." Eva looked calm as she faced Simon. "We've hit a wall here. The best way to learn more about Rockley is through more fieldwork."

"She's got a point," Jack said. Riling the nob was part of his motivation, but he did see the logic of what Eva said. "I know that bastard's patterns. If any of it changes, if he goes anyplace different, then something's up."

"Makes sense," said Marco. "Dalton's our asset. He can help us keep a tail this time."

"Then I'll go," Simon insisted. "Or Lazarus."

Eva raised her brows, looking like a queen staring down at a dirt-smeared upstart. "You seem to doubt my ability to do my job, Simon."

"Not a bit," he blustered. "But, it's just that . . . you're a woman—"

"That comes as a tremendous surprise." She tugged on her gloves, still cool as the moon.

Jack couldn't stop his grin. Oh, he enjoyed this. Watching her set the toff down with just a few words and icy looks.

"Dalton's stronger than you," Simon complained. "While you two are following Rockley, Dalton could decide he's had enough. Overpower you and flee."

"He could overpower *any* of us, even you. If Mr. Dalton truly wanted to run, he could do so at any moment, regardless of who's accompanying him. Besides," she continued, looking into the mirror as she pinned on her hat, "two men following someone appear more suspicious than a man and a woman out for a stroll through this fine city of ours. Who'd ever suspect an ingénue such as I could be capable of any mischief?" She turned and batted her amber eyes at Simon.

Jack knew she was doing it as a lark, but the sight of her fluttering her lashes and giving herself an innocent look sent a twist of hot need right through him. Maybe it was because he knew she wasn't any such thing as innocent, but whatever the reason, he spun around and busied himself with finding his new jacket so he wouldn't face the temptation she offered.

She tugged on her coat, then pulled a watch from the pocket. "It's nearly quarter past twelve, which doesn't give us much time to get to Rockley's home before he sets out for the day."

"Wait." Simon grabbed a sheet of paper, then scrawled something on it. He shoved the paper toward Eva, looking as happy as if he'd eaten boiled rat. "My society contacts confirmed that these are the gatherings Rockley's been invited to tonight. He could go to all of them or none."

She looked over the list, then folded it neatly and tucked it into her handbag. "Are you ready, Mr. Dalton?"

"I'm ready."

He'd put on his coat and done up the buttons of his collar. He knotted a simple tie around his neck, conscious of her gaze on his hands. With her watching him, his fingers felt thick and clumsy.

These clothes were a bit better than the doll's rags they'd stuffed him in yesterday, but he still wasn't comfortable. It wasn't the clothing that made him feel squeezed. Punching on that jury-rigged bag had helped burn off a small bit of his restless energy, but not enough. Not nearly enough. He wouldn't feel at all easy until Rockley was dead.

And he couldn't feel calm in Eva's presence. As soon as he'd clapped eyes on her today, he'd been on edge, nerves strung tight. It didn't make sense. He knew plenty of women. They didn't ruffle him. Usually, all he had to do was give a female a look or crook his finger, and they'd come running. And if they didn't want him, it didn't matter. There were always more women.

The only reason he could figure was that he hadn't really been around a woman since before he got sent up to Dunmoor.

That wasn't true. Before Eva had shown up earlier, he'd been around this woman Harriet. She might be a few years older than Jack, but she was handsome and had a good figure. He didn't even blink when Harriet was around.

But Eva had him tied up. He was all knots.

And now he was going to be alone with her.

"Don't you have a hat?" She looked critically at the top of his head.

Most decent gentlemen didn't go out of doors without a hat. He'd favored a smart bowler before he'd gone to prison. A swell topper for a gent without too many airs.

"Everything I'm wearing now was given to me by you lot."

"We'll have to find you something suitable. No use making you look even more like a ruffian." She sent another disapproving look at his uncovered head.

He resisted the urge to smooth his hands over his hair. He'd wet it down earlier, but he'd been due for a haircut from the prison barber, and his dark curls resisted efforts to be tamed.

She stepped to the front door. Simon looked as though he wanted to raise more objections, but a cutting glance from Eva made the nob shut his trap. That wasn't the kind of look someone just knew how to give, not without experience in giving it. What was that other life Eva had mentioned, the one she needed to protect? It was a mystery he wanted to solve.

"Coming, Mr. Dalton?"

Jack's heart beat hard within his chest. He was about to go outside, *truly* outside, into the London streets. Him and Eva, on their own. Two days ago, the most excitement Jack had in his day was whether or not he'd find a maggot in his ration of meat. Now he was back in London. Stalking the man he wanted dead. With a beautiful, thorny woman at his side.

"Wouldn't miss it," he said.

The pounding of his heart didn't ease once he and Eva stepped outside of the chemist's shop. Nor when they got into a hackney cab and headed off toward Mayfair. It only got worse, his heart like a drum hit by a mallet. He saw all the familiar sights of London, all its parks and churches, squares and omnibuses and carts and people. In the daylight, the city was just as filthy and splendid as ever. He couldn't decide if he wanted to drink it all in or tear everything down.

Daylight hours meant that Eva couldn't be seen riding in a hansom, so they'd hailed a four-wheeler. The growler was bigger than a hansom, and had a musty smell and threadbare squabs, but it still felt too small and didn't offer much room, especially for a man Jack's size. It seemed even smaller than the carriage they'd ridden in during his escape from Dunmoor. Now he'd shift and bump against Eva, reminding him of her presence. As though he ever forgot her. She spent much of the ride to Mayfair watching him with that too canny gaze of hers. It fair set his already tight nerves closer to snapping.

"Waiting for me to either make a run for it or tear your clothes off?" he rumbled.

"I know a number of ways to disable a man," she answered, "so I'm prepared for either eventuality."

"Don't that set my heart at ease."

"It wasn't supposed to."

He lapsed into a moody silence, staring out the dirt-streaked windows as they traveled west. The streets got wider, the people walking down them more posh. Coachmen drove pretty broughams and elegant landaus, the passengers radiating self-importance like overdressed suns. He'd never seen a landau until he started working for Rockley. He hadn't known such luxury existed.

Mayfair was exactly the same place of spotless marble and shining glass, broad streets that made a body feel insignificant, and servants walking their mistresses' tiny dogs. Nothing had changed. Which he supposed was the point. Street trash like Jack and Edith Dalton were blown about, consigned to rubbish heaps and forgotten. These here were gentry folk with ancestors going back to the time of . . . he didn't know about any long-ago kings, but doubtless Rockley's family had been employed hundreds of years past as the Royal Arse Wipers, and they were damned proud of it, too.

What was it Rockley said to him once? He'd been dressing in his evening clothes, or rather, his valet had been dressing him. Rockley had stared at himself in the mirror the way a hawk might admire its own feathers, and drawled, "There's nothing more permanent than blood, Dalton."

"Whatever you say, m'lord," Jack had answered.

The bastard had been referring to ancestry and heredity, but he could have been talking about the other kind of blood. The kind that flowed in his veins, the kind that spilled out of Edith, stained the floorboards, stained his memories. That was permanent, too.

Jack's gaze kept flicking toward Eva. She said they were going to follow Rockley, but what if she had something else planned? She'd already said that taking him to the coppers was out, but maybe she had some other scheme in mind. He needed to stay vigilant around her.

The cab came to a stop on Grosvenor Street. A few footmen minding the front doors sent baleful glances toward the hackney, but no one chased them off.

"That's it." Jack nodded out the window to a house in the middle of the block. "Rockley's place."

Eva leaned forward to gaze out the window, as well. Her fresh, light scent took away some of the mustiness of the cab, and he breathed it in. Still, it wasn't enough to quiet the clamor within him. Because he was sitting in a hackney halfway down the block from the home of his sister's murderer.

There were fancy terms for the columns and little projected roof that stood outside Rockley's front door, but Jack didn't know them. The door itself had been polished so much it was a black mirror, reflecting the swept front steps and street. Two potted trees stood on either side of the door. Tall windows set in the stately brick faced the street, the curtains inside pulled back to let in Mayfair sunlight. The first time Jack had seen the place, he'd been struck dumb. People truly lived like this? And yet they also were crammed ten to a room in Bethnal Green? How could it be possible? But it was.

"We've done surveillance here," Eva said. "Managed to get the plans to the house, as well, so we know the layout."

"Plans don't tell you that he keeps an armed man in the hallway outside his bedroom, and that he'd go through the mews when he'd come home late at night."

"I don't see extra guards outside his house now."

"You wouldn't. But his men would be on the inside. He didn't want his posh neighbors to know he paid a bunch of East London toughs to watch his arse."

She nodded, taking in this information.

"Look there." He pointed to one of the second-story windows. "That shadow against the glass? That's the hallway. His bedroom faces the back, where it's quieter. But I'd stand in that hallway there outside his room as Rockley got dressed for the day. He's got someone doing the same job."

"So he's still at home." She checked her pocket watch. "Twelve-fifty. Just like you said."

"And in about five minutes, the coach'll come around and wait for him by the front door."

"Unless he's concerned about your escape and chooses to leave through the mews."

Jack shook his head. "He's got his patterns. May be hard to follow him if you don't know 'em, but he always starts his day the same way. He'll go about his business as he usually does, to send a message. He won't let a piece of filth like me disrupt that."

She looked at him sharply. "Why would you say that?"

"Because to Rockley," he said, spreading his hands, "there's nothing more important than appearance."

"No, I mean, why would you call yourself a piece of filth? Do you really think of yourself that way?"

He blinked. "I don't think of myself in any way. I just am."

The idea seemed to flat-out puzzle her. "You've got to have some conceptualization of yourself. Some idea of who you believe yourself to be."

He gave a quick bark of laughter. "Self-reflection—I think that's the word for it—that's a luxury for them that don't have to worry about their next meal, or whether the rain will come through the holes in the roof. There's only survival. And if you don't fight to survive"—he shrugged—"you don't."

"Not once during those nights listening to the rain did you ever ponder who you were, or what you were meant to be doing? Something beyond survival."

Shifting on the creaking squabs, he glanced away from the amber knives of her eyes. "I may've," he allowed. There had been dreams, plans. Hopes for a life beyond the crowded, dirty alleys he'd known. His own boxing academy, for one. Like the kind Maclaren had, but instead of just training men, it'd be a place where boys could get off the streets, away from the gin palaces and dicing games. Someplace where they could feel safe and have dreams of their own.

He shook his head, clearing away the cobwebs of old hopes. "Doesn't matter, anyway. It's all led me here."

"But I—" Her words stopped abruptly. She sat up straight, her gaze fixed on something out the window.

Everything within Jack tensed. He knew what she saw. Slowly, he turned his head to look out the window.

A footman held open the front door, and a big, strapping bloke stepped outside. It wasn't Fowler, Curtis, or even Voss. Probably they'd moved on to other jobs, or died. Men like them—men like Jack—never lived long, despite their size. A hazardous life, one might call it.

This new chap wore a checked suit and a bowler hat. Jack didn't know him by name, but names signified nothing. Five years ago, Jack had been that man. Like him, he'd looked up and down the street, scanning for any signs of trouble, body primed to fight if danger arose. No mistaking the telltale shape of a gun in the hired man's coat. Jack had favored an Enfield Mk II, if his fists couldn't finish the job.

Jack ducked back as the hired man's gaze swept past the hackney cab.

"That's Fred Ballard," Eva said. "His main bodyguard." She glanced at the carriage. "Rockley's moving on."

Turning back to the window, Jack saw Ballard give a quick nod to someone standing in the doorway.

Rockley emerged.

Fire roared through Jack's veins, and his vision hazed. A fist seemed to close around his throat. He wanted to launch himself from the cab. He could already feel the crunch of bone against his fist as he smashed it into Rockley's handsome face. He could smell the blood as it coated the spotless front steps, hear the wet gurgle as Rockley struggled to breathe through the ruin of his aristocratic nose and mouth.

"Dalton."

A woman's gloved hand closed around his wrist as he grasped the handle to the cab door. He stared down at the female's hand.

"Dalton," the woman repeated, her voice an urgent whisper.

He looked up. A woman stared at him intently. She had sherry eyes and wheat-gold hair and he didn't recognize her. Not at first.

"You can't go out there," she said, her words tight. "The moment you do, Rockley's thug will shoot you down."

Eva. That's right. The woman was Eva.

"Might get to him before that." He spoke through clenched teeth.

"It's nearly a hundred feet between the cab and Rockley. More than enough time for his thug to fire off several rounds." Her hand tightened around his wrist. "Don't take that gamble, Dalton. Don't throw this entire mission away."

"Edith—"

"Would want her brother to stay alive," she finished. "Remember what I said earlier? You have to *think* if you want Rockley to pay. Rushing him in the street has only one result: your death."

"Goddamn it," he snarled. Because what she said made sense. Rockley always made sure his bodyguards were good shots. Jack would be a corpse before he made it half the distance.

His hand made of rusted iron, he unwound it from the door handle. Slowly, Eva released him.

"Good," she said after a pause. "Good."

"Don't feel good," he growled. "Feel like tearing up lampposts."

Glancing out the window again, Eva said, "He's getting into his carriage."

Jack followed her gaze. Rockley was, in fact, stepping into his waiting vehicle, with the footman waiting to close the door behind him. The bodyguard sat beside the coachman, his arms folded across his chest, his eyes constantly moving. Once Rockley had seated himself, the footman closed the door. The coachman snapped the ribbons, and the two matched bays responded, setting off at a trot.

Eva leaned forward and opened the small sliding door mounted at the front of the cab. "Driver, do not lose that carriage. And make sure they don't see us. There's a guinea in it for you."

With that kind of carrot, the driver hurried to follow. The hackney sped after Rockley's carriage.

Jack gripped the leather straps mounted on both sides of the hackney's walls, stretched out like a man on the rack. His muscles felt as though they'd burst right out of his clothing, and his heart slammed inside his ribs. Goddamn it, Rockley looked the same, exactly the same as he had five years ago. Everything had changed for Jack. Nothing had changed for Rockley.

Tall and elegant in his perfectly made, stylish clothes, his hair shiny and combed beneath his top hat, sporting an elegant mustache, Rockley was the model of a flawless aristocratic gentleman. Handsome, too, the blighter. Dark hair, blue eyes. The kind of face that women push each other aside to get close to. Hundreds of years of breeding pretty people gave him a face that truly got away with murder.

"You did the right thing," Eva said.

"Still want to rip his fucking guts out through his mouth," he gritted.

"I'm sure you do. But we have to keep our sights on our objective. This is my eighth mission for Nemesis, and I've learned that success relies upon logical, precise thinking."

"Logic and precision ain't my usual way of doing things."

"And you wound up in prison as a result."

He cursed under his breath. "Got a point there. But it don't make me skip with joy."

"I'm . . ." She appeared to labor to speak. Her gaze slid away from his. "I'm sorry."

He stared at her. Grudging as her words had been, they seemed genuine. Maybe this ice palace of a woman wasn't as cool as she let on.

They rode on in silence, following Rockley through the city. Jack already knew where they were heading. Toward Lincoln's Inn Fields, where Rockley's man of business kept offices. The hackney journeyed from Mayfair's wide, dignified streets into the bustling heart of London's legal world. Men wearing sober coats and dour expressions paced up and down the avenues, sheaves of papers bound with red cloth tape tucked under their arms.

"Tell the driver to park on Portugal Street," Jack said. "We can ditch the cab there and keep an eye on Rockley from a little shop on Portsmouth Street."

"That way Rockley's driver and guard won't see our hackney again and get suspicious. Wise thinking." She repeated Jack's instructions to the driver, who did as he was told.

They got down from the hackney. Jack was about to hurry down the street when Eva hissed at him, "Offer me your arm, damn it."

Right. Even without him wearing a hat, they'd attract less attention if it looked like they were a couple out on errands together.

Feeling strangely clumsy, he held out his arm. She looped her arm with his, her hand resting lightly on his sleeve. He could barely feel the pressure of her fingers upon him, but he sensed them anyway. Heat crept up his neck and spread across his face.

They walked briskly down the street. She matched his stride easily. Just as he'd known, Rockley's carriage had parked outside the red-brick building that housed the offices of Mr. Mitchell, his lordship's man of business. The coachman waited with the vehicle.

"Where's Ballard?" Eva asked.

"Waiting outside Mitchell's offices." He held open the door to the crooked little shop perched on Portsmouth Street, and she stepped inside. Neither of them paid attention to the clutter of goods piled up on every available surface. Both he and Eva stared out the shop's window. It offered them a good view of the front of Mitchell's building.

"Doesn't that attract attention?" She peered past the copper pots and china mugs lined up in the shop window. "Not many gentlemen walk around with hired guards."

"I got a few queer looks, but no one said anything. Rockley's the heir to some huge title and estate. If he wanted to walk around with a peacock on his shoulder, wasn't nobody going to tell him he couldn't."

"He's the Duke of Sunderleigh's son," she said. "That title goes back to the time of the War of the Roses."

He frowned, pictured the flower sellers in Covent Garden firing mortars at each other. "An old title, then," he guessed.

"One of the oldest. I suppose if he had a few odd habits," she murmured, "they'd just be dismissed as the eccentricities of the elite."

"Like killing girls." He fought the bile that climbed his throat.

"Or ruining them, with no one to stop him." She glanced up at Jack. "But we'll stop him."

"There's no extra security out front," he said, trying to get a hold of his rage. "If there's something, some piece of evidence, that Rockley's trying to protect, it's not here."

She nodded. "He'd station more guards wherever he keeps his documentation of his misdeeds."

"He should just destroy any evidence, if it's going to link him to a crime." He picked up a tiny china box, the outside painted with flowers so fat and mean-looking he expected them to have teeth.

The shopkeeper came bustling forward. "Can I assist you, sir?"

"No," Jack snapped. The man jumped.

"That is," Eva said, her tone soothing, "my cousin and I are simply perusing right now. We will be certain to ask for your assistance should we need it."

"Yes, ma'am." The shopkeeper hurried away, looking almost grateful to make his escape.

Eva glanced at Jack as he put the little box down.

"What?" he demanded.

"I'm not going to play Pygmalion with you," she answered. "But you're going to have to smooth down your manner."

He didn't know who that Pygmalion lady was, and wasn't about to ask. "It never hurt me before."

"You lived a different life before, where being unseen didn't matter. But now"—she gave him a look that started at the top of his head and went all the way down to the toes of his boots—"a great big unmannerly brute of a man is the kind that shopkeepers tend to notice and remember. We don't want anyone recalling you, should they ever be questioned. And if we want information from anyone, they're more inclined to give it if we deal with them courteously."

He narrowed his eyes. "Ought to think about being a teacher."

To his surprise, she tensed, and seemed wary. "Why do you say that?"

"Lecturing comes natural to you."

She gave a quick glance to make sure no one in the shop was looking their way, then, certain they weren't being watched, she made a rude hand gesture at Jack.

Which startled a laugh out of him. And also attracted the attention of his groin. Something about seeing a prim and proper lady giving him the two-fingered salute made for an intriguing contrast. It made a bloke think about what other kinds of naughty things the lady knew.

"But no," she continued, "Rockley wouldn't destroy any evidence about the government contract. He couldn't have gone into the deal alone, and he'd want to keep documentation as leverage in case anyone tries to cross him."

"You've got your hands around my neck, but I'm gripping yours, too."

"Exactly."

They continued to watch the front of the building that housed Mitchell's office. Foot traffic sped by, carriages and wagons in the street, and an occasional customer came into the shop.

"Never heard what Rockley and Mitchell talked about," he said. "Like I said, if he's in for fifteen minutes, it's a normal day. Ten if Mitchell has good news."

"He might be in there longer today. Rockley knows you're out, so he may be making special provisions."

"A will, if's he's smart."

Several minutes later, Rockley came out of the building, with his hired man in the lead. As before, Rockley got into the carriage and Ballard climbed up beside the coachman.

"How long has it been?" Jack demanded. He didn't have his pocket watch any longer to keep track of the time.

She consulted her own watch. "Fifteen minutes."

"He'll be going to the Carlton Club next, then."

"We need to get back to the cab now," Eva said.

They left the shop, and Jack was fairly certain the shopkeeper muttered a little prayer of thanks to have

them gone. Fortunately, the hackney driver had decided they were a ripe pigeon to be plucked, and still
waited for them on Portugal Street. Eva jumped into
the cab with the same speed and strength she'd demonstrated since Jack first had met her. As he climbed in
after her, he realized with a start that he'd only met her
yesterday. Seemed like much longer than that. A half-
dozen lifetimes, at least.

"Stay with that carriage," she called up to the driver.

In an instant, they were off again. It didn't seem as
though Rockley, his hired muscle, or his coachman
noticed the hackney in pursuit.

"I get the feeling our cabman's done a spot of tailing
before this," he muttered to Eva.

"If it keeps Rockley from seeing us," she answered,
"let's be thankful for the dubiousness of his character."

Christ, there was something about the way she
talked that made his blood go hot. He couldn't understand it. There was nothing about her that was like his
usual type of woman. He preferred them light and friv-
olous as soap bubbles—the rest of his life was tough
and harsh. When it came to female company, he didn't
need challenges, just thoughtless pleasure. But Eva
dared him at every turn, and damn him if he wasn't
starting to look forward to her next bit of cheek.

"We definitely appear to be heading toward Pall
Mall," she noted, looking out the window.

"It's giving me a twitch." Digging his knuckles
into the padded seat, he felt the scratch of horsehair
through the threadbare cushion. "All this shadowing
Rockley but not making a move. If we ain't going to
hit him, I can just take you everywhere he goes. See if
he's added more men for security. Then we don't have
to wait for him. Could be done in half the time."

"He may have altered his schedule in five years," she said. "Or he might break from his usual patterns today, knowing you're at large. If he does anything unusual, we have to be there to see it."

Jack glowered at the passing streets. "Going to need another go on that punching bag the toff set up for me."

"His name's Simon."

"He your man?"

She raised her brows. "Good God, no. Not that my personal life is any of your concern."

"So, you don't have a man."

"How tiresome this subject is." She studied the stitching on the seams of her gloves.

"That means, no, you don't." He didn't like how glad that news made him. "But you run around with dangerous blokes at all hours of the day and night."

She rolled her eyes. "I had no idea that they instilled such puritan values in prison."

Jack snorted. "We had chapel once a week. They stuffed us into these little stalls that weren't more than standing-up coffins, and made us listen to some dry old stick of a chaplain lecture us on meekness and humility and Christian duty. Didn't feel so Christian when they'd flog you for talking too much. Or stick you in the dark cell just 'cause a warder didn't like your look." He fought a shudder.

The physical pain of being flogged was easier to bear than the long days and weeks spent in utter darkness, with nothing to drink but water, and nothing to eat but bread. He'd never slept well, always caught in a haze of exhaustion—men in the dark cell didn't get mattresses or blankets, just a hard wooden board set into the wall. And the silence. God Almighty, the silence. The lack of contact with others. Just thinking of it now made his throat close. Prison was never a chatty, cheerful place, but the absolute void of sound and human contact within the dark cell made many lads snap.

"Spoken as one who'd suffered such punishments," she said quietly.

"Aye." Had the marks on his back as proof. And a hate of complete darkness. He tipped up his chin. "Didn't break me, though. They tried, but never could."

She tilted her head as she gazed at him. "That must've taken some extraordinary strength on your part."

"Strength, or being pigheaded." He shrugged. "Whatever you call it, it got me through five years without losing my mind."

Her look was troubled, thoughtful. "I don't know if I could have survived that."

"You would've," he answered at once. "If only to drive the matrons barmy."

Her quick smile came as a surprise. "I do believe you're right, Mr. Dalton."

He could not lean back, couldn't be easy, not so long as he trailed after Rockley like a wolf denied its prey. Yet there was something oddly gratifying about having Eva with him on this mad hunt, talking with her as he'd never talked to another human being. Those five years at Dunmoor must've changed him, far more than he'd realized.

From the cab, Jack and Eva watched Rockley go up the steps and into the imposing Carlton Club. The footman at the door bowed at Rockley's entrance, then gestured toward his carriage to wait for his lordship around back. It wouldn't do to have carriages lined up outside like a common opera house, even if the carriages were the gleaming vehicles of England's elite, drawn by horses that cost far more than a working man could make in a year.

"Ballard is staying with the coach," Eva noted as the vehicle rolled away toward the mews.

"Even a bloke as high in the instep as Rockley can't argue with the club's rules. Only members and the club's servants are allowed inside."

"Surprising that he'd feel comfortable there," she murmured, her gaze fixed on the daunting stone arches that lined the building's walls, "without his paid muscle to watch his back. Unless he could put his paranoia aside long enough to rub elbows with the conservative elite."

"What's *paranoia*?" Jack asked.

"An irrational or overinflated sense of persecution. Excessive suspiciousness."

"That's Rockley, all right." He sneered. "He uses his paranoia to make the world safer for him. Only it ain't safe. Not from me."

"Or Nemesis." She studied the outside of the club. "So he wouldn't be able to post additional men here."

"If he had evidence of something, he wouldn't keep it at the club."

Still, they had to wait for him. As they did, Eva stepped out and purchased them all several pies from a shop a few streets over, even bringing food to the cabman. They ate their luncheon without speaking, still sitting inside the cab. He still couldn't quite get used to eating in front of another person, and had taken his breakfast in his room, but he'd spoken truly last night. It was easier to eat in front of a woman than a man.

"All this Nemesis work's pretty dangerous," he said between mouthfuls. "Surprised that they'd let women be part of it."

She scowled. "Harriet, Riza, and I want to see justice served just as much as any man. More so, since so much harm is perpetrated against women, and little protection. My God, they only just repealed the Contagious Diseases Acts."

He'd heard some of the prostitutes complaining bitterly about those acts, and how they could be forced to go through humiliating medical examinations, or worse, locked up against their will, if found to be carriers of disease.

"Don't doubt there's plenty wrong done to women," he said, "but what if you or Harriet get hurt?"

"Just like any army, all the operatives of Nemesis are trained for many months before becoming officially part of the group. Simon has an estate outside of town we use for training. Firearms. Hand-to-hand combat. A few other skills I'm not at liberty to divulge."

"And you went through this training, too?"

She gave him a cold smile. "Test me."

He smiled right back. "Be delighted to."

They resumed their meal in silence, but the dare hung between them like a lit fuse.

Some hours later, Rockley emerged. They followed at a distance, but after making several turns and doubling back twice, the cabman opened the sliding door that allowed him to talk to his fares.

"Sorry," the driver said, voice tight with apology, "but that blighter slipped away from me."

Eva cursed. "This kept happening to us before. He could be heading anywhere."

"Not anywhere," Jack said. "Did you see him, when he came out of the club? He ran his hands down the front of his waistcoat and patted his stomach. That means he'd had a big luncheon. But he don't like feeling all stuffed and lazy. He'd want to go to his gymnasium next. It's on Church Street, right by the river."

Her eyes widened. "Don't tell me. Tell our driver."

Jack repeated his directions to the cabman, and they were off again.

They reached Church Street a few minutes later. Jack couldn't stop the small bit of pride that swelled in his chest when he and Eva spotted Rockley's carriage outside a two-story stone building. A brass plaque read CHELSEA GENTLEMEN'S GYMNASIUM.

"The ace up our sleeve," Eva murmured. No mistake about it—respect shone in her eyes when she looked at Jack.

And he liked it.

"After this," he said, "he always goes home to bathe. The driver might change the route up, but Rockley don't care for being mussed."

Which proved true. Though the hackney lost Rockley's carriage on the return trip, when they reached his home on Grosvenor Street, they were just in time to see Rockley head inside.

Eva pulled out a folded sheet of paper. "This is Simon's list of parties Rockley's been invited to tonight. A dinner given by the industrialist Edward Cole. Another dinner, this one hosted by Lord and Lady Scargill. A ball at the home of Lord and Lady Beckwith."

"He'll bathe and change for his night out, then."

They continued to wait. The sun had lowered itself behind the skyline, throwing long shadows, and the street lamps came on to push those shadows back.

"Can you stop shaking your leg?" Eva didn't try to hide her annoyance.

He hadn't been aware he'd been doing so, his leg restlessly jiggling. "I'm going round the twist, sitting here like this."

"Distract yourself."

"I can think of a way or two you could distract me." He gave her a wicked grin.

"Goodness," she said, yawning, "with that kind of poetry, what woman could resist you?"

"Not many did." It wasn't a boast, but the truth. He never lacked for female company.

She leaned forward, and lamplight filtered in through the glass, touching along the clean line of her cheek and the fullness of her bottom lip. He'd spoken automatically a moment ago. Making bawdy suggestions came naturally when you were from the shabby, low parts of town. Cheap and ready coquetry was thrown out like so much tinsel. It was a way everyone related to one another when life was tough and fast— the common currency of flirtation.

But he realized something just then. He wanted her. Not simply because he hadn't had a woman in five years, and she happened to be handy. No, with her gold eyes, fancy words, and mind like a cutthroat's blade, she set a fire to him, a fire that could only be quenched by discovering the feel and taste of her.

"Not many women resist you?" Her lips curled into a smile, causing heat to shoot to his cock. "Congratulations, Mr. Dalton. You've just found a woman who can."

CHAPTER SEVEN

Eva didn't know whether her words were for Dalton or herself. A measure of both, she supposed.

She needed to remind herself that he served one purpose, and one purpose only: finding evidence of Rockley's embezzlement, and with that, gaining restitution for Miss Jones along with the downfall of the nobleman. These alone were Nemesis's objectives. She must think of Dalton as simply a means to achieve those objectives. He was no more than a lever or pulley in the construction of Rockley's ruin, as other men had served Nemesis's purposes before.

Yet, as he stared back at her within the dark confines of the hackney, the shadows and lamplight shaped him into a man both menacing and alluring. She didn't know a man could be both. The flinty contours of his face could soften with a smile, the hard gleam of his eyes could glint with unexpected humor or feeling.

Impossible to deny the animal allure of his physicality, as well. He inhabited his body with full awareness. She already knew what he looked like without his clothing, and as she returned his gaze, she had an aching awareness of his big, strapping frame, of how flimsy everything seemed in comparison to him.

Perhaps she ought to have taken Simon's advice and

had him or Marco accompany Dalton today. No—just as she'd told Dalton, she was a trained operative who had been actively recruited by Nemesis. If she had an inconvenient attraction to him, she could master it. She could not let anything cloud her judgment.

"You go throwing out a challenge like that," he rumbled, "I have to take it. Don't forget, love, I broke out of prison. Getting into your bed won't be as difficult."

"Correct," she said. "It will be *more* difficult. And it isn't a challenge, but a statement of fact."

"All facts can change."

She nearly admired his audacity. Overcoming obstacles, finding the possible in the impossible—these were things that had drawn her to Nemesis in the first place. She never took the path of least resistance, and had to respect anyone who chose the same. But there were exceptions, especially when the resistance he faced was her own will.

"Something hasn't changed, though," he said, his gaze suddenly fixed out the window. "Rockley's taking up one of the invitations he received."

The man himself emerged from his house in evening finery, his shirtfront pristinely white, his black wool evening dress absorbing light.

She suppressed a groan. Her limbs were stiff and aching from a day spent in a poorly sprung four-wheeler, but it looked as though the night was far from over.

"Can't aristocrats spend a quiet evening at home?" she muttered.

"This lot don't have work or jobs," Dalton said. "Not so far as I've seen. They got no reason to get up with the sun."

"Which is it to be, then?" She peered at Rockley as he gave instructions to his coachman, but he was too far up the block for her to hear what he said. "Dinner with the industrialist? Will he dine with Lord Scargill, instead? Or is it the ball hosted by Lord Beckwith?"

Dalton grumbled. "This part I never knew. Always a different posh place each night."

Her thoughts racing, Eva went over the list of names. She tried to place herself in Rockley's mind, vile though that location was. He might take up the iron magnate's offer, but she doubted Rockley wanted to associate with new money or men who made no secret of working for their wealth. Lord Scargill was a lesser nobleman of slim influence. As distinguished as the Carlton Club was, it permitted plutocrats who supported Tory causes as well as noblemen with ancient but trifling bloodlines. Rockley could have had enough interaction with those varieties of men whilst at the club. Yet Lord Beckwith was an earl, and while such titles were losing their importance, his hadn't diminished.

"He'll go to Lord Beckwith's," she said.

Dalton looked skeptical. "You sure?"

"No. But all we have at this point is instinct, and mine says Beckwith's soiree. His mansion's on Curzon Street."

That seemed to mollify Dalton. He reached behind and slid open the door that allowed passengers to communicate with the cabman. "Oi, Palmer. We're on the hunt for the toff again. Curzon Street."

"Right you are, guv," the driver answered with surprising cheer. As Rockley's carriage pulled away, the cab followed.

Dalton sat back in his seat and crossed his arms over his wide chest. It shouldn't astonish her that he'd learned the name of their cabman, especially considering they'd been with the driver all day. The two seemed to share the camaraderie of the working man, and though Eva's own circumstances were far from luxurious, she could never have that common ground. She couldn't deny its utility, though. The inducement of a guinea for a day's labor might buy the use of a man's time, but it couldn't buy his goodwill. She had secured one, Dalton the other.

They didn't have far to go. Rockley's carriage queued up behind a line of others outside a massive home in Mayfair. Lights and music poured from the tall windows, and a column of women in glittering gowns and men in evening clothes marched up the stairs like the world's most elegant battering ram.

The cab stopped a discreet distance away.

"I've been here before," Dalton said. "Not a lot, but I remember this place."

"Only the upper echelons are invited to Lord Beckwith's gatherings," Eva said. To which Rockley clearly belonged. She sighed. "And his parties usually go on until three in the morning."

Rockley alit from his carriage and joined the sparkling crowd heading inside. He exchanged nods and greetings with those near him. He was taller than most of the other guests, so following his progress into the mansion proved easy. At last, he went in. Ballard slipped down from the carriage and disappeared through the mews.

"He'll be going in through the servants' door in the back," Dalton noted. "The rule was: stay nearby but out of sight. I got real talented at keeping myself hidden."

She eyed his broad shoulders skeptically. "As though anyone could overlook you."

His grin flashed in the darkness. "A man of many gifts, I am. I can show you a few."

Most assuredly she would *not* respond to that. Opening the cab door, she said, "Let's have ourselves a closer look."

On the street, she made sure to keep close to the

shadows, though one or two eyes turned in her direction. If anyone from the soiree were to glance out into the street, they'd hardly notice a woman in a plain day dress and short woolen cape. She might be mistaken for a governess, which suited her fine. Sending a quick glance behind her, she noted with approval that Dalton had a natural instinct for finding shadowed places. Amazing that man of such sizable proportions could hide himself at all, yet he did, and with an unanticipated agility.

They moved silently along the street, skirting around the edges of Lord Beckwith's property. She slowed in her steps, allowing Dalton to catch up with her.

"Don't suppose we'd be able to get in through the service entrance," she whispered.

"This place was always kept tighter than a thief's purse. Even the bloke at the back door had a list of who could and couldn't go in, servants included." He narrowed his eyes, gazing into the darkness. "There's a house next door—it's dark now."

"Sir Harold Wallasey's home. He and his wife are out of the country on a diplomatic mission—I read it in the paper. Probably left a skeleton staff."

"See that window there?" He pointed one blunt-tipped finger toward a second-story window. "It'd have a right clear view of the ballroom."

"Which would presuppose us being inside a private residence, uninvited, in order to utilize it." At his grin, she demanded, "What?"

"Those fancy words you use." His gaze heated. "I like 'em."

Of all the responses to her vocabulary, this was the least expected, especially from him. The frank desire in his eyes stirred embers within her. And all she could say in return was the very articulate "Ah."

He seemed to enjoy confusing her, for his smile widened. "You Nemesis lot said you'd do anything to see justice done."

Straightening her spine, she said, "Of course."

"That include breaking and entering?"

She rummaged through her handbag, which was, admittedly, a bit larger than the average lady's purse. From its depths she pulled a slim silver case. She opened the case, revealing its velvet-lined interior, and held it up for his perusal. "This is Nemesis's official policy for housebreaking."

Dalton gave a low whistle.

Lock picks of every shape and variety were arranged neatly within.

"No one's in the kitchen." Eva peered through the windows. "Can't even see a light down the hall. Perhaps even the butler and housekeeper are gone. The house seems empty."

Beside her, Dalton said, "Seems downright rude not to take 'em up on the invitation."

She stepped lightly to the door. Just to be certain, she tried the doorknob. It was locked. After a final glance around, she bent close to examine the lock.

"This won't take long," she murmured.

"Not that I don't appreciate the view," he said, leering openly at her backside, "but I'd like to give that lock a go."

She eyed him dubiously. "The house might be empty, but we can't linger or make too much noise. Kicking the door down would assuredly call attention."

He gave her an affronted look. "Thought you trusted my brains."

"I do—"

"To a point." He held out one large hand. "Hand them picks over."

"Do you know how to use them?"

After tugging on the knees of his trousers, he crouched down in front of the lock. "Spent years as a screwsman," he said quietly. "'Course, none of the places I broke into were half as fine as this one, but locks are like ladies. Fancy or common, they all yield to a man who knows how to use his pick."

"I think you left an *r* out of that last word."

He chuckled. "I never leave anything out." On no occasion would Dalton suffer a lack of confidence. She handed him the picks.

Eva clasped her elbows and watched as he sorted through the different picks, then began to slowly, carefully manipulate the lock. He frowned in concentration as he worked the picks. She fought the absurd impulse to push back a curl of dark hair that fell across his creased forehead.

The sounds of chatter and a string quartet from next door filled the small courtyard in which she and Dalton stood. Voices from the Beckwiths' garden also glided over the wall separating the two properties—the melodic rise and fall of genteel conversation, most of it inconsequential. If there was the brokering of power to be done, it usually happened in card rooms and studies, where alliances and factions could be sealed with cigars and brandy.

Hearing a girl's giggle followed by a man's lower murmur, she recalled there were other ways of forming alliances.

"There's a sweetheart," Dalton said as he pushed open the door.

Together, they entered the darkened kitchen, Dalton

quietly shutting the door behind them. A massive enclosed cooking range lurked against one wall, and shelves were lined with copper molds and pans. She gripped his sleeve to catch his attention. Silently, she pointed to the long table that ran the length of the kitchen. A kettle and two cups had been left out.

"Could be they've been sitting a while," he whispered, standing close. His breath fanned warmly over her face.

"Or were used this afternoon."

Cautiously, they left the kitchen and entered a darkened corridor. They passed closed doors that led presumably to the butler's pantry and housekeeper's office, and other storerooms. No lights shone out from beneath the doors, but Eva couldn't allow herself to breathe easy. They climbed the stairs winding out of the service areas.

They emerged in a cavernous hallway, draped thick in the atmosphere of wealth. Everywhere she looked, she espied priceless artwork, the gleam of gilding and marble, and the labor of scores of servants. From the banisters to the baseboards, everything maintained scrupulous cleanliness. Branching off from the hallway were other spacious rooms, plush with carpets and overstuffed furniture. But the room they sought was on the next floor up. She glanced toward the wide staircase, and he nodded in agreement.

The walls were far too thick to admit any sound of the gala next door, and all she could hear was the ticking of a clock in some distant study. Otherwise, the huge home was utterly still.

True to his word, Dalton moved easily through the silent house. He seemed an odd combination of contrasts, and every time she believed she understood him fully, he defied her definition.

On the next floor, she let Dalton take the lead. They passed rows of stern portraits, and tables whose sole purpose seemed to be holding fragile vases. When the family was in residence, no doubt the vases would burst with hothouse flowers, rigidly patrolled lest any of the flowers have the temerity to wither and die.

Dalton opened a door and she followed him inside. She shut the door behind them quietly. None of the lamps were lit, the curtains were drawn. The chamber was thick with darkness. She stood still for a moment, allowing her eyes to adjust. Stumbling blindly forward might find her colliding with furniture.

She blinked as light suddenly glazed the room. Dalton stood by the window, holding the curtain back with one arm. She hadn't heard him moving through the chamber, not a single stumble or muttered curse as he knocked into a table, yet he'd appeared by the window as if conjured. More of his skills as a housebreaker.

With illumination from Beckwith's house filtering in, she saw that the chamber in which she and Dalton stood was a sitting room. Or she surmised it was. Holland covers draped over the furniture, but a couch's gilded legs peeped from beneath the white fabric like a debutante's attempt at flirtation. A mahogany escritoire awaited a lady's correspondence, and a folding screen stood in one corner, with an easel holding a partially completed painting behind it, as though the room's usual occupant liked to create a separate space for their art.

"Prime spot for snob watching," Dalton murmured when Eva joined him at the window.

So it was. From their position, they had an excellent view of Beckwith's ballroom, its rows of huge windows acting like a proscenium arch for the theater of elite Society. She could faintly hear the strains of an orchestra. The ballroom blazed with the light of not merely gas lamps but chandeliers, throwing everyone within into high relief. Men formed a uniform mass of black wool evening clothes, their hair shining with liberal applications of macassar oil. The women wore frilled, pastel confections, jewels winking from their throats and hair. They fanned themselves continuously, vainly trying to cool themselves. It had to be an inferno in there.

"Where's Rockley?" she asked, scanning the crowd.

"Just coming in."

Their quarry appeared at the entrance to the ballroom. The moment he did, people swarmed around him—upper-class young men, their faces shining with drink and entitlement, gray-whiskered gentlemen of gravitas, matrons pressing their marriageable daughters forward like white-swathed sacrifices. Everyone, it seemed, wanted the notice of Lord Rockley.

"Dung attracts flies," Eva said.

Dalton gave a soft snort. They both watched Rockley slowly progress into the ballroom, people trailing after him. Little wonder that he garnered so much attention. Even if one didn't know his title and wealth, he radiated power. From the set of his shoulders to his upright spine, the way he held his head and gestured with his white-gloved hands, his every move spoke of confidence, of authority. Who wouldn't want to bathe in the lambent glow of his privilege?

He was an attractive man, as well. Could give Simon a run for having such aristocratic features, but Rockley was dark where Simon was fair, and that held its own allure.

Eva couldn't look upon Rockley and see anything but an unblemished rind disguising a rotten fruit. His good looks seemed an affront and a deliberate lure, enticing people—women, especially—to their doom.

"He'll be making his rounds of the room for a while,"

she said, observing his passage farther into the ball-room. "Some idle conversation. Unlikely that he'll join the dancing right away." She pointed toward a door leading off the ballroom. "All those men are heading to the card room. They want as little to do with dancing as possible."

"Made a thorough study of these gentry folk, you have," said Dalton. He shot her a chary glance. "You one of 'em?"

She scoffed. "There are many worlds between May-fair and Bethnal Green."

"If they ain't your people, how d'you know so much? All their names, where they live, how their little parties play out."

"Most of Nemesis's targets come from the ranks of the elite. I have to know my enemy." She waved a hand toward the ballroom. "Those are not my people, as you call them."

"Then who is?"

She studied him. "Why do you want to know? If you're looking for leverage to use against me, it won't work, I've made certain there are no loose ends to make me trip."

Though he kept his gaze on the ballroom, his brow lowered. "Blackmail and leverage are Nemesis's meth-ods, not mine. I want to know about you on account of me being curious. Been trapped together in a hackney all day. It makes a man's thoughts wander."

"And they wandered toward me?" Best to be overt, face the issue head-on so it couldn't control her.

"Only other person in that cab was myself, and we both know my history. Seems only fair," he added. "Got a file at headquarters about me. This thick." He held his fingers apart, just as Simon had done when illustrating Dalton's dossier.

She debated. Deliberately, she'd spoken little of her life and upbringing with the other Nemesis operatives. Their questions to her were always met with vagaries. It made her somewhat removed from them. Which was as she wanted it. It was safer that way, not just for the sake of Nemesis and its missions, but for herself. No chance of being hurt when someone truly didn't know you.

Yet she felt a strange need to share something of herself with Dalton. She knew he desired her—he'd made no secret of it, and, if she wanted to be truthful with herself, she'd been thinking about what it would be like to run her hands all over his body and feel his mouth on hers.

She understood lust. Had felt it many times. One could share one's body without revealing one's heart. This compulsion urging her now, this need to reveal herself to Dalton, had another origin besides desire. In this darkened chamber, illuminated by the ambient light from the ballroom, with *this* man, she could allow something of her true self to emerge.

"My parents were missionaries," she said finally. She kept her gaze on the swirling crowds within the ballroom. "They ran several charities here in London. For women. The poor. Ventures like that are always short of resources. They made frequent rounds of all the Society ladies, soliciting funds."

"They took you with 'em," he said.

"A good guess. And an accurate one."

He shrugged. "Beggars do the same. Got a little raggedy tyke beside 'em, making big sad eyes at the passers-by. Get more coin that way."

A humorless laugh escaped her. "In that, we were just like the poor souls they were trying to help. It worked, too. Though my mother always felt we could have done better if I smiled more at the rich ladies. Never felt much like smiling, though," she murmured. "I saw how they lived, how they acted. The same way you learned about Rockley from watching him, I did the same with those wealthy women. They seemed so . . . jaded, so weighed down with apathy. Searching for something to do with themselves."

She and Dalton watched them now, the ladies of the elite. Forming clumps at the edges of the ballroom, or whirling across the floor in the patterns of dance. Some of the women looked bored. Others had rapacious and judging eyes.

"Never had no truck with those women," he rumbled. "Can't say as I was sorry about it."

"Some were decent, genuinely compassionate. Others, less so. Just like anyone. But it teaches you something about pride, continually having your hand out, asking for help."

He grunted. "Aye. Tastes like quinine."

"Or lye." She nodded toward the ballroom. "He's dancing now. Unless he's in the market for a wife, he won't dance with the same woman twice."

Rockley made a fine figure on the dance floor. He easily guided the young woman in his arms through the waltz, and she beamed up at him, surely feeling that she was the envy of all the other girls at the ball. Eva half expected the young woman's snowy gown to be stained by Rockley's moral pollution.

"He didn't want to be leg-shackled," Dalton said. "Doubt that's changed."

"It's so much easier to ruin girls without having a wife at home." She couldn't keep the bitterness out of her voice.

They were silent again, observing the strange rituals of another culture.

Yet Dalton, it seemed, wanted more details about Eva. "They still in London, your parents?"

"Africa. Nigeria, to be more specific, doing good works." She'd had a letter from them a month ago describing the school they'd built—with considerable assistance from the local populace. Clasping her elbows, she spoke quietly. "I didn't follow in their footsteps. I believe . . . I'm a disappointment to them."

It stunned her that she'd said the words aloud, when she hadn't fully articulated them to herself. And of all the people she should confess this to, she had not anticipated her confessor would be Jack Dalton.

She waited for his scorn, telling herself it didn't matter if he jeered at her or said something cutting. It would teach her a lesson about revealing too much of herself to him, to anyone.

"If Nemesis does what it claims," he said gruffly, "if it makes injustices right, and if you're part of Nemesis, then you *are* doing good."

"But I'm not bringing faith to the ignorant, or clothing those who've only known nakedness."

He grunted. "Bollocks to that. You're working for the needy here at home, where you're wanted. Not trying to force belief down the throats of people who might not even ask for it."

Stunned, she unclasped her elbows and let her arms hang down her sides. "I never thought of it in those terms."

"About time you did."

She could hardly believe it. He was defending her work. Defending *her*. When he had no reason to do so. She knew when someone lied, told her half-truths, or spoke with the intent to flatter and deceive.

Dalton had meant every word.

Without thinking, she brought her hand up to press

in the center of her chest. As if she could hold back the pieces of self-protection that crumbled from around her heart. She didn't want to like him, or feel grateful for his understanding. She didn't want to feel anything for him.

It couldn't be helped, though. He'd found a vulnerability.

And he didn't even know it. He continued to stare into the ballroom. His lip curled as he watched several bejeweled matrons gather in a circle, fanning themselves. "Every now and then, do-gooders would come parading through Bethnal Green, clanging bells and clapping hands. Women like that lot. The way they treated us," he scoffed, "like we were idiot children."

Giving herself a mental shake, she brought herself back to the conversation.

She knew precisely what he meant. Some missionaries thought of their charges as little better than animalistic brutes, and it was their duty to elevate them. Not as high as the missionaries themselves, but out of the mud of their ignorance. Her parents, at least, were not so blinkered in their ideology.

Dalton said, "Then they'd get angry when they figured out that us poor folk weren't as simple as they wanted. We couldn't be shaped into what they wanted us to be. And more than a few of us didn't care for their sort of *charity*." His jaw tightened. "Most of 'em lost interest after a bit. They'd find another charity or just give it up altogether, like they were bored of poor people."

"When my parents and I would return to some ladies," she said, "asking for more donations, they'd look at us with this *confusion*. Wondering why we'd come back. As though giving a handful of pounds or a few dozen blankets should suddenly, magically cure poverty."

"Or that we should be grateful to find jobs that barely paid nothing. *Honest* work, they called it. Anything to keep us low." He tugged on the silk fabric of the curtain, a swath of fabric that, if sold at a second-hand shop, could feed a man for months. "We couldn't dream of having this for ourselves. Couldn't aim for anything beyond just a roof over our heads and a measly bowl of mutton for supper."

"And you?"

He frowned. "What about me?"

"You must've aimed for more than a roof and mutton." If she was coming to understand anything about Dalton, it was his ferocious determination. A man like him wouldn't be satisfied with crumbs. He'd want the whole banquet.

"Always had bigger plans for myself," he admitted. "I wanted out of Bethnal Green, and no dirty factory job was going to make that happen. So I became a housebreaker, then a fighter. Nothing aboveboard, only underground brawls they'd hold in deserted buildings. Earned me the name Diamond Jack, on account of being hard as one of them stones. After that, I came on as Rockley's bodyguard." His sneer of disgust seemed aimed not just at Rockley, but at himself. "The most money I'd ever had, all to watch some toff's back. I took it, and gladly. Didn't matter to me what the bastard did, so long as I kept him safe and got my wages."

The bastard in question had ended his waltz and stood talking with two men she recognized as top parliamentary figures. One of the men laughed at something Rockley said, and gestured toward the card room.

"Maybe those nobs are in on the scheme with the cartridges," Dalton said, nodding toward the men talking with Rockley.

"They aren't afraid of him," she said. "You can see

it in the way they look at him, the ease of their laughter. He doesn't have any hold over them."

Dalton grunted softly, a sound partway between amusement and reluctant admiration. "Ought to consider becoming a card sharp, the way you read folks."

"The late hours would interfere with my work for Nemesis. And I don't care much for the smell of cigars."

Rockley and the other two gentlemen strolled from the ballroom, seemingly eager to immerse themselves in the masculine world of importance.

"Damn," Eva muttered. "There isn't going to be another room in Sir Harold's house that will have a view of the card room."

"He'll have to come back through the ballroom to leave," Dalton noted.

They wouldn't know who Rockley spoke with in the card room, but at least she knew he couldn't slip away unnoticed.

Eva leaned forward, bracing her elbows on the windowsill. "Did you ever think about being anything other than hired muscle?"

A fleeting look of contemplation crossed his face, something almost wistful. But it was gone before she could be certain. "Nah. Folks always knew me as a bruiser, and that's what I became. Either in the ring or on that nob's payroll." He held up his fists. "These have always been more valuable than this." He tapped the side of his head.

"You overvalued the wrong commodity," she said.

His expression was confused, as though she suggested paying for oxygen. "Muscle is all I'll ever be."

Unaccountable anger surged through her. "Stop calling yourself that."

Again, he looked mystified. "Don't know why you're getting so cross. What difference does it make to you how I think of myself?" He folded his arms across his chest as he gazed at her.

Why, indeed? She couldn't answer him. Only that it *did* upset her, far more than she would have believed. He seemed to accept the role he'd been given, a role that vastly underestimated his capabilities. No one, it appeared, ever told Jack Dalton that he could be anything more than a brute for hire.

But he had a brain. A very good one. And it had lain fallow for far too long.

She saw examples of wasted potential every day. One couldn't live in London without seeing the mudlarks, crossing sweeps, match girls, or men sitting on curbs when their jobs had been made redundant. It always stirred her. But never as much as Dalton did.

"I just don't like to see squandered possibility," she muttered.

"A missionary at heart," he said, wry.

If that's what he believed, she wouldn't disabuse him. Better that than him thinking she had more than a professional interest in his welfare.

A faint noise sounded in the corridor outside, the creak of floorboards beneath carpet as someone made their way down the hall. Both she and Dalton stiffened, exchanging glances with each other. From beneath the door, light gleamed. Something jingled. The housekeeper's keys.

Dalton dropped the curtain immediately, throwing the chamber into darkness. Both he and Eva raced for the shelter of the folding screen. The screen itself wasn't particularly large, but Dalton was, so they had to stand close together, her back pressed against his front. His arm wrapped around her, beneath her cape, and his hand spread across her stomach.

The moment they settled into place, the door opened.

More jingling and footsteps as the housekeeper walked into the room. A small glow spilled upon the walls—she must be carrying a lamp.

Eva tensed and felt Dalton do the same. Had the housekeeper heard her and Dalton and come to investigate? If so, behind the screen would likely be the first place the housekeeper looked. Talking their way out of the situation wasn't possible, and Eva didn't want to subdue and tie up the poor woman—though if it came to that, she was prepared.

The footsteps stopped, and the housekeeper sighed. Yet she didn't look behind the screen. More light filled the room.

Cautiously, Eva peered around the edge of the folding screen and saw the housekeeper standing exactly where she and Dalton had been moments earlier. The older woman gazed out at the ballroom across the way, a wistful look upon her face.

"My, isn't that lovely?" She sighed again, then hummed along with the faint music, swaying slightly.

Eva edged back. She and Dalton hadn't been seen. And so long as they stood behind the screen, they wouldn't be. Yet she couldn't feel calm, not until the housekeeper left. From the expression on the older woman's face, rapt with attention, it appeared that might be a while.

She kept herself still, willing her breathing and heartbeat to slow. But as she did, she became aware of Dalton's nearness. With so little room behind the screen, their bodies pressed against each other. Knowing that she was going to be in and out of a carriage all day, she'd worn a small bustle, and it now kept a minor distance between her and Dalton. Yet her back leaned fully against his chest. His heat spread through her, and the hard, broad muscles of his torso formed a living

wall. She caught the scent of soap and wool and . . .
him.

Her every part was aware of him—his size, his
strength, the potency of both his body and his will. Her
own flesh felt tight, sensitive, and when his breath
curled warmly over the back of her neck, she fought a
shiver of burgeoning arousal.

His palm was large and hot against her belly.
She shifted, adjusting her footing, and his thumb
brushed against the underside of her breast. Heat
streaked through her. Such a simple, light touch, yet it
spread through her in quivering waves. She was half
afraid, half desirous that his hand would move higher,
cupping her breast.

His hand stayed where it was. She felt and heard a
slight catch in his breathing. He was as affected as she.

She could sense that his mouth was barely an inch
from her nape, and had a powerful urge to lean back
even more so his lips could touch her flesh. What would
his lips feel like? Rough? Soft? Or both? Yet, despite
her desire to find out, she held herself motionless.

It was all she could do to keep her eyes open. She
felt both languorous and inflamed, conscious not only
of Dalton but also the fact that they had to remain quiet
and still. They couldn't be discovered by the housekeeper.
They couldn't take this attraction any further.

After what felt like ten lifetimes, the housekeeper
sighed again and let the curtain fall. She walked back
to the entrance to the chamber, paused for a moment at
the doorway, then closed the door behind her.

Both she and Dalton waited as the housekeeper's
footsteps faded down the corridor. Another minute
passed, yet neither she nor Dalton moved. Eva told herself it was merely to ensure that the housekeeper didn't
suddenly return.

Finally, when a suitable period of time passed, she stepped—stumbled—from behind the screen. Her legs felt unstable, her head light.

She heard Dalton's muttered curse behind her. It sounded as though he were making adjustments to his clothing—specifically, his trousers.

Immediately, she went to the window and pulled the curtain back to look into the ballroom.

"Rockley's still there," she said in a low voice. "We're safe."

"Wrong about that, love." Dalton appeared beside her, his face hewn into hard angles. Dark stubble lined his jaw. He was the embodiment of uncompromising masculinity.

"You and me," he continued in a rumble, eyeing her, "we're dangerous as a loaded gun."

CHAPTER EIGHT

The night yielded nothing. Nothing useful, anyway.

At two in the morning, Rockley had finally left the ball and gone home. No other side trips. No late-night secret meetings in riverside warehouses. No visits to one of his preferred brothels. Just home.

Far as Jack could tell, all he'd gained was an even greater hate—if it was even possible—for Rockley. The bastard continued on with his life just as he'd always done. Protected, privileged, Society's untouchable ideal. Finding a way to ruin him would be one hell of a miracle.

The other thing Jack had gained tonight: a fierce hunger for Eva.

As he lay in his narrow bed at Nemesis headquarters, staring up at the patterns of light on the ceiling and listening to Lazarus snoring in the room down the hall, he still ached with wanting her. Having her pressed up against him, smelling so sweet, feeling her curves . . . it had been a temptation almost no man could've resisted. Somehow, he had, but it didn't help that she'd shown him far more empathy than anyone ever had before.

Through the whole of that day, dragging back and forth across London, stuck in a small hackney, his awareness of her kept growing. Like a weed, poking through the stone wall of his anger.

She seemed cold as frost on the moors, but beneath that was a woman of determination, of passion. What would it be like, stripping away all her layers, thawing that frost? What kind of woman would be underneath?

A hot-blooded one. And damn him if he didn't burn to uncover her.

Lying in his bed, he let his mind travel down the path he hadn't taken behind that folding screen. He pictured it: his mouth on the back of her neck, kissing, biting her silky skin, his hands cupping her breasts, feeling their shape and softness. He pretended that her corset didn't cover her breasts, so that when he played with her nipples, he'd feel them grow hard beneath his fingers. She'd lean into his touch.

Jack closed his eyes, allowing himself to fall deeper into his fantasy. He reached down and took his aching cock into his hand.

His hands would pull up her skirts as she continued to stand in front of him, and he'd touch her legs until he found where her stockings ended and her bare skin began. There'd be her drawers, too. Little frilly things, he decided. He'd find the opening in her underwear and then he'd find her sweet, hot pussy, glossing his fingers with her wetness.

He stroked himself now, imagining what it would be like to dip his fingers between her lips, feel her heat and response. She'd fall back against him as he touched her, her head turning to the side so he could take her mouth with his. He'd slide his fingers inside her. Hell, she'd be deliciously tight, and his fingers were thick. She'd squirm against him, her hips pushing into his hand, but they'd have to be quiet, so quiet. Not a word or sound to give themselves away.

He thrust harder into his hand, brutal, as he pictured her twisting and silently gasping with pleasure. She'd reach back and undo the buttons of his trousers, then grasp his cock and stroke him, just as he touched her. Faster, now. She'd be a little rough, just the way he liked it, the way he touched himself now, but her hand would be so much better, slim and soft. They'd stand like that, behind the screen, pleasuring each other, moaning noiselessly into each other's mouths, until she tightened around his fingers and gasped as she climaxed.

Jack snarled as he and his imaginary self came. He bent up from the bed, body stiff, as his seed shot from him in a hot arc. But in his mind, his come didn't splatter on his stomach and chest, but over Eva's fingers. And then she licked them, one by one, her eyes on his.

He fell back onto the mattress, panting. Looked down at himself. He'd never come this hard before, not from his own hand.

"Christ," he muttered. He used a corner of the sheets to clean himself off, before lying back in bed.

Usually, when he had himself a nightly wank, it took him only minutes to fall asleep afterward. It had been a long day, too, exhausting him with its frustrations and anger. But now he found himself wide awake, wondering if Eva was thinking about him, too. If she was in her own bed, remembering how he felt against her. If she also pictured what might have happened between them, and if she touched herself, too.

At the very thought of her hand drifting beneath the covers to nestle between her legs, Jack was hard again.

"Fuck." He tried to ignore it, but it was like ignoring a telegraph pole sticking up from his groin. No other choice, then. He took hold of his cock once more and pumped it, knowing it was going to be a long, frustrating night.

* * *

"Did you learn anything?"

Sitting at the table in the parlor, Jack glanced up from hunching over his cup of coffee. Simon stood in the doorway, throwing his hat and coat onto a nearby chair as he glowered at Jack. After the rubbish night he'd had, Jack had the strongest need to hit the toff right in his pretty face.

Just as he was about to open his mouth and tell Simon to piss off, Eva came up the stairs. The day outside must be a raw one, for her cheeks were rosy and she carried the scent of wind and rain on her.

Or maybe her cheeks were pink for another reason. She looked at Jack and more color came into her face.

If he thought he'd wanked her out of his system, he was wrong. He couldn't stop staring at her, not as she also took off her hat and coat, not as she bustled into the kitchen to pour herself some coffee. And when she came back into the parlor, his gaze refused to go anywhere else.

He caught Simon's dark frown and curled his lip in response. Let the nob try to do something. Jack wouldn't mind a good, healthy brawl right now.

Lazarus and Harriet also entered the parlor. The swarthy-looking bloke, Marco, hadn't appeared all morning. Had another mission, Jack supposed, or he could be floating in the Serpentine. Jack didn't much care.

Cradling her cup of coffee, Eva sat on the arm of a cushioned chair. Pale purple smudges ringed her eyes. Had she been thinking about him last night, and that's what had kept her awake? Or was it the fact that their operation against Rockley had stalled before it'd truly begun?

The fact that they hadn't made any progress soured

Jack's mood further. "Didn't learn bollocks," he rumbled.

"Not entirely true," Eva said. Her voice shivered over him, and he tore his gaze away from her to glare into his coffee. Inconvenient, this attraction. Bloody inconvenient.

Continuing, she said, "We saw that he spoke with two high-ranking parliamentarians, and they clearly weren't under his thumb. None of Rockley's usual haunts have additional security, either. Which means that wherever he keeps the evidence of his embezzling is not part of his standard schedule."

"Unless it doesn't exist," Harriet noted.

"It does," Eva said, confident. "He'd be certain to keep documentation in case any of his collaborators try to turn on him."

"And if Rockley knows that Dalton's on the loose," added Lazarus, "he'd be sure *not* to go where the evidence is stored, so he doesn't lead Dalton right to it."

Jack had to admit that the old soldier spoke wisely. Still, "That don't help us one bit," he growled. "We can't track down all the places Rockley *doesn't* go. It'd take a bleeding eternity."

"Perhaps," Eva said, thoughtful, "the answer isn't with Rockley, but his collaborators. They might not be as cautious as Rockley in covering their tracks."

"We've already been through the public records of those involved with the government contract." Simon spoke from where he stood next to the mantel, arms crossed over his chest. "Only Rockley's name was mentioned. If anyone else had been listed, we would've investigated them already."

The highborn gent's peevish tone rankled Jack, especially since it seemed directed at Eva.

"The other chaps in the deal could've been involved on the sly," he fired back, "outside of public record. Rockley dealt with lots of blokes. They'd come to his place all the time. Any one of them could've been part of the contract."

Though Simon scowled, the other members of Nemesis nodded thoughtfully, including Eva. A flicker of satisfaction glowed in the center of Jack's chest.

"The contract with the army was consigned six years ago," Eva said to him. "Exactly when you were still working for Rockley. Whoever was also involved with the contract must have been to see him during that time. So you would have seen the collaborator, as well. Maybe heard him, too, talking to Rockley about the contract."

"Lots of gents met with that bastard. He'd be at home once a week in the afternoon for private business. Didn't want to go to anyone's office or have meetings at the club." Despite his tiredness, he felt edgy and restless, and got up to pace. "But there were too many blokes who came and went. Ain't possible for me to remember them all. And I sure as hell don't know what they talked about. They'd go into Rockley's study. I just stood outside and kept guard."

"You never listened in?" Simon looked disdainful.

Jack wheeled around with a snarl. "They didn't pay me to eavesdrop. I earned my coin by beating men until they soiled themselves." He gave Simon a mean smile. "And I was good at my job."

Before Simon could do something stupid, like take a swing at Jack, Eva spoke. "The key to Rockley skimming from the army contract is in those meetings."

"Told you," Jack said. "I don't know what they talked about."

"We don't need to know what they said," Eva answered, "only who met with him. Once we know who they are, we can start building from there."

"It was six years ago, love. I didn't write it down in my journal." He hated admitting to anyone that he couldn't do something, especially her, but there was no use in pretending he could dredge up the names of men he barely met and from so long ago.

"Another go at the punching bag?" Harriet suggested. "That might help you recall them."

"I could punch this building down to splinters," Jack said, "but it still wouldn't help me remember."

Eva frowned in consideration for a moment, then set her coffee down on the floor. She walked over to him and took hold of his wrist.

Memories from last night seared his brain. Easy to think of her gripping something else on his body with that same remarkable strength. Reasonable thought drained out of his head and went south.

When she said, "Come with me," and pulled him toward the stairs leading to his bedroom, his brain stopped working altogether.

She wants to do this now?

So what if she bloody well does? You're not going to stop her.

An ugly thought crept into his head—she had to know the effect she had on him. Was she using that to manipulate him? Make him more biddable? He needed to be cautious, particularly because his wits seemed to cloud whenever she was near him.

When they reached his room, she let go of his wrist and went quickly to the small table. Not the bed. Opening a drawer in the table, she pulled out some paper and a pencil.

He held up his hands and shook his head. "Not

touching that stuff. I thought we already proved that
I'm no good at writing and thinking."

"Because we were going about it the wrong way."
She indicated the chair in front of the desk. "Just take a
seat, Mr. Dalton—"

"Jack," he said. "Since you had your arse up against
my meat and veg, it's only polite to call me by my name."

She glared at him. Heat climbed up his neck, and he
realized what he felt was shame.

"That was . . ." He searched for the word. "Crude of
me. I had a rubbish night, and I took it out on you."

"I'm not a delicate lily," she said, "but I won't tolerate anyone being disrespectful."

"You shouldn't," he answered.

Slowly, the hot anger in her eyes cooled, and she
nodded.

He found himself strangely anxious, oddly yearning
for her to speak his Christian name. No one had said it
in years, and he wanted to hear it from *her* lips, in *her*
voice.

"Take a seat," she said after a moment, then added,
"Jack."

It was a peculiar thing, this mix of gratitude and
desire. For to listen to her say his name gave him back
a part of himself, a personal, hidden part kept safe
from the rest of the world. He wasn't Diamond Dalton,
the hired muscle. He wasn't D.3.7., the convict. He
was . . . himself.

And it was intimate, too. Watching her lips shape his
name, hearing it with that refined accent of hers, in her
low, husky voice. As though they were lovers.

Hard to remember his caution when thoughts like
that filled his head.

With some difficulty, he sat at the table. She set the
paper and pencil down in front of him.

"We're going to try a different method to help you remember these men," she said, standing behind him. He stared at the blank sheet of paper, her nearness making his own mind as empty as the page.

"Start with a face," she continued, "or something else you remember about each of the men that used to meet with Rockley. Could be anything. The mole on his cheek. The kind of waistcoat he wore. If he had a deep voice or a high one. It doesn't matter if it seems important or not. Whatever pops into your mind. Write it down."

"And if I can't remember anything?"

"You can." She placed her hands on his shoulders, and there went his brain again, fizzling away. "You were able to think through and recall Rockley's schedule yesterday. I know you can do this."

"I—"

A clock somewhere in the house chimed ten.

"Damn," she muttered. "I have to go. We'll continue this when I return at five."

He stood as she hurried toward the door. "The hell are you going?"

"My other life." With that, she was out in the corridor and down the stairs. Jack stood on the landing, listening as she spoke briefly with Simon.

"Want me to flag a cab?" the man asked.

"God, no. I've already spent more than I should on hired carriages. There's an omnibus that'll take me right to Sydney Street."

"What about Dalton?" Simon asked in a low voice. "Does he have the mental capability to do what we need?"

Though Jack wanted to leap down the stairs and plant his fist in Simon's face, instead he strained to hear Eva's equally quiet response.

"He's far more intelligent than anyone gives him credit for. Including himself."

The door opened, then shut.

"Did you get all that, Dalton?" Simon called up the stairs.

"Especially the bit where you're a needle-pricked nob," Jack called back.

There was a pause. Then, "Get to work, Dalton."

"Go bugger yourself, Lord Cuntshire." Jack stalked back to his room. Just because he could, he slammed his door. He hadn't had a door to slam in years and it felt damned good, if petty.

With Eva gone, restlessness seethed through him. He paced the small bedroom, sometimes stealing glances at the sheets of paper on the table. They seemed to mock him, those pieces of paper, taunting him with the fact that he couldn't remember any of the men who'd gone into Rockley's study. It hadn't been his job to pay attention to those toffs. But somewhere in their ranks was the one man who'd lead them to the incriminating evidence. Who?

There'd been that one bloke, the one with the bushy eyebrows. He'd met with Rockley on an unseasonably warm day in March, dabbing at his low, sweaty forehead with a handkerchief embroidered with the initials *JSY*. "A glass of lemonade, Young?" Rockley had asked, laughing.

Young!

Jack strode to the table and wrote the name down on the paper. As usual, his writing looked more like an animal's claw marks than actual letters, but he could read it. He stared at the name in shock.

She'd been right. A piece of recollection at a time, and it led him to the name.

For the next hour, he ran himself through the process

of picking through his memories, like a dustman sifting through heaps of debris, searching for anything valuable. He'd catch a glint here and there, the reflection off the sheen of a particular memory, and clean it off until at last he came up with a name.

Columns of names now filled two sheets of paper. He held them up as though he'd conjured them from magic, and, in a way, he had.

Striding to his door, he flung it open and hurried downstairs. Simon and Harriet sat at the parlor table, several newspapers spread out before them. They both looked up, equally guarded, when he appeared.

Jack shook the papers in his hand. "Got enough brains to write up a list of thirty-four names."

"Excellent, Mr. Dalton," Harriet said, plainly surprised.

Simon, however, looked skeptical. He held out his hand. "Give it here."

"Eva sees it first," Jack said.

"She won't be back until five." Simon glanced at the clock. "Hours from now. We don't have time—"

"Eva and then the rest of you lot." Jack didn't know why he wanted Eva to be the first to see his handiwork, but it felt vitally important.

He didn't let Simon answer. Turning, Jack thundered back up the stairs and into his room, giving the door another satisfying slam. Even with banging the door shut, Jack couldn't get calm or settled. He paced around his small bedchamber, trying to distract himself until Eva returned from . . . wherever it was she went.

Brompton. He remembered that. And she had mentioned Sydney Street to Simon. The map in Jack's head unfolded, and he envisioned that exact street. It had rows of genteel houses—where artists and writers often lived and rented rooms. That's where she was now.

At her job? He didn't know what it might be. An artist's model? Not quite respectable, that, and the daughter of missionaries would be sure to find respectable work. What, then?

God—could time move more slowly? It felt like an eternity had passed. It had only been fifteen minutes.

He couldn't wait. He had to show the list to Eva *now*.

After tucking the folded papers into his pocket, he went to the window as quietly as he could. Pulled it open, slowly, to keep from making noise. The window looked out onto the small yard below. He leaned out and saw that a very narrow path led from the yard toward the front of the building, and onto the street.

Turning sideways so he could fit his shoulders through the window, Jack eased himself through. He gripped the window from the outside, using the strength of his upper body to hold himself upright as he pulled his legs through. It was an awkward business, him twisting and hanging on to the wooden frame, then the bricks, and a trickle of sweat worked its way down his neck. He found footing, wedging his boots into the gaps in the masonry, then climbed down.

Two stories stood between him and the ground. He had to edge across and then down to ensure he didn't pass in front of any other windows and give himself away to the Nemesis people within. He hadn't done this much climbing around since his old housebreaking days.

As he passed next to one of the windows, he heard Lazarus. ". . . least he's quieted down . . ."

Jack smirked to himself. And when he had only half a dozen feet between him and the ground, he let go of the wall and jumped down, landing in a crouch.

He stood, and saw a pair of wide eyes staring at him from over the top of the fence bordering the yard. A little boy watched him, his look more curious than frightened.

Jack placed his finger to his lips. The boy nodded in agreement. Jack winked, and then ran.

"What's the capital of Portugal?"

Two blank little faces stared back at Eva. The girls shifted on their chairs and plucked at the stitching on their pinafores. They weren't particularly engaged in their lessons today, but then, Eva wasn't particularly interested in tutoring, either. She couldn't stop her thoughts from circling back to Dalton . . . Jack. Normally, she compartmentalized very well, going back and forth between her current mission with Nemesis and her daily work here, in her rooms.

Yet she found herself rushing the Hallow daughters through their lessons, growing impatient when their attentions wandered. The longer it took to get them through their tutorial, the longer it would be before she could return to headquarters, and Jack.

"Come now, Elspeth, Mary," Eva said. "We've been over this before. It has a lovely castle with crenellations, and a basilica, and a pantheon called Santa Engrácia." She held up a few pictures of the landmarks, hoping to jog their memory.

"Barcelona," said Elspeth.

"No, stupid." Mary rolled her eyes. She was nine and knew everything. "It's Madrid."

"Don't call your sister stupid, Mary. And Madrid is the capital of Spain, not Portugal."

"I know!" Elspeth, the younger of the two, kicked her heels against her chair's legs. "Lisbon!"

"Very good." When the younger girl beamed, Eva continued, "And what happened in 1755 that nearly destroyed the entire city?"

There was a pounding on the stairs outside, as though someone were leaping up them two at a time, but she ignored it. Likely a workman was running late to make repairs on Miss Siles's rooms. The writer had left her window open the other night, allowing rain to get inside and damage the floorboards. Eva suppressed a sigh. Writers were the most forgetful lot. And now Eva would have to contend with the sounds of a workman's hammer throughout the day—as if she weren't already distracted.

"An earthquake," Mary answered.

At that same moment, a loud knock sounded on Eva's door. She never locked it during the day, in case any of her pupils came early, and she didn't want them waiting out in the hall. Before she could ask who it was knocking now, however, the door swung open.

Jack Dalton stood in her doorway.

For a moment, all she could do was gape. His chest rose and fell quickly, and his hair was disheveled. It looked, in fact, as though he'd been running.

Running. Through the city. Looking for her.

And now here he stood. In her rooms.

A quick, stunning burst of pleasure at seeing him, followed immediately by tension and wariness. She stiffened in her chair. Oh Lord, he'd come all the way from the Nemesis headquarters. Did Simon or the others know he was here? What did he want? How had he found her? Were the police chasing him, given that he was an escaped convict? Worst of all—would he give her identity away to Mary and Elspeth Hallow?

Frowning in puzzlement, he crossed the threshold and shut the door behind him. His gaze traveled from her to the wide-eyed girls to the lesson papers arrayed over the table.

Eva slowly rose from her seat.

"We're learning about Lisbon," Elspeth said brightly. "It's the capital of Portugal."

"Is it, now?" asked Jack. He took a few cautious steps closer, staring at the girls as if they'd dropped out of the sky.

Could she hurry him out the door, before the girls asked questions, before he said anything to reveal her other life?

"Who are you?" asked Mary.

Eva started to answer, a cover story already constructed, but Jack spoke first. "I'm here for schooling, like you."

The girls giggled. "You're too old for lessons!" Mary insisted.

Jack's gaze moved from the girls to Eva, and held. "You can learn new things at any age." He broke the contact, turning back to the girls. "Never been to Portugal. Have you?"

"We've been on holiday in Ramsgate," said Elspeth. "I had some barley candy and Mary put sand in my hair."

"Sisters can be the very devil sometimes," Jack said. "Mine used to follow me everywhere. Couldn't turn a corner without running right into her. Like a puppy, she was." Though Jack spoke cheerfully, his eyes were melancholy.

A hard knot lodged itself in Eva's throat.

"What about you, miss?" Jack directed the question to her. "Do you have any devilish sisters?"

She narrowed her eyes. With the Hallow daughters gazing at her eagerly, he had her in a perfect place for interrogation.

"No sisters. Nor brothers." None that had lived past infancy, anyway. "I'm all alone."

"Ah," Jack countered, "but you've got me and Miss Mary and Miss . . ."

"Elspeth," the girl filled in.

"That's three friends. So you're not alone."

Jack was most assuredly *not* her friend. Yet, with him talking so genially with the children—hardly the picture of a tough street-bred ruffian—and being so circumspect in preserving her secret, she had to wonder. Seeing him like this, she felt he became even more real. More . . . human. Careful demarcations blurred, like a hand-drawn map left out in the rain.

"All right, girls." She gathered up the lesson papers. "I think that's enough for today. This nice gentleman's come for his lessons, and I don't want to be rude and keep him waiting."

Mary and Elspeth jumped up from their chairs. "Hooray!"

The utter joy on their faces made her heart sink. It would always be an uphill battle to teach them. But then, most children didn't care for school or learning. She couldn't take their reluctance to be there personally. Dentists had it worse. Barely.

Eva helped the girls into their coats and bonnets and walked them to the door. "Don't forget to study your French verb conjugations."

"We won't, Miss Warrick," Mary said with all the sincerity of a politician. And then she and her sister were off, running down the stairs. A maid of all work always waited for them at the tea shop down the street, ready to escort them home after their lessons. Eva had met the maid a handful of times. She was barely older than the girls, which was usually the case with families of small means. Teenage maids were far cheaper than their older counterparts.

"No running," Eva called after the girls. Their footsteps slowed for a second, then sped right back up again.

She closed the door and turned to face Jack. He stood near the table, examining her tutoring materials. The books looked fragile and strange in his hands, yet he flipped through them, frowning in concentration.

"A teacher, then." He looked up at her.

"A tutor."

His smile, rueful as it was, still sent a curl of heat through her. "Got the right amount of high-handedness for the job."

"I'm purposeful, not high-handed." She crossed her arms over her chest. "How did you find me?"

He paced through her rooms, making everything strange and small by his presence. She'd never thought of herself as a particularly delicate or overly feminine person, yet having him here made her conscious of the differences between them and how transitory, almost feeble, the objects she'd gathered around herself were. As though he were far too elemental, too primal for such things as her chintz-covered sitting chair or the painted china roses given to her by a grateful student's parents.

It wasn't a particularly comfortable sensation. Especially the way he looked around her rooms, at her belongings, as if drawing out hidden truths about her. Today, he'd learned one, no, two: where she lived and what she did to make a living.

Yet she'd read his dossier. She knew far more about him than he about her. Or did. Perhaps now they were even.

"Jack," she said, drawing his attention. "I never gave you my address."

"You said you lived in Brompton." He plucked up a bottle of toilet water from her nightstand and gave it a sniff before setting it down. "And I heard you talking to Simon. You mentioned Sydney Street."

"And how did you figure out in which building I lived?"

"I asked a costermonger. A short chap with a red beard. Said I was in from the country and was here to surprise my cousin, but I couldn't remember her address. He was cagey at first, since we don't look related, but I told 'im about your parents being away doing good works and them asking me to look after you."

He looked over at her bed, the bed where she slept each night. Or didn't. Last night, she'd lain awake, weary but keenly aware. She'd closed her eyes, only to see Jack, dangerous as the darkness, as he'd lurked in the shadows of the drawing room. She had actually looked on her abdomen to see if his hand had left an imprint, for she'd felt his touch continually afterward, like a burn.

"You sneaked past Simon and the others. Escaped headquarters."

His grin widened. "One little flat compared to a whole prison is nothing." He prowled over to her dresser and opened it, revealing her clothing.

She stalked over and closed the door before he could reach into the dresser and fondle her petticoats. "Tell me what you're doing here. Obviously you thought it couldn't wait until I came back to headquarters later."

From his pocket, he produced two squares of folded paper. He held them out to her. No denying the look of pride on his face as she took the paper.

She scanned it. Lines of pencil scratches covered the paper, lines that could've been writing in English or possibly Chinese mathematics. "I don't know what I'm looking at."

He scowled as he snatched the paper back. Jabbing

his finger at the markings, he said, "John Young, Victor Skidby, Matthew Branton, John Gilling. I can read 'em off to you, if you can't figure my writing."

She glanced between him and the documents he held. "This is the list of men who visited Rockley."

"Thirty-four names. Don't know if it's all of 'em, but that's a fair number." He added, almost bashful, "That method for remembering, the one you told me, it worked."

Carefully, she took the papers back. It took a bit of squinting, but she began to decipher the scrawl that passed for Jack's writing. Aside from the nigh illegible quality of his penmanship, the list itself was organized and thorough, grouping names together by the time of year in which they met with Rockley and the quantity of meetings they had with the nobleman.

She couldn't deny it. "I'm . . . impressed."

God protect her, but when a look of pride softened his rough features, her heart tightened. He'd never been praised for thinking his way through a situation.

Self-preservation made her say, far more lightly than she felt, "Perhaps I should start tutoring adults, as well."

"Like to think that I'm a special case." His voice deepened, his gaze holding hers, and she recalled with pristine clarity what he'd felt like last night, pressed close behind her as they'd hidden themselves behind the folding screen. The heat and size of him. The response of her own body at his nearness, and its burgeoning hunger to learn more of his touch.

Having him here, in her private space, the only man who'd truly seen both halves of herself—it soothed and troubled her at the same time. To draw someone near, for the first time, brought forth a longing she hadn't known she possessed. But she feared that desire, too. She needed to keep herself whole, complete.

For all the unexpected connection they shared, Jack was still an unknown. Not fully trustworthy, not truly.

He came here, a voice in her mind insisted, *instead of trying to get to Rockley on his own.*

Because he realizes it's too dangerous right now.

She didn't know what to think, only that she needed him out of her rooms, out of this facet of her life.

"We ought to get back to headquarters," she said brusquely. "If the others have found you missing, they might call the constabulary. You're a wanted man, and if you're taken into custody, or killed in the pursuit, then the mission is over."

His look shuttered. "Don't want any coppers searching for me."

"No, we do not." She put on her coat and gloves, then pinned her hat into place. She strode to the door, with him following, but hesitated before opening it. Turning back to face him, she said quietly, "Thank you."

His brow wrinkled. "For what?"

"For not giving me away." Her gaze slid toward the lesson plans. "You could've made things very difficult for me, but you didn't. I'm . . ."—she struggled with the word—"grateful. I'm in your debt."

Opening the door, he said, "Ah, now that's a mistake, love." His smile over his shoulder was captivating in its wickedness. "You never know when I'll want you to make good on that debt. Or what I'll ask for."

CHAPTER NINE

Silence met them at Nemesis headquarters. Eva paced through the rooms, calling names, but no one was there.

"Maybe they've all taken themselves off to the pub for a pint," Jack suggested.

A pleasant scenario, but unlikely. Though she doubted they had gone to the authorities. Jack didn't know it, but alerting the constabulary about him was one of the last things anyone wanted to do. It would turn all of their lives into a thorn-covered bramble, rife with evasions, explanations, and half-truths. As well as the possibility of exposure.

Just as she was about to head outside to see if any of the operatives were near, the door opened. Simon, Marco, and Harriet entered. The moment they saw Jack, everyone began shouting at once.

"Where the hell have you been?" Simon bellowed.

"We've been combing the city, looking for your miserable hide." Marco's olive skin darkened with anger.

Harriet glanced back and forth between Eva and Jack. "Did you know about this?" Her voice was accusatory.

"Can't keep me chained up like a dog in a yard," Jack fired back.

"I'd no idea," said Eva. "Not until he showed up at my door."

This drove Simon apoplectic. He could barely form words. "At your . . . how did . . ." He rounded on Jack. "Goddamn you—you nearly put everything at risk."

To Eva's surprise, rather than punching Simon, Jack calmly folded his arms across his chest. Disdain replaced his rage. "It was you who let me escape. And it was *you* who underestimated my brains." He studied his nails, the picture of bored derision. "Seems like you ought to be angry with yourselves, not me."

While Simon blustered and Marco and Harriet gaped, Eva had to bite her lip to hide her smile. Only yesterday, Jack had been convinced he hadn't any value beyond his bodily strength, and now here he was, finally taking credit for his intelligence.

"There's no time for wasting on accusations and interrogations," she said. "Jack's written up a list of the men who met with Rockley, and we need to cross-reference it with what we know of his business dealings."

A brief silence fell, fraught with speculative glances. Eva realized that she'd called Jack by his Christian name—a clear indicator that he'd become more than a pawn in their game. After seeing him in her rooms, watching him with the Hallow daughters, she felt he was no longer merely the embodiment of vengeance. More than a fierce masculine force possessing a dark, mysterious allure. He was . . . a man. Jack.

Troubled by her own complex feelings, she pulled the list from her handbag and set it on the table. "I'll need you to read it to me," she said to Jack, "so I may transcribe it and make it a little more legible."

As the other Nemesis agents calmed themselves, she

and Jack worked at copying his list. There were disgruntled rumblings from Simon and Marco, and a few inquisitive glances from Harriet, but Eva and Jack were able to complete their task quickly. Once they had done so, and Lazarus had returned from his own search of the city, the next few hours were occupied with reviewing the names.

Harriet brought out the sizable dossiers that had been compiled on Rockley, including as much of his financial and business connections as possible. The file itself was the product of countless hours of information gathering, not all of it aboveboard. Eva herself had posed as a clerk and sneaked into the record vaults of several corporations in order to obtain vital intelligence about Rockley's numerous business ventures.

Going back and forth between Jack's list and combing through the thick dossiers was tedious, slow work. Yet Jack surprised her—and everyone—with his dedication to the process, scanning through piles of documents and making notes. His notes could only be read by himself, but when he spoke them aloud, they made perfect sense.

By the time the sun had begun to set and the lamps inside had been lit, they'd gone through all the names Jack had provided. Every one of them had legitimate and known business connections to Rockley. Except one.

"John Gilling," Eva said. "What do we know of him?"

"A barrister and a minor figure in the social world," Simon answered, ticking off points on his fingers. "Shares chambers near the Inner Temple. The third son of an old landowning family."

"Shares chambers?" Marco rubbed at his neatly trimmed goatee. "Then his practice isn't exactly flourishing."

"For a man his age," Simon confirmed, "he ought to be farther along in his career. He's a regular during the Season, but always looks a bit shabbier, a bit more threadbare, than most."

"Sounds like the type of bloke who'd want a little something extra in his pockets," Jack said.

Eva studied the papers in front of her. "We've checked all the other names, and Gilling seems the most likely candidate. Gilling's in need of funds, and that would work to Rockley's advantage. But Gilling's position would give him access to other contractors' bids—that's why Rockley would approach him in the first place. Gilling's got to be the key. He's surely Rockley's partner in the government contract. But we need to be certain."

"How?" asked Lazarus, gnawing on the stem of his battered briar pipe. Harriet shot him an annoyed look, which only made him gnaw with more gusto.

"Bluff," Jack said. "Then see how much he reveals."

"The best way to do that is to catch him off guard." Eva tapped her chin as she ran through the sundry scenarios that would best work to Nemesis's advantage. Abruptly, she looked at Simon. "You were able to find out which social events Rockley was invited to. Can you do the same for Gilling? I'll need to know if he'll be attending any balls within the next few days, and be certain that Rockley won't be attending the same events."

"Of course," he answered immediately. "What are you planning?"

Eva stood and stretched. She didn't miss the way Jack's gaze lingered on her, or the answering heat within her body.

"Last night, Jack and I watched an elegant soiree from the outside. But now it's time for us to get a closer

look. You and I," she continued, directing her words to
Jack with a grin, "are going to a ball."

Jack stared at himself in the mirror, not certain if he
liked what he saw. The fabric was covered with chalk
marks and looked like something a chap might wear
when performing at the music hall. Didn't look much
like a fancy suit of clothes at all. He shifted, and bit
back an oath as pins dug into him.

"Careful, sir." The tailor kneeling at his feet spoke
without looking up from adjusting the hem of Jack's
trousers. "It's best if you stay still until we're done fitting you."

"Don't like staying still," Jack muttered. To distract
himself, he took stock of the small tailor's shop in which
he now stood, his gaze moving restlessly over bolts of
fabric, dress mannequins, and half-completed suits. The
shop smelled of wool and tea, and pale sunlight crept
past the crowded front window to pool on the floor. The
whirr of a sewing machine droned through the shop as
another tailor made what would be some gent's coat.

"You've got no choice." Simon, bored, leaned against
a counter. "The ball Gilling's attending is tonight, and
if we want your evening clothes done in time, you'd
better cooperate."

Likely, the toff had grown up having suits especially
made for him, and had perfected the art of standing
motionless while some tailor stuck a measuring tape
right against his tackle.

Not Jack. He'd gone with Rockley to his tailor on
Old Burlington Street. That place was a palace compared to this cramped little shop, all carved wood,
thick carpet, and armies of tailors bowing and smiling.
Once a month, Rockley would go to be fitted for new
clothes, with Jack standing guard, as usual. Tailors had

swarmed over Rockley, measuring, cutting, murmuring toadying nonsense, and he'd just stood there like a god accepting worship as if it were his due.

Now it was Jack's turn to be turned this way and that, and grunted at as if he were cattle being considered for purchase and slaughter.

"Are you certain you can get his suit ready in time, Mr. Olney?" Simon asked the tailor. "We need it by no later than eight tonight."

"It won't be easy," Olney answered, frowning at Jack's trousers. "But I'll get it done. Nemesis helped me out when those men were demanding protection money, and I owe you all a debt of thanks. Mind," he added, giving Jack an up-and-down look, "this chap's terrifically big. Getting evening clothes to fit him properly will be a challenge."

Jack was about to tell Olney that the British prison system had made him this *terrifically big,* but decided that the fewer people who knew about his time at Dunmoor, the better. At least the tailor didn't ask too many questions.

"There's no better tailor in North London," Simon replied. At least the smile he gave Olney looked genuine.

The tailor reddened from the praise. "Too kind, Mr. Addison-Shawe." He cleared his throat. "I'll just . . . get back to it, shall I?"

Simon waved his hand, the kind of gesture rich folk seemed born knowing how to do. Olney immediately returned to his work.

Or tried to. "Sir," he said to Jack with a strained smile, "I can't measure your legs properly if you hold that stance."

Jack bristled. "This is how I always stand." His legs were braced wide, and he balanced on the balls of his feet.

"You're standing like a boxer." Simon pushed away from the counter and paced around the shop. "Bring your legs closer together. Closer," he snapped when Jack shifted slightly.

"I feel like a sodding fool," Jack growled. Once again, he was out of his element, an ignorant outsider—and the one person he felt slightly comfortable with was all the way on the other side of town. "This whole scheme's ridiculous."

The haughty look on Simon's face slowly changed, becoming almost kind. "I remember the first time I was fitted. Couldn't have been more than seven or eight. Everyone was very cross, shouting at me not to move, telling me how to stand. My father was . . . displeased." Simon's mouth twisted. "He expected better from an Addison-Shawe."

Jack stared at Simon for a moment. He hadn't been expecting that. Especially not from Simon.

Frustration dimmed. "So, I stand like this?" Jack asked, changing his stance.

Simon considered his posture, then nodded. "That will suffice." He returned to the counter and carelessly flipped through a magazine.

For a while, the only sounds in the shop came from the scattered traffic outside and the hum of the sewing machine inside. Olney continued to pin and mark what would eventually become Jack's evening clothes.

He'd never owned a special suit for going out at night before.

"If this party we're going to tonight is so flash," Jack said, "does that mean Eva's got to wear some fancy gown?"

"I suppose," Simon answered from behind his magazine.

Jack recalled the women at the ball from the other

night, in their frothy gowns, delicate as frosted cakes, and tried to picture Eva in something similar. But she seemed too hard-boiled for things like lace fans and silk flowers. He smiled to himself, imagining her striding into a ballroom, bold as brass, with a pistol tucked into her velvet sash. Maybe she'd make it a pearl-gripped pistol, for formal occasions.

"She got a man?" he asked.

Frowning, Simon lowered the magazine. "Eva's private life is her own."

"So," Jack said, raising one eyebrow, "you don't know."

"Of course I know. As much as she tells me," Simon added on a mutter.

"Keeps herself close." Jack watched as the tailor continued to make adjustments on his clothing, little nips and tucks whose purpose only Olney seemed to understand.

"Trying to get her to open?" Now it was Simon's chance to lift a brow. "I've news for you, Dalton: it won't work. Eva's the toughest woman I know. Hell, she's the toughest *person* I know, male or female."

"Someone hurt her," Jack guessed. "Someone in her past." The thought made his fists clench with the need to beat the bastard, whoever he was.

"Nothing so melodramatic. She simply . . ." He shrugged. "She doesn't trust many people. That's how she's always been. The most unsentimental woman I've ever met. Won't form intimate attachments."

It sounded very much to Jack as though it meant Eva didn't have a man. Which made him glad, indeed.

"You tried, though," he said. God knew that if Jack worked side-by-side with her, day after day, he'd try to form an *intimate attachment*. Hell, he'd only known her for less than a week, and he couldn't stop wondering about the taste of her lips, the texture of her skin. His nights had become damned restless because of her.

Just because she kept everyone at arm's length didn't mean she lacked desire or passion. He'd seen it, felt it. But she couldn't keep it buried forever.

Simon straightened, tugging on his coat. "I might have. But she rightly pointed out that people who work together oughtn't mix the personal and professional."

Jack snorted. "Maybe it's on account of her type not being polished toffs. Maybe she needs someone a bit more rough around the edges." He studied himself in the mirror, in his strange piecemeal evening clothes.

"Dalton, if you were any more rough, you'd be serrated." Simon's reflection appeared in the mirror behind Jack. They couldn't be more different, him and the fair-haired nob. Even the easy way Simon wore his perfectly tailored, fashionable clothes showed how unalike they were.

Jack never let himself feel ashamed or small because of his low background. He couldn't change the particulars of his birth. Nobody picked who their mother was going to be, whether she was a genteel lady or a whore. Far as he could tell, there wasn't much difference between either. Both were just women. Neither good nor bad.

Fathers were even more unpredictable. He didn't know who his was, and neither had his ma. Could've been a navvy who dug trenches to build roads, could've been a lord looking for cheap pleasure far away from Mayfair's knowing eyes. Whoever he was, he never knew that his one night with Mary Dalton eventually brought Jack into the world.

It didn't matter. All that mattered was who Jack was now.

He'd spent the past five years wanting only one

thing—to destroy Rockley. That hadn't gone away. But a new fire burned within him, just as bright.

He desired Eva. Wanted her to want him.

Uncharted territory, this. She might not fancy him. Could give him the cold shoulder. That'd be a bad business.

He'd just have to make sure she wanted him in her bed.

Looking into his own eyes, he vowed that he would succeed in all his goals.

Jack had faced off in the ring against Iron Arm McInnis, a bruiser with a 35–0 record. He'd taken on three blokes armed with knives and broken bottles in an alley brawl. Hell, he'd confronted the possibility of death or imprisonment as he'd walked, manacled, into the courtroom.

His heart beat harder now than it ever had. He thought it would burst through his chest, right through the starched shirtfront he wore.

Pacing around the parlor in the Nemesis headquarters, he kept checking the clock on the mantel. She'd be here any moment.

He started to rake his hands through his hair.

"Don't!" Marco yelped. "You'll get pomade all over your gloves."

Jack's hands paused in midair, then he slowly lowered them. "Never going to get used to this," he muttered. Pomade slicking his hair back, white gloves, starched collars and shirtfronts. Slick-soled shoes that gleamed like ebony mirrors. The kind of clothes worn by the upper crusters he'd see through doorways, windows. Not his own sort.

"You don't have to get used to it," Lazarus said, sitting beside the fire. "It's only for tonight."

Right. It was a disguise, meant only to get him into
the ball at some gentleman's house, where he'd find
Gilling. And then, they'd proceed with the next step of
their plan.

Many things could go wrong tonight. He could
be barred from getting into the ball. Gilling might not
be there. Or Gilling would be there and shout the house
down the moment Jack made his move. The investigation against Rockley could collapse, leaving them with
nothing and no means of bringing him down.

But what truly made Jack's skin feel tight with nerves,
what made his heart pound, was thinking about what
Eva might do when she saw him in his new evening
clothes. Would she laugh at him, say something snide
about stuffing a bear into silk and wool? It oughtn't
matter what she thought. Yet it did.

Footfalls sounded on the stairs. A man's and a woman's. She was here. Simon had gone to fetch her, and
now he was back. With her. Their muted voices came
through the door.

Jack stopped his pacing and stood in the middle of
the parlor. He felt big and ham-fisted, uncertain. But
his chin rose and he pulled his shoulders back when the
door opened and Eva appeared.

She stopped abruptly, causing Simon to nearly collide
with her. When she didn't move any further, Simon
sidled around her and into the flat. But what the blond
toff did after that, Jack had no idea. All he saw was Eva.

He felt as though someone had punched him in the
chest. Hard. He couldn't speak or breathe. Could only
stare.

She wore a dress of shiny golden fabric, with dark
blue velvet ribbons along the low neckline and trimming the ruffles of her skirts. Golden beads glittered
on the front of her gown. She'd put fresh flowers in her

elaborately pinned hair, roses with pale yellow petals.
The dress left the slopes of her shoulders exposed, and
even in the harsh gaslight, her skin gleamed like a
pearl. Long white gloves came to just above her elbows, and the skin of her upper arms was just as gleaming as her neck and shoulders. Her neck was bare, but
she wore a glittering pair of earrings that caught the
light with each turn of her head.

It wasn't the fanciest dress he'd ever seen—the ladies
from the other night had had more ruffles and bows
and beads—but, by God, he'd never seen any woman
look more beautiful.

"I see"—she cleared her throat when her words
came out in a rasp—"Olney managed to get your suit
ready in time. He did an . . . excellent job."

There wasn't a full-length mirror in the flat, and
Olney had delivered the evening clothes. Jack had caught
glimpses of himself in some of the smaller glasses but
he had no idea what he looked like once he'd put everything on.

Judging by the way Eva looked at him now, he looked
like a juicy steak, and she was starving.

Her gaze moved over him, and he felt it as surely as
if she'd taken off her gloves and run her hands up and
down his body. Her appreciative look lingered on his
shoulders, then traveled lower, down his chest, and
lower still. She wet her lips. In response, his cock thickened, snug against the wool. He clenched his teeth to
keep from groaning aloud.

If he'd felt awkward before, now manly confidence
surged through him. He liked the way she stared at
him. An improper look if ever there was one. And the
ideas spinning through his head weren't proper, either.
They were downright indecent.

Did she have silken drawers on underneath that

gown? Were they white, pale blue? Trimmed with ribbons or plain? He wanted to grab up big handfuls of her golden skirts and find out.

"What a pretty gown," Harriet said, coming out of the kitchen. She approached Eva and tugged playfully on the narrow band of her sleeve. "What on earth are you doing with it?"

Pink crept into Eva's cheeks. "It was an indulgence. I've no real need for it."

"You do tonight." Harriet glanced back at Jack, who still couldn't move or get his mind to function, and winked. "If a gown could be a weapon, yours is a Gatling gun."

Jack felt more like he'd been knocked clean off his feet by a sledgehammer.

"When are we going to see you in something like that, Harridan?" Lazarus chuckled.

"Be grateful that you won't," she fired back. "Because if you did, you'd expire of ecstasy on the spot."

Simon held up a printed card. "Present this invitation to the butler, and you'll be permitted entry. Be very careful not to lose it."

Eva took the card and examined it. "This must be a valuable commodity. How did you obtain it?"

"It's the art that appears not to be art," the blond man answered. "*Sprezzatura,* the Italians call it."

Marco grimaced. "Your pronunciation is abominable." He repeated the Italian word, and even Jack had to admit it sounded like music when spoken by Marco.

"That card might get you in the door," Simon counseled, "but once you're inside, the rest is up to you." He looked at Jack pointedly. "Genteel behavior is essential."

For all Simon's helping Jack with the fitting, it was plain that he still didn't trust Jack. Suited him just fine. He didn't trust Simon, either.

Jack rolled his eyes. "Here I was planning on having a belching contest in the middle of the dance floor."

"Next time," Eva said. She looked at the clock, and again Jack was struck by the slim curve of her throat. He hadn't missed the swells of her breasts, either, the tops just visible at the dipping neckline of her gown. Nice handfuls they'd be, soft and full. He ached to touch them, to hold them, to tease her nipples into tight beads.

Damn it. At this rate, he'd be strutting around the ball with a cockstand all night. He needed to get control of himself and his thoughts.

"It's just nine now," she said. "The dancing's already begun, which means it's the perfect time for us to arrive."

He was starting to know the ways of polite society, and stuck out his arm for Eva before she had to ask. What was it the gentry said? Ah, that's right. "Shall we, my lady?"

"Oh, we shall." She rested her hand on his arm, and smiled up at him. He felt dizzy. "Time to infiltrate the serpent's nest."

Eva took one step. Then another. Slowly, slowly, she and Jack ascended the stairs outside Lord Chalton's ball. They were sandwiched between guests waiting to present their invitations to the butler. Music and light spilled out the door, combining with the chiming of flutes of champagne and equally bubbling conversation. Within minutes, she would show the butler her invitation and come up with identities for herself and Jack. She'd worked something out earlier in the day, and rehearsed it to herself in the carriage ride over, but she hoped her cover story held beneath the butler's imperious stare. The upper servant could have her and

Jack tossed out onto the curb if he so desired, invitation or no invitation.

Her pulse raced and her palms dampened her gloves as she and Jack went up another step. The woman standing in front of them continued throwing glances over her shoulder, the plumes in her hair bobbing with each movement. Compared to the splendor of the woman's Ottoman silk and velvet gown, Eva's ensemble was almost austere, and she stiffened beneath her regard. But it wasn't Eva's simple gown that kept drawing the woman's gaze. It was Jack.

Had the plumed woman's escort known the way she looked at Jack, he would have been mortified, if not livid. Eva herself wanted to throw her gloved fist into the woman's face.

Yet she couldn't blame the plumed lady's interest. In his evening finery, Jack looked . . . dangerous. The severe black-and-white of his clothing, the excellent cut of his coat across his wide shoulders, and the fit of his trousers over his long, muscled legs—all of it emphasized how very wild he truly was. Evening clothes only highlighted the difference between him and all the other elegantly attired men waiting to attend the ball.

His dark hair had been tamed and slicked back, revealing the hard contours of his face—square jaw, crooked nose attesting to his life as a fighter, heavy brow. Though his lips were somewhat thin, their curves hinted at carnality.

A rough man in evening dress. She'd never seen anything more arousing.

Keep alert, she reminded herself sharply. They were here for the mission.

Difficult to remember that when Jack kept looking at her with blatant hunger. She didn't feel quite so plain in her simple gown when he did that.

At last, they reached the top of the stairs. The butler held out his hand, and Eva gave him the invitation.

"Your name, madam?"

Monarchs would cower at the butler's haughty tone.

Summoning her own hauteur, she sniffed. "Mrs. Eloise Worthington, of the Northumberland Worthingtons."

The butler glanced at Jack, who glowered back.

"And this is Mr. John Dutton," Eva said. "The cattle magnate from Australia."

The butler studied him. Beneath her hand, Jack's muscles tensed as if preparing to knock the butler flat. Gently, she squeezed his arm in silent communication. They'd agreed ahead of time that he would speak as little as possible. Since he seemed comfortable with silence, he'd agreed, but she hadn't extracted a promise from him not to hit someone.

After an excruciating pause, the butler waved toward the staircase behind him. "Supper has already been served. Dancing is in the ballroom at the top of the stairs. Good evening."

She and Jack moved on. They crossed the threshold and stood in the vaulted foyer, where footmen relieved Jack of his coat and hat and took Eva's wrap.

She sent Jack a meaningful glance, which he returned. They'd done it. Gotten past the first obstacle. But they hadn't crossed the Rubicon.

He offered her his arm again, and together they ascended the curving stairs that led to the ballroom.

"Why Australia?" he said in a low voice.

"Much of that country was settled by transported convicts." She shrugged. "It would stand to reason that someone of your physique might be their descendant."

"If I have to talk to someone," he pointed out, "they'll know I'm English."

"Most of these people have as much experience with Australia as they do Bethnal Green."

"None," he said.

"Exactly." They reached the landing, and followed the trail of guests and music toward a set of wide double doors that stood open. In wordless understanding, they both paused and took a breath. Then stepped into the ballroom.

"Bloody buggering hell," Jack breathed.

"Agreed," Eva murmured.

While not as large as the Beckwiths' ballroom, the chamber was still impressive in its size. White and gilt columns rose up toward a coved, equally gilded ceiling, from which hung crystal chandeliers that hurt the eye with their brilliance. The parquetry floor shone like a mirror, reflecting back the forms of men and women in their evening best. Liveried footmen bearing trays of champagne stood against the walls, as much part of the furniture as the upholstered chairs placed for wallflowers and dowagers.

Everywhere was a sea of black wool, lustrous silks, and jewelry that twinkled like the unfeeling stars. Some men wore military uniforms, drawing young girls in white like a plate of cakes. Conversation draped over the chamber. Long patrician vowels mixed with the gliding strings provided by the orchestra. A screen of potted palms had been placed at the farthest end of the chamber, discreetly concealing the musicians.

"Smell that?" Eva drew a deep breath, and Jack did the same.

"Beeswax. Sparkling wine." He breathed in again. "Soap and starch."

"Privilege."

When a footman passed by with his tray of champagne, Jack grabbed two glasses. Despite his genteel gloves, the flutes looked tiny and fragile in his hands.

She sipped at her champagne and was relieved to see that Jack did the same rather than gulp it down.

"I don't see Gilling," she said. She'd studied a picture of him earlier to familiarize herself with his appearance. "Let's take a turn around the room."

They moved through the guests milling at the edges of the chamber. She made certain to nod regally at those they passed, trying to convey with only her bearing that she belonged here as much as anyone. It was like wearing someone else's face, someone else's body. Yet she must have been reasonably successful, for no one sneered at her, and she even received some polite nods in return. Murmurs of speculation trailed after her and Jack. In the narrowly defined world of the elite, new faces were bound to incite interest.

She saw more than a few ladies gazing at Jack avidly. Her response was an icy stare. But why should the other women's interest bother her? She'd no claim on him. Not in the slightest. Yet it sparked a cold fury when a particularly pretty brunette in rose-hued taffeta gave Jack a look of blatant invitation.

To his credit, his gaze never lingered anywhere. Not on any thing or person. He was at all times watchful, assessing. And when a gentleman or two spent a little longer gazing at her, Jack's glower had the men hurriedly looking away.

"What's going on between Lazarus and Harriet?" Jack asked abruptly. "The two of 'em snipe at each other regular as the bells of St. Paul's."

She chuckled softly. "It's obvious to everyone that they fancy each other, but they're both too bullheaded to admit it."

"Where's the harm in it?"

"It's not a good idea for Nemesis operatives to become romantically involved. But I also believe they're afraid."

"On account of that combat training you receive."

She pursed her lips. "If either Harriet or Lazarus took the initiative and declared themselves, and was rejected . . . I don't think either wants to risk that pain. So they just taunt each other and amuse the dickens out of the rest of us."

Jack was silent for a while, but then said, "If they want each other, then to hell with the rules and to hell with getting hurt."

She felt her brows rise. "Do you really believe that?"

He shrugged. "Life's got a habit of slipping through your fingers, slippery as an eel, and leaving you with nothing. Maybe if we're offered a chance at something good, we should grab it while we can."

Unsure how to respond, she sipped at her champagne. Was he referring just to Harriet and Lazarus, or something more?

Damn it, I can't think about that now.

"Still no sign of Gilling," she said quietly.

"If he scuttles around the edge of the upper crust," Jack answered, "he'll be here. We can wait him out."

They continued to stroll leisurely at the perimeter of the ball, watching the highest echelons of British society in the rituals of their arcane culture.

"That woman," she murmured, "over by the punchbowl. The one in the diamonds and green satin. She's paid off a blackmailer three times so no one finds out about the son she had before she was married."

"Bloke standing next to the third window," Jack said. "With the belly and bushy sideburns, looking snobbish."

"Sir Denholm Braunton." A baronet, she recalled,

known for his particular hatred of policy intending to help the poor.

"He pays a whore twenty pounds to whip him. Or he did five years ago," Jack added. "Maybe now the price has gone up to thirty pounds."

She smiled darkly over the rim of her glass. "Secrets. Everyone here has them. From the blushing debutante to the venerated patriarch." There were sexual peccadilloes, financial misdeeds, addictions, thefts.

He snorted. "Wouldn't know it just to look at 'em. They swan around as if gold comes out their noses when they sneeze."

They both stopped and faced the dance floor, where couples decorously spun.

"When I used to solicit donations with my parents," she said, watching the dancers, "I'd suspected that there was another face to Society. Then I joined Nemesis, and I learned that Society has many faces. None of them real."

"But people like us," Jack said, "we know the truth. Who they really are."

"They aren't *all* bad," she noted. "Only fallible. Like any human."

"Fallible?"

"Capable of making mistakes."

His expression darkened. "Aye. God knows I've made plenty of those."

The opening strains of a waltz drifted out across the ballroom. Couples took their places upon the floor. Once, waltzing had been considered scandalous, something only for fast women and men of questionable morals, but now spotless debutantes clasped the hands and shoulders of irreproachable young bachelors as approving parents looked on. The waltz began, and the couples started their turns across the floor.

The sight, Eva had to admit to herself, was a pretty one, a whirl of pale silk and dark evening clothes. Dancing was part of an aristocrat's education, and everyone moved with precision through the ballroom like an intricate mechanical device. Ladies both young and not so young beamed up at the faces of their partners, while the men were afforded the opportunity not only to put their hands upon a woman's back, but to converse with her with a small degree of privacy. The perfect medium for courtship or flirtation.

As the couples spun by, Jack said, "The dancing we did in Bethnal Green was a bit more rowdy."

"I can teach you later." The moment the words left her mouth, she realized that she'd actually enjoy showing Jack how to waltz. "You're probably a natural." And he would be, too. Though he was large, he moved with uncommon agility.

"If it means I get to look down the front of your dress," he said, "then I'm for it."

"Poetry, Jack." She affected a sigh. "Pure poetry."

His mouth formed a hard line. "Don't know how to say pretty, fawning words," he said gruffly. "All I know is that I like looking at you."

Heat fanned across her cheeks. Such simple words, given in a surly tone, yet they moved her, far more than she would have expected.

As she struggled to think of some response, a middle-aged man with a sash adorned with medals and considerable white eyebrows approached them. He looked faintly puzzled at their appearance, as well he should. He was the host of the ball.

"Lord Chalton," Eva said, sinking into a curtsy, then offering the baron her hand. "Such an honor to receive your invitation."

He took it and bowed, though he still looked baffled. "The honor's mine, er . . ."

Eva laughed as though he were making a joke, then her laugh trickled away as if realizing that he wasn't joking. "Mrs. Worthington," she supplied. "Eloise Worthington. From Alnwick. Lawrence Worthington's widow. He used to speak so fondly of you and your days together at Cambridge, winning blades together in the college boat club. Surely you haven't forgotten!"

For a moment, the baron said nothing, but Eva smiled at him pleasantly, utterly assured that her late husband and Chalton had spent many an hour rowing on the Cam.

"Mrs. Worthington, of course." Chalton nodded. "Delighted you could attend." He glanced nervously at Jack.

"I hope it wasn't too presumptuous of me to bring along a friend," she said, smiling. "Lord Chalton, this is Mr. John Dutton from Sydney. You've heard of Dutton Cattle Company, naturally."

Jack, impassive, stuck out his hand.

"Naturally," Chalton echoed. He shook Jack's hand weakly, and it was like watching a terrier shake hands with a wolf. "Ah, I see that Lady Addington could use more champagne. If you'll excuse me . . ."

"Your reputation for hospitality is not exaggerated," Eva trilled. "But, if I may, before you go . . ."

Chalton, who had been sidling away, stopped, though he looked pained to do so. "Yes?"

"I understand that John Gilling is here tonight. My brother-in-law's cousin is a great friend of Mr. Gilling, and I'd like to pass along Stamford's good wishes."

"You'll find him in the card room," Chalton answered, then, with a quick bow, hastened away.

It would look gauche to hurry across the ballroom immediately after their host had moved on, so Eva stood calmly fanning herself and smiling serenely at the room. From the corner of her eye, she caught Jack staring at her.

"What?"

"A damn neat trick you just played there, Mrs. Worthington." Admiration was clear in his voice and eyes. "I knew you were sly, but I didn't know *how* sly."

Oddly, it was one of the best compliments she'd ever received. But she couldn't revel in his praise, not while they still had a job to do.

Eva steadied her nerves. They had scaled partway up the mountain, but were far from the summit. Every step brought them closer to their goal. It also meant they had farther to fall.

"We passed the card room on the way to the ball-room," she said.

Jack held out his arm, and she took it, enjoying the feel of iron-hard muscle beneath the expensive fabric. "Time to hunt down our prey."

CHAPTER TEN

The card room at a Society ball seemed an incongruous place for a criminal. Overstuffed men sat in overstuffed chairs, crowded around tables as they played genteel games of whist. Some silver-haired dowagers were scattered here and there like antique pearls, content with their cards and sherry. Decades had passed since those women had taken their turns upon the dance floor, and yet nothing truly had changed save for the stiffening of their joints. Greater comfort and amusement could be found here, among women their own age and men who had no interest in flirtation.

For all its gentility, nearly everyone within the card room held a secret. Most were innocuous. Others . . . unlawful.

From the doorway, Eva and Jack scanned the chamber.

"Table by the bookshelf," he said in a low voice. "The bloke with the gingery hair and scrawny hands. That's Gilling."

The man in question appeared as inoffensive as the room in which he played cards. The two other middle-aged men at his table were equally unexceptional.

"Seems a likely partner for a scheme to defraud the government," she said. "He'd do whatever Rockley wanted." A collaborator with strong ideas and opinions would prove more difficult to manage.

"We don't know if he's the link we want," Jack noted. "One sure way to find out, though." He took a step into the room, but Eva stayed him.

"Let me bring Gilling out," she said. "We can't have this play out before a roomful of witnesses, and if he recognizes you and bolts, the plan's shot to hell."

Though he looked unhappy with having to wait a few moments longer, Jack gave a nod. He pointed to a shadowed corridor leading off the main hallway. "Get him over there. I'll take care of the rest."

She didn't like the ominous sound of that. "This scene has been scripted, Jack," she warned. "Don't decide to change the performance in the middle of the play."

His expression darkened. "Still thinking of me as Nemesis's puppet."

"I only want this mission to succeed."

"Then goddamn trust me." He stalked off.

Eva took a moment to collect herself. Had she spoken out of turn? Did Jack merit her confidence? He'd already proven some degree of trustworthiness, and an exceptional intelligence. Yet she kept holding fast to her mistrust. It made their roles more easily defined. Simpler.

The question she needed to answer now was whether or not Gilling was the man they could use to ruin Rockley.

She glided into the card room, offering whoever looked her way a bland smile. A few men glanced up at her, their gazes lingering, but she politely ignored them as she pretended to idly watch the games in play. She meandered around the chamber, taking her time. Finally reaching the table where Gilling sat, she feigned observing the game.

"I hope I'm not disrupting, gentlemen," she said. "But I'd grown weary of dancing and thought to amuse myself with other pursuits."

Gilling looked up from his hand and gave her a quick perusal. Liking what he saw, he said hastily, "No disruption at all, madam. We could deal you in, if you like."

Marco had taught Eva how to cheat at dozens of card games, including whist. If she so desired, she could strip these men of every coin they carried, perhaps even take their signet rings and pocket watches. All the while they'd have no idea she swindled them. A clever rogue, that Marco. But then, the British government had trained him to be.

"I've no head for cards," Eva said. "But I have every respect for those of you who do have that talent. Clearly," she added, smiling, "you have an abundance of talent."

Gilling's pale cheeks flushed and he mumbled his thanks.

"Oh, do continue your game," Eva urged as the other men became restive.

After glancing at her again, Gilling resumed playing. Eva made appreciative murmurs whenever he won a trick and exclaimed in dismay when he didn't. Gilling preened beneath her attentions.

When all the tricks were played, and Gilling emerged the winner, Eva clapped then fanned herself.

"I never would have believed whist could be so exhilarating," she trilled. "I find myself dreadfully overheated. Some fresh air would benefit me." She gave Gilling a meaningful glance.

"There is a balcony," he said, standing. "Would you do me the honor of allowing me to escort you?"

"You are kindness itself." She took his offered arm.

A few men muttered, "Lucky dog," and shot Gilling

envious, incredulous looks. Apparently, bold widows did not usually make appearances in card rooms.

Together, she and Gilling left the chamber, his steps hurried.

"There's a shortcut," she said, pointing her fan toward the darkened corridor.

Needing no further urging, he led her into the passage. The hallway must be used mainly by servants, for the doors were narrow and the walls sparsely adorned. The sounds of the ball faded, the shadows thickened. There was no sign of Jack.

Gilling stopped and looked around, frowning. "Perhaps we ought to find another way. This seems wrong."

A door opened behind them. They turned to see Jack stepping out of a chamber, blocking their path back to the ballroom. His brutal smile was calculated to frighten, and, judging by the stunned look on Gilling's face, it was a success. Even knowing Jack as she did, Eva herself felt a shiver of fear.

"It's very right, Gilling," Jack said. "I've been waiting for you."

Like a bloody coward, Gilling immediately broke away from Eva and stepped backward. The sod actually put her between him and Jack, as if taking shelter behind her.

"You know who I am," Jack said.

"J . . . Jack Dalton. You're supposed to be in prison." Gilling's voice turned high and thin.

"Decided I'd had enough of bread and rock breaking." Jack flexed his hand. "Rather break Rockley instead."

Gilling stared at Jack's arms, his shoulders. "I warn you," Gilling piped, "if you attempt any violence I'll—"

"That ain't what I'm here to do. And I never *attempt* violence." Jack's mean grin widened.

Gilling swallowed hard. He shot an accusing glance at Eva. "You led me here! To *him*!"

"This is far more interesting than a game of whist," she answered, and Jack loved the cold deliberateness in her voice. She seemed to hold many different women within herself, and yet all of them were her. He could explore her for a lifetime and never fully know all of her.

"What do you want?" Gilling demanded again.

"Same thing everyone these days wants." Jack rubbed his fingers together. "The means to make myself comfortable."

"A bottle of gin should see to that," snapped Gilling, then looked terrified by his brief display of cheek.

"But it isn't very lasting, is it, Mr. Gilling?" Eva asked. "What we're proposing is a good deal more permanent."

"Your money for my silence," Jack said. He took a step toward Gilling, and the man sidled backward.

"Blackmail?" Gilling's eyebrows rose. "There's nothing you can hold over me. Certainly not someone of your class," he added.

"Folks of my class know all sorts of valuable things," Jack said. "Like the fact that you and Rockley skimmed your contract with the government. Took home a fine profit for yourselves while soldiers fired shoddy cartridges."

"Utter nonsense!" Gilling countered. "I have no idea what you're talking about!"

"Your left eye twitches when you lie," Eva said pleasantly. "Just a little. I saw it whilst you were playing cards. Not much of a bluffer."

"I'm not lying!"

Jack crossed his arms over his chest and stared at Gilling. The same look he'd give his opponents when they stood at opposite sides of the boxing ring. A match could be won before a single punch had been thrown.

Gilling turned even paler. "See here," he gulped, "even if your allegations were true—which they aren't—I haven't any money to give. You'd be better served blackmailing someone else, someone with property and wealth."

"That's exactly what I'm doing," Jack said. "What you're going to do is help me get money out of Rockley."

If Jack had a pen, he could've written on Gilling's now paper-white face. The man's mouth opened and closed.

"Just go to him yourself," Gilling stammered.

"Too dangerous," Eva said.

"Rockley and me," Jack explained affably, "we've got what you'd call a history. You know that. I couldn't get anywhere near him. But you can. You'll be my middleman."

"But how am I to get you any money from him?"

Jack said, "That's your worry."

"And if you don't do as instructed," Eva continued, "your involvement with the government contract will be brought to the attention of very interested parties. I imagine it wouldn't be difficult to have you arrested on charges of treason."

Looking hunted, Gilling tugged at the collar of his shirt. "I still have no idea what you're talking about."

"We've got written proof, Gilling," Jack said. "The records you kept. They're ours now."

"Oh, God," Gilling croaked. "I . . . I must go. I have to think."

He stumbled past Jack and Eva, heading back toward the main hallway. Jack didn't try to stop him, easy as the task would've been. Yet as Gilling lurched down the corridor, staggering around other guests, Jack and Eva followed wordlessly at a distance through the house. Gilling hurried down the front steps and into the street.

If Gilling arrived in a carriage, he didn't wait for it to be brought around. Instead, he waved down a hansom and flung himself into it. He shouted instructions at the driver. The cab drove on.

With Eva right behind him, Jack ran for their hired carriage parked in the nearby mews.

"Don't lose that hansom," he called up to the cabman.

As soon as he and Eva were in the growler, it took off in pursuit. The cab raced through the streets, rocking from side to side. Jack braced his legs against the seat in front of him, and Eva held tight to the strap beside her. Neither of them spoke. He liked that she kept her silence while they were on the chase. No useless gabbing for the sake of hearing her own voice or making dull comments about obvious things. She had the calm, focused look of a hunter. A hunter in gold-colored silk, with yellow flowers in her hair.

Looking out the window, he noted the neighborhood. "St. John's Wood," he said aloud.

"Wonder what's here," she murmured.

He had a pretty strong suspicion what that might be, but he'd wait until they'd reached their destination before saying anything. He didn't want to look like a fool. Not in front of her.

The growler came to a sudden stop.

Both Jack and Eva peered out the window. Fine-looking brick houses lined the quiet street. A little ways down the block, Gilling had jumped out of the hansom. He hurried up the walk of one of the houses. Lights shone beneath the drawn curtains, but the house itself looked as decent and well behaved as any of its neighbors. Looks couldn't be trusted, though.

"Do you know that place?" Eva asked.

"It's Mrs. Arram's."

"Ah," she said with understanding. Mrs. Arram's brothel catering to wealthy gentlemen had been on the list of Rockley's favorite haunts.

"Perhaps Gilling needs to blow off steam," Eva suggested, "so to speak."

The man knocked on the door to the brothel. The door opened, revealing two huge men. Gilling spoke to them, looking frantic, but it was too far away for Jack to hear what was being said.

"They've got more security than normal," Jack noted. "Usually it's just one chap at the front door and another at the back."

"One of them might be Rockley's man," Eva mused.

"It's Wednesday, and not even ten o'clock," he said, shaking his head. "Rockley never went to Mrs. Arram's on Wednesday. And he never went to any brothel before midnight. Gilling would know that."

"Then why come here? Unless," she said, thoughtful, "he's here to check on the evidence."

Jack took his gaze away from Gilling, still speaking with the guards, and frowned at Eva. "You think the proof of them skimming on the contract would be at a whorehouse?"

"It's a sensible location to store something highly valuable," she explained. "Secure, as you noted. Most genteel brothels are better guarded than any bank. The men who go there have only one real purpose in mind, and it isn't searching for incriminating documents. Yet if Rockley ever needed access to those documents, he could have it without attracting any attention. Likely he pays Mrs. Arram a substantial fee to keep the documents at her establishment, but with a strong warning that she isn't to know or ask about what those papers contain."

Damn him, but it made sense. Jack said, "We'd been looking for places where Rockley might've added security, but we searched in the wrong places. We didn't even know if the evidence existed, but it does, and it's here." He snorted. A brothel. A sodding brothel.

"Gilling has to know it," Eva said. "When you told him you had the evidence, he came straight to Mrs. Arram's to check on it." She peered out the window. "It looks as though the guards aren't going to let him in, however."

Gilling, looking more and more upset, was shouting at the men standing watch, trying to shove past them. One of the guards pushed him back. Gilling stumbled backward. Before he could try forcing his way in again, the door slammed in his face. For a few minutes, he pounded on the door, but it stayed shut.

Finally, Gilling gave up. He sulked down the walkway and flagged another hansom. He got in and drove away.

"Same story here, my lad," Jack called up to the hackney driver. "A nice bit of coin for you if we stay on him."

"Right you are, sir."

This time, as the cab sped through the streets of London, Jack and Eva weren't silent. As soon as they set off in their pursuit, she said, "Rockley knows you've escaped prison. You're out there. He also knows that you'll never be able to touch him, not physically, anyway. But his one vulnerability would be the evidence of his embezzlement. So he bulks up security at Mrs. Arram's to make certain you have no way of getting to that evidence."

Jack snorted. "Hell of a rotten bastard."

"One of the worst I've ever encountered," she said. "And I've encountered quite a lot of rotten bastards."

It didn't surprise Jack when Gilling's cab came to a stop outside Rockley's home. However, after Gilling pounded on the front door, he was allowed to go inside.

"They let him in," Jack murmured. "But Rockley won't be there. He's never home at this time. Doesn't usually get back until three or four." That was hours away.

"Perhaps the butler is allowing Gilling to wait for Rockley's return," Eva suggested.

"Rockley didn't like having folks in his home when he wasn't there. But if the butler's letting him stay, there's got to be a reason."

"More proof that Gilling and Rockley were partners in the scheme to swindle the government," she said darkly. Her lips tightened. "I don't particularly fancy the idea of sitting in this hackney for five hours, doing nothing."

"Where next?"

"Home." After she gave the cabman the direction for Nemesis headquarters and the carriage moved on, she sat back against the squabs, her expression shuttered as it usually was when she was deep in thought. Jack liked watching her think, the tumblers of her mind turning.

"We did pretty well back there," he said. "Working Gilling like that."

Her smile flashed in the dimness of the cab. "It did go rather nicely."

"Sound surprised," he noted. "Thought you Nemesis lot all partnered together doing these jobs of yours."

"We do. I have. Usually I partner with Simon, but I've gone into the field with almost everyone else."

His mouth curled. "So it's me you didn't expect to work out."

"All quantities are unknown until tested," she answered.

"Guess that means I passed the test," he said dryly.

She hesitated before saying, "It's ongoing."

He couldn't blame her for being chary. Earning someone's trust—especially someone as cautious as Eva—could take lifetimes. A handful of days wouldn't change much. He wasn't sure he could trust her, either. Having spent his life in the company of thieves and good-for-nothings, he'd learned that the only person he could fully have faith in was himself. Always somebody ready to sell him out for their own profit.

Nemesis had already proved they'd do anything to make sure they saw justice served. They'd throw him under the wagon wheels if they thought it'd help their purpose.

But he wanted Eva's trust. He wanted her secrets. He wanted . . . everything.

In the darkness and light of the carriage, he saw her sitting opposite him in that golden gown of hers, her shoulders slim but not fragile, the soft shadows between her breasts. Something big and hungry curled in his stomach.

"How'd you get involved with Nemesis?" he asked. "Missionaries' daughters don't seem the sort to throw in with ruthless bastards who dish out vengeance."

"When I was helping my parents in the East End, I'd heard rumors someone was grabbing Chinese boys off the streets. I told my father and mother, but they didn't want to get involved."

"But *you* did."

"I made some investigations and crossed paths with Simon. Thought he was one of the kidnappers at first. But when I found out what he was doing, that he was trying to help the boys, too, we worked together. He didn't think I could handle myself." She smiled darkly. "I proved otherwise. Simon and I put an end to the trafficking. Then he offered me a place with Nemesis. I didn't hesitate."

Of course she didn't.

"How often did you visit brothels with Rockley?" she asked suddenly.

It took him a moment to realize she'd asked him a question. "Like I said, he had four he usually went to. Kept it interesting, is what he told me. Depending on what fancy struck him, we'd go every other day. Didn't watch him, though, if that's what you're asking. Only kept guard outside." Jack had gotten far too used to hearing Rockley fucking, to the point where he'd barely noticed it, standing out there in the hallway and thinking of what to eat for supper or whether he'd have time to grab a pint on his way home.

"And when you were there, did you . . ." She waved her hand.

"Sample the merchandise?"

Her jaw tightened at his mocking tone. "Never mind. I was only curious about the running of a brothel, the logistics involved." She made a show of picking off a piece of fluff from her skirts. "If Rockley was a regular patron, I thought perhaps it would be a good business strategy to keep the men in his employ happy, as well, but it truly does not—"

"I didn't."

She stopped fussing and gazed up at him. He wondered if she knew how hopeful she looked. "You can tell me the truth," she said.

Anger flickered to life. "I've never lied to you. When I say that I didn't fuck any of the whores, I mean it."

She didn't blink at his crude language. "You must've had opportunity."

"Plenty. But I don't pay for sex." He tore his gaze away from hers, folding his arms over his chest. "When she couldn't make enough coin from doing sewing and mending, my ma walked the streets. I swore I wouldn't let the same thing happen to Edith. Tried to keep her from that . . . life." He spat the word.

"Didn't matter, though," he continued, glaring out the carriage windows. He didn't see the fine shopfronts and flats of the West End, but the narrow tumbledown hovels of Bethnal Green and the hollow-faced women who walked its filthy streets. "She became a whore, just like our ma. I told her, *Be a shopgirl, go work at a factory.* Gave her money. But she wouldn't leave it. She said, *The only way a girl like me's going to get anywhere is on her back.*"

His words like rusty nails in his throat, he said, "So, no. I didn't sample the merchandise. Because the damned merchandise was someone's sister. Someone's ma."

His sodding eyes burned. His goddamn chest ached. He'd spent five years on the rack of his own thoughts, his own condemnation, but it hadn't been enough. It was never enough.

He started when Eva's hand cupped his face. Caught up in his self-blame, he hadn't noticed that she'd moved to sit beside him. But in an instant, it was all he was aware of.

The cool reserve surrounding her fell away. Her gaze searched his. It almost killed him, seeing the compassion and sadness in her eyes—he couldn't stand anyone's pity. He didn't want it. Pity was for weakness.

And yet . . . she showed him a kindness that went beyond pity into something deeper. A shared understanding.

"I should've tried harder," he rasped. "Nabbed her

off the street and locked her up somewhere, a place far away in the country. But I chose to believe her lie when she said she was happy at the brothel where she worked. It was a fancy place, a place where gentlemen went. The girls there looked healthy and comfortable. So I let her stay. I fucking let her stay," he growled. "And then she'd been killed. By my own sodding boss. He liked his bedsport rough. Must've gotten too rough that night. I didn't warn her to stay away from him. I may as well have stuck the knife in her."

"*Rockley* killed Edith," she said quietly. "Save your anger for him, not yourself."

"Oh, aye," he said, bitter. "I'm a goddamn hero."

"I never said that." Her mouth curved into a soft, bittersweet smile. "But maybe you'll become one."

He took up most of the seat, so she squeezed tight next to him. Her hand still cupped his cheek, and though he wished she weren't wearing gloves, he still soaked up the feeling of her touching him.

He became, suddenly, conscious of everything. The sensation of her leg pressed against his. How she was warm and cool at the same time, and smelled of flowers and her own satiny skin. The desire for her he'd been feeling as a continuous pulse now thundered through him.

Though shadows were heavy in the carriage, he was close enough to her to see the widening of her pupils, hear the low, edged catch of her breath.

The atmosphere between them changed. She'd been offering kindness a moment before. Now, kindness turned to hunger.

He raised his own hands. Slowly. Cupped the back of her head with one, and curved the other around her neck. She stared up at him, her breath coming fast.

Then he put his lips on hers.

He'd watched iron-hulled ships being built in dock-yards, and how, when the welders had put torch to metal, sparks had showered everywhere. Liquid light.

Those same sparks, that same heat and light, poured through him now as he felt and tasted Eva's mouth for the first time. She was silk and steel, and so delicious he wanted to gulp her down. He traced his tongue across her lips, catching the flavor of champagne. Her lips opened to him, and he sank farther in. Where she was wet and fever-hot.

He didn't think she'd resist him—he'd seen the de-sire in her face—and she didn't. More than that, she kissed him with the same hard hunger that burned in him. She gripped his shoulders, pulling him closer. He growled. *Yes.*

It was everything and not enough. Roughly, he pulled her onto his lap. She moved to wrap her arms around him, but he held her back. Holding her gaze with his, he used his teeth to take off his gloves and tossed them aside. He wrapped one hand around the back of her neck. The other pressed against her chest, just beneath her collarbone. She gasped, and he gave another growl. He urged her down for another kiss.

Gliding his hand down the span of her chest, feeling the pounding of her heart, he dipped his fingers be-neath the neckline of her gown. At his first touch of her breast, his whole body ached with need. And when his fingertips found the hard point of her nipple, she moaned, pressing closer.

Goddamn him, but he'd never touched or kissed a woman as fine as her, or known this keen fire. She also pulled off her gloves, and they joined his on the floor of the carriage.

"Eva," he rumbled, when her own hand slid beneath his evening coat to grip his shoulder through the thin cotton of his shirt, her nails digging into him. "Good bloody Christ."

"Blasphemer," she murmured, then nipped at his mouth.

He took his lips from hers, running them over the line of her jaw, then down her neck. Her smell made his head spin and his cock ache. He scraped his teeth across her skin, and she made a sound of pleasure as she writhed against him. The carriage swayed as it jolted down the street, the rhythm urging both Jack and Eva on. She rocked her arse into his groin. He pinched her nipple and caught her pleasured cry in his mouth.

He knew, he *knew* it would be like this between them. Hot and wild. Not pretty but honest and bare. And he also knew that if he wasn't inside her, *now,* he'd lose his damn mind.

He released his hold on the back of her neck to reach for the hem of her skirts. The carriage shuddered to a stop.

"Here we are," the cabman called down.

Gasping, Eva broke away. She stared at Jack through lowered lids, and color spread across her cheeks. With slow, rigid movements, she moved off his lap to sit on the opposite seat. Her hands shook as they struggled to smooth her hair and skirts.

Jack also panted as if he'd gone twelve rounds in the ring. He watched her try to tidy herself, and all he wanted was to pull her onto his lap again, have her straddle him. There were other options, too. She could brace her arms on the seat, and he'd lift her skirts, baring her from behind. She could sit, and he'd bury his face between her legs. They'd both get very, very untidy.

"Change of plans," Jack called up to the driver. "Take us to Sydney Street."

"Right, gov." The cabman clicked his tongue at his horse, and the carriage began to move.

"Wait," Eva exclaimed. "Don't go anywhere yet, driver."

"All right, madam." The cabman sounded puzzled, but the hackney stopped rolling.

"I'm not taking you to bed in that place," Jack growled. "Not where every sodding person can listen in."

"You're not taking me to bed in *any* place," she said.

Disbelieving, he stared at her. "Right. Because some other lady was grinding against me, not you." He provoked her on purpose, needing some kind of reaction, some response that showed she was as affected as he was.

She blew out a breath. "It can't. This cannot go any further."

"Because you're a lady and I'm street trash."

She looked at him scornfully. "Have you ever heard me say that? I don't think of either of us in those terms."

"I want you," he said, his voice so rough and low he hardly knew himself. He took her hand in his, running his thumb back and forth across her wrist. Her pulse came quick and fast beneath his touch. He wanted to pull her across the narrow space of the carriage and start up where they'd left off, with his hands beginning their journey up her legs and her gasps in his ear. "You want me. Simple."

"Not simple," she countered. "Complicated. I work for Nemesis, and getting involved with you compromises that."

"Nobody has to know." Back and forth went his thumb, learning the softness of her skin.

"*I* would know. And it would throw off my judgment.

Stop it." She tugged to free her hand from his grasp. "I can't think when you do that."

"You need to think less." He wouldn't release her. "Stay too much in your head, and the rest of you dries up and blows away."

A sudden hurt shone in her eyes. "My thoughts and my work are all I have. I can't give them up." She gave her hand another tug, and he let her go. A second passed, as if she waited for him to continue arguing or reach for her again.

He said nothing. There'd be naught to gain this night. He hadn't known how damn close she kept herself, walled up even more than Dunmoor Prison.

"We'll go up," she said after a few moments. "Tell the others what we've learned tonight."

Reaching over, he opened the door to the carriage, noting the way she held herself still when he moved nearer. But he didn't touch her, only waved toward the open door, letting her go. Maybe gentlemen got out of carriages first and helped ladies down. But Jack couldn't walk comfortably. Not yet. And his will had already been sorely tested. Touching her made him want more.

She cast him a wary glance before climbing down. As Jack took several calming breaths, willing his body to quiet, she paid the cabman and thanked him for his service.

That thought niggled him again. Was she using the attraction between them to keep him controllable? The closer they got to Rockley, the more Jack wanted his blood. But when Eva kissed him, touched him, thoughts of everything but her fled. He'd be willing to do anything, if only to taste her again.

She wouldn't rook me like that.

"Coming, Jack?"

"Aye," he grunted. He stepped down and nodded at the driver before the hackney rolled on.

As Eva unlocked the door to the chemist's shop fronting the headquarters, Jack stood on the curb, watching her, hands in his pockets. Her back was straight, as if she expected an attack. No, not an attack. An escape.

The door to the shop opened, and they walked inside, passing the rows of silent bottles and the scale.

She really was like Dunmoor Prison, closed up tight, containing walls within walls. It was herself she kept locked away. Afraid of what might happen if she were to break free.

Tonight, he wore a gentleman's evening clothes, but that hadn't changed who he was: an escaped convict. He was glad of that. Glad he knew how to break out of prison. It meant that he could help her escape her own. But she was strong, an unknown to him in plenty of ways. She had to demolish her own walls.

CHAPTER ELEVEN

Marco stalked into the parlor and threw a newspaper onto the table.

"It's over," he snapped, pacing.

Eva set aside her tea then picked up the paper and read aloud for the benefit of Simon, Jack, and Lazarus, also drinking their morning tea. "'QUEEN TO MAKE RARE PUBLIC APPEARANCE.'"

"Page four," said Marco curtly.

Turning to the appropriate page, Eva scanned the columns. What she saw made her curse softly.

"What's happened?" Jack demanded, getting to his feet.

Eva continued reading. "'John Gilling, a barrister of the Inner Temple, was discovered early this morning near his chambers, cruelly murdered. The poor gentleman had been stabbed to death.'" She gazed up from the paper, stunned.

Everyone made noises of shock and disbelief. Her heart pounded in her ears as she went on. "'Mr. Gilling's corpse was discovered in an alley by one Harry Peele, dustman, as Mr. Peele went about his morning circuit. Though Mr. Peele has been taken into custody for questioning, the chief suspect is the notorious criminal Jack Dalton, who has recently escaped from Dunmoor Prison.' "

"Does it say any more?" Simon asked.

She quickly looked over the rest of the article. "Only some editorializing about the sad state of our fair city, where respectable men could be murdered near their place of business by fugitives from the law, et cetera." She flung the paper onto the floor.

Jack, who had joined Marco in pacing the floor, kicked the offending newspaper, though it didn't travel far. "Rockley."

"So it appears," Eva said. She rubbed at her tired eyes.

Sleep had been scarce last night, her mind and body both too stimulated to allow her any rest. Thoughts of the evidence against Rockley had crashed against remembering Jack's hands, his mouth, the honeyed ferocity of his kiss. She'd ached everywhere, craving his touch, wishing she'd taken him back to her rooms where they could have stripped out of their evening finery and finally given in to their mutual desire. But she'd made the right decision by refusing him. Or so she'd told herself as she drifted into fitful slumber.

He hadn't shaved this morning, and he looked so dangerously alluring with stubble darkening his hard jaw, it had taken considerable self-control not to drag him up the stairs to his bed. To save her sanity, she'd kept her gaze away from him, their conversation to a minimum.

Yet she couldn't stop watching him pace like a caged animal, seething with brutal fury.

"Rockley killed Gilling?" Lazarus wondered, frowning. "When?"

"Sometime last night," Eva answered. "After Jack and I left Rockley's place." She knocked the side of her fist against the table, making the teacups rattle. "Damn it, we should've stayed."

"And done what?" Simon asked. "You would've seen Rockley go into his home, but there wouldn't have been any way to know he'd murder Gilling. Or any way to stop it. It's easy enough to sneak a body out of a house under cover of night, and if you've got men of criminal reputation in your employ. Which Rockley has."

"But *why* would he kill Gilling?" Lazarus pressed.

"On account that Gilling went to Rockley and told him about me," Jack said, still stalking up and down the parlor. "Just as we wanted. We light a fire under them both, and get Gilling to put the squeeze on Rockley. Gilling's more afraid of what the government will do to him than he is of Rockley."

"But to Rockley, the weak link becomes Gilling," Eva added. "He knows about the government contract, knows about the evidence, which makes him a liability to Rockley. Since he can't get to Jack, he can silence Gilling. So he does."

"He's ruined women and killed a prostitute," Marco said, "but we don't have any evidence that he's killed a man before."

"Now he has," Lazarus said, shaking his head. "Jesus."

"Could have been done by one of his bodyguards," Simon suggested.

"Thugs would beat a man to death, not use a blade," Jack said. "If it came to it, a bodyguard would shoot a man. We don't go for knives. But Rockley," he added with a snarl, "he's fond of 'em. Seems to be his preferred way of killing."

The truth of this sank in, and everyone looked appalled.

"He pins it on you," Eva said, "and gets the Metropolitan Police to do his dirty work." She picked up her teacup, then set it back down. She'd no desire for tea. Or anything else.

Marco swore in extravagant Italian, his favorite tongue for foul language. "With Gilling's death, we've lost our way to strike at Rockley. Worse, security around Rockley and the evidence is going to be impenetrable. He'll throw everything he has at keeping his person and the documentation secure."

"This whole operation is fucked," muttered Lazarus.

Cursing viciously, Jack spun around and threw his fist into the wall. Reverberations shook the parlor.

At that moment, the door opened to reveal a young woman in a cloak and bonnet. She stared at Jack, her eyes wide, a gloved hand raised in shock.

"Mr. Byrne downstairs recognized me and said I should go up. Perhaps," she said weakly, "I ought to come back another time."

Eva jumped to her feet and hurried to the girl. "No, no, please come in, Miss Jones."

Jack pulled his fist back, revealing the hole he'd punched in the plaster, and a new web of cracks marring the wall. Despite the plaster dust coating his hand, he appeared to be fine. The wall, however, was not. He hid his hand behind his back as Miss Jones took a few tentative steps into the room.

"We're, ah, making excellent progress on your case," Eva said, guiding the young woman to a chair. "Might I get you a cup of tea?"

Miss Jones shook her head. "No, thank you." She made no move to take off her bonnet or cloak. No plans to stay long. She sent Jack a few cautious glances as she sat.

"This is Mr. Dutton," Eva said quickly. "He's assisting us with your case."

"That's precisely why I've come." Miss Jones picked at a loose thread on the tablecloth, studiously avoiding everyone's eyes. Which prevented her from seeing the looks of concern shared by the Nemesis operatives.

"Are you certain you wouldn't like some tea?" Eva pressed, knowing that the delay in fixing the girl a cup would give her time to collect herself.

"All right." It was a capitulation, not an agreement. Though Miss Jones had come to Nemesis a somewhat timid creature, she seemed even more so now, her shoulders slumped, her hands trembling as they rested on the table. Her skin was paler, too.

Eva went into the kitchen to prepare tea. No one in the parlor spoke, and in the strained silence, it felt as though she were banging on a timpani drum rather than stirring milk into a delicate china cup. When she finally emerged from the kitchen, she set the cup down in front of Miss Jones and took a seat beside her.

The girl picked up her tea, but her hand shook so much the liquid spilled over the rim and onto the tablecloth. "I'm sorry." She blinked back tears as she set her cup back down with a clatter.

Oh, this wasn't good. Eva laid her hand over Miss Jones's. "It's all right," she murmured.

"It isn't!" The young woman looked martyred as she stared at Eva. "It's terrible! Worse than terrible. Disastrous."

"We'll soon make everything right with Lord Rockley." Simon gave Miss Jones a reassuring, kind smile, which only made the girl appear even more miserable.

Miss Jones took a shuddering breath, as if steadying herself, then spoke in a rush. "Whatever it is you're doing to get me justice, however you plan on extracting recompense from Lord Rockley—I want you to stop."

Stunned silence followed. Eva could only blink her

astonishment, seeing equally baffled expressions on everyone else's faces.

"Why?" she finally asked.

"Lord Rockley . . . he . . ." Miss Jones covered her mouth with her hand.

Rage poured through Eva. "Did he hurt you again?"

Eva's anger must have shown in her countenance, for the girl said quickly, "Not physically, no. But," she added, "he's been making threats. Warning me that if I try to take any further action against him he'll make my life even more hellish than it already is. I won't be accepted anywhere. My father's business will be ruined."

"Does Rockley know about Nemesis's involvement?" Marco asked.

The young woman shook her head. "He knows only that I've made allegations against him. And that I haven't left London. Yet that is exactly what I intend to do. Leave the city. Perhaps even leave England. I just want to disappear, to bury it all."

"You've spoken of this to your father?" Eva said.

"Papa thinks I'm having tea with a friend today. He's no idea I'm here, or what I'm asking you to do. But, please," she said, turning imploring eyes to Eva, "stop pursuing Lord Rockley. No good can come of it."

Fury the likes of which Eva had never known surged through her. Only the presence of Miss Jones kept her from unleashing a torrent of foul language. She had a strong urge to throw her fist into the wall, just as Jack had done. What she truly wanted to do was beat Rockley into a syrup. Bad enough that he'd ruined Miss Jones, but now he intimidated and threatened her into silence.

He had the blood of at least two people on his hands. Jack's sister, and now Gilling.

"We cannot stop," Eva said. "Rockley must be

brought down. He'll just keep hurting more girls, girls just like you."

"If I demand it?" Miss Jones pressed, her voice quavering.

Frustration and sympathy warred within Eva. Words tried to form, words that would give Miss Jones the necessary strength to continue in their pursuit of Rockley. But the young woman was fragile, and anything Eva could think to say might sound bullying and cause the girl to crumble even more. Judging by the silence from the other members of Nemesis, they were struggling with what to say, as well. None of them wanted to abandon the case.

Jack suddenly grabbed a chair and pulled it near Miss Jones. He turned it around to straddle the chair, bracing his arms on its back. The girl looked startled, almost ready to flee, until he gentled his expression to something verging on kindness.

"Did you have plans for yourself before this business with Rockley?" he asked.

His question caught her off guard. After a moment, she answered, "My parents wanted me to marry. They were hoping to find me a respectable tradesman and see me settled as a wife and mother."

"And what did you want for yourself?" He asked this softly.

She cast her gaze down to the floor. "I . . . wanted to be a teacher. It didn't matter to me if I married or not. But I'd hoped to find some mill town school where I could teach the children of the workers. Give them a chance at life outside of a mill. It doesn't matter anymore." She dabbed the corners of her eyes with her sleeve. "No one will hire a ruined girl. And now Lord Rockley threatens not only me, but my family. I've lost my dream, but I can't let my parents suffer for my mistake."

Eva's heart contracted, feeling the sharp loss of the girl's dream and her desire to do good.

"It wasn't your mistake," Jack said. "Never say that. This Nemesis lot brought me on board because I've got information on Rockley that no one else has." Fortunately, he made no mention of Nemesis blackmailing him into cooperating. "More than that, I've got my own reason for wanting to ruin that bas—that scoundrel. He harmed someone important to me. More than harmed her. He stole her life. Killed my sister with his own hands."

Miss Jones gasped. "Did you go to the police?"

He smiled bitterly. "The police don't bother when the victim's a whore. And Rockley had 'em all in his pocket. They'd never touch a bloke with so much power."

"What did you do?" the young woman asked.

"Tried to get my own justice. It didn't work, not the first time, but that don't mean I won't stop trying. See, Miss Jones," he continued, his dark eyes serious, "men like Rockley think they can do whatever they want. Hurt whoever they want. Girls like you and Edith. That's why we can't stop going after him."

Miss Jones's forehead pleated with concern. "I don't know," she said doubtfully.

"His threats now are a storm that's got to be weathered," Jack went on. "Ultimately, he won't be able to do you any more harm. You and your family will be safe. Me, and the others here, we're fighting for you. For Edith, for all the girls Rockley's harmed. If we don't bring him down, he'll just go on, using and throwing away women. Taking their reputations, their lives."

He shook his head, raw anguish etched into his

features. "I couldn't save Edith, but there are so many other girls I *can* help. That *you* can help. But that'll only happen if you let us get on with our work."

Eva, watching all this, felt the hot knife of sorrow in her own chest. She remembered what he'd said last night, about failing to protect his sister. He carried the pain with him always.

Outside in the street a wagon rolled by and two women stopped to converse in brisk, cheerful voices—the noises of everyday life. Within the Nemesis headquarters the fire in the grate popped. Miss Jones stared at Jack, her hands clenching in her lap.

Eva held her breath. So did everyone else in the room.

"All right," Miss Jones said after a long, long silence. Her shoulders straightened, her back drew up taller, and she lifted her chin. "All right. We'll go on. We'll ruin that bastard." She blushed at her own crudeness, but kept her gaze steady.

Eva didn't sigh in relief, though she felt like it. Once Nemesis was on a mission, almost nothing kept them from pursuing it to the very end. A villain like Rockley had to pay for his crimes, whether Miss Jones wanted vengeance or no. They wouldn't have stopped in their quest for justice. But it made their role less difficult when they had their client's support.

"There's a lass," Jack said, patting Miss Jones's hand.

The girl blushed again. And no wonder. The warm approval in Jack's gaze was a potent thing.

"You've made the right decision, Miss Jones," Eva said.

The young woman blinked, as if she'd forgotten that Eva, or anyone else besides Jack, was also in the room. His words had held her spellbound.

She rose, and Jack and the other men also stood. Though she still looked pale, a new resolve shone in her face and revealed itself in her upright posture. "I ought to go. Papa will be expecting me soon."

Eva got to her feet and walked Miss Jones to the door. "We will keep you apprised of any new developments."

The girl gave a small laugh. "I think it best if I don't know the details of your methodology."

Smiling, Eva said, "Probably safer that way." She opened the door. "Thank you, Miss Jones."

"It's I who owe you my thanks." She looked past Eva to Jack. "You've given me a new courage, Mr. Dutton."

"It was always in you," he answered. "Just got a little shaken, is all."

Miss Jones ducked her head, his compliment making her shy. "I'm sorry about your sister."

"Me, too," he answered. "But we'll make it right, you and me."

The girl gave Jack a tentative smile, then turned and walked down the stairs.

Eva closed the door and leaned against it. She couldn't take her eyes from Jack. He'd done what she and the other Nemesis operatives hadn't been able to accomplish—convince Miss Jones to push past her fear. And he'd done so without raising his voice, without frightening or coercing. The strength of his words and conviction alone had done it.

Marco, Simon, and Lazarus looked at him as if he'd just calmed a herd of stampeding horses.

"Commendably done," she said. "And you've a new admirer. She looked at you as if you rode in on a white charger, holding a lance and shield."

Jack gave an unchivalrous snort. "A knight in rusty armor."

She wondered if he'd ever see himself as anything more than that.

"That was well done," Simon allowed. He picked up the discarded newspaper. "But whether or not Miss Jones agreed to continue with the case is irrelevant. We're still at an impasse with Rockley now that Gilling's dead; security is even tighter than before and the police are on the lookout for Dalton. So long as Rockley knows Dalton's out there, we won't be able to make any progress."

Jack crossed his arms over his chest. "What was your plan for me when the job against Rockley was finished? Throw me back into Dunmoor?"

"God, no," she answered, appalled. Although Nemesis hadn't precisely been forthcoming about their intentions. The way they'd been treating him, he'd expect them to toss him aside like so much rubbish. "We were going to counterfeit your death and give you a new identity."

Jack appeared to consider this idea. She'd tipped Nemesis's hand, but there was no choice for it. He needed to know.

"We're going to lose Rockley," he said. "He'll bury himself so deep, we'll never be able to get anything out of him. Unless . . ."

"Unless?" Marco prompted.

"We fake my death now," said Jack.

He didn't think they'd cheer at the idea. Turned out, he was right. Grim silence met his announcement. Eva, in particular, looked troubled.

It oughtn't annoy him. She was part of Nemesis, and he was just a pawn in their game. Made sense that she'd fret over the notion. He saw it in her eyes. Once Jack was "dead," they'd have no more leverage over him. He'd have his liberty, and that was something they didn't want. He wouldn't be their leashed dog anymore.

From the beginning, he'd made it clear that if he could find a way free of them, he'd take full advantage. Of course she wouldn't like that.

Still, it riled him to see her uneasy about taking off his collar. For all the hunger he and Eva felt for one another, they didn't share trust.

"Makes sense," Simon mused. "If Rockley believes Dalton's dead, he'll think the threat against him is gone. The police will back off, and he'll loosen security, giving us an opportunity to get our hands on the evidence."

Though Marco and Lazarus nodded, Eva continued to frown. "There must be another way," she said, "or some different strategy we can use."

"If you've got a suggestion, love," Jack said bitingly, "don't keep it to yourself. We'd all like to hear how to keep me on a tether."

"I . . ." She glanced away. "I don't."

"Settles that, don't it?" He planted his hands on his hips. "It's time to kill me."

He never forgot the smell. Long after he'd left the narrow, grimy streets of the East End, when he'd kept a fine little flat in St. Luke's, and even when he'd been in prison, where the air smelled of lye and porridge, he'd never quite gotten the scent of Bethnal Green from his memory.

As he and Eva stole through the twisting lanes, darkness hanging over the alleys like a sulk, he was drowning in smell, in memories. Coal smoke, mud, fried fish, human filth, and here and there, the sweet stench of opium.

He knew all of it. And bugger him if it didn't force a small blade of sorrow between his ribs. It hadn't changed here. Five years away, and the poor of London still lived like animals, hopelessness a dark slime that coated the uneven streets and ran down the crumbling walls.

This was the place that had been his home, the place that made him. The streets were more his parent than his ma and nameless father had ever been.

He didn't feel a sense of homecoming, skulking through the lanes and alleys of his old neighborhood. He felt only a cold, distant sense of anger, that anyone should be forced to live ten in a room, with the only water coming from a filthy old pump, and babies crying all night because their bellies were empty.

In a drab wool cloak, Eva kept silent beside him. Weak light from a gin palace spilled across her face. He looked for signs of disgust or shock in her expression.

There were none. He remembered that she'd been raised by missionaries, and had probably spent too many hours in places like Bethnal Green and Whitechapel. She already knew how low people could sink.

Still, her gaze was wary. That showed she was smart.

Two men stumbled out of the gin palace. Jack put out an arm to shield her from the drunkards as the men threw wild punches at each other. Too busy beating each other to notice Jack and Eva, the drunks took their fight down into the gutter. But the brawlers blocked the way.

Jack shoved them aside with his boot heel. They rolled away, still throwing punches.

Someone inside the gin palace laughed, a high, shrill sound.

"Keep moving," Jack said in a low voice.

Eva hurried on, with Jack right next to her.

"I've studied maps of the area," she said. "I've even been here before. But I have no idea where we are."

"Don't worry. I do." He turned down a snaking alley.

"The maps you've seen, they'll never show you the real lay of the land. Streets are alive down here. Always twisting, never where you think they're going to be."

She stepped over a puddle of some unknown liquid. "So if they keep changing, how do you know where to go?"

"Got the same animal blood in my veins," he answered.

They continued walking, passing three women who sat upon a stoop. A gang of almost a dozen children of all ages stood and played in the street. The clock might've chimed after midnight, but that didn't mean young babes were snug and safe in their cradles. Three kids wearing only ragged shirts dragged sticks through the muck caking the road. When an infant started to cry, a small, thin girl scooped him up into her arms, trying to soothe him.

They all stopped and stared as Jack and Eva passed. Half the children ran after them, their hands outstretched. He made sure to keep an eye on the pack he carried. Little hands made the best pickpockets.

"Penny, sir? Spare a penny, miss?"

Jack reached into his pockets. There were two coins in there, and he had to save them for later.

"Here." Eva pressed coins into the children's open palms. The money disappeared right away. "That's all I have, so none of you follow and ask for more."

Like startled pigeons, the kids ran off, their bare feet slapping through the mud.

Eva watched them disappear into the darkness. "Hard to believe that we have homes lit by electricity, surgeries can be performed without the patient aware of a single cut of the scalpel, and so many other modern wonders, yet these children live as if it were the twelfth century."

"Time don't mean anything here," he said. "Not politics or science or anything else. Only keeping alive from one day to the next. That's the only measure."

"It's a goddamn sodding abomination," she said with sudden, quick heat. "It's a wonder anyone here survives childhood."

"A goodly number don't." He kept to the shadowed side of the lane. Though it'd been years since he'd last walked down the streets of Bethnal Green, he was still known in these parts. His tracks needed to stay covered. "Them that do find a way to keep living, somehow."

"Like you," she murmured. "Not merely bare subsistence, but rising above it."

He used to think so. Think that he'd dragged himself up from the gutter into a swell life. Clean, healthy, properly fed. Women in his bed when he wanted them. A job that put money in his pocket. What else did he need?

Something more than that, he realized. Something that made a difference past his own needs.

Bloody hell, these Nemesis blighters are getting inside my brain.

Not just Nemesis, but Eva. His body ached with wanting her. Yet it went beyond basic lust. Her drive, her backbone and daring. He'd thought someone could only feel greed for things—wealth, a fine carriage of one's own—but that wasn't so. You could be greedy for a person, too.

Right now, he needed his thoughts sharp. Trouble was cheap and abundant in this part of the city, especially for a wanted man.

"Down here." He nodded toward a set of stairs that led toward a basement at the foot of a building. The blackness was even thicker at the bottom of the steps, making the door there barely visible.

Eva stayed close behind him as he went down the stairs and rapped the side of his fist against the door.

It creaked open, revealing a skeleton of an old man. His face looked even more skull-like as he lifted a low-burning lamp.

"One bed or two?" the old man demanded as he stepped aside to let Jack and Eva enter. "We're almost all full up for the night. An extra bed'll cost you."

Jack dipped his head to keep from banging it on the low beams inside the long room. Shapes lined up in rows on the floor. Coughing punctuated the silence, and the mutterings of drunkards sleeping off their latest trip to the bottom of a bottle. Someone hushed a fussing baby.

He glanced at Eva beside him. Her mouth pressed into a tight line as she took in the dim, stale room and the two dozen people using it as their home until daylight. In all her visits to the slums as a missionary, she probably hadn't seen places like this one.

Beds was a nice way of saying a mound of moldy straw and a thin, tattered blanket crawling with lice.

"No bed," Jack said. "I want to know where the fight is tonight."

The old man eyed him suspiciously. "Don't reckon what you're talking about."

Jack held up a shilling. "The fight," he prompted.

"Abandoned slaughterhouse," the old man answered quickly. "A half mile from here. Want me to point the way?"

"I know it." Jack dropped the shilling into the man's bony hand. He and Eva turned to leave.

"Sure you don't want a bed for you and your lady?" the old man cackled. "Nice an' comfy for the both of you."

Jack didn't answer, escorting Eva back up the stairs.

He'd sooner carve a portrait of the queen into his chest with a dull knife than have Eva spend a night here.

Back on the street, he guided them through a maze of alleys toward the old slaughterhouse.

"Did you ever sleep at a place like that?" she asked quietly.

"After my ma died," he said. "Me and Edith spent more than a few nights there, or wherever had a few beds open. Usually didn't sleep well, on account of the rats biting on my fingers and toes."

She visibly shuddered, but at least she didn't give him any pitying looks or try to say something consoling.

An empty yard surrounded the old slaughterhouse, where the pens used to be. The wood that made up the pens had long since been scavenged. The slaughterhouse itself was a large brick building, parts of its roof caving in, with tall wide doors through which the condemned animals once had been driven. The business itself had shut down when Jack had been just a tyke, but some of the old-timers remembered the way the terrified cows used to bellow before they met the knife.

Now, the sounds of men's rowdy voices echoed around the yard.

As Jack approached the building, he cast a wary look at Eva. He'd no doubt she could take care of herself, but he was leading her right into one of the roughest, meanest places he knew. At the first sign of trouble, he'd get her out of there.

"Stay close to me inside," he warned. "And don't say much. Your accent is a dead giveaway you ain't from these parts."

She nodded. Thank God she was sensible, and not one of those teacake-brained females who'd go charging into an unfamiliar, dangerous situation, convinced they had all the answers.

Jack pressed his last shilling into the hand of the dead-eyed bruiser guarding the door. The bloke squinted at Jack for a moment, trying to place him.

"Don't I—"

"No," Jack said, cutting him off. "And you don't want to."

The bruiser likely heard threats all the time, but after looking at Jack for a second longer, he realized that Jack could actually make good on them. He stepped aside and let Jack and Eva enter.

A wall of shouts met them as soon as they stepped inside. Outside it had been cold enough to leave a crust of frost on puddles, but inside was hotter than Satan's own chamber pot, and smelled as good, too. The air stank of sweat, tobacco, and cheap whiskey. At least a hundred men crowded around a ring that had been scratched in the dirt.

Within the ring, two men faced off. They'd stripped down to the waist, and their bodies glistened with sweat and blood as they circled each other, fists upraised. The eye of one of the fighters had swollen shut. The other looked like he favored one leg. Probably he'd taken a hit there—low blows were counted just as much as any other.

Swollen Eye danced forward, fists at the ready. He bobbed to one side as Hobbled swung a left hook, then he jabbed at Hobbled's bad leg. His opponent sank down onto one knee. Swollen Eye darted closer and plowed his fist into Hobble's jaw, sending the other man sprawling onto his back. The crowd roared in approval.

"They don't follow the Marquess of Queensbury's rules," Eva called to him above the racket.

"Only rule is that you have to stop punching a man when he blacks out," he answered. "And no knives in the ring."

That didn't stop fighters from trying to smuggle in weapons. Jack's hair covered the scar he had on his left temple, a souvenir from a piece of pig iron one of his opponents had gripped in his fist. But the bugger hadn't held on to his advantage for long. After he'd been cut, Jack had knocked the sod to the ground and ground his boot heel onto his opponent's wrist, until his fingers had spasmed open and Jack had kicked the pig iron away.

Jack watched the fight now. Swollen Eye took advantage of Hobbled's prone position, crouching over him and raining blows. Hobbled could barely lift his arms to protect himself as blood spurted. The crowd continued to cheer.

He glanced at Eva. The sight of blood was common here, and between that and the heat, he half expected her to look faint. Instead, she watched the fight with a frown of concentration. He should've known that the sight of two men pummeling each other into paste wouldn't upset her.

Looking back to the ring, he noticed something. "The idiot's lowering his guard," he muttered to himself.

Swollen Eye, confident in his victory, dropped his hands to taunt his opponent. Hobbled managed to raise up just enough to throw a right jab. It crashed into Swollen Eye's face. With a groan heard above the shouting, Swollen Eye toppled backward into the dirt. He didn't move. Not even when three men scurried into the ring and slapped his face as they shouted at him.

Hobbled staggered to his feet. He waited as the three men continued to slap and yell at the downed fighter. Eventually, one of the men glanced over and shook his head. Hobbled grinned, showing big gaps in his teeth, and raised his hands in victory.

The throng watching the match bellowed its approval. As Swollen Eye's limp body was dragged off by his friends, Hobbled limped around the ring, accepting the crowd's tribute.

Hell, he remembered that. The flood of sound and praise that would wash over him as he stood with his arms lifted, spattered with the blood of his opponents. The spectators would roar at him, and he'd roar back. A bloodstained champion.

He caught Eva watching him. Saw the understanding in her eyes. For as long as a match lasted, he'd been a god. Something more than another piece of slum trash.

"You miss it," she said.

"Not the bruises and broken bones, I don't." But they both knew that wasn't the truth. "Come on, the next fight's about to start and I want to find Charlie before then."

She followed in his wake as he shoved through the crowd, clearing a path for her. "And Charlie is . . . ?"

"Old friend of mine," he said over his shoulder. "Bookmaker."

"It's only legal to gamble at racetracks."

He threw her a dry look. "Because everything else here's strictly aboveboard."

A corner of her mouth turned up. "Right."

"But Charlie's more than a bookmaker. If there's something you want or need, anything at all, Charlie can get it for you."

As he pushed through the mob, he saw more than a few blokes give Eva the eye. She'd kept the hood of her cloak up, but women always snared attention at fights. Aside from her, only a handful of females were scattered through the crowd, and most of them looked like the sort who charged for their company.

Jack glared down anyone who gave Eva more than a passing look. Just let one of the bastards try anything. He hadn't had a decent fight in a long while.

No one tried anything.

At one edge of the building, men gathered, shaking handfuls of money at someone standing in the middle of the circle. A voice rose up above the crowd. "It's six to one for O'Connell. Twelve to one he knocks Arkley out in the first five rounds. What'll it be, lads?"

There'd be no getting to Charlie until all the bets had been placed. Men surged forward, ready to have their wagers written down. This went on until someone beat a pipe against a metal bucket, signaling that the fight was about to start. The crowd around the bookmaker thinned as the spectators all turned toward the ring.

The bookmaker stood there, writing in a battered notebook and holding a huge fistful of banknotes. Even though she was dressed in a skirt, she also wore a shirtwaist, tie, and a man's waistcoat. Her dark hair had been tucked up into a bowler hat, and she held a cigar between her teeth.

"Betting's closed," the bookmaker said as Jack stepped closer.

"What're the odds you've got the clap?" Jack asked.

Her mouth dropped open as she looked up, and her cigar fell to the ground. "Diamond Jack!"

"Hello, Charlie," he said.

CHAPTER TWELVE

"*This* is Charlie?" Eva demanded. She hated the shrill note in her voice, as if she were some melodrama heroine, but, *damn it,* Jack had caught her by surprise. She had to wonder if he'd done it on purpose, just to see her look shocked. No doubt her eyes were round as oranges and her mouth hung open.

"Charlotte Linton," the bookmaker said with a cheerful grin, "but everyone round these parts calls me Charlie." She appeared to be somewhere in her late thirties, possessing a sharp-edged attractiveness both at odds with and in perfect harmony with her rough surroundings.

The crowds cheered as two more men proceeded to pummel each other in the ring.

Charlie turned to Jack with an expression of stunned but pleased disbelief. "It's really you, Diamond Jack?"

"Must be," he answered, "because I've got on his trousers."

The bookmaker threw back her head and laughed. Then grabbed Jack by his shoulders and pulled him into an embrace. Eva noted sourly that Jack enthusiastically returned the hug.

"Blimey and bloody hell," Charlie cried, "it *is* you! Got bigger, though." Pulling back, she gave his bicep an appreciative squeeze. Eva wanted to shove her to the ground. "Didn't think it was possible. If we had weight classes here, you'd have been at the top."

"Breaking rocks either wears a man down to a nub or builds him up," he said, a hint of pride in his voice.

"Word was you got sent to the clink for trying to do in that toff." Charlie used her thumb to tilt back her bowler hat. Eva would have thought the combination of men's clothing with a woman's skirt might appear silly, but Charlie looked raffish and daring, curse her. Eva never considered herself a particularly conventional woman, but standing next to Charlie made her feel like a vicar's prim daughter.

"It was him that killed Edith," Jack growled.

"So I heard," Charlie said somberly, "and I'm right sorry about it. But I didn't think they'd let you out of stir."

"Let myself out," Jack replied, and Charlie laughed again.

"'Course you did!" She punched him in the arm affably. "No sodding prison walls can hold Diamond Jack, the fighter with one of the best records in Bethnal Green."

"His escape is not something we'd like to advertise," Eva said through clenched teeth.

As if suddenly remembering that Eva stood watching the whole exchange, Charlie glanced at her. Taking in Eva's deliberately drab cloak, Charlie said, "She don't seem like your usual style of bird, Jack. Looks a bit frowzy."

"I'm blending in with my surroundings," Eva snapped. "And I'm not Jack's *bird*."

Charlie grinned. "Got a mouth on her, though."

"Don't I know it," Jack said.

Eva fought to keep from ramming her knee into his

groin. "The mouthy bird wants to know if Charlie's going to help us or not."

"That all depends," Charlie answered. "What kind of help do you need?"

Jack stepped closer, and lowered his voice. "We need to steal a body."

Charlie refused to leave until the boxing match had been concluded.

"There's friendship and there's business," she said, watching the ring. "I got to earn my beer, too."

Eva smothered her impatience as the pugilists fought. She'd never been to an underground boxing match, and if the circumstances weren't so urgent, she could easily devote hours to studying the environment and the participants. London existed in countless variations at all times—a thousand cities that held the same space on the map. They lived side by side, and you could spend your whole life here without learning all the different Londons.

This London was brutal, vicious, yet pulsating with invisible energy. A masculine place, pared down to its elemental self, where men proved themselves by trouncing challengers in the most primal, unrefined way possible. It made perfect sense that this place, and others like it, had created Jack.

She'd no doubt that he could set foot in the ring right now and defeat anyone here. Including the other fighters—fierce-looking men lined up near the ring, shadowboxing or watching the current match. None of the fighters would make for pleasant company if encountered in a dark alley.

And Jack could thrash any of them.

Despite all her books, the many languages in which she could converse, her pride in her higher reasoning, the desire she felt for him was far from intellectual. Seeing him here, knowing that he once ruled this rough, wild place, kindled a hunger within her.

"None of these blighters could touch you," Charlie said, echoing Eva's thoughts. She shook her head mournfully as she watched the fighters swing at each other. "Wasn't nobody better than Diamond Jack. Undefeated, you were. A bloody shame when you retired."

"Couldn't stay in the ring forever," he answered. "The money was better being a bodyguard, and I didn't get my nose broken every two weeks."

"But you were the Leonardo da Vinci of brawling," Charlie complained. "You don't take da Vinci's paintbrushes away just 'cos he hurts his pinkie finger."

"Jack's got more to offer than his fists," Eva retorted.

Charlie sent her a cunning smirk. "Oh, I know that, darling."

Would anyone notice if, in the middle of the fight, Eva hauled off and punched Charlie? Or would the crowd gather around and place bets?

"The match's ending," Jack said quickly.

He and Eva retreated to the edge of the building as Charlie settled with the bettors. Volumes of money changed hands with a speed that would shame the most experienced bank clerk. Despite the fact that Charlie was one woman amid a sea of men—some of them angry over the results of the fight—she looked comfortable, confident, laughing over bawdy jokes and shouting down anyone who complained about their bets. She seemed to know everyone, and they knew her. A woman like Charlie could be a valuable resource for Nemesis.

Eva would sooner chat with an adder than approach Charlie for information.

"Green's a nice color on you," Jack said, chuckling.

"I'm not jealous," Eva answered at once. She had no right to that emotion, not where he was concerned. Yet acid seemed to be burning through her veins.

"A lot of time's passed since me and Charlie."

"You could take up with her again tomorrow and it wouldn't matter," she said airily.

His eyes narrowed as he gazed at her. "Didn't figure you for a liar."

The impulse to deny it gripped her. Yet he deserved far better than that. So did she, for that matter. "Perhaps I'm jealous," she admitted, then added hastily, "But I've no right to be. It's completely irrational."

His gaze heated. "Nothing rational about you and me wanting each other. That don't stop us, though."

"No," she said, "it doesn't." She wasn't accustomed to feeling this strongly about anything besides her work—certainly no man ever engendered this kind of response. It was a strange vocabulary, this kind of emotion, one with no words, no logic or syntax. How could she make sense of it?

She couldn't. The thought made her stomach clench.

Once her business concluded, Charlie drifted over toward Jack and Eva, meticulously counting a stack of pound notes. A family could live for a year on the money Charlie held, the take from a single night's work. Compared to the wages she might make in a factory or some other drudge work, it was no surprise a woman as clever and ruthless as Charlie would turn to criminal employment.

Charlie stowed the wad of cash. She glanced toward the ring, where more fighters took their positions. A man with a scraggly mustache collected bets—where on earth did the spectators find so much money, when it was clear from their grimy, threadbare clothing that they hadn't much to spare?

"You better be prepared to pay, and well," Charlie said. She sighed, watching the mustached man collecting wagers. "I'm losing the best part of my night."

"Can't you consider it a favor to Jack?" Eva asked, irritated. "Being old friends."

"Even old *friends* got to pay," Charlie replied.

Eva's mouth twisted. "Sentimentality doesn't have a high value."

"Not with me, it don't." Charlie peered at Jack. "You know how it is, don't you, Diamond?"

He gave a fatalistic shrug. "Nothing's changed around here. But I'm short on funds right now. I'll have to owe you, Charlie."

The bookmaker grinned in a way Eva didn't like at all. "Owing me is a recipe for trouble."

"I'll be sure you're amply compensated," Eva said tightly. Nemesis didn't have a large budget—they pooled their funds from their sundry other employment—but if paying Charlie out of her own pocket kept Jack out of the bookmaker's debt, Eva would gladly shoulder the cost. "The night's moving quickly, so let's get to business."

"Normally I take all payment in advance," Charlie drawled. "Given that Jack's an old chum of mine, I'm willing to wait for the sake of—what's the word you used?—sentimentality."

"What a sterling example of benevolence," Eva growled under her breath as Charlie led them out of the building.

The bookmaker picked her way through the yard full of detritus and debris, with Jack and Eva following. Jack kept his gaze moving and vigilant.

"Can we trust her?" Eva asked in a low voice.

"No," he said without hesitation. "But Charlie's the best. Anything you want, she can get. No questions asked."

What had Charlie procured for Jack? "That must come in handy."

"I ain't going to tell her about Nemesis," he said, frowning, "if that's what's got you fretting."

They left the yard and trailed after Charlie through thick shadows congealed between ramshackle structures.

Eva whispered. "It's *you* I'm concerned about. She could turn you in for a reward."

"Only thing Charlie won't do is rat someone out. Murder's out, too," he added.

"Well, *that's* a relief," she said tartly.

Jack glanced at her from the corner of his eye. "So, you're worried about me."

She didn't miss the faint, very faint, note of hope in his voice. How many people had ever felt genuine concern for him? He'd been alone, reliant on no one, for most of his life. For all her parents' preoccupation with helping others, she'd always known that they cared for her. Loved her.

Had Jack's sister loved him? Had she fussed over his bruises from the boxing ring? Or had he sat wearily on the edge of his bed and held a compress to his battered body, because no one else had been there to do it for him?

"I . . ." She forced the words out, words she wanted to hold close for her own protection. Yet he needed them. "I *am* concerned about you."

Even with the darkness heavy around them, she could see the look of wonderment on his face. A fissure spread through her heart. God, he'd had so little.

He stopped walking and turned to her, his expression turning fierce. "Eva—"

"Lively, you two!" Charlie called over her shoulder.

They continued their trek, leaving behind the twisted,

gloomy streets of Bethnal Green and heading southwest, toward the river. The neighborhoods through which they passed were marginally better, with fewer people aimlessly wandering the streets, and stained brick buildings lit by gas lamps.

"Oi," Charlie hissed as they hurried down a block. "Coppers patrolling."

True to her word, patrolmen's lamps appeared at the end of street. Charlie slipped into a narrow alley soundlessly. Eva did the same, forcing herself to ignore the stench of rotting cabbage wafting from the alley's recesses. For a moment, Jack eyed the tight, dark space warily. Given his experience with dark, confining places, his reluctance was understandable. But the police neared.

Grabbing Jack's hand, Eva tugged him into the alley. They pushed farther back into the alley and hunkered behind a pile of discarded mattresses. The smell emanating from the mattresses was even worse than rotting cabbage—and she didn't want to know why.

She held her breath as she heard the patrolmen's footsteps on the pavement. With his escape from prison, Jack was already a wanted man. Now that Rockley had framed Jack for Gilling's murder, the Metropolitan Police would be eager for Jack's arrest.

The patrolmen walked past the alley, their lamps sweeping across. Jack's breathing became ragged. Crouched behind him, Eva placed her hand between his shoulder blades, silently willing him to be calm. A reminder that she was with him. Seconds later, tension lessened in his muscles and his breathing evened.

The beams of the police lanterns pierced the alley's darkness. She kept her head down, praying that Charlie and Jack did the same. An eternity passed.

Finally, after she had aged fifty years, the police moved on.

She wouldn't exhale, or breathe at all if she could help it, until the patrolmen were long gone. After their footsteps faded and several more minutes elapsed, she, Jack, and Charlie stumbled out of the alley, all of them gasping and coughing to clear their lungs.

Jack looked ashen, his knuckles white where he gripped the strap of his pack. The confined space had taken its toll on him.

Smiling, she took his hand and nodded toward the alley. "We ought to swap Simon's mattress out for one of those."

As she'd hoped, Jack chuckled, the pallor fading from his cheeks.

Turning, Eva discovered Charlie watching them curiously, as though they were a pair of cats who'd suddenly begun playing dice—entirely unexpected.

Eva tilted up her chin in wordless challenge. With a shrug, Charlie resumed striding down the street, and Eva and Jack followed.

The heavy smell of river water slunk through the air as they neared the Thames. A two-story official-looking building crouched a block from the Embankment, its columns and pediments streaked with soot. Spiked iron fencing encircled the structure, though the building itself was so gloomy and imposing, it seemed unlikely that anyone would fight to get inside. Only one light burned in an upper window.

Rather than lead them toward the main entrance, Charlie skirted around the building until she came to a side basement entry. She scraped her nails down the metal door.

Jack shifted restlessly beside Eva as they waited.

She kept herself tense and waiting, alert should Charlie lead them into a trap.

Clanging like a knolling bell, the door opened and revealed a sallow man in a gray, baggy suit. His thin hair clung to his skull. He glanced first at Jack and Eva, wariness in his sunken eyes, then at Charlie with a dim flare of recognition.

"Charlie," he intoned.

"Evening, Tiffield," she answered briskly. "We've come to do a bit of shopping."

The sallow man held the door open, and their party trooped inside. They found themselves standing in a long, tiled hallway, a few lamps burning dimly. The night had been chill, but within the building, it was even colder. A sweet, rank smell combined with the acrid scent of chemicals.

Tiffield unlocked another metal door and waved them in. Silently, they entered a dark, windowless chamber, and here the smell became stronger. Tiffield turned on the lamps.

No mistaking the contents—or rather, occupants—of the chamber. Rows of tables were covered with heavy waxed cloth, human bodies forming distinctive shapes beneath the fabric. There had to be at least three dozen corpses in here.

A morgue. Charlie had taken them "shopping" at the morgue.

"Looking for something in particular?" Tiffield asked with the same bored intonation as a shop clerk.

Charlie looked expectantly at Jack. Eva half expected the bookmaker to say, "Tell the man what you want, Jack."

"A bloke about my size," he answered. "Even better if he's got dark hair and eyes."

Scratching the skin behind his ear, the morgue attendant considered this for a moment. "May have a few who fit the bill." Tiffield muttered to himself as he walked between the rows of cadavers.

"You all right?" Jack asked Eva quietly as they trailed after the morgue attendant.

"Perfectly," she said. Though that wasn't entirely true. She was no stranger to death, but she'd never been surrounded by its presence like this.

He looked concerned, yet didn't press, for which she was grateful. He seemed to have an instinctive understanding of what she needed. The more someone coddled her, the more she struggled, their concern feeling like a pair of hands closing around her neck. But Jack let her breathe.

Tiffield stopped beside a table and, without preamble, flipped back the covering to reveal a body. "How about this one?"

"Seems a bit scrawny to me," Charlie said critically.

"Hair color's not right, either," Jack noted.

"That can be dyed," the morgue attendant suggested.

Eva pressed her fingertips to her mouth to hold back an inappropriate giggle. A dead man—someone with a whole history, a life now gone—lay in front of them, and they spoke as if discussing the suitability of a sofa. She'd thought herself hardened by her work with Nemesis, but clearly there was more for her to learn.

"Got anything else?" Charlie asked.

Tiffield flicked the cover back over the corpse and moved farther through the rows of bodies. The procedure was repeated as he uncovered another cadaver, and Charlie and Jack debated over its merits.

"This one's throat is all torn up," Jack complained.

"Got it cut over a woman," Tiffield explained. "She didn't come to claim 'im, though."

"We need something with not too many visible wounds," said Jack.

The morgue attendant heaved a sigh. "Sure got a lot of requirements."

"It's important," Eva said dryly.

Tiffield covered the body and moved on to another. He pulled back the cloth, revealing the corpse beneath. "This here chap might suit. Come in earlier tonight. Was a bully for a bawdy house who got pushed down some stairs by a customer that argued the price. Snapped the bully's neck. Think of it, a big bruiser like this gets done in by a man half his size." Tiffield shook his head. "Ain't no logic."

The dead man had no argument for the morgue attendant. Whoever he was, whatever his name, he did closely match Jack's size and build. It made Eva shiver, to see someone so like Jack stretched out in the indifference of death, his strength now utterly gone. To reassure herself that Jack was very much alive and strong as ever, she glanced up at him as he studied the body. He must have been entertaining similar thoughts, for his gaze was shadowed.

"Dark hair," Charlie noted. "That's good. But the mustache's got to go."

"Think there's a razor somewhere about," Tiffield said.

Without inflection, Jack said, "Go get it."

The morgue attendant took a step, then asked, "You sure this is the one you want?"

"He'll do," Jack answered.

Tiffield scurried away, presumably to find shaving implements.

"Won't someone notice if a body's missing?" Eva asked.

"Not these lads." Charlie waved an unconcerned hand

at the rows of covered corpses. "No one comes to claim
'em, and the police don't care about some dead—what's
the word?—reprobate. They're unwanted."

It seemed London was full of superfluous men.

"A hard world, this," Jack murmured. His gaze met
hers over the body. It was clear they thought the same
thing—it could just have easily been him upon the table,
unclaimed, growing colder, with no one to mourn his
passing.

I would, she told him silently. *For whatever solace it
brings you, I would find the loss of you to be a hard
burden.*

Perhaps it was enough. She couldn't know, but there
was some satisfaction in his eyes, dark as darkest night.

She realized suddenly that there would come a time
when she would lose him. When the mission was over,
he couldn't stay in England. He'd have to start his life
over, somewhere far away. And she could never leave
Nemesis—their work meant too much to her. Which
meant that someday, if the mission was successful, she
and Jack would never see each other again. The thought
hollowed her.

Bustling in with a cup of foam and a razor, the
morgue attendant set to work shaving the corpse's face.
"I ain't a mortician," he grumbled, "making a body
pretty for a funeral." Yet Tiffield didn't stop in his task.

Once the dead man had been shaved, Jack produced
a bundle of clothing from the pack he carried and
tossed them toward Tiffield.

"Put those on him," Jack said.

The morgue attendant studied the wad of garments.
"They look just like your clothes."

"Never you mind that," Charlie snapped. "Just get the
stiff dressed."

Tiffield complained under his breath again, but

pulled the garments onto the cadaver. Eva winced at the rough, impersonal way the morgue attendant handled the body, as if it were nothing more than a haunch of meat at Smithfield Market. Her one consolation was that rigor mortis hadn't yet set in.

"There," Tiffield announced. "All nice and handsome for you."

"Needs one more thing," Charlie said. From a pocket in her skirt she produced a flask, and splashed strong-smelling whiskey across the body's chest and face. "Now he ain't dead, just dead drunk."

Though the words felt odd and sour in her mouth, Eva asked, "How much do we pay you for the . . . body?"

Tiffield started to speak, glanced at Charlie, then stopped. After a moment, he said, "Nothing."

Eva looked back and forth between the morgue attendant and Charlie. Clearly, Tiffield was in some kind of debt to the bookmaker, but whether it was a financial debt or another kind of obligation, Eva wasn't certain—nor did she want to know. The many faces of London were often ugly, and possessing a certain amount of believable deniability often worked in one's favor.

Before Tiffield could change his mind, Jack hefted the body onto his back. "Blimey, he's a heavy bugger," he said through gritted teeth.

"We weighed him yesterday," the morgue attendant said. "Over sixteen stone."

"Me, too," Jack muttered.

"Got to go now, Tiffield," Charlie announced. "Standard terms apply."

"I know" was the sullen answer. "I never saw you. I don't remember anything."

Charlie strode to Tiffield and patted his face. "Good lad."

The woman could give lessons in sheer audacity, Eva decided.

In short order, they were back outside. Eva breathed out in relief to be away from so many corpses, but her sigh was short-lived as she pointedly remembered the dead man Jack carried. She, Jack, and Charlie gathered far away from incriminating light.

"Where do we send payment?" she asked Charlie.

"Don't trouble yourself about it," the bookmaker answered.

"I don't carry debts," Jack growled. "Tell me what I owe, and it'll get paid."

Charlie's smile was singularly ominous. "Sorry, ducks. The where, when, and what—that's up to me to decide." Cheerfully, she said, "Good to see you out of the clink, Jack. And it's been a pleasure, Miss Prim," she added with a wink. "Have a charming evening."

Before Eva could object to her unflattering sobriquet, Charlie seemed to melt into the shadows. One moment she was there. The next, nothing. Eva strained to hear even the lightest footstep on the pavement. But Charlie had vanished.

Eva wasn't sorry to see her go.

Grunting, Jack shifted beneath the weight of the body. "Feels like I'm carrying my own corpse."

"You are." Despite her cavalier words, she felt all too aware of the similarities between him and the dead man.

Jack snorted. "What do the toffs say? Indubitably. Now let's go get me killed."

The gaming club was the sort of place gentlemen liked to frequent. It trod the line between seedy and smart that seemed to draw well-heeled blokes by the cartload. Not

quite as elegant as the clubs of St. James's, not as un-
savory as the dens clustered near Covent Garden. Jack
knew from experience that the club kept a few girls
upstairs, but for the most part the men came to play
cards and roulette, drink too much and laugh too loud.

Rockley was inside. He came here every Thursday,
but just to be certain, he checked the mews behind the
club and saw the bastard's carriage. The hour approached four, when Rockley usually left and headed
home to sleep the sleep of the conscienceless. Eva was
in place. All Jack had to do now was wait in the shadows across the street.

Except he'd done far too much waiting in the past,
and it scratched him now. If everything went well in
the next few minutes, he'd be that much closer to finally gaining vengeance. If everything didn't go well,
tomorrow Tiffield would be showing off his corpse to
some new interested buyer.

A sick despair climbed up his throat, and he spat
upon the ground to rid himself of it. Now wasn't the
time to think about the shortness of his life, or how
he'd leave this world without a soul to care whether he
was alive or taking up space in the city morgue.

No, that wasn't true. There was Eva. He'd seen how
she had looked at him back in that place of death. As if
he mattered to her. More than a pawn in Nemesis's
game. More than a former brawler, failed murderer,
and escaped convict.

New energy moved through him. Like he used to
before a fight, he danced lightly on the balls of his feet,
shaking out his arms, stretching his neck. He had to
succeed. He'd never lost a match back when he was a
boxer. He wouldn't take a dive or lose this one.

He kept himself loose, even when the clock struck
four and Rockley's carriage drove up to the front. The

bastard himself emerged from the club, gleaming in his evening clothes. His bodyguard took the lead, scanning up and down the street, then giving Rockley a nod that everything was clear. Rockley moved toward his waiting carriage.

Now.

Jack darted out from the shadows with a burst of speed. He ran in front of the club, close enough for Rockley and his bodyguard to see him but not close enough to be within decent firing range. His legs burned with the urge to carry him *to* Rockley, not past him. Maybe he could try it. Maybe he could be fast enough to smash the son of a bitch's head against the stone steps before his bodyguard could shoot.

No—he had to stick with the plan. He halted in the middle of the street and stared at Rockley. The bastard had to see him in order for the scheme to work.

Rockley looked at him. Jack looked back. A distance of only twenty feet separated them.

For a moment, time shuddered to a stop. The street fell away, the club, the whole sodding city.

Jack hadn't been this close to him in years. He'd aged a little—more lines fanned around his eyes and a few bracketed his mouth—and wrinkles in his evening clothes revealed it had been a long night.

Rockley's eyes widened when he saw Jack. And Jack had to pretend that he was just as surprised to be spotted—as though he'd been spying on Rockley and had been accidentally caught while trying to slip away.

Despite his plan to simply be seen and then run away, Jack snarled, "Filthy murderer. I'm still going to make you pay."

Rockley's shock vanished, replaced by a look of bitterest hate. "Trash is all you are, Dalton. All you will ever be. You cannot touch me."

"Don't want to touch you," Jack spat. "Just kill you." His feet carried him closer, his hands already curving to wrap around Rockley's throat.

Rockley paled and took a step back. He smacked his silver-topped walking stick against his bodyguard's arm. "You idiot," he growled. "Take care of him!"

Ballard shook his head like he was rattling his thoughts straight. Then reached into his jacket and pulled out a big, mean pistol.

Thoughts of crushing Rockley's windpipe scattered as soon as Jack saw the gun. Right. The plan.

Time to go.

He ran. Speeding down the dark, empty street, he listened to make sure the bodyguard followed. There. The tread of thick boots—like his—on the pavement. Ballard ran with the grace of a heavy wagon. Instinct shouted to run as fast as possible, lose the thug in the maze of streets leading toward the river. Instead, Jack paused at an intersection, waiting for Ballard to catch sight of him.

The bodyguard shouted, "Oi!" He leveled his pistol.

Jack ducked as a shot rang out. The bullet slammed into the wall behind him.

Cursing at his missed shot, Ballard rushed toward Jack. Jack spun around and ran. After waiting and watching for so long, and not having enough action, it felt almost good to throw himself into this chase, his blood pumping, his body moving.

There, just up ahead, he spotted the Embankment. If he ran straight toward it, he'd corner himself. If he turned down this alley, he could shake off Ballard.

He headed to the river. It was a thick, black snake twisting in front of him, a few small wherries bobbing over its surface.

At the edge of the Embankment, Jack spun around to face the approaching bodyguard.

Ballard's steps slowed as he got Jack in his sights. He lifted his gun. "Diamond Jack Dalton," he jeered. "You ain't so grand. *I'm* protecting his lordship now."

"You'll be pulling his knife out of your back soon," Jack said. "Unless you wise up. But maybe you *can't* wise up. Maybe you're too sodding stupid."

Ballard sneered. "I ain't the one who went and cornered myself." He pointed his revolver. Cocked the hammer.

Jack's heart slammed inside his chest as he waited. This had to be perfectly timed. *Wait. Wait.*

The gun fired. Three times.

Jack toppled backward into the water. The river closed around him, dark and heavy as death.

CHAPTER THIRTEEN

From her position a hundred feet down the Embankment, Eva stiffened when she heard the shots, then the splash of a person falling into the river. Did someone cry out? Had Jack been hit?

She peered down into the black water, straining for any sight of him. Her arms wrapped about her waist, tight, as if to hold herself back from jumping into the river and searching for him. Vile as the Thames was, she'd readily swim it to find him and end the doubt that clutched at her stomach. But she couldn't. She had to stand here in the shadows, her only company a corpse that eerily resembled Jack, and wait.

God—it had been too long. "Where is he?" she muttered. A hundred fears assailed her with their sharp, poisoned claws.

A darker shape appeared in the water. The chains around her stomach eased, then she growled in frustration. Only a large river rat swimming through the refuse that floated atop the Thames.

Then—something broke the surface, gasping. It moved toward the bank.

She threw off her cloak and hurried down the waterman's steps leading to the river. A man swam toward her. Jack. He didn't appear to be injured, either. *Thank God.*

Relief robbed her of breath, as though a fist squeezed her lungs.

Dropping to her knees, she reached out, grasping his arms, and attempted to haul him out of the river. She panted with the effort. He did indeed weigh sixteen stone, if not more. Both she and Jack struggled to get him onto the shore. Finally, with a heave and groan, he pushed himself out of the water.

She fell backward, with him sprawled atop her. Long moments passed as they lay like this, him huge and wet, gasping, with enough presence of mind to brace himself on his elbows so his full weight didn't crush her. The front of her dress was instantly soaked, and clung to her damply. The chill water smelled dank and fetid, but she hardly noticed the scent.

He was on her, his legs between hers, their bodies pressed close. His clothes were plastered to him, and with her own sticking to her skin, she felt everywhere the movement of his muscles, his raw animal strength. Their hearts seemed to be battering their way toward each other. His heat burned away the river's chill.

They stared at each other, both still panting, their breath mingling, intimate as a confession. Hardly any light reached the riverbank, yet she was powerfully aware of the darkness and ferocity of his eyes, the hard contours of his face. His curved lips, so close to hers.

Pinned as she was beneath him, she could hardly move, yet didn't want to. Not when he lowered his head just as she raised hers, and their mouths found each other.

Heat and hunger. It felt as though it had been years, not days, since last they kissed. Ravening need tore through her, its edge whetted by the press of his massive body, his demanding mouth. For all that they lay upon a grimy, wet slab of stone beside a musty river, she knew only his taste, his feel. The unfettered power of Jack.

She ought to have been terrified or intimidated. He was so much bigger than her, so phenomenally strong. Yet desire made her strong, too, every bit his equal. She squirmed her hands free and wove her fingers into his wet hair. A low, deep rumble resonated from his chest and into her.

Yet he pulled away with a feral sound. He rolled onto his back, leaving her wet and chilled. They both lay there, panting, staring up at the night sky dulled by clouds, listening to the slap of the water against the stone landing. She risked a look at his groin. His cock was clearly outlined through his damp clothes, and she tucked her hands beneath her to keep from reaching for him.

He laid his arm over his eyes, his hand clenched into a fist. "Bloody buggering hell," he said roughly.

"Exactly," she answered.

It would be easy to blame their kiss on the excitement and uncertainty of the night, but she'd been on assignments equally exciting and uncertain with other Nemesis agents. She hadn't clawed hungrily at any of them afterward. Only Jack roused this mad need, this loss of control.

She struggled upright, her body feeling oddly heavier without him atop her.

"It worked, then," she said.

"Rockley saw me, his man gave chase, and I made sure he thought he plugged me. I heard him on the edge of the Embankment, looking to see if I surfaced. So I floated like a corpse for a minute—out of shooting distance—before sinking down again." He grunted as he rose to standing. Wincing, he adjusted his cock, and her cheeks heated at the matter-of-fact way he handled himself. A sudden image of him with his cock in his hand made her mouth dry, her breasts feel tight and sensitive. Did he ever do that? Touch himself in the middle of the night? And did he think of her when he did it?

God, she might lose consciousness if she considered it.

She started to rise. He stuck out his broad hand, offering assistance. Normally, she refused such gestures from men, but she couldn't seem to pass up any opportunity to touch him. She slid her much smaller hand into his, shivering at the sensation of his rough palm against hers. As easily as he might heft a puff of milkweed, he pulled her to her feet.

"You're all wet," he said, staring at the front of her dress. His gaze avidly took in how the fabric molded to her body, her breasts and hips.

"Because of you."

A hot light burned in his eyes. She was certain that same light burned in hers. But there was more to do this night, and she needed her wits. She turned away.

Good Lord, there was a corpse at the top of the waterman's steps, not fifteen feet away, and she'd been writhing around with Jack, not even caring. He was an opiate.

"Dawn's nearly here," she said.

He shook himself like a dog, scattering water, then pushed his wet hair out of his face. "Let's finish this job."

They climbed up the slick stairs, his boots squishing with each step. It struck her then how dangerous his part had been tonight. He could just as easily have drowned in the perilous river as been hit by a bullet.

At the top of the stairs, the body waited for them,

sprawled upon the ground. The night was cool, but not as cold as it had been in the morgue. Decay would set in soon, and rigor mortis.

"Give me your gun." Jack held out his hand.

"I've shot it before," she objected. "I've even hit people."

"Shooting a dead man's a nasty business, and I don't want you doing it."

She considered holding on to her revolver, then, sighing, passed the weapon to him. "The bodyguard shot three times."

"Lost count on my way into the water." He stood beside the body, cocked the gun's hammer, and pressed the muzzle to the corpse's chest.

"Wait!"

Frowning, he lowered the gun. "What?"

She gathered up her cloak, forming it into a bundle. "Put this over the muzzle. It ought to dampen the sound."

"It'll ruin your cloak."

What an odd streak of consideration he possessed. "Need a new one, anyway."

He did as she suggested, placing the bunched-up cloak between the gun and the body. "Sorry, mate," he said to the corpse. Then he fired. He put one more bullet into the cadaver's torso.

"Three shots," she reminded him.

"I'm going to get him in the face so he's harder to identify." He sent her an apologetic look. "It'll be messy."

"Do whatever you have to." Despite her bravado, she shut her eyes when he fired the last shot.

"Keep 'em closed," he advised.

Though she didn't quite take his advice, she kept her gaze on the toes of her boots while he picked up the body. From the corner of her eye, she saw him go back down the waterman's steps, then heave the body into the river.

"All right, love," he said, after coming back up the steps. "It's done." At least he didn't chide her for not looking.

They both watched as the body drifted out farther into the water, then sank from view.

"Whoever he was," she murmured, "I hope he absolves us."

Jack turned away from the river. "That's the problem with the dead. When we need their forgiveness, only thing they got for us is silence."

The sun broke over the eastern horizon, spreading light like an illness. Eva and Jack began the long walk back to headquarters as London woke.

Jack studied his face in the cracked mirror as he ran the razor along his jaw. It wasn't a pretty face, never had been, and he hadn't been living a life of ease and luxury. Even when he scraped away the last of his stubble, he still looked rough and mean. The sort of man who'd once dominated underground boxing matches, dealing out vicious beatings on a weekly basis, and taking his share of punches, too. Who could shoot a corpse point-blank without a blotch on his conscience.

He'd fallen into bed with the first rays of dawn and slept deeply. His dreams had been only of Eva, and the depraved, filthy things he'd like to do with her.

Bending over his washbasin, he splashed water on his face, rinsing off the shaving soap. Didn't some faiths believe you could just have a priest or preacher dunk you in water and you were reborn, clean down to your very soul? Religion never called to him, not when he was too busy trying to survive this life to think about the next one, but right now the idea of starting over, utterly spotless, was a tempting thought.

The door to his room opened. Eva stepped inside, her face shuttered. His back was to her, but he could see her in the mirror above the basin.

Her gaze moved over him, hot and quick. All he wore was his unbuttoned shirt and trousers, his braces hanging down. In the mirror, he watched her watching him, how her look caught on the span of his bared chest, then moved lower, lingering over his arse and down his legs. All the way to his bare feet, which made him feel oddly exposed. Big feet, he had, and hairy. More proof he was a brute, not a nice man.

But what she saw pleased her. She looked at him as if he were a sweet she wanted to suck on. He went iron-hard in an instant.

She shut the door behind her and leaned against it. Turning, he pressed a towel to his face to dry himself. Her gaze flicked back down to his chest, then farther south. When she saw how her study of his body affected him, her cheeks turned pink—and not from embarrassment.

He didn't care that he could hear the other Nemesis folk downstairs, talking and going about their daily lives. He didn't care that it was broad daylight. Only thing he did care about was getting Eva in his bed. His bed that was only steps away.

He started toward her. As he did, her expression went distant again and she held something out. A newspaper. It had been opened and folded to show one of the inner pages.

Taking it, he scanned the paper. It was easier for him to read when he said the words aloud, so he did, though he struggled over some of the longer words. " 'The body of infamous criminal and escaped prisoner Jack

Dalton was pulled from the Thames today. Though the corpse was somewhat disfigured by his injuries as well as his immersion in the river, he has been positively identified by authorities. The discovery of Dalton's body comes as a considerable relief following his murder of John Gilling, barrister.' "

There was more, but he'd read all he needed.

It had worked. The world believed him dead. Rockley must think he was dead, too. The police would've told him straightaway.

Jack was free.

For some reason, it became important for him to carefully refold the newspaper, then set it on his wash-stand. His body felt strange, awkward, as though it belonged to someone else, and he tugged on strings to make the limbs move.

"Where will you go now?" Eva asked. Her voice seemed to come from far away.

"Go?" he repeated. He faced her.

She paced to the window and stared out at the yard. "We've got no leverage over you anymore. Nothing can keep you here, short of force." She drew her finger down the dusty windowpane, leaving behind a bar of clean glass.

"Maybe Nemesis doesn't need me anymore."

"I—*we* do. You still know more than any of us about Rockley's habits, his movements."

"So I'm still useful," he said.

"We need you more than you need us," she continued in that strange, toneless voice. "I'm sure Rockley's lightened his security. That was the point of last night's endeavor. It would be fairly straightforward for you to extract your revenge upon him. The kind of revenge you've wanted since the beginning."

He stared at her back, the line of her neck, and the

shapes of her shoulder blades beneath her dress. A slim woman, but a fortress. "He'd be dead, but that wouldn't help Miss Jones get her life back."

Eva turned her head, showing him the line of her profile. "Miss Jones never meant anything to you."

"Maybe not at the beginning." He took a step toward her. "But I've been thinking it's *her* I'm doing this for. I didn't help Edith, but I can help Miss Jones. She's what's keeping me here."

"Miss Jones," Eva said, finally turning to face him. "You care about her?"

"What if I do?" he fired back. "Think a thug like me can't care about someone?"

"I know you can," she said quietly.

His heart beat hard within his chest as he stared at her. Sunlight poured into his room, uncovering everything. Brightness everywhere. It caught in the honey tumble of her hair and amber of her eyes, those damn shrewd eyes that saw too much but maybe not enough. He knew the sharp beauty of her face like he knew the shape of his own dreams.

"I ain't going nowhere," he said, low.

"For Miss Jones."

"Does it matter why?"

She stepped nearer, until only a few inches were between them. Reaching out, she pressed her palm against his chest. Her touch was fire and frost, tearing through him.

"No," she said after a moment. Then raised herself up on her toes and kissed him.

He'd grown addicted to her kisses, how they revealed her true self—not controlled and calculating, but wild and hungry. Unrestrained. Her kisses spoke to the animal in him. He growled now, pulling her close.

He slicked his tongue into her mouth, and she opened

even more to him. She tasted sweet, but he wasn't fooled. She was spice, too. The kind that robbed him of his wits. He'd do anything to have her taste, to feel her. If she kissed him like this, taking and giving, whatever she asked of him, he'd do it.

Wait . . .

He broke the kiss. His hands went to her shoulders, holding her away from him.

Her eyes blinked open, convincingly glazed.

"Don't," he rumbled. When she frowned, as if confused, he said, "You don't need to gull me like this to keep me around."

Her expression changed. From muddled with desire to confusion, and then to fury. She twisted away from his grasp.

"I was wrong," she said angrily. "Here I'd been defending your intelligence to everyone, but it turns out you're the world's biggest imbecile."

Before he could speak, she pulled open the door so hard it bounced against the wall, then stormed from the room. She ignored the other Nemesis members asking her if she was all right, then slammed the front door behind her.

Seconds later, Simon raced up the stairs and into Jack's room. Grabbing a fistful of Jack's shirt, he snarled, "What the hell did you do?"

Jack felt his mouth curl. "Remember how I said I can read? Turns out I can't." A bitter laugh scraped his throat. "Not a damn word."

From the shadows across the street, Eva and Jack watched the front of Mrs. Arram's brothel. It was a slow night, for they'd been keeping vigil for the past half hour and not a single customer had knocked on the front door.

"The hell is everybody?" Jack muttered.

"Perhaps the gentlemen of London have suddenly developed an attack of morality," she answered.

His snort of disbelief indicated just how much he thought that was likely.

They fell back into strained silence. She burned with impatience to just stride up the walkway to the brothel's door and barge her way in. Yet they couldn't approach until they were certain that the security had been lightened.

Fortunately, keeping an eye on the brothel meant she didn't have to speak much. She wasn't certain she could say anything to Jack that wouldn't sound angry or reveal how his suspicion had cut her deeply. She couldn't give him that power. At all times, she must protect herself. His accusation had only reinforced this belief. A moment's vulnerability left her with a raw, red wound. She'd not be so foolish again.

"Eva—" he began, then stopped as a carriage appeared on the street and stopped outside Mrs. Arram's.

An unknown man stepped down from the carriage and, after glancing up and down the street, approached the brothel. Judging by his hat and the cut of his suit, he was some sort of prosperous banker. Using his walking stick, he knocked lightly on the door. It opened almost immediately.

Eva sighed with satisfaction. Only one bully guarded the door now, not two. Security had indeed been reduced since the last time. Jack's "death" had served its purpose.

The bully spoke with the customer for a moment before stepping aside to allow him inside.

After the door had closed again, Eva fussed with her clothing, making certain that she looked tidy and presentable. She tugged on her gloves and adjusted the veil on her hat. Satisfied, she turned to Jack and smoothed down the lapel of his coat. He held himself motionless.

Her hand stopped in the middle of her attentions. What the hell was she doing? Fussing over him like the attentive wife she was about to impersonate?

She turned away. "Time to get our evidence."

They crossed the street and, with his hand on her elbow, walked up the path to the front door. Her heart set up a fast rhythm. Anger, anticipation, Jack's nearness and touch—they all combined within her. As they mounted the steps, she forced herself to take deep, regular breaths. She couldn't let her inner turmoil affect the mission.

Once they stood before the door, Jack exhaled and stretched his neck from side to side, as though readying himself for a fight. Despite his respectable checked suit and slicked-back hair, he still resembled the brawler he had been. She didn't want to take pleasure in the way he easily inhabited his size and strength, or the gleam of determination in his eyes, or a thousand other details that called out for her admiration. But what she wanted and what she actually did were very different things.

"Ready, missus?" he asked her.

It troubled her how much she liked hearing him call her that, especially after what he'd said earlier. "Get on with it."

He sent her an inscrutable look, then knocked. As it had before, the door opened. The bully stood there, a large man with a face that appeared as though it had been on the receiving end of a concrete slab.

"Yeah?" the bully demanded.

"We're here for the strawberries," Jack said.

The bully narrowed his tiny eyes as he looked back and forth between Jack and Eva. He looked hard at

Jack, then paused to study her. She offered him her best
uncertain smile, just the sort a woman might bestow
when stepping into unknown territory. As much reassuring herself as whoever looked at her.

Whatever he saw seemed to satisfy him, for the
bully stepped back and held the door open. "Awright.
Go on to the parlor an' have a chat with the lady of the
house."

She and Jack moved into the foyer. It resembled the
foyer of any successful businessman's home, complete
with umbrella stand, large mahogany coat rack, and
vases of fresh greenery. Piano music and the trill of
women's voices floated down the hall. A central staircase led to two more stories—presumably where the
girls did their work. Somewhere in this building was
Rockley's private room, and in that room they'd find
his strongbox containing the evidence of his crimes.

"Parlor's that way," the bully said, motioning down
the hall.

She and Jack exchanged a look. They could try to
make a break for it right now, but that would bring the
whole house down on their heads. Security may have
been lightened, yet it still existed. Other guards were
posted throughout the brothel. Better to try to get as far
in as possible without struggle.

They were taking a chance, bringing Jack here
rather than Simon or Marco. As Rockley's former
bodyguard, he might be recognized, but he knew the
layout of the brothel. He also knew how the bullies
would fight, if it came to that. She hoped that it didn't.

Together, they walked down the carpeted hall and
arrived at the parlor. The place still resembled a businessman's home—dark furniture, floral wallpaper, and
overstuffed chairs and sofas—except lounging on the
furniture were nearly a dozen girls in robes and negli-

gees. Three of the young women played cards, another yawned into her hand. A girl sat on a man's lap, idly toying with his mustache. In the corner, a young woman with dyed red hair played an upright piano. It was dispiriting how good a musician she was. Eva could easily guess that she'd been some clerk's daughter who'd been modestly educated in music, painting, and French, but some fall from grace had led her to this place.

Difficult to ascertain their age with the amount of paint they wore, though some couldn't have been more than fifteen.

An older woman in burgundy silk approached, smiling. "Welcome, sir, and"—she glanced at Eva— "madam."

Eva dropped her gaze, as if embarrassed.

"How might we gratify you this evening?" Mrs. Arram sounded halfway between a procuress and a grandmother offering tea and biscuits.

Though Jack had doubtless been in many brothels, he looked suitably abashed. "The wife and me, we were, ah, thinking maybe . . ." He chuckled nervously.

"Of course!" Mrs. Arram said to Eva, "We've only girls here, madam. Were you interested in watching, or were you considering a more participatory role? Or," she added, "did you and your husband want an audience? There's a wonderful room with plenty of hidden vantage points. A girl could be in the room with you, too, watching. Whatever you desire."

For a moment, Eva found herself at a loss for words. From the corner of her eye, she saw Jack redden.

She was seized by a rather wicked impulse. "Perhaps we could find a girl for me, and my husband could watch?"

He made a strangled sound, and she smiled inwardly.

"That could easily be arranged," Mrs. Arram said. "We have many fine girls . . ." Her words trailed off as she looked at Jack with a frown.

It was only a moment, an expression so quick and fleeting as to be nearly unseen. But Eva saw it. The smallest widening of Mrs. Arram's eyes.

Jack and Eva exchanged glances. He understood.

"Let me ring for Genevieve," the madam continued, cheerful. She strolled toward a bell pull. "She's just the girl for you."

"Don't," Eva said, darting forward. But too late. Mrs. Arram lunged for the bell pull and tugged on it.

A door concealed within the wall's paneling swung open and a hulking man with thinning hair barreled into the room. He stalked toward Jack. "Lady of the house wants you out," he said, with a bored tone of voice that spoke to the number of times he'd been called upon to roust unruly customers.

But he'd never dealt with a customer like Jack. Thinning Hair reached for him, and Jack immediately plowed his fist square into the bully's chest. His would-be assailant staggered back, gasping.

Screaming, the prostitutes leaped up from their seats. The lone customer in the parlor unceremoniously threw the girl in his lap to the floor as he jumped to his feet. He darted out the side door without a backward glance.

"Behind you," Eva called to Jack as the smashed-faced bully from the front door came thundering into the room. Smashed Face brandished a heavy cudgel and saw immediately that Jack was the threat.

"It's Diamond Jack Dalton!" the madam screeched.

Both guards' faces briefly paled with fear as they realized whom they confronted. Eva had known Jack possessed a reputation, but she hadn't understood its true scope until that moment. These two paid thugs, both clearly hardened criminals, were frightened of him.

But they were rough men, too, and their fear turned to rage. Thinning Hair pulled a knife from a sheath on the back of his belt. Snarling, he waved it at Jack.

Eva stepped forward, intending to help Jack with his two opponents, but saw the madam reaching into the drawer of a table. Metal glinted. A gun. Before Mrs. Arram could pull out the pistol, Eva drove her fist into the woman's face. The madam went down noiselessly, dropping the gun. The weapon skittered under a heavy cabinet.

In a flurry of lace and perfume, the girls in the parlor fled, shrieking like terrified parrots.

Whirling around, Eva saw Smashed Face charge Jack. The bully swung his club. Fast as fire, Jack lashed out, grabbing hold of Smashed Face's wrist and preventing the bully's strike from connecting. Jack seized hold of the other end of the club. Using his hold on the bully's wrist, he flung Smashed Face to the ground. Smashed Face grunted as he went down hard, and Jack twisted the club out of his hand.

Armed with the cudgel, Jack faced off against Thinning Hair. The bully slashed at him with his knife, gaslight gleaming lewdly off the blade. Jack parried the blows, holding his assailant back with swings of the cudgel. Back and forth, they traded feints and strikes. Eva longed to run to his aid, but if she tried to insert herself into the fray, she'd only distract Jack and likely get them both hurt in the process.

And to watch him fight like this, tough and dirty, mesmerized her. He had a natural skill, an innate understanding of when the next strike might be coming, and he battled back with a street-born warrior's grace. There were no civilized rules, no gentlemanly principles at play. He only meant to hurt his opponents, by any means.

Thinning Hair took a step back, pushed away by Jack's assault. But Smashed Face was getting to his feet, preparing to join the fight.

"Jack!" Eva called in warning.

He acted so quickly, so fluidly, she barely discerned the movement. Hardly a moment after Thinning Hair slashed at him, Jack struck the bully's leading shoulder with the cudgel. In nearly the same motion, he kicked Smashed Face in the chest. The power of Jack's kick sent the bully careening backward. His head slammed into a heavy wooden side table. Groaning, Smashed Face fell to the ground. His eyes rolled back as he lost consciousness.

Jack didn't spare the insensate man another thought. He turned back to Thinning Hair, grinning viciously. Seeing his colleague sprawled oblivious on the floor stoked the bully's fury. He slashed upward with his knife. Jack dodged the strike, then brought his cudgel down on Thinning Hair's wrist. A sickening crunch filled the parlor, and the bully screamed. The knife dropped from his hand.

Jack smashed his fist into the bully's jaw. For a moment, Thinning Hair fluttered his eyes like a parody of a coquette. Then he crumpled to the floor, out cold.

Spinning around, Jack readied himself for another assault. But none came.

"That's the lot of them," Eva said.

"There'll be more." He glanced at the madam, lying across the carpet, then at Eva. His grin returned, a flash of white teeth that, combined with his fighter's stance, made her pulse kick.

She had to keep her head on straight. She was still angry with him, and they had to find the evidence. "Now where?"

"Rockley's private room is at the top. Whatever we're looking for, it'll be up there."

She started toward the door to the parlor, but as she passed, he gripped her elbow, stopping her.

Nodding toward the side door, he said, "That leads to the servants' stairs. Faster."

She nodded and waved for him to lead the way. Only minutes earlier, the parlor had been filled with feminine chatter and the melodic strains of a Schubert waltz. Now it was silent and empty, save for the three unconscious people splayed upon the floor. Eva smiled to herself. Nemesis had been here.

No—Nemesis couldn't take credit for the force of nature that was Jack Dalton.

She followed him through a narrow servants' hallway. A few frightened maids peered out from doorways before slamming them in terror. They'd been too well trained to go to the police for assistance. Then she and Jack arrived at the steep, cramped stairwell reserved for servants. He bounded up them, continuing to hold the cudgel. Her own revolver was still in her handbag, but only as an eleventh-hour resource. Firearms in enclosed spaces were extremely dangerous— they had a habit of hitting the wrong people, or being wrenched out of one's hand. Her gun would stay in its secure place unless absolutely necessary.

As soon as they reached the second-floor landing, the door there burst open. Another bully charged into the stairwell, armed with a heavy pipe.

At once, Jack and the guard swung at each other. There wasn't much room to maneuver, and Eva winced as the pipe connected with Jack's shoulder. He only grunted. He moved to strike at the bully with his cudgel, but the stairwell was too narrow to get a decent swing. He dropped the club and gripped the bully by his lapels, then hit his head against the wall. The guard's head was thick, however, and the strike didn't knock him out. He dropped his own weapon and also grabbed Jack by the lapels. Pushing away from the wall, the bully slammed Jack against the stair's railing, the banister driving right into the small of his back. He pounded Jack against the rail once more, forcing a pained groan from Jack. He struggled to keep from being thrown over the banister onto the steep stairs below.

Eva dropped to the ground, fumbling between the men's heavy boots as they fought. There! Her fingers closed around the pipe.

She rose up behind the bully, then brought the pipe down onto the base of his skull. The guard made a gurgling sound before sinking to the floor. Jack caught himself before he toppled backward, his hands gripping the railing. Once he'd righted himself, he bent over the slumped bully, his ear to the man's mouth.

"Is he dead?" she asked.

Jack straightened. "He'll want to make friends with a bottle or ten of whiskey when he wakes up." Eyeing the pipe in her hand, he said, "Should consider myself lucky you didn't do anything like that to me."

She hefted her acquired weapon. "It's early yet."

A corner of his mouth curved up. "Will I get any warning?"

In response, she waved toward the stairs. "Keep climbing, and find out."

He nodded and started up the next flight, with her following. Either he was foolish, or he truly did trust her. And Jack was no fool.

But they still had farther to go, with a fight every step of the way.

CHAPTER FOURTEEN

The commotion roused the rest of the house. As Eva and Jack continued to ascend the servants' stairs, she could hear women's panicked voices and irritated and alarmed men hurrying out. No one wanted to stay in a brothel under siege.

At the very top of the stairs stood a baize-lined door. Cautiously, Jack eased it open, holding his body in readiness if another bully tried to attack. All they found was an empty carpeted hallway. As they stepped into the corridor, it was eerily silent. Two doors faced each other across the passage. Presumably, one of the doors led to Rockley's private chamber, and in that chamber was the evidence.

But where was the guard? Surely there had to be one. Even with Jack supposedly dead, a man as paranoid as Rockley wouldn't leave dangerous documents unprotected.

Jack nodded toward one of the doors. He placed his finger against his lips. She nodded in understanding.

They edged beside the doorway, backs to the wall. Jack stuck his foot out and pressed down on the floorboards directly in front of the door. The floorboards obligingly creaked beneath his weight.

From within Rockley's private room, four gunshots

rang out, bullets flying through the door. Splinters flew. Eva flattened herself tight to the wall to keep from being hit by both the shattered wood and the bullets.

Then more silence. The guard inside waited.

Jack tensed, readying himself to storm into the chamber. She stopped him with a hand on his arm.

"Oh, my God!" she screamed. "You killed 'im! You killed the madman!"

The door slowly creaked open. Leading with the gun in his hand, the guard poked his head out. Jack struck instantly, grabbing the bully's hand and slamming it into the door frame. The guard's hand opened with a pained spasm, and the gun dropped from his grip. Eva lunged for the gun just as Jack shoved the guard back into the chamber.

She caught the pistol before it hit the ground.

A tremendous crash sounded from inside Rockley's chamber. Inside, she found Jack and the guard furiously trading punches. This guard was just as big as Jack, just as brutal a fighter. The two men threw vicious blows, pummeling each other as if they were in a Bethnal Green brawl rather than an elegantly furnished bedroom in St. John's Wood. She immediately discarded the idea of taking a shot—with the two men locked in combat, she ran the risk of hitting Jack rather than the bully. But she kept the gun, just in case Jack got himself into a tight situation.

She had to make use of the time he was buying her. Dodging the men as they threw each other into walls and furniture, she checked under the four-poster bed and behind the framed paintings. No sign of a strongbox or vault.

She tugged open a dresser's drawers and dumped their contents on the ground. Bile rose in her throat as floggers and restraints tumbled over the carpet. She had a feeling that Rockley wielded rather than received the flogger. And he'd never consent to be restrained.

Eva jumped aside as Jack and the guard crashed into the dresser. The sound of breaking wood filled the room as the dresser broke apart beneath their weight. Neither of the men seemed to notice. They hauled themselves to their feet and resumed fighting. Blood dripped from the corner of Jack's mouth, and the guard's eye had already begun to swell shut. Yet they didn't slow or stagger as they brawled.

At this rate, they'd tear the house down around them before she could find the evidence.

"Damn," she muttered to herself, glancing around the chamber. "Where the hell is it?"

Her gaze caught on a small door that presumably led to a closet. Flinging it open, she found several men's jackets hanging there. Useless. But on the floor of the closet . . .

There sat an iron strongbox, roughly the size of a traveling valise. Two locks secured its lid, and handles were on either end of the strongbox, making it relatively easy to transport. But the strongbox wouldn't be traveling anywhere in a hurry—a locked chain secured it to a metal ring mounted to the wall.

She crouched down and removed her lock picks from her handbag.

Fire suddenly spread across her scalp as someone gripped her roughly by the hair and jerked her back. "You ain't getting in there," snarled the guard.

Her eyes burned, and her hand came up automatically, grasping her own hair to lessen the force of his tugging. Twisting around, she jabbed the fingers of her free hand into his unprotected windpipe as he bent over her. He gagged and his grip on her hair lessened. She kicked at his knees at the same moment she brought the side of her hand down onto his forearm.

Howling in pain, he released her. And then he wasn't there anymore. Jack slammed into the guard, tackling him to the ground. Jack pinned the bully's arms with his knees as he knelt over him. If Jack had been fighting viciously before, he was rage personified now, his face dark with fury as he landed blow after blow to the guard's face.

Though the sight was brutally fascinating, she had her own task to accomplish. She turned back to the lock fastening the chain to the strongbox. Forcing herself to ignore the wet, crunching sounds of Jack's fists pounding into the bully, she worked her picks on the lock. She'd never before had to pick a lock when someone in the same room was administering a relentless beating, and she strained to sense the tiny clicks and barely perceptible movements of the lock's mechanism as Jack unleashed the full extent of his fury on the guard.

The man's groans stopped, but Jack's assault didn't. She glanced over her shoulder. The bully was unconscious, blood flowing from his nose and mouth. But Jack kept going.

"Jack," she said sharply. "He stopped fighting back."

Snarling, Jack whipped up his head. The moment his gaze fell on her, the mask of rage fell away.

"Don't add murder to your list of crimes," she said.

"He . . . hurt you." His words were a low rasp.

"I hurt him back."

His scowl slowly faded. "So you did."

"Now stop distracting me." She turned back to her work, fighting for calm when she felt anything but. He'd been on the verge of killing the bully, and all because the guard had tried to harm her. He'd been callously efficient when fighting with the other guards, but this had been personal.

The lock's tumblers clicked into place. She unfastened it, separating the strongbox from the chain that bound it to the wall. Her arms strained with effort as she struggled to pull the heavy container out of the closet. It might be the size of a valise, but it was far heavier, as though someone had packed the case with bricks instead of clothing.

"I'll see to that." Jack grabbed the strongbox's handles and hefted it easily.

Getting to her feet, she said, "Now you're just showing off."

He started to grin, but winced from the cut at the corner of his mouth. "I want a look at what we've got on Rockley, but we ain't opening this here."

"A neighbor may have notified the constabulary," she said in agreement. "Between the gunfire and this"—she gestured at the ruined bedchamber, where every single piece of furniture had been destroyed by Jack and the bully—"we've made enough noise to summon the entire Metropolitan Police. The army, too."

She stepped around the prostrate form of the guard, and together she and Jack left the bedroom. They hurried down the main stairs, Jack in the lead as he carried the strongbox. The house stood silent. Either everyone had fled, or the women cowered in their rooms.

Eva and Jack reached the ground floor. The front door was only steps away. But as they crossed the foyer, Smashed Face charged. Jack didn't slow his steps. He swung the strongbox at the attacking guard. The metal container caught the bully right in his gut. He grunted and careened backward, gagging. As she and Jack sped through the front door, the bully didn't try to stop them.

They hastened out into the street. Whistles and the clanging bell of the Black Maria police wagon broke through the night's silence. She and Jack ran in the opposite direction, toward the hansom they'd hired for the night. The cab waited for them in an alley, and moments after they'd clambered into the vehicle, the strongbox settled across Jack's knees, the driver snapped the reins and they were off. If anyone looked askance at a woman riding in a hansom, Eva didn't give a damn.

She'd just stormed into a brothel to steal incriminating evidence from an embezzling nobleman. Reputations were just bits of tissue paper in comparison.

She didn't relax against the seat until they were well out of St. John's Wood, with no sounds of pursuit. Only then did she give a long, slow exhale.

Jack's smile flashed in the darkness. "Haven't had that much fun since all three O'Leary brothers challenged me in the ring."

Given what she'd just witnessed at the brothel, she had no doubt how that fight had concluded.

"It's serious business, what we do for Nemesis," she answered. Then grinned. "But that *was* fun." She couldn't admit that to anyone—except Jack. Yet the excitement of what they'd just done continued to course through her.

"Could use a pint after a dustup like that," he said with a grin.

"Me, too," she said, wistful. But there'd be no drinks until after they reached headquarters.

"We could share a pint or two at the pub." His expression sobered. "What I said before, about you trying to gull me—"

Her mood plummeted. She glanced away. "Don't."

He put his fingers on her chin and turned her to face him. Rough, the pads of his fingertips against her skin, and his eyes were dark as mystery, filled with fire. Heat settled low in her belly.

"Goddamn it," he rumbled. "Listen. I'm . . . sorry about what I said." He shook his head. "Where I'm from, ain't no one as ruthless and manipulative than women. Men got nothing on them. But the women, they have to survive, any way they can. That's what I know."

"I'm not like them," she said tightly.

"You ain't like any woman I've met," he answered, heated.

His gaze searched her face, and she marveled at the contrast between the man who'd relentlessly cut through the guards at the brothel and this man, who looked at her with desire and admiration. Yet they were the same man. Brutal but honorable in his way. Capable of base violence and fierce emotion. Including the emotion he felt for her.

"I *am* sorry," he said. "I oughtn't have said that to you, and I hate that I did."

She clasped his wrist and leaned closer. Then kissed him. Because she had to. Because every part of her wanted it, wanted him. She tasted his blood in the kiss, metallic and earthy.

His grip on her chin tightened, and his growl traveled from deep in his throat into her with low, dark reverberations.

"You're like no one I've ever known, either," she whispered against his mouth.

"A pair of rare birds we are," he agreed. "Not birds—wolves. Rare wolves."

She glanced down at the strongbox. "Wolves who are in possession of dangerous, perhaps even ruinous, information."

Both his eyes and teeth gleamed in the shadows. "A wolf's got to have fangs."

* * *

At Nemesis headquarters, no one wanted to wait until morning to open the strongbox. Everyone gathered around Eva as she sat at the parlor table, using her picks to open the two hefty locks securing the strongbox's lid.

Jack leaned against the wall, holding a damp cloth to his busted lip, watching. Impatience burned at him to see what, if anything, the coffer held—but he didn't want to be one more body breathing down Eva's neck as she worked.

It was a damned pretty neck, though. What he wouldn't give for a proper time and place to run his mouth over it, breathe in its scent. But proper times and places were in bloody short supply.

All he could do was wait and seethe, slowly torn apart by his hunger for Eva and his need to learn what was in the coffer.

Could be that the strongbox contained nothing more than a few dirty French photographs or letters from mistresses. If that was true, then everything he and Eva had done was for nothing, and they'd be no closer to destroying Rockley than they'd been at the beginning. No—they'd be worse off, because they had nothing to hold over the bastard, their hand played.

He wasn't the only impatient one.

"Give us a go at that," Marco urged. "I cracked the Turkish embassy's safe in Paris in less than three minutes."

"If you'd stop chattering at me," she said without looking up, "I'd get this done much faster."

"Shut it and let the lady work," Jack snapped.

Marco scowled at him, but at least he stopped talking.

Finally, the telltale snick of the locks opening sounded in the quiet room. Everyone crowded closer to the table, Jack included, as Eva opened the lid. Tension was sharp and tight when she held up what was inside.

Stacks of paper.

"What are they?" Harriet demanded.

Eva sorted through them. "A list of London's most elite courtesans, and their even more elite clients."

Simon plucked that sheet of paper from her fingers. "Top-ranking ministers, heads of major corporations, bishops." He whistled. "This could wreak considerable damage if it fell into the wrong hands."

"'Course that's why Rockley has it," Jack muttered. "Anyone tries to make a move against him, and he's got 'em by the stones."

Eva held up two official-looking documents. "Deeds. One to a property here in London—a town house in Knightsbridge by the looks of it—and a house in Somerset." She studied them closer. "The name of the deed holder has been left blank."

"He must've swindled them from someone," Lazarus suggested.

"It's a veritable trove of villainy," Harriet said, shaking her head.

Jack clamped down on his edginess. "None of this's what we're looking for."

More silence as Eva rifled through the papers. It seemed Rockley had gotten involved in a sodding heap of crime, or at least liked to hang on to evidence of other people's offenses for his own use.

It took them nearly half an hour to go through all the documents, sorting them, studying them.

Finally, Eva said, "Yes. This." She untied a cord binding a set of papers. It appeared to be columns of numbers, with notations scribbled beside the figures.

"Is that it?" Simon demanded.

"A full accounting of the government contract for the cartridges." She scanned the documents and muttered a curse. "That son of a bitch. He and Gilling took more than half the money allocated for the production of the cartridges. Rockley got the lion's share, but Gilling made a profit, too. With the rest, they purchased substandard manufacturing materials from foreign suppliers. Bills of sale, as proof." She pointed to several sheets of paper.

Simon examined the bills, and his upper-class features twisted with a snarl. "He fucking sold out British soldiers. How many men died because of him?" He flung the papers onto the table. "I'll kill him."

Jack smiled grimly. At last the toff understood the fury and need for vengeance that ate at him. "Get in the queue, mate."

Slowly, Eva got to her feet. She gathered all the papers and set them back in the strongbox. "No one's killing anyone. We've got the evidence we need against him, and we're going to make use of it. He will be made to pay for his misconduct."

He bristled. "You sound so bloody calm about it."

"I'm feeling anything but tranquil," she answered, meeting his gaze. In the lamplight, she looked carved from golden marble. It was the coolness, he realized, she used to shield herself, a kind of armor she made with her mind. The more the world threatened to shatter apart, the calmer she became. "He's kept a good record of his crimes—and there are many. When it comes time to lead the charge against him, I'll be right there, sword in hand."

Her voice was flat, detached, but he understood now. He saw it in her eyes, and could feel it in the fury that turned her so perfectly still—when it came time for

Eva to unleash the fierceness within herself, God help whoever stood in her way.

And damn him if he didn't want to be there to see it.

Returning to her simple, ordinary rooms after the events of the night felt as though she were visiting someone else's life. And she was—except the life she visited was her own. There, on her table, were lesson plans and books. There, propped upon the mantel was a photograph of her parents that had come in their last letter. Unsurprisingly, her father and mother looked stern and righteous as they posed outside the school they had built in the depths of Nigeria.

Their letter, penned by her mother, was tucked into the top drawer of Eva's nightstand. Once again, her mother had urged her to join them, to give up tutoring for a higher calling. *Your talents are too exceptional to be wasted on the bored daughters of the bourgeoisie,* Elizabeth Warrick had written. *There is a young missionary here who is in search of a wife and helpmeet. I should be very happy to pass along your permission for him to write to you. Use your life for some greater purpose.*

Eva hadn't yet replied to the letter.

Clad now in her nightgown but unable to sleep, she strode to her desk, preparing to finally answer. Yet before she wrote a single line, she flung her pen to the desk and leaned back in her chair, staring at the ceiling.

What would she tell them? How could she describe her and Jack storming into a brothel to steal documents belonging to a corrupt nobleman? And what would she say about Jack, the escaped convict who fought like a brute but had a soul of incomparable depth. And the way he kissed her . . . heat streaked through her, simply remembering the feel of his lips against hers, how he seemed to breathe her in, taking her into himself as though she were a vital part of him he couldn't survive without.

She'd hated having to leave him at headquarters an hour ago. She wanted him here, with her. In her bed. But with all of Nemesis watching, she couldn't very well take him by the hand and lead him out the door. They'd question her judgment—Simon most of all—in entangling herself with Jack whilst in the middle of a mission. She questioned her judgment, too. There wasn't anything wise or careful about wanting him. And she had ever been wise and careful.

She started at the sound of a tap on her window. A dark shape loomed there. Grabbing her pistol, she edged closer. Perhaps Rockley had been able to find her and send one of his thugs in pursuit. Her rooms were on the top floor of her building—whoever it was had skill in climbing.

A face appeared in the window. Jack.

Exhaling raggedly, she moved to the casement and unfastened the lock. As soon as she slid open the window, Jack climbed inside with that surprising agility given his size. She stepped back to give him room.

He'd found some dark clothing, and with his black hair and stubble-shadowed jaw, he appeared to be the night come to life. She'd never seen such fire in his eyes. In her tidy little rooms, he looked big, dangerous—irresistible.

His gaze flicked down to the gun still in her hand. "Reminds me of the first time I met you."

Turning away, she set the pistol on a nearby table. "I usually don't receive visitors at this hour. Especially not at the window."

She tried for flippancy, a final measure of self-protection, but even to her own ears she sounded breathless. No need to ask him how he'd gotten here. He already knew how to escape from headquarters without being seen, and he knew where she lived. He didn't have any money, but she could well imagine him running through the streets, dark as the shadows themselves. Intent on one purpose—her.

He came up behind her. She didn't hear him move, but *felt* him there, the warmth of his body, the hot intensity of his presence. His skin and clothing carried the scent of cool night air. Already her flesh became tight, achingly sensitive, her body reacting to his nearness alone. Yet she couldn't turn around. Couldn't face him. Not much frightened her, but he did. No, not him, but the way she responded to him, the way he made her feel.

They both knew why he was here in her rooms. She ought to demand that he leave. Threaten him with the gun if he didn't. But she couldn't do that. She wanted him here, so badly that she was rooted to the spot, unable to do anything but look at her pistol on the table and listen to the sounds of their roughened breathing.

The floorboards creaked beneath him. He'd done that deliberately. Giving her time to choose. Move away or stay.

She stayed.

He stood directly behind her, his heat seeping into her body, yet they didn't touch. She heard the slight shift of his clothing as he moved. She braced herself, expecting him to be rough and urgent.

Instead, his large hand slid slowly, deliberately up her back. From the small of her back all the way along her spine, tracing her shape, until his palm rested just beneath her nape. She gasped at the sensation, as though his touch were flame.

He tugged her robe down her shoulders and she helped push it to the ground. Then he repeated his touch along her back, with only the thin cotton of her night-gown separating her flesh from his, and her gasp turned into a moan. His palm moved along her shoulders, her arms, as if learning her. When he stroked along the curves of her buttocks, he rumbled.

"I knew it," he said, his breath on her neck. "Knew you'd have the sweetest round arse. Wanted my hands on it since the beginning."

She exhaled a laugh. Leave it to Jack to speak only the earthiest of poetry. And it aroused her, far more than pretty metaphors or lyrical praise.

Deliberately, she took a step back, bringing their bodies together. His chest against her back. Her buttocks against his groin. Despite his clothing, she felt the shape of his hard, thick cock as it nestled against her. An animal growl escaped him.

His hands curved over her ribs, then up. She held herself in eager anticipation as she waited, waited, and then, oh yes, his hands covered her breasts. For a moment, he simply held her, as though reveling in the sensation of her breasts in his hands, but his stillness didn't last long. He cupped her, stroked her, arousing her nipples into stiff points. When he pinched them, his teeth raked her neck.

Arching her back, she couldn't stop her moan. The sensation of his teeth and fingers shot through her, gathering hotly between her legs.

She twisted her head to the side. "Kiss me, damn it."

He chuckled quietly, then took her lips. Open-mouthed, they kissed, ravenous, as he continued to caress and stroke her breasts.

She needed more, of him, his touch and hunger. She fumbled with the buttons lining the front of her nightgown, her fingers shaking, but she managed to undo them to her waist. The fabric gaped open.

Clever as she'd always known him to be, he took the invitation for what it was, peeling back the cotton to bare her breasts. Then they were in his hands, his incredible, big hands that were callused and not at all refined, and she seemed to spin away, lost in the feel of him touching her this way, skin to skin. He rolled her nipples between his fingers and caught her gasp in his mouth.

One of his hands drifted from her breast, moving down her torso over the curve of her stomach. Then he gathered up the hem of her nightgown and stroked between her legs. A cry broke from her at his intimate touch.

"God," he rasped in approval, "you're so goddamn wet." His fingers slipped between her folds, sliding over her soaked flesh. When he rubbed her clit in slow, deliberate circles, pleasure clawed through her. She had to lean against him or else slide to the floor.

He worked her like this, one hand caressing her breast, the other stroking between her legs, and his mouth on hers, swallowing her every moan and whimper. She never thought a man like him could be this way, commanding and tender, touching her as though they belonged to each other and this was only right, only proper.

He slid a thick finger inside her and at once her body tightened, readying itself for release.

But then he took his finger away, and she cried out in protest.

When he spun her around to face him, his face was carved, brutal with desire. He kissed her, hard, then said, "The first time you come, it'll be with my mouth on you."

Her face flamed, while another heat poured through her. She started toward the bed, but he scooped her up in his arms with shocking ease. Instead of taking her to bed, he strode to the table and sat her down upon the edge. When he knelt down before her, her heart beat thickly in her chest and breath became scarce.

She stared down at him, so impossibly big, kneeling yet far from subservient. They both held power. Never had she felt stronger than at that moment, seeing the hunger and need in his gaze and the rigid line of his jaw. For her. All for her.

He stroked up her thighs, pushing her nightgown back. Revealing her legs and then—

"Ah, there it is," he rumbled. He teased her pussy with his fingers, and his eyes blazed. "Know how many nights I've thought of nothing but this? How much I've wanted to taste you? This gorgeous cunt. My tongue on your pretty quim, eating you up."

"I've wanted that, too," she gasped.

"Hell." One hand he used to continue to stroke her, the other flew to the buttons of his trousers. She watched, fascinated, as he tore them open and pulled out his cock. It was huge and dark and beautiful, straining upward in a thick curve. He pumped it as he caressed her.

The vision of his broad length in his own hand as he knelt between her legs—she nearly climaxed from the sight alone. And when he bent his head to her, and licked her in one long, slow stroke, she had to bite down on her lip to keep from screaming.

He feasted on her, licking, tracing her with his supple tongue. She draped her thighs over the unbending breadth of his shoulders. Sounds of approval and pleasure rumbled from him. He took her clit between his lips and sucked.

She bowed upward, no longer able to hold back her climax. It was a tightening and a release, as expansive and devastating as time itself. And endless. For he continued to lick and taste her, taking her to ecstasy too many times for her to count. She knew only the feel of him and how he drank of her with a brutal reverence.

She kept her eyes open, watching him, his mouth on her, his hand on his cock. She clutched the back of his head with one hand, and the other she used to stroke and rub her nipples.

He pulled back enough to say hoarsely, "You hide this, don't you? Won't show anyone what you're really like. How wild you are. How hot you burn."

"Not with you," she moaned. "Can't hide . . ."

"That's right." His voice was deep, unyielding. "Only *I* get to see this." He licked her again, and another climax shuddered through her.

"Enough," she said when she could speak again. She pushed him back, and his eyes blazed.

"We ain't done," he growled.

"We surely aren't." She pointed to the bed. "Take off your clothes and lie there."

His eyebrows rose at her imperious tone, but he did as she commanded. He stood and stripped off his clothing, flinging everything aside with flattering haste. His coat, waistcoat, shirt. Trousers and boots. Then he was naked. Standing in the middle of her rooms completely nude.

She'd seen him without his clothes once before, but they had been in a dark carriage, and she hadn't had the luxury of time and light to truly look at him. Now she had both, and what she saw filled her with raw, female need.

His every muscle stood out in hard relief, from the round caps of his shoulders to the planes of his chest and down to the sharp delineations of his abdomen. He was everywhere muscled—arms, thighs, calves—and he was wondrous and stunning and not a little frightening. Without his clothing, he became the most primal essence of masculinity, timeless and potent.

As he turned to kick aside his clothes, she saw his back. Scars traversed it, the thick indelible mark of the lash. Her heart contracted.

He turned back to her, and her gaze followed the line of his hip as it arrowed down to his groin. His cock stood at full attention and seemed to twitch beneath her perusal.

He took a step toward her, but she pointed once more at the bed. "Go on," she commanded.

He shot her a look that seemed to indicate he didn't appreciate being ordered about, yet he moved fast enough, climbing onto her bed. As he did so, she took a selfish moment to admire the flex of his firm buttocks. The springs creaked and the mattress sagged beneath his weight. There was a very good chance they'd break her bed tonight. She didn't care in the slightest.

"Bed's too damned small to lie down," he said.

"Sit at the edge."

When he did so, and looked at her expectantly, she pulled off her nightgown and tossed it onto a nearby chair. He growled in response.

"Better not turn down the lights," he said, staring at her, "because I've waited too long to see you like this."

"I've wanted to be seen."

She let him look his fill, reveling in the way he drank her in with his eyes. He was a man, so of course his gaze lingered on her breasts and between her legs, but he also traced the lengths of her arms, her legs, even taking note of her bare toes.

But there was only so much admiration from a distance either of them could stand.

"If you don't bloody get over here, right now," he said, "I'm coming to get you."

"I don't like being ordered around, either," she answered.

She sauntered toward him, feeling the sway of her hips, the measure of her own power. And the way he watched her, as though she contained every answer to every mystery, filled her with strength.

His hands curved over her hips when she stood between his legs. Leaning forward, he nuzzled her breasts, the bristle of his jaw deliciously abrasive against her skin. He ran his tongue around her nipples, alternating between them, and she threaded her fingers into his hair, holding him close. More heat spiraled through her—feeling him, seeing him.

Reaching down, she grasped his cock. He rumbled against her breast as she encircled him. He was iron-hard, filling her hand. She stroked the wide head, down the shaft, then back up, lightly raking her nails over him. Sharply, he inhaled, his hips rising up. Ah, he liked that. So she did it again, punctuating her strokes with careful scrapes up his shaft.

His hand clamped down over hers. "Have to stop," he grated. "Or I'll go off in your hand."

She smiled wickedly. "I wouldn't mind."

"I would, damn it. Enough talk—need to be inside you." He pulled her closer.

As he sat on the edge of the bed, his hands on her hips, she straddled him, her legs wrapping around his waist. Their bodies pressed close, and they both groaned at the feel of his chest against her breasts, his flat abdomen and rigid cock tight to the curve of her stomach. She didn't take him within her, not yet. For a lifetime it seemed she had waited for this, and she wouldn't rush.

Canting her hips, she guided his cock between her folds. Up and down she moved, sliding him along her lips, over her clit, coating him with her wetness. Exquisite sensation flooded her to feel him like this, to watch the agonized pleasure on his face as she deliberately tortured them both.

"Ah, God, Eva," he gasped. "That's . . . *God* . . ." Yet even as they both shook with pleasure, he had reached his breaking point. Hands almost cruel on her hips, he lifted her up, notched his cock at her opening, then brought her down, surging into her.

She cried out.

Instantly, he stilled. "Hurting you?"

"I only need . . . a moment." He was huge within her, stretching her to her utmost. Thank heavens she was soaking wet, for she doubted she would've been able to accommodate him otherwise. She breathed deep, willing her body to relax. In a moment, the pain ebbed, and she was left with only sensation, wonderful sensation.

"Better?" he asked.

"Best," she murmured.

"Good, because I've got to do this." He thrust up, and she cried out again, this time from pure pleasure. "And this." He moved once more, filling her completely.

She clung to his shoulders as she rode him, his hips meeting hers, his cock exquisite within her. His thrusts were measured but fierce, and she gasped with each one.

Looking down, she watched his cock plunging in and out of her. *Yes.* Everywhere, heat. Sensation. She ground her clit against him as he continued to fuck her relentlessly. White-hot, her climax tore through her. He clapped his hand over her mouth, muffling her cries.

When the last filaments of her orgasm faded, she found herself flipped onto her back, her knees up and feet on the mattress. Jack knelt on the ground, his hands continuing to grip her hips. She gazed up at him through pleasure-glazed eyes. Sweat glossed his body. Brutal desire hollowed his cheeks, and his expression was fierce. A beast ready to claim its mate.

More than lust shone in his eyes. A kind of searching, a need. And when he thrust into her, that need blazed even higher.

She gripped the mattress for support as he drove in and out of her. The room was filled with the sounds of flesh against flesh, and their commingled cries. Light gleamed on his muscles as they flexed with effort. Primal. True and real.

With a groan midway between anguish and ecstasy, he suddenly pulled out of her. Hot seed shot from him, coating her belly. He threw his head back as his climax raged on.

At last, he released his grasp of her hips—there would be bruises, but she didn't care—and planted his hands on either side of her head, his body bowing over hers. Their kiss was molten, deep. She wanted to lose herself in this moment, every inch of her thrumming with satiation.

But he pulled away. She could barely stir as she watched him pad across the room to search for and retrieve a towel from a cabinet. He returned, and sat beside her as he gently, thoroughly, cleaned her.

"Thank you," she murmured, "for having sense to . . ." She glanced down at her stomach meaningfully.

A corner of his mouth turned up. "Only sensible thing I've done, when it has to do with you."

When he'd cleaned her, he put the towel aside and gathered her up in his arms. The bed was too small for him, but he managed to twist and turn himself so that they lay cradled together, his front to her back. His lips ran back and forth over her neck, his hand curved at her waist. After the heated activity only minutes earlier, they were quiet now, listening to the predawn birds stirring in the trees outside.

She wondered if, when the sun came up, her landlady would ask her to leave. No mistaking what she and Jack had been doing. Well, she could find someplace else to live. A small price to pay for what had been the most extraordinary experience of her life.

And Nemesis? Would they ask her to leave, too? *That* would be a bitter cost. Nemesis meant everything to her. She couldn't leave them. She had to continue with their work.

Yet she couldn't regret what she'd done, what she and Jack had done together. She didn't know what it meant, or what the future might bring, but for now, she could allow herself this moment of repletion. She had unleashed her true self, without fear. It had been . . . remarkable. Jack was remarkable.

Yet the mission was ongoing. She had no idea if it would succeed or not. And if, by luck and determination, they were successful in their plans, then Nemesis would have no further use for Jack, and he would have to go. It would be far too dangerous for him to remain in England. And she'd never leave.

"Wish I could stay," he said drowsily.

"I wish you could, too." But it was impossible. Everything about the two of them together was impossible.

CHAPTER FIFTEEN

Tired, sated, his brain fogged with weariness and thoughts of Eva, Jack climbed in the window to his room. Dawn was minutes away, and all he wanted was to crawl into bed and sleep for a year.

He tensed the minute he got inside his room.

Simon leaned against the wall, watching the window, arms folded over his chest.

"Whatever you got to say," Jack muttered, peeling off his coat, "say it quick. I ain't in the mood for lectures." He threw his coat and waistcoat onto a chair and did the same with his shirt. He had a mad impulse to press his shirt to his face. It might carry Eva's scent, and he wanted to pull it deep into his lungs.

Instead, he made himself move to his washstand and pour water into a basin, which he splashed on his face.

"No lecture." The toff's voice was dangerously quiet. In the mirror, Jack saw Simon's gaze roam over his back as if looking for the best place to stick a knife. "A warning."

Turning around, Jack dried his face on a cloth. "Threatening me ain't very smart, gov."

"I don't make threats," Simon answered, still in that deadly soft voice. "When I say I'll do something, I'll do it. So mark me, Dalton," he continued, pushing away from the wall, "if you hurt Eva in any way, I *will* kill you."

Though the nob didn't have Jack's size, it was clear Simon knew how to scrap. Only a real fighter stood the way Simon did now, body and hands loose but ready. His sharp blue eyes revealed a fighter's confidence. Jack could beat Simon, but the toff would give him a hell of a brawl.

Fury boiled through him at the idea that he might hurt Eva. "Think she can't take care of herself?"

"I know she can. I've known her far longer than you have, and I'll still know her after you've gone."

Jack didn't want to think about that, about when the work against Rockley was over and what it meant for him. He could only live in each moment as it happened.

"That's your plan, then," he sneered. "Move in after I leave and help nurse her broken heart. Offer a shoulder to cry on, then offer her a lot more." The thought of Eva with Simon—or her with anyone else—made Jack want to break every piece of furniture within ten miles, then smash down the walls of every building.

To the toff's credit, he looked appalled. "Christ, no. Eva's my friend. I'm not looking for a way to get under her skirts."

"You did."

"Years ago. I don't think of her in that way any longer."

The cage of anger loosened slightly around Jack's chest. He sat on the edge of his bed and tugged off his boots, letting them fall heavily to the floor. "Then tell me what the hell this is about."

Simon pointed at him. "This is about you not hurting Eva. Not making her promises you can't keep."

Jack knocked Simon's hand aside. "No one's promised anyone anything." How could he? He'd nothing to offer, nothing to vow. All he had was vengeance, and when that was fulfilled—*if* it was fulfilled—he'd have nil. Not even his name, since he was believed to be dead. Of course he'd leave when the mission was over. He had to. He couldn't expect anything else.

But Simon, goddamn Simon, had planted seeds in his head. About things that could never happen.

Eva—his. And him being hers. Not just for a few weeks of pleasure, though God knew how incredible that pleasure was. But for months, years. Maybe longer.

His heart beat heavy beneath his ribs, thinking of this. But when the mission was done, and if he still lived, he'd have to move on. Staying would be too dangerous, even if the coppers thought he was dead. There was always a chance someone might recognize him, and he'd be on the run again.

"She understands what's what," he said, more for his own benefit than Simon's. "It's all temporary."

Simon exhaled. "As long as that's recognized by both of you. Once the mission is over, you're not useful to Nemesis anymore. You leave, and she can move on without regret. Without you."

"Believe me, gov," Jack said, "no one knows that more than me."

In Bethnal Green, happiness wasn't handed out like pints of ale. You had to find it—or make it—for yourself. It was either that, or live in a constant state of rage and misery.

When Jack awoke, he let himself lie in bed for a few moments, his gaze roaming around this cramped little room that had become, for a short while, his home. Simon's warnings still rang in his ears, and their reminder that he could only have Eva for a short while longer. The thought sent a sharp pain through his chest.

He rubbed the heel of his hand between his ribs, but the pain wouldn't recede.

He made himself focus on what good he did have, same as he'd done back on the streets of Bethnal Green.

Last night . . . His body stirred and his pulse hitched just thinking about it, about Eva, and how she'd finally let free her wildness, her heat. With him. That had been best of all, knowing that she'd shared that secret part of herself only with him. They might not have as long together as he would've wanted, but he'd take everything he could get and be glad of it.

And they finally had the evidence against Rockley they needed. Revenge was like vinegar on his tongue. Close. So damn close. He'd been waiting five years. Within a handful of days, he'd see Rockley topple. What would happen afterward, he didn't know, but he wouldn't think about it now. Now was for savoring the anticipation of that bastard's ruin. It might not be as satisfying as killing him, but maybe Nemesis was right and having Rockley live in shame and disgrace could be better. He could sit and stew and let regret tear the flesh from his bones, the way Jack had done in prison.

Was this happiness? No. Jack never knew that feeling. But it was as close to it as he could get.

He rose from bed, and got ready for the day. Judging by the ash-colored light, it was already late afternoon. He smiled—his life had always been lived at night. Only when he got to Dunmoor did that change, rising with the dawn, working all day, and collapsing onto his cot soon after sunset. But he was claiming himself back.

He hurried downstairs, hoping that the rest of Nemesis had gathered so they could talk about the next steps with Rockley. They'd have a plan. They always had a plan.

His steps halted when he found Eva already in the parlor, standing beside the fireplace. He barely noticed Simon and Marco sitting at the table. She didn't blush or look away, but met his gaze boldly, with unmistakable heat.

It was like invisible hands grabbed him, pulling him toward her. He needed her mouth, the feel of her hands, the warm scent that clung to her neck.

Marco coughed. Loudly. A reminder that Jack and Eva weren't alone. Goddamn it.

Though he didn't care what either Marco or Simon thought, Jack couldn't go to Eva, not even to stand beside her. He'd have to touch her, and one touch would lead to more, and more. Instead, he grabbed a chair, swung it around and straddled it, his arms braced across the back.

"The next steps need to be planned carefully," Simon announced. "We're close now. Too close to get sloppy."

"He'll have been told that the evidence was stolen," Eva said. "The madam identified Jack, too. Rockley will know Jack isn't dead."

Marco asked, "Won't he go to the police with that?"

Jack snorted. "And tell them I was spotted busting up a whorehouse where he keeps damning papers? No—he'll keep his muzzle shut."

"If he feels the walls caving in around him," Simon pointed out, "he'll lash out, try to protect himself."

"We have to move first before he can." Eva frowned in thought as she looked into the fire. "It's time to—"

Everyone silenced as footsteps sounded on the staircase outside. It could have been Lazarus or Harriet, but Jack didn't recognize the tread. He stood.

Eva opened the door, revealing Byrne. The chemist stood on the landing, his forehead all creased with worry, and held out a slip of paper to her. "This came for you. Not you specifically, miss," he added, "but I was told to give it to the folks upstairs."

"Told by whom?" she asked.

"The boy that delivered it. He ran off before I could ask who sent it."

"Thank you, Mr. Byrne." She took the note.

"What's it about?"

She shook her head. "Policy, Mr. Byrne."

Contrite, the chemist smiled. "Right. Less I know, the safer I am." He gave a little bow and then trundled back down the stairs.

After Eva closed the door, she unfolded the note. Jack, Marco, and Simon all watched her as she scanned it. A troubled look crossed her face. "It's from Miss Jones. 'It is vitally important that you come immediately,'" she read aloud. Glancing up, she added, "The handwriting's hers, but it's shaky."

"She wants us to go to her home?" Marco wondered. "She and her father have always met with us here."

"Something must be wrong." Simon got to his feet and put on his hat. "Eva and I will see what's the matter."

"I should go, too," Jack said.

"He did help by talking with her last time," Eva noted.

Instead of arguing against Jack's presence, Simon just nodded.

Maybe Jack had earned the toff's confidence after all.

But it was the look of trust in Eva's eyes that Jack truly prized.

Pretty suburban neighborhoods like Hammersmith always made Jack's skin crawl. It was all so bloody normal, so orderly and neat. Even now, as he, Eva, and Simon walked toward the house of Miss Jones and her family, they passed men returning from their work in the city. The sun hung low on the horizon, and all the good, respectable men of business hurried home for supper. Through the lit, lace-covered windows, Jack watched as women greeted their husbands, taking their hats and coats, offering dutiful kisses on the cheek. Children in clean, starched pinafores clung to their fathers' legs until they were shooed away by their mothers. The men retired to front parlors, where they read newspapers and smoked pipes.

These were the people who decorated advertisements pushing health tonics, soap, cocoa. Perfect little kingdoms in perfect semidetached houses, and far from anything he'd known.

"Do you envy them?" Eva asked as they passed one house, with its brightly lit front window showing the people inside like actors on a stage.

"There ain't no thought in it," he said. "They're all doing what they think they're supposed to, but what's the fun of it? Where are the guts?"

"Perhaps they don't want fun or guts. Perhaps all they want is security, certitude."

"Only one thing's certain," he said. "We're all going to wind up in the ground. Way I figure it, that leaves us free to do what we want. Not shut ourselves away in tidy boxes."

"Radical notion," she answered. "You might be a revolutionary."

"Don't go picking out my crate and setting me up on Speakers' Corner," he warned. "I'm just trying to survive, not change the world." The world could take care of itself. He had his own skin to look after.

But as he, Eva, and Simon walked down a tree-lined street, heading toward Miss Jones's house, a kick of worry beat beneath his pulse. Worry for the young lady. Eva had said that the girl's handwriting looked shaky, which meant she'd written her note in a state of distress. Rockley might have threatened her again, or done worse. Jack knew that Eva could take care of herself, but most females hadn't been given much to defend themselves. They were at the mercy of men and the law, neither of which seemed to care much about the fate of women.

But that's why Nemesis existed.

Miss Jones's house was one of the smaller buildings on her block. Unlike most of the other houses, only a few lights burned in the windows. Simon knocked on the door, and after a minute, the girl herself answered the door. Pinched lines showed on either side of her mouth. She looked as if she'd aged ten years in just a few days. Her face was pale, and she twisted a handkerchief in her hands. She definitely didn't look happy to see any of them on her front step.

"Come in, please," she said, holding the door open. "I've sent our maid out, so we're alone."

They all stepped into the entryway as Eva asked, "Where are your parents?"

"Also out."

"Tell us what this is about," Jack said.

Miss Jones turned and moved down the hallway. "I've got some tea ready in the kitchen."

Jack, Eva, and Simon all shared a look after she disappeared through a door.

"Don't like it," Jack muttered.

Eva frowned. "She's acting oddly, that's true."

"Odd behavior or no," Simon noted, "she's our client. If Rockley's threatening her further, we need to help."

"Will you come?" Miss Jones asked, reappearing in the doorway.

Feeling restless and ill at ease, Jack followed the others as they filed into a medium-sized kitchen. Racks of pans lined the walls, and an iron stove took up one side of the room. A round table stood in one corner, surrounded by chairs, and beside the table was another door that looked like it led to a pantry.

Miss Jones waved toward the table. "Please sit."

Jack glanced around the kitchen. "Where's the tea?"

"I beg your pardon?" the girl asked, looking even more pale despite the heat of the stove.

"You said you'd made tea." Eva nodded at a kettle, still hung up on its hook. "It's not even on the fire."

Miss Jones's face seemed to crumple. She pressed the handkerchief to her mouth. "I'm sorry!"

Jack heard them before they came into the room— men. He spun to face the door just as three huge bruisers wielding clubs came barreling through. Two more blokes charged from the pantry, one of them holding a lead pipe and the other sporting a pair of brass knuckles.

It was as though someone had rung the bell to start the match—everything became instinct. He grabbed a heavy long-handled pan from its rack and swung it at the three men. From the corner of his eye, he saw Simon tussling with the bloke holding the pipe, ducking to avoid the swinging blows and throwing punches of his own. Eva had a chair in her hands and jabbed its legs at the chap with the brass knuckles, holding him back.

Jack weaved to the side as a club-wielding thug swung at him. He countered by striking with the pan. The thug wasn't fast enough to dodge the hit, and took the pan hard on the side of his head. He staggered. Jack cracked the pan onto the bloke's arm. The thug shouted in pain, and his club went flying, smashing into the racks on the walls and sending pots and pans crashing

to the floor. The bloke sank to his knees, whimpering
as he cradled his broken arm.

Miss Jones shrieked, flinging her handkerchief into
the air.

Jack didn't pay her any mind as he faced the other two
near the kitchen entrance. They rushed him at the same
time. He picked up an iron spit that lay on the ground,
and, armed with the pan in one hand and the spit in the
other, parried the bruisers' strikes. One club caught
him across the back, and he grunted with the impact.
But he wouldn't release his makeshift weapons. He kept
swinging at the two thugs, holding his ground when
they tried to force him back into the corner.

Simon wrestled with the bloke holding the pipe,
grabbing hold of it with both hands and using it as leverage to shove his attacker into the wall. Once he had
his opponent pinned against the wall, Simon rammed
his knee into the bloke's gut. As the thug doubled over,
Simon punched him in the nose. Blood spurted, bright
red, and Miss Jones screamed again, louder than the
bloke with the smashed nose.

As Jack continued to fight with the two other bruisers, he saw Eva swinging the chair at Brass Knuckles.

"Careful with that, little miss," the thug sneered.
"Might hurt somebody."

"Like this?" She brought the chair up and raked the
points of its legs across Brass Knuckles's knees. He
staggered, then landed on his hands and knees right in
front of the stove. She leaped to him and opened the
stove's door, slamming it against his head. Brass Knuckles shouted in pain, but his shouts stopped after Eva
gave him a few more good knocks against the iron
stove and he collapsed onto the tile floor.

Well, goddamn Jack if the sight of Eva pummeling a

thug into unconsciousness wasn't one of the prettiest things he'd ever seen.

He still had his two club-holding attackers to worry about, though. When one of the blokes lunged for him, Jack slapped the length of the spit against his belly. As the thug crumpled, Jack plunged the spit in and out of his shoulder. The bloke clutched at his wound as blood seeped through his fingers.

That left one remaining thug. He looked at Jack, then at Eva, then at Simon, and finally at his friends writhing in agony on the floor of a suburban kitchen. Dropping his club, he ran from the room.

Jack chased him to the front door. The thug pushed a passing man to the ground as he raced down the street, and Jack shouted at the bruiser's retreating back, "You tell that fucking bastard that nothing's stopping me!"

The thug turned a corner and vanished.

As Jack started to shut the door, a bobby marched up the walkway. He tensed, readying himself to fight or run if the copper tried to nab him.

"No need for that language, sir!" the bobby snapped. "This is a respectable neighborhood."

Before he could say anything, Eva appeared at Jack's side. "Thank God you're here, Constable. There was an attempted burglary, and we only just managed to escape unscathed."

The copper blew on his whistle, and in a few minutes, half a dozen patrolmen milled around inside Miss Jones's kitchen. Jack kept a good distance between himself and the police, hovering at the edge of the room, keeping his face in the shadows.

"What the hell happened?" one of the bobbies demanded, staring at the groaning, wounded thugs. "Beg your pardon, ladies," he added, glancing at Eva and Miss Jones.

"We were visiting our friend when these horrible men burst in and demanded our valuables," Eva said in a shaky voice. "It was simply dreadful!" She ran and threw her arms around Jack, burying her face against him, and he patted her back. It didn't help that his blood was high after the fight, and feeling her pressed against him made him want another kind of action.

"Looks like you did a number on them," another copper said, sounding chary.

"I was at Rorke's Drift," Simon said flatly.

The constables all looked suitably awed and impressed, and Jack had to admit he was, too. He hadn't known that about Simon—if it was true. It had to be. That wasn't the kind of thing a bloke lied about.

"And you?" the first constable asked Jack.

Simon spoke before Jack could. "He was my batman." With a shrug, Simon added, "It's impossible to lose a soldier's instincts. When these men attempted to rob us, we acted according to our training."

"Thank the heavens for it!" Eva added. "These criminals would have stolen our valuables and murdered us, had it not been for these gentlemen's quick thinking."

"Whose house is this?" the constable asked.

"M-mine," Miss Jones stammered. "It happened j-just like they said. Please—take these men away."

"We'll need you to file a report, miss."

"It will have to wait until tomorrow." Simon's tone wouldn't take a refusal. He sounded exactly like the upper cruster he was. "The women are clearly distraught."

The coppers all blustered their agreement. After clapping restraints on the thugs, the police carted them off in a Black Maria. Cramped and uncomfortable, those vans were. Jack had slammed around in it like a caged dog when they'd taken him away, as if he could have knocked the metal sides down. But the blokes inside now were too injured to do more than groan as the van drove off.

"I'm sorry," Miss Jones cried once they were alone again in the wrecked kitchen. Weeping, she covered her face with her hands. "I'm so very sorry. I had no choice."

As Jack and Simon stood with their arms crossed, Eva held out a fresh handkerchief. "Tell us what happened."

The girl blew her nose. "I saw in the paper that a criminal's body was pulled from the Thames, and I recognized Mr. Dutton—that is, Mr. Dalton—from the picture accompanying the story." She glanced at him. "You were so kind to me, and I believed for certain that Lord Rockley had killed you. I was . . . horrified. Outraged. I knew I had to do something."

Eva pinched the bridge of her nose. "God, tell me you didn't."

Miss Jones gazed at the broken crockery scattered across the floor. "Clearly, I did."

"And clearly, I ain't dead," Jack said.

"I know that *now*," the girl answered.

Jack snorted. "Don't sound so glum about it."

Clenching his jaw, Simon said, "You should have come to us."

"I thought it was my involving you that led to Mr. Dalton's death," Miss Jones replied. "I was determined to see an end to this. So I summoned my courage and went to Lord Rockley." She held up a hand before Jack, Eva, or Simon could scold her for such stupidity. "It was dangerous and injudicious, I know, but I believed

I could handle the problem on my own. I said that I knew he'd murdered Mr. Dalton, and that he had to turn himself over to the police at once."

"Which he didn't do," Jack said.

"He laughed at me," the girl confessed. " 'Dalton's an escaped convict, a menace,' he said. 'I've done the law a favor by killing him. They'll give me a commendation for ridding the world of such scum.' "

Fire raced through Jack's veins to hear Rockley's words—though they weren't a surprise. If ever two men had been placed on this blighted earth to hate each other, those men were Jack and Rockley.

"Then he threw me out," Miss Jones continued. "He said I was to tell no one, or he'd make my life even more miserable than it already was. I was so . . . ashamed . . . and frightened, I couldn't leave my home or speak to anyone. Not even my parents. But then, this morning, Lord Rockley showed up at my door. He said that I had to summon the people I had working for me, and that he would take care of the rest."

"And if you disobeyed him?" Eva asked.

"He'd hurt my parents." The girl's eyes and voice were pleading. "I had to do it. You must understand that." She broke down into another round of sobs.

"The bastard put it together." Jack swore under his breath. "The girl goes to him on account of him 'killing' me, then I show up at the brothel to take the evidence."

"So he connects you and the blackmailing to Miss Jones," Eva said.

"And Miss Jones to us," Simon finished.

"He might not know Nemesis's name," said Eva, "but he realizes that there's a larger force behind her attempt at retribution. What could be easier than luring us to her home and killing us all in one fell swoop?"

Jack wished there were more of Rockley's thugs around so he had something—some*one*—to hit.

"We can't wait another bloody minute," he snarled. "It's got to end. Now."

"It will end." Eva's gaze moved to the small windows set high in the wall, where the last shreds of daylight died. "Tonight."

Eva knew the threat had never been higher. None of them could discount the possibility that Rockley had Miss Jones's house watched. They'd instructed the girl to take her family and go somewhere safe for a few days. Things with Rockley had escalated, so the Joneses needed to be out of harm's way.

Eva, Jack, and Simon took a twisting, circuitous route back to headquarters—doubling, sometimes tripling back, changing carriages, riding omnibuses, and going on foot. By the time Eva, Jack, and Simon reached the chemist's shop, it had been hours since sunset.

When she reported to Marco, Lazarus, and Harriet about the ambush at Miss Jones's home, the first response was shocked silence. Followed by every voice raised at once. All of Nemesis had an opinion, and they spoke it—loudly.

Eva raised her hands, demanding quiet. "We're finishing this. Immediately."

"I've got a note here," Simon added, "that will be delivered to Rockley within the hour. We're arranging an exchange: ten thousand pounds in return for the evidence."

"That won't do any sodding good," Jack rumbled. "Saying he doesn't double-cross us—which he will— all we're getting out of him is money. He'll continue grinding people into the dirt. Nothing's going to keep him from hurting more women."

She pulled out a metal strongbox, smaller than the one taken from the brothel, and removed a packet of documents. Handing the papers to Jack, she said, "Have a look at these."

He studied them. "It's what we took from the whorehouse."

"Duplicates," Marco said. "Forgeries, actually."

"I ain't an expert," Jack murmured, examining the papers, "but they look exactly the same."

Marco smirked. "One of my specialties when I was still in her majesty's employ. A good forgery can be worth more than the original."

"That's what Rockley will be given," Eva explained.

"Someone gets the real things," Jack deduced.

Simon revealed, "I've high-up contacts within the government. Men who haven't been touched by Rockley's influence. By midnight tonight, they will be in possession of the real evidence."

Taking the forgeries back from Jack, Eva said, "His treachery will be revealed. Tomorrow morning, everyone shall know about his perfidy. He'll be utterly ruined."

"But he won't know that when we do the swap," Jack said. "We bilk him out of ten thousand quid, and still get to destroy the son of a bitch." He looked around the room with a vicious smile. "I think I like you Nemesis lot." His gaze lit on her, the cold light of retribution warming to something much more personal.

She could get far too comfortable seeing that heat and intimacy. She could start to crave things she shouldn't have, and leave herself open to immeasurable pain.

Yet her bones, her heart—they ached with wanting him. In the midst of all this madness, the flame of her need burned even brighter.

She busied herself putting away the forged documents, striving for the control that had served her so well for most of her life. The only time she truly lost control was with him. A hazardous thing.

"Now isn't the opportune moment for celebrating," she said briskly. "It's almost certain that if Rockley agrees to the exchange, he'll try something. We've got him cornered, and that makes him dangerous. Today at Miss Jones's was proof. This juncture is critical, so we cannot let our guard down."

Jack said, "I don't get . . . what's the word . . ."

"Complacent," Eva filled in.

"Yeah. Nobody complacent survives Bethnal Green."

"Or escapes from prison," added Harriet.

"Or ascertains the patterns in seemingly random vagaries in a man's schedule," Marco threw in.

"Or fights his way in and out of a heavily guarded brothel," Simon said.

Jack tipped his head in acknowledgment. It warmed her to think how, when first she'd met him, he hadn't given much value to his intelligence, and neither had the others in Nemesis. A radical evolution had transpired.

Simon headed for the door. "I'll use our usual means of obfuscation to have this note delivered to Rockley. I won't wait for a reply, but there will be no way for him to trace the note back to our location."

"How will we know if he agrees to the drop?" asked Harriet.

"He'll go for it," Jack said with certainty. "He won't play by the rules, but if he thinks he's got a way to take us out, he'll grab any chance. Make sure he knows that I'll be the one doing the drop. That'll definitely bring him out, not just his thugs. He'll want to see with his own eyes that it's been taken care of."

Nodding, Simon slipped out the door. Harriet, Lazarus, and Marco tried to fill the time by discussing a mining town under the thumb of despotic owners and managers, but all of them were tense, distracted. Her mind spinning with dozens, hundreds of possible outcomes for tonight, Eva couldn't join in with her colleagues' talk. Through it all, Jack stood off to the side, massaging his hands in preparation for a fight, his expression distant and brooding.

Needing some way to occupy herself, Eva said to him, "Show me how you escaped from here without anyone knowing."

He considered it for a moment, seeming to debate whether or not it was a good idea to reveal his secret to her and to Nemesis. Then, "Awright."

Yet instead of going up to his room, he went downstairs, with Eva following. They walked through the chemist's shop. He stepped outside, and she trailed after him as he went through the narrow space that ran alongside the building. They emerged in the little yard behind the structure. Their breath steamed in the cold night air, as though she and Jack had become half dragon.

He pointed up to his room. "Just opened the window, climbed out and down. Simple."

"Not so simple." She stared up at the thirty-foot climb. "There isn't much to hold on to, and if you'd fallen, you could have broken something. A leg, or your neck."

He shrugged. "Something any housebreaker worth his picks knows how to do."

Rolling her eyes, she said, "Let me be impressed, damn it. For a man with so much braggadocio, you can be ridiculously modest sometimes."

"Bragga—"

"It means swagger, confidence. Arrogance."

He snorted. "Yeah, I've got that. But I don't see the point in talking up something that anyone can do."

"Not anyone." She glanced around the yard, dark and bare. "Desmond—he's on assignment, so you haven't met him yet—he tried to start a garden out here. A vegetable patch and some flowers."

Jack scraped the toe of his boot through the dirt. "You couldn't grow rocks out here."

"For a year, Des kept at it. We'd find him out here at all hours, digging in the dirt, muttering over seeds and soil composition." She nudged a dried, twisted root with her shoe. "But nothing took. Drove him half mad."

"My ma said her grandda could grow anything anywhere. He'd drop a pebble into the dust and a whole cabbage would spring up, or so she told us."

"Did you know him?"

Jack stuffed his hands into his pockets and scuffed around in the dirt. "He was long dead by the time me and Edith came around. And Ma hadn't seen or spoken to her kin since she was a girl. She came to London looking for work." He made a low sardonic sound. "Turned out right dandy for her. Wasn't no more than six and twenty when she died."

A long life, by Bethnal Green standards. Daily, Eva had evidence of the cruelty of humanity, yet it never failed to pierce her whenever she confronted it again. Was it any wonder she fought so hard to keep herself protected?

Looking over at Jack as he moodily contemplated the barren soil, that same piercing sensation struck her. She was too vulnerable to him—yet she couldn't stop herself from wanting him.

They both turned at the sound of footsteps. Lazarus appeared at the edge of the yard. "Oi, you two. Simon's back."

Upstairs, they found Simon surrounded by the others. He was keen as a knife about to be thrown. "It's done. We're meeting Rockley at two in the morning, at the Tower Bridge construction site. No one will be there at that hour, so there's less chance of a passerby getting caught in the crossfire."

Nobody disputed that there *would* be crossfire.

The clock on the mantel showed the hour to be several minutes past ten. Fortifying themselves with coffee, the members of Nemesis and Jack gathered around the table to discuss strategy. Lazarus drew up a map of the construction site, and they used this to plot out their positions and tactics. Every eventuality was considered—but no one had the gift of precognition. Situations might arise that no one could foresee. The consolation was that everyone had enough training to handle the unexpected.

By midnight, the air had grown thick with strategies and possibility, dense as the smoke from Lazarus's pipe.

Simon leaned back in his chair, his fingers laced behind his head. "The only chance we have to ensure the success of this mission is if everyone acts in accordance with the plan." He looked pointedly at Jack.

As much as they'd grown to trust Jack, he was still the wild card. He'd be within striking distance of the man who killed his sister. Such an opportunity might be too difficult to pass up.

"I know my part, gov," Jack muttered. "Didn't come this far just to botch it within spitting distance of the end."

"You've done all right by us, Dalton," Lazarus said.

"It wasn't your welfare that interested me," answered Jack.

Blunt as always. One of the things she liked about him.

"But yours does." Jack nodded at Eva. "I don't like the idea of you coming to the drop."

"Pity," she said, "because I am."

"It'll be sodding dangerous."

"But the rest of this mission has been safe as a nursery." When he scowled, she continued. "Gilling surely told Rockley about me, and the thug that attacked us at Miss Jones's house saw me, too. Rockley knows I'm part of this operation. I need to be there at the exchange. If I'm not at the drop as your backup, he'll know that you'll have people stashed out of sight. He'll see you standing by yourself and then call off the exchange."

"Then have Simon in plain sight," Jack countered.

"I have to be there," she insisted. "I've worked on this mission from the beginning, and I'm not crawling away to hide now that we're almost at the end. The decision isn't yours to make, but I need you to have faith in me."

"I've got plenty of faith in you," he said. "It's Rockley and his men I don't trust."

"Me, either." She lowered her voice. "And that's why I need to be there to make certain you're safe. No one I trust with your safety more than me." She glanced at Marco and Simon. "No insult intended."

Both men held up their hands. "None taken," said Marco.

Jack was dourly silent for a long moment. Then he muttered, "Goddamn it."

As acceptance went, his wasn't particularly enthusiastic. But she didn't care if he adored the idea of her coming to the exchange. All that mattered was ensuring the success of the mission and protecting Jack.

She glanced once more at the clock. Less than two hours until they met Rockley for the exchange. Despite her assertive words to Jack, her heart rammed against her ribs. In all her missions for Nemesis, none of their adversaries had been as unpredictable, as dangerous as Rockley. There was nothing he wouldn't do to ensure his security. A wealthy—and desperate—man. He'd already tried to kill them. Anything could happen tonight. Any of them might be wounded. Or worse.

Her gaze lingered on Jack, dark and austere as he moodily stared at the map of the construction site.

She'd faced risk before, but never had the stakes seemed so high. If anything were to happen to him . . .

The walls of the parlor suffocated, the tick of the clock deafened. She felt herself on the verge of angry recklessness. It beckoned to her with pointed fingers and glassy eyes. No—she needed control of herself. Yet to spend another minute inside would see the fine threads of her reserve snap.

"Where are you going?" Jack and Simon asked in unison as she bolted for the door.

"I'll be back for the exchange," she managed to say, "I just—"

And then she was out the door, down the stairs, and out into the night.

CHAPTER SIXTEEN

Jack was a man of instinct. He acted as his gut steered him to do. So when he saw Eva bolt from the room, he immediately went after her without a second thought.

She was a fast one, though. By the time he reached the bottom of the stairs, the door to the chemist's shop had already swung shut behind her. He was out on the sidewalk a second later, just in time to see her figure disappearing into the shadows at the end of the street.

Calling her name would just wake the neighborhood. Instead, he ran in pursuit, along dark streets barely lit by flickering lamps. He followed the sound of her boots on the pavement, his own heart pounding in time. He kept seeing her face the moment before she'd run from Nemesis headquarters. A kind of wildness and fury he'd not seen in her eyes before. Worry gripped him like a fist around the throat. She seemed capable of anything.

He turned a corner and caught the flash of her skirts in the lamplight. She headed toward a little park dense with trees and shadows.

The hell with it. "Eva!"

She turned at the sound of his voice. Her eyes were like an animal's—an animal that would tear your hand off if you tried to feed it. She backed into the park, until the darkness swallowed her.

He sprinted into the park and plunged through the shrubbery, shoving aside branches that scratched at his face, until he emerged in front of a small brick shed surrounded by grass.

Eva paced back and forth in front of the building.

He moved toward her slowly, step by step, the way one might approach a hawk caught in a snare. How was he supposed to get close to her? She seemed ready to bolt at the smallest movement. Some small words, then.

"How many missions have you been on for Nemesis?" he asked.

His question seemed to catch her off guard. "Eight."

"You always get this nettled before a face-off?" He took another step closer.

She shook her head. "This is the first time."

"Then what's got you so riled?"

Her pacing stopped. Fitful light barely pushed through the trees and shrubbery. She looked more shadow than flesh, the details of her blending into darkness. Yet he could feel her, knew all of her—a map carved into his chest. He took one more step toward her.

"I've never had so much to lose before," she said tightly. "You could get hurt. Or you'll survive, but then you have to leave. Either way, I lose you."

There was a crashing inside him like a carriage accident, spilling pleasure and fear and anger all out onto the pavement in a heap of confusion.

"I don't want it to happen," she went on, "but it will, and it makes me so damn *furious*."

He was silent. How could he get her to burn that fury out of her? Rage was a dicey thing—it motivated or derailed, and he didn't want her so distracted by it that she might do something dangerous.

"Hit me," he said.

"I'm not going to *hit* you," she said, appalled.

"When anger's eating me up and got me so I can't think, best way I know to get rid of it is to hit something. You'd break your hand if you punched a tree or the wall. So, best thing for it is to hit me." He stood with his arms at his sides, presenting himself as a target.

Still, she hesitated. So he held up his hands, palms out. "Use these. Like sparring pads."

For another moment, she didn't move. Then she landed a jab in his palm. He kept his feet, but the strength in her punch came as a surprising certainty.

"I can't let myself lose control," she said, keeping her knuckles pressed against his palm. "I can't disappoint Nemesis. I can't let *you* down."

A throb made itself at home between his ribs, the pain much greater than the dull ache in his hands. "Won't happen." He closed his fingers around her fist. Held it against his palm.

She stared up at him. He lifted his free hand up to cradle the back of her head and kissed her, swallowing her doubt with his lips. She tasted of night and spice, and he drank her down, wanting her breath to replace his own, needing the feel of her mouth. He'd meant the kiss to be some kind of comfort, but hunger roared to life the moment he touched her.

She returned the kiss with her own sharp need. Her mouth opened to him, her tongue slicked against his, and he felt that stroke all the way down to his cock.

Releasing her fist, he curved his hand around her waist. When he pushed his hips against hers, she widened her legs. He walked them backward, until she leaned on the brick wall, and he pressed himself against her. Her hands gripped his arse, fingernails digging into him as she urged him closer. He groaned at the feel of her cradling him and her desperate demand. Not shy, his Eva.

Hazily, he was glad of the hour's lateness. No one was in the park except him, Eva, and the nighttime. No one to hear her gasps as he rocked his hips into hers, or his animallike sounds.

Something seemed to drive them, some urge that pushed them both. A wild hunger that wanted to defy the danger looming ahead. Within the next few hours, either they'd win out against Rockley or everything would go to hell.

He wanted all of her. For as long as he could have her.

As she seemed to want him. Their kiss grew more urgent, starving.

With a brutal groan, he pulled back. "Need to be inside you."

"Yes," she gasped, undoing the buttons of his trousers. They kissed, mouths open, panting with need. His body pressed against hers as they leaned against the wall. She was slim and strong beneath him, her fingers wrapping around his cock the sweetest thing he'd ever felt. As he gathered up her skirts, he felt the shaking in his hands. Hunger for her shuddered through him.

If only the damn world could stop. If we'd just have this forever.

He stroked up her legs, over her stockings, until he found the bare skin of her thighs. She shook, too. He tugged her drawers down, and she kicked them away. And then he ran his hands over her hips, her arse. His fingers found her pussy's wetness. They both moaned as he stroked between her lips and rubbed the hard bud of her clit.

"Now, Jack," she demanded breathlessly. "No more waiting."

Grateful for his strength, he lifted her up, his hands

on her hips, fitted himself to her entrance, and then brought her down onto him in one hard thrust. Oh, God, she was so slick, so tight around him. She gasped, her breath hot on his neck and her arms around his shoulders.

For a moment, he couldn't do anything, couldn't move, only felt her surrounding him and the beat of her heart against his. Then she shifted, a slight movement of her hips, and he was gone.

He thrust up into her, using the wall for leverage. Her heels hooked around his calves. He sank into her with thick, deep strokes. *Too rough?* Yet she only held him tighter, and her gasps came quick and hot with every thrust.

"*This* is for you and me," he growled. "We'll never lose this." He punctuated his words with his hips driving against hers.

She moaned his name—the best thing he'd ever heard. As contained as she kept herself, only he could make her feel this way, could push her beyond the limits of her control.

He shifted, making sure that with each thrust, he ground against her clit. Her whole body tensed, and just in time, he covered her lips with his, swallowing her cry as she came. But he couldn't be satisfied, not until she cried out again, and once more.

As she continued to tremble, he lifted her up and off him. She was pliant, her eyes gone heavy-lidded, as he turned her around and placed her hands on the wall. Gazing back at him, she arched her back, lifting her hips in bold invitation.

"Never seen anything prettier," he rasped.

He grasped her hips, then drove into her. Already pushed to the edge of his restraint, he couldn't keep himself from moving hard and fast, his strokes into her almost brutal. Yet she met him eagerly, pushing herself back onto him as if she couldn't get enough of him.

He could never have enough of Eva. The heat of her, this hidden wild woman who was his alone. That they were both fully dressed but bare in the most important places only sharpened his excitement.

It took more control than he knew he had to pull out a moment before his seed shot from him, his orgasm hot and relentless. God, how he wanted to come inside her. But even lost in pleasure and need, he had to be smart.

Still, he bent over her, her back curved against his chest, as they struggled to breathe. She felt small beneath him, almost delicate, but he wasn't fooled. She was every bit as strong as him, maybe stronger. Such a fighter, his Eva, so full of fire.

He nuzzled her nape, inhaling the scent of her skin, her sweat, and when he scraped his teeth over the skin, she gave a little tremble of pleasure. His own legs felt shaky.

Time slipped away. Nothing either of them could do to stop it.

Fishing around in his pocket, he found a handkerchief, and used it to clean them both. Slowly, they collected themselves, righting their clothing.

"They'll know what we've been up to," he said, tucking strands of her hair behind her ear.

"Can't bring myself to give a damn."

He bent and kissed her. "That's my lass."

A flash of loss crossed her face, and he realized that he'd spoken of something that couldn't ever be. She wasn't his lass. Just as she'd said, surviving tonight meant they'd have to go their separate ways—her to the life she'd built for herself and him to an unknown future. He'd never given much thought to what the future held for him. As he and Eva left the park and walked back toward Nemesis headquarters, he saw that if he did live past tonight, the time ahead without her would be emptier than the heath surrounding Dunmoor Prison.

As Eva and Jack neared Nemesis headquarters, she felt herself sharpen and focus—as though she were a telescope aimed skyward and the blurred forms of stars were gaining clarity, precision. The riotous, angry pounding of her heart steadied with each step.

He had done that. Or rather, *they* had, with the heat of their bodies and the strength they drew from each other. She trusted her Nemesis colleagues, but somewhere during this mission, she'd learned to trust Jack with a conviction that reverberated all the way to her marrow.

Natural as oxygen, he'd taken her hand for the return journey to headquarters. She glanced down at the sight—his hand so much bigger than hers, roughened from hard labor—and a sudden, sharp throb pierced her calm. How had this happened? She'd been so careful. But it had. Losing him would be a wound she'd carry with her the rest of her life. But she had to stay here, in London, with Nemesis. This was her work, her life. She couldn't turn her back on it. Not even for her own happiness.

She made herself concentrate on what was to come. If her thoughts strayed, she put herself and her team in danger. Yet both she and Jack were tensely silent.

They approached the chemist's shop, and Marco and Simon emerged from the shadows. Simon had slung his rifle on his shoulder, as he had when he'd been in the army. It was the same Martini-Henry he'd used at Rorke's Drift, and she knew he trusted the weapon far more than most people. He never lost his military bearing, but with the rifle on his back and his expression blade-sharp, he looked every inch the soldier.

Marco appeared unarmed, but she knew that he had a revolver in a special shoulder harness he'd constructed—his preferred method of carrying weapons. Where Simon favored forthright military tactics, Marco held fast to the methodology of subterfuge. The vestiges of being a spy.

Neither men spoke as she and Jack approached. Simon and Marco both gazed at Jack's and Eva's joined hands. Difficult to read her colleagues' expressions in the darkness. They were all of them expert in hiding their emotions. Unblinking, Eva returned their opaque looks.

Jack, however, wasn't as adept at concealment. His jaw formed a hard, square line, and he seemed to grow even larger, more intimidating. A deliberate challenge. His body language said plainly, *I'm not sorry, and if you've got something to say about it, I'll make you hurt.*

Damn, there was that pain in her heart again.

At last, Simon gave a brusque nod. He held something out to Eva. Her gun and a pouch of ammunition.

She took the weapon and bullets and tucked them into her pockets. "I didn't bring you anything."

"Next time."

Marco handed Jack a revolver, ammunition, and a leather portfolio. "These are the forged documents."

Rifling through the papers, Jack said without looking up, "He's going to double-cross us."

"Certainly he will," she said. A man like Rockley would never hold to his word. Of course, Nemesis also planned on deceiving Rockley. He didn't know that, however. Rockley would want his money back and his blackmailers—particularly Jack—dead.

"We'll make the swap," Jack continued, stashing the

revolver in the inside pocket of his coat. "And he'll give some kind of signal. The blokes he'll have stashed somewhere will start shooting."

"How will you recognize his signal?" Simon asked.

"I'll know it when I see it."

It was a measure of everyone's faith in Jack that none of them questioned his instinct.

"When Rockley gives his signal," Jack went on, "I'll give mine. That's when you lads lay down some cover for me and Eva."

"What's the signal to be?" Eva asked.

Jack thought for a moment. *"Bollocks,"* he said with a smirk.

"It couldn't be something a little more elegant?" Marco complained. *"Bach,* perhaps? Or *Bernini?"*

"He'd know for certain something was up if I start talking like a toff."

Marco glowered.

"Bollocks it is, then," said Eva.

"No heroics, no attempts on Rockley's life," Simon cautioned. "We'll provide enough cover for you two to get out of there, and then all of us retreat."

Jack scowled at that word.

"This is how it's got to be," Simon continued.

"So long as we all make it out alive"—he glanced quickly at Eva—"then I'm happy as a goddamn Sunday roast."

She made herself ignore the shard of fear that embedded itself in her heart, thinking of Jack hurt or worse, and pulled a timepiece from her pocket. "It's approaching two. We need to arrive with enough time to get Marco and Simon into position."

As she spoke, a hackney clattered to a stop in front of them.

"To the minute, sir," the driver said, tipping his hat

at Simon. The weapon on Simon's back made the cabman start, but he didn't drive off.

Marco climbed lightly into the carriage. The vehicle
tipped, however, when Jack did the same. Before Eva
could take a step into the cab, however, Simon's hand
on her elbow stopped her.

He said in a low voice, "If there's the slightest
chance—"

"My mind is clear," she replied. "I won't endanger
anyone on the team."

He frowned. "It's *you* I'm concerned about."

"Have I ever fallen short?" she countered.

"You've never had such a distraction before."

"He's not a distraction."

"And she can bloody well take care of herself," Jack
added with a snarl, sticking his head out of the carriage.

Simon exhaled through his teeth. "I know that."

"Then get the hell in the cab," she said.

Fortunately, Simon made no further comment. But
he was still gently raised, and so he insisted she climb
into the carriage before he did. Once they were all inside, Marco rapped on the roof, and they were off.
Jack was a solid, warm presence beside her in the carriage. She did not care if Simon and Marco watched as
she took Jack's hand. All that mattered was surviving
the next hour.

In the darkness, the Tower Bridge construction site
looked as if some massive creature had fallen dead beside the Thames and rotted away, leaving only jutting
bones. Scaffolds in various states of assembly clustered
on the bank. Girders stacked atop each other, and cranes
waited like vultures. Metal tracks crisscrossed the
ground, partially completed. Construction had only re-

cently begun, with the support structures still being built before the real work could start. Eva had seen sketches of the proposed bridge in the newspaper, but it was difficult to imagine such an engineering marvel could emerge from this chaos.

That was a concern saved for the construction workers and engineers. Right now, she was more worried about the number of places Rockley might hide his own hired guns, and the treacherous terrain. With the moon waning and only a few lamps casting dim pools of light here and there, shadows were too abundant. But the darkness could be Nemesis's friend, too.

She and the others approached on foot, having left the cab several blocks back. The shapes of the scaffolds rose up out of the night, and the only sounds came from the river slapping against the pilings. The site was deserted.

"I'd expect this place to be patrolled," she whispered to Jack.

"Wager Rockley paid off the guards," he answered under his breath. "No witnesses."

The swap was to take place in an open expanse, with the river on one side and a grouping of temporary buildings that served as construction offices on the other. Crates and piles of timber formed the final boundaries of the site. Jack and Eva would meet Rockley in the middle of the expanse.

With a silent hand signal, Simon had them stop. He pointed to the tallest scaffold, a structure three stories high. More crates clustered at the very top of the scaffold. It would make an excellent vantage for someone armed with a rifle. By the time Eva glanced back at Simon, he'd already disappeared.

Marco nodded toward a tall stack of metal sheets near the exchange site. It would serve as good cover for him as he kept an eye on the proceedings. Then he, like Simon, melted into the darkness.

Jack and Eva were alone.

The time was nearly two, but she allowed herself just a moment to simply look at him, just as he looked at her. He'd grown no less large or powerful in the time she had known him. The lamps' flickering light only highlighted the hard contours of his face, the breadth of his shoulders. To anyone first seeing him, he seemed exactly like the kind of man one didn't want to meet in a dark, deserted place.

Yet, only an hour earlier, they'd given each other a fierce, desperate pleasure, and it still resonated through her body. He'd kissed her with passion and care, his big, rough hands cupping her face tenderly. And he stared at her now with an expression both warm and fierce.

"Can't kiss you now." His voice was a low rumble, meant for her ears alone. "If Rockley's watching—"

"We won't give him any advantage." A personal attachment could be exploited.

"But, God, how I want to taste you again. One last time."

"Not the last time," she insisted. "We stick to the plan, we punish Rockley, we survive."

"Holding you to that," he said.

She drew in a breath. "The orchestra's tuned. Now we play the final movement."

They were silent for a moment. Then, together, they walked toward the exchange site, weaving between the stacks of building materials and crates, until they reached one end of the open area. The space itself was the length of three train cars and exposed enough to give any hidden gunman a decent shot.

Two men appeared at the other end. One of them

was the hulking tower of muscle, Ballard. Despite the other man's dark clothing, she recognized him immediately: Rockley. He held a case, presumably containing ten thousand pounds.

Jack muttered a curse. Hatred seemed to pour out of him in unseen surges. But he didn't rush toward Rockley. He kept his ground, waiting.

"He's got more men with him," Jack said, low enough for only her to hear.

"I see two lurking behind those crates to the right," she whispered back.

"And two more off to the left."

Not unexpected, but still troubling. They were outnumbered. At the least, they had Marco and Simon to help. "It's going to be a fighting retreat."

"Always knew it would be." He seemed eager for it, in fact.

"Ready?" Eva whispered.

He nodded, terse.

Yet they hadn't taken more than a step before Rockley's command cut through the stillness. "Just you, Dalton. The woman remains behind."

She and Jack exchanged a look, his gaze showing clear reluctance to leave her, but they knew they'd have to capitulate in order to complete the trade.

"Then your man stays put," Jack shouted back.

A taut silence, and then, "So be it."

Jack inhaled, and moved to take a step.

She couldn't stop herself. "Jack."

He stopped without looking back.

"Be careful." Minimal words, but they were all she could offer.

After a moment, he said, "Same to you."

She smiled faintly to herself. A fine pair of poets they were.

Her smile died as Jack walked away. There was nothing for her to do now but wait, watch, and hope.

Jack felt every step like an earthquake. He wondered why the scaffolds didn't collapse and the ground didn't shudder. It seemed as if he could break the whole sodding planet apart with each step forward.

The distance between him and Rockley narrowed. It was dark, so Jack couldn't see the bastard's face very well, but it didn't matter. Rockley's polished, handsome features were burned into his mind. He knew his face, his gait, his voice. He was like one of those diseases that ate a body from the inside out, always there, impossible to fully remove. Rockley was Jack's sickness. After tonight, either Jack would be cured, or the disease would kill him.

He and Rockley faced each other. A distance of five feet separated them. Such a small distance. Jack could snap his neck before any of Rockley's men could make a move. But this was about more than blood for blood.

Jack held up the portfolio. "Got the papers. I want to see the money."

Rockley lifted the case. "It's here. But I want to verify the documents are genuine."

"And I don't want you giving me bundles of newspaper topped by a few pound notes."

Jack and Rockley edged close enough to each other so that they could reach for the cases. Both of them were silent and tense as they extended their arms, then made the swap. He and the lord eyed each other warily as they examined their respective goods.

Flipping open the case, Jack saw rows of ten-pound notes neatly bundled with ribbon. He pulled out one of the bundles and ran his thumb over the money, then did the same with all of the packets. It was all there. Ten thousand pounds.

All the more reason to distrust Rockley. The son of a bitch would never part with that much money, despite the fact that he could afford it ten times over.

Jack watched Rockley carefully as he examined the sheaf of documents, looking for any sign that Rockley suspected them to be forgeries. After a moment, Rockley stuffed the papers back into the portfolio.

"It's all there," Rockley said.

Jack silently exhaled. Marco's forgeries had done their job.

Now he asked the question he'd wanted to ask for five years. "Why the hell did you kill Edith?"

Rockley's lips tightened. "Edith was . . . a mistake. She panicked like an idiot when things got rough, and we struggled. Hurting her was an accident."

Sickness burned Jack's throat. Sickness and rage. "You should have called a damned doctor instead of letting her bleed to death on the floor."

Staring at him, appalled, Rockley said, "I'd never risk my own reputation, my family name for a whore from Bethnal Green."

Jack had to walk away. Before he killed Rockley.

"We're finished here," he growled.

A smug little smile danced around Rockley's mouth. The bastard had never been a good card player. "Yes, we are indeed finished."

Holding the portfolio, Rockley turned away. He took a step, then dropped the portfolio to the ground. The sound echoed through the construction site, loud as a cannon.

"Bollocks!" Jack shouted, and ran for cover.

* * *

Gunfire rang out. Eva sprinted toward the shelter of several crates. As she did, she cast a glance over her shoulder, looking for Jack. He took a step toward her, but more gunfire held him back. With clear misgivings, he ran in the opposite direction, finding cover behind a stack of lumber.

Making an escape was impossible. The intelligence they'd gathered about the configuration of the construction site must have come from an earlier date, because the lumber and equipment were in different arrangements. The only way out would mean she and Jack had to cross a huge, exposed stretch, making them easy targets. All she and the others could do was fight.

Ducking behind the crates, Eva took stock of the situation. Rockley had disappeared, but his hired muscle shot at Jack and Eva from their positions. There were two thugs plus Ballard closer to Jack, and two men nearer to Eva. She waited for the telltale muzzle flash of their weapons before shooting back. But she had to be judicious. She possessed a limited number of bullets. Each shot had to count.

One of the thugs closer to her made a break from his cover and ran right toward her. A high whine from a rifle's bullet pierced the air, and the thug turned and ran back to his cover. Simon. She'd be sure to thank him later.

Eva heard grunts and more gunfire from Jack's side of the construction site. Her heart lodged itself firmly in her throat. Jack was the one with the money. He'd be the primary target. *Need to help him.*

Rising up out of her crouch, she readied herself to break from behind her cover. As she did so, a large, dark shape loomed in front of her. She dove to the ground a moment before a pistol barked and a bullet slammed

into the crate behind her. Had she been any slower, that
bullet would've gone right through her skull.

Eva hit the ground and fired at the same time. The
muzzle flash illuminated one of Rockley's thugs lunging toward her. Then he groaned and fell heavily to the
ground.

Getting to her feet, she warily approached the fallen
man. He clutched his shoulder, blood dripping through
his fingers.

She picked up the thug's gun and shoved it into her
handbag. A quick patting down of his body uncovered
no other weapons. He wouldn't be going anywhere.

More shots rang out from across the construction
site. She heard Jack's cursing and the thumps of fists
meeting flesh. From the sound of things, he was outnumbered. After making certain that her gun was fully
loaded, she ran toward him.

CHAPTER SEVENTEEN

The instant the first shot rang out, Jack's only thought was for Eva. It didn't matter that he knew she could take care of herself—he acted on instinct, and that instinct demanded he protect her. But the gunfire kept him from going to her. No choice but to find his own cover and hope like hell she did the same.

He threw himself behind a stack of wooden planks and immediately returned fire. Strange to fire a gun again after so long. It'd always been a last resort.

No sign of Rockley. The bastard had snuck off. His men stayed behind, though, trading shots with Jack and the other members of Nemesis. Jack's only relief came when he saw the flash of Eva's gun from the other side of the construction yard.

Firing guns in the middle of the night was a sure way to attract the coppers, and it didn't surprise Jack when Rockley's hired men stopped shooting. Tense silence fell. He crept forward, snaking his way between crates and piles of metal. The damned escape routes weren't where they were supposed to be. A fight it had to be, then.

The thugs had to be taken out. They'd keep coming after him, trying to get the money back, unless he stopped them first.

He needed to lure them out into the open. Reaching down, he grabbed a heavy piece of metal and threw it. It landed with a loud clang in an open space between several crates. Two of the thugs rushed out of the shadows, thinking to ambush him. But they stood in confusion when they found only the wrench lying on the ground.

Wordlessly, Jack charged the men from behind. He rammed his elbow into the head of one of the men, and the bloke went sprawling. With a punch to the jaw, Jack knocked him out. That left the second chap. The thug raised his gun to fire, but Jack snatched up a piece of wood and flung it at him. The board smacked against the man's forearm, throwing off his aim. As the shot went wild, Jack lunged.

He twisted the gun out of the bloke's hand. As soon as the gun fell, he plowed his fist into the thug's chest. As the man gasped, Jack grabbed his hair and rammed his head down onto Jack's knee. Wasn't a move he used often in the ring, being quick and not particularly showy, but he was after far more than prize money here. And he was fighting with only one hand, since he had to keep a good grip on the case full of money. The chap was out before he hit the ground.

Two blokes down. Got to get to Eva.

Ballard stepped into his path. "His lordship wants his blunt back."

Jack stared at the younger version of himself. He may have been younger, but he was still as big as Jack, with arms as big around as pier pilings. There was experience in Ballard's eyes, though he hadn't yet seen the worst of life. Ballard still had the shine of possibility, as if he could face down whatever this world threw at him. Enough time with Rockley would change all that.

"Got the sound of Seven Dials in your voice," Jack

said. "That's how Rockley likes it. Too poor to care that we're being used."

"If it ain't me," Ballard said, "it'll be someone else."

"Don't make it right."

The young bloke only shrugged. "Right don't keep a roof over my head or pay for beer."

"There's more in the world than beer and keeping the rain out." Jack didn't know why he tried to talk to the chap, instead of simply laying into him. But he'd seen too many echoes of himself lately, too many roads he could've taken.

Eva's influence. That words could mean as much as fists. What would she make of him now, trying to have a conversation with Ballard instead of just pummeling the bloke? Jack didn't feel softer—he felt as sharp as ever, but with a more precise edge.

Ballard frowned. "Here now, don't you go trying to confuse me. His lordship says to get the blunt back, and to kill you. And that's what I aim to do."

Without another word, Ballard attacked.

To hell with being nice.

They threw themselves at each other, trading punches. Ducking one of Ballard's fists, Jack had to admit that the bloke knew his business. He'd trained, just as Jack had, his strength almost equal to his. Jack landed an upper cut, making Ballard's head snap back, but the younger man came back quickly with a right hook that caught Jack square on the side of his jaw. His mind and vision fogged.

Carrying the case full of money hindered Jack, leaving him dependent on using just one hand to fight. But he had the use of both elbows, knees, and feet. He didn't have a gentleman's pretty rules about fighting. So after shaking his head to clear it, he countered Ballard's attacks, kicking at the weakest points of the bloke's body.

Ballard grabbed his collar, and threw him into a crate. The wood shattered around him. Thick splinters jabbed through his coat and into his back. Grimacing, Jack struggled to his feet. He could feel blood running down his skin as he leaped at Ballard. They locked together, grappling, careening from crate to piles of girders to stacks of lumber. All the while, they threw punches and rammed knees and elbows into each other, with Ballard fighting to get the case from Jack.

Jack swallowed a groan as Ballard slammed an elbow into his ribs. Something cracked, filling him with a red film of pain.

A damn good fighter, Ballard. Even the brawl with the bullies at Mrs. Arram's hadn't been this rough, and none of those blokes had held back.

If Jack could walk away from this fight, he'd consider it a damn miracle. But he had to keep going. He had to get to Eva. He shoved at Ballard, trying to break free.

A revolver barked. He turned just in time to see one of the other hired thugs fall to the ground, gripping his bleeding thigh. The gun he'd been holding now lay upon the ground. And standing over him, Webley in hand, was Eva. Jack saw it all in an instant: the thug had been drawing a bead on him while he fought with Ballard, and Eva had shot the bloke before he could pull the trigger.

She now picked up the thug's dropped gun and stuck it in her handbag. From the sound of metal clanging on metal, she'd added the weapon to a growing collection.

Eva's presence distracted Ballard long enough for Jack to land a punch right in the center of his face.

Blood shot from the other man's nose as the bone crunched beneath Jack's fist. But the chap didn't go down. He stayed standing and fought. If Jack wasn't on the receiving end of Ballard's punches, he'd be impressed by the bloke's heart. No wonder Rockley had picked him out of all the other bruisers. Ballard took a lot of punishment, and dished out plenty of his own.

He should give the case to Eva, but that'd make her more of a target. He had to hang on to it. Drawing a breath, Jack steadied himself before launching into another round of blows. It was going to be a long fight.

Eva had never seen two men more determined to beat the hell out of each other. She'd witnessed Jack in some brutal fights before, but none of his opponents had been so much his equal. As he and Ballard continued to brawl, she had the mad notion that the whole of London would succumb to the ravages of time, collapsing around the two men as they fought.

If she tried to get in the middle of it, even to help, she'd only make Jack's job that much more difficult. She'd be a liability.

Behind her, she heard the ping of Marco's gun ricocheting off a metal plate, followed by someone returning gunfire. Was it Rockley? Another of his hired brutes? With the darkness heavy over the site, it was difficult to know who was where. Even an expert sniper like Simon would have trouble spotting his targets.

She whirled as heavy footfalls approached. There wasn't time to reload or aim before one of the remaining thugs, running from Marco's shots, plowed into her. She went sprawling, losing her gun and her handbag. *Hell.*

She just had time to clamber to her feet before the

thug swung at her, and she ducked beneath the blow. They danced like this, as he threw punches and she evaded the hits. He had size, strength, and reach on her. Impossible for her to match him that way.

Light spilled on the ground behind the thug, cast by one of the lamps.

She waited. Until the precise moment when the thug threw another punch, and his equilibrium was off. Then she moved. She hiked up her skirts and kicked him in the chest. Unbalanced and propelled by the momentum of the kick, the thug stumbled backward, right into the pool of light.

There was the crack of a rifle. Her attacker jerked as a bullet hit his arm. He shouted in pain. The thug looked at her, then into the darkness where the shot originated from. Cursing, he ran off, vanishing into the night and leaving behind only spatters of blood upon the ground.

Eva couldn't risk exposing herself, not when Rockley might still be lurking around the construction site, but she vowed that when she saw Simon later, she'd thank him for his expert marksmanship.

Picking up her gun, she spun back to help Jack and saw him standing over Ballard, splayed on the ground. The other man struggled to get to his hands and knees, but his limbs collapsed beneath him. Jack himself was covered in cuts and already darkening bruises, his coat torn, and blood dripping from the corner of his mouth. But he was alive. He still held the case of money.

Glancing up, he saw her. He took a step toward Eva. Then stopped when Rockley emerged from behind a crate with a pistol trained right at Jack's head.

"My money," he snapped. "Hand it over."

Eva raised her gun.

"Get that thing on the ground and kick it toward

me," Rockley hissed over his shoulder at Eva, "or I'll plant a bullet in his brain."

She had no choice but to set her gun down and push it to Rockley with the toe of her boot. Leaving Jack wounded and vulnerable as he faced off against his greatest enemy.

Jack glared at Rockley, hate pumping through him. Leave it to the bastard to step in after his hired bruisers had softened Jack up.

"Hand over my money."

Jack's entire body was tense as iron. He was aware of Eva, watching him. He felt the weight of the case in his hand. It carried more than pound notes: a means for Miss Jones to rebuild her life, and some way to put Edith to rest.

But the gun pointed at his head had its own convincing argument.

Jack stepped forward quickly and swung the bag, slamming it into Rockley's forearm. The gun flew from Rockley's hand. Before the weapon even hit the ground, Jack wrapped his hand around Rockley's throat.

Eyes bulging and face red, Rockley scrabbled at Jack's fingers, trying to break his hold. But Jack kept his hand tight around the bastard's neck. He lifted him up, so Rockley's feet dangled.

"Feels good," Jack growled. "Just a fragile bit of bone and flesh. So easily crushed."

"Dalton, please." Rockley could barely gather enough breath to wheeze. "Give you . . . anything."

"Can you give me Edith? Can you give me back five years of my life?"

Rockley only stared at him with wild, terrified eyes, his hands clutching at Jack's wrist.

"You're scared," Jack rumbled. Pure, clean hate burned through him. "Want to live. Feeling alone, desperate. This is what Edith felt. As she slowly died. And now you feel it, you son of a bitch. I want you to feel it. I want you to look at my face, and know who's killing you and why."

Softly, Eva said, "Jack." Not a plea or a demand. Just the speaking of his name.

His hand still tight around Rockley's neck, Jack lowered him to the ground.

"But I ain't going to kill you," Jack said. "Killing you's too merciful. I want you to live. You're going to suffer, Rockley. Every moment of every day. Edith's at peace now, but you won't have any. Never again."

Jack uncurled his fingers from their grip on Rockley's throat. He took a step back and watched the nobleman gag and cough like a chimney sweep.

He turned at Eva's approach. She held a hand out to him. "Let's go."

Jack reached for her. Their fingers barely brushed, then impact jarred through him. Ballard's heavy weight bore down on him. The bloke looked like raw meat, cut and bleeding, yet he was relentless, pinning Jack in the dirt, his arm across Jack's throat.

"You and me ain't done," Ballard muttered.

Jack tried to plow his knee into Ballard, but the younger man twisted to avoid the blow. Jack continued to thrash, striving to get a hit in somewhere. Didn't help that he was already battered and exhausted from their earlier brawl.

Out of the corner of his eye, he saw Eva pull a revolver from her handbag.

Then the gun fell from her hand, clattering to the dirt, as Rockley grabbed her from behind. He wrapped one arm around her, pinning her arms to her sides. In his other hand, he held a long, thick nail, and pressed its tip against Eva's neck.

She twisted, trying to break free, but he dug the sharp tip of the nail into her skin. A bead of red appeared.

Jack's eyes clouded. He thought he'd been angry before.

"A little less fight," Rockley spat. "That means you, too, Dalton."

Fury tore through Jack. It burned along his veins, set fire to his muscles. Gave him strength beyond any he'd ever had. He grabbed Ballard's wrist and shoved the man's arm off his throat. He twisted Ballard's entire arm. The man groaned as something in his limb snapped.

Jack pushed to standing, throwing Ballard off. Fist like a freight train, he rammed it into Ballard's face. Bones crunched beneath Jack's knuckles, and the hired muscle collapsed onto the ground. Black spatters of blood landed in the dirt. Ballard's eyes rolled back. Though his chest moved, the rest of him didn't.

Panting, steaming with hate and swaying on his feet, Jack faced Rockley. Eva held herself still beneath the sharp point of the nail, but she looked as angry as Jack felt. Marco and Simon had to be holding their fire, concerned that they might hit her.

Rockley glanced at Ballard's prone form. "No wonder I hired you, Dalton. You were always the best at administering beatings."

"Saved one for you."

"I'll decline your generous offer." His gaze flicked to the case Jack held. "Let's try this again. Hand me the money. And if you make the slightest move, the merest twitch, then I give this woman a new means of breathing." He pressed the nail harder against Eva's neck. She didn't make a sound as more blood welled and dripped down beneath the collar of her dress.

It was all Jack could do to keep from launching himself at Rockley and tearing the bastard's head clean off his body. But the long night had taken its toll on him. His legs felt so goddamn heavy. He wouldn't be fast enough to reach Rockley before the son of a bitch stabbed Eva.

Moving stiffly, Jack closed the distance between him and Rockley. As he got nearer, he saw white lines of rage around Eva's mouth.

"Slowly," Rockley warned as Jack lifted his hand holding the case.

Jack did as Rockley commanded, moving at a drugged pace. Rockley snapped out his free hand and grabbed the case. Still holding on to Eva, he edged back, putting distance between them and Jack.

"Now you let her go," Jack growled.

"I may as well put a gun in your hand if I do." He glanced down at Eva. "She comes with me. The same terms apply. If you make a single move, or," he added, raising his voice, "if your friends out there try to shoot me, then I stab her. Am I clear, gentlemen?"

There was a long silence before Marco's and Simon's voices came from out of the darkness. "Clear."

Rockley started walking backward, taking Eva with him.

Enraged at his own helplessness, Jack could only watch as Rockley crept farther away, holding Eva.

"I'll make you pay, Rockley," Jack said through gritted teeth.

"No you won't" was the answer.

Eva released her hold on Rockley's arm. She speared her hand between her throat and the nail, pushing her palm against its tip. Blood dripped down her hand as she tried to shove Rockley's arm away.

Jack leaped forward. He grabbed Rockley's arm and pulled it back. As he did, she ducked out from Rockley's grip.

Knowing she was safe, Jack launched himself at Rockley.

He and Rockley crashed into a stack of girders. Jack pinned him against the metal beams. As Rockley struggled, snarling and cursing, Jack pried the nail out of his hand.

Holding Rockley's gaze with his own, Jack rammed the nail into the bastard's chest.

Rockley's eyes went round and wide. He stared down in disbelief at the nail sticking out between his ribs. Blood soaked the front of his elegant shirt. He dropped the case. Feebly, he clawed at the nail, trying to pry it from him, but blood made the metal slippery, and he couldn't find a good grip.

Jack stepped back. He watched Rockley slide down the stack of girders, until the man sat on the ground with his legs sticking out like a doll. The case filled with money lay beside him.

"You can't . . ." he gasped.

"I did," Jack answered.

Rockley turned his glassy eyes to Eva, who came to stand beside Jack. "Please . . . as a woman . . . you must help . . ."

"As a woman," she said, "I'm happy to watch you die. You won't hurt any more of my sex. Ever again."

"One final thing." Jack strolled over to Rockley and crouched beside him. He reached into Rockley's coat and pulled out the folio containing the documents. "All these? Forgeries. The real evidence is already in the government's hands. Papers are going to be full of it tomorrow morning—your treason. I'm just sorry you won't be around to see it."

Rockley's face turned even more chalky. His lips moved, but no sound came out.

"Look at me, Rockley," Jack said. "I'm the last thing you're ever going to see. Take the image of my face with you to Hell. I sent you there because of what you did to Edith. The moment you killed her, you killed yourself."

Rockley gasped, shuddered, and then went still. His gaze became vacant. His chest stopped moving.

He was dead.

Slowly, Jack got to his feet. He stared down at Rockley's lifeless body. The elegant nobleman sprawled in a pool of his own blood, his handsome face now waxy. Jack waited for the feeling of triumph. It didn't come. All he felt was tired.

"Jack." Eva took his hand, tugging him away. "The police will be coming."

He turned from the body to look at Eva. The exhaustion wrapping around him disappeared. She was scratched, bloodied, beautiful. And alive.

All he wanted to do was wrap her in his arms and never let go. But the coppers' whistles cut through the air.

He grabbed the case of money, took her hand, and together they ran into the night.

The back room at Ockham's public house was filled with odd and broken debris: tables missing legs, chairs whose backs had broken off, half a poster advertising Greywell's beer. Currently, it also held all the members of Nemesis, some of whom looked just as damaged as the furniture. Too tired to sit, Eva leaned against a wall, while the men arranged themselves throughout the cluttered room, talking in low voices.

A note had been sent to Miss Jones and her family, telling them to meet Nemesis here, rather than at headquarters. With Rockley's mysterious death all over the morning papers, it was the safer option.

Those papers were now spread across several listing tables. NOBLEMAN'S TREACHERY! LORD ROCKLEY MEETS A BAD END AS BETRAYAL IS JUSTLY REWARDED.

Sunlight trickled through a high window as Harriet finished bandaging Jack's back. Despite the fact that his wounds were more severe than Eva's, he'd insisted that Eva be treated first. The cut at her throat wasn't very deep and wanted only some cleaning and a salve. Her hand, however, bore a deep puncture, and was swaddled in bandages. It would be a few weeks before she'd have full use of her hand. But this was all inconsequential compared to the damage Jack had taken.

He sat on one of the backless chairs while Harriet made her last adjustments to his dressings. Gauze crisscrossed over his bare chest. He was bruised, battle weary—a warrior.

Jack had fought for her, been willing to do anything to keep her safe. Warmth centered in her chest and spread outward.

He caught her looking at him, but he didn't smile. Just stared right back. She wanted to press her lips to his bandages. Feel the thrum of his pulse beneath her hand, and swallow his breath. The seconds kept creeping forward, toward a time when she'd no longer know the texture of his skin or hear the rough rumble of his voice. She had to gather close what she could while she still had time.

"If you rest and not push yourself overly hard," Harriet cautioned him, "you'll be healed within a few weeks."

Jack grunted softly. "Don't know what you mean by *rest*."

"Familiarize yourself with the term." Harriet patted him on his shoulder, missing the sharp glance Lazarus aimed at her.

Jack stood and was slipping his arms into the sleeves of his shirt when Miss Jones and her parents entered. The young woman and her mother took one look at a partially dressed Jack before they immediately turned their gazes to the floor.

"Perhaps we ought to come back a little later," Mr. Jones suggested, red faced.

"Be done in a trice." Jack quickly did up the buttons of his shirt, though his face tightened in pain from the effort. "There. Presentable as a sermon."

It was still scandalous for a man to talk to anyone without a jacket, let alone tucking in his shirt, but they'd long moved past social niceties by this point.

"You've read the papers," Eva said to Mr. Jones.

"So we have," he answered, somber. "A very bad business."

"Given the evidence of Lord Rockley's treason," Simon noted as he came forward, "there isn't going to be much of an investigation into his death. Imagine you're rather shocked by it all."

"Glad, more like," Miss Jones said with surprising vehemence. "But Lord Rockley's fatality . . . did any of you . . . ?" She glanced at Jack.

Before he could speak, Eva said, "Nemesis always protects its clients, even after the job is done. The less you know of the circumstances surrounding his demise, the better."

"So, it's all over, then?" Mrs. Jones asked. She gripped her daughter's shoulder. "My girl is safe?"

"From future threats by Lord Rockley, yes," Eva said. Unfortunately, a woman's reputation was a fragile thing, easily broken and difficult to repair. Everyone in the room knew this, acknowledging it with a brief silence.

"You may find it easier to begin again in a new city," Marco suggested gently.

"I've a brother in Wolverhampton," Mr. Jones said. "He's been after me to join his business there for years. Perhaps now is the time to take him up on the offer."

"We've many contacts in Gloucestershire," Simon added. "If you ever have need, they can assist you."

Mrs. Jones said earnestly, "I cannot find sufficient words to thank all of you for what you've done for us."

"Wasn't no more than you deserved," Jack said. "Than any wronged woman deserves."

Eva handed Miss Jones the case. "And here's something that might make the transition into your new life a bit easier."

With a puzzled frown, the young woman set the case on a table and opened it. She gasped. Her mother took one look at the contents and tottered over to a chair, with her husband fanning her using his hat.

Miss Jones stammered, "But . . . that's . . . it's . . ."

"Enough to start over," Jack said.

Coldness seeped through Eva. "One more thing." She gave Miss Jones an envelope. As the girl examined the papers inside, Eva explained, "A deed to a country estate. It's yours now, to keep or to sell, as you see fit."

For a moment, Miss Jones could not speak. Holding the deed, her head bowed in thought, she walked the length of the room then back again. "I know precisely what to do with it." She glanced at her parents. "I won't be going to Wolverhampton."

Mr. and Mrs. Jones exclaimed in surprise, but Eva, Jack, and the other Nemesis operatives kept quiet, waiting.

"I aim to take possession of this estate," the young

woman continued. "With the money you've given me, I'll start a school—a refuge, for girls who've been abused. I can help them gain new lives, as you've given me mine."

"Are you certain, my dear?" her mother asked.

"I am," came the confident answer. "This is what I've always truly wanted to do."

"An excellent idea," Marco said, and the sentiment was echoed by everyone in the room. This, Eva felt, was Nemesis's true purpose—that no one person or organization should be responsible for addressing wrongdoing, but that everyone labored together for justice. Eva's own parents could not fault her for wanting this.

Miss Jones suddenly looked abashed, and glanced shyly at Jack. "Mr. Dalton, if you wouldn't mind . . . I'd like to name the school after your sister. But . . . I'm sorry, I can't remember her name."

"Edith," he said. "Edith Dalton."

"The Edith Dalton Home for Girls," Miss Jones said, trying out the name. "Would that be all right?"

Eva's chest tightened at the look of pure, humble wonderment on Jack's face.

"I'd . . ." He cleared his throat, but his voice was still hoarse when he spoke. "That'd be an honor. A right honor. Thank you."

"Thank *you*." Miss Jones gazed around the room, looking at each of the Nemesis agents in turn. The youthful fear had left her face, replaced by confidence and purpose. "All of you."

"What of payment?" Mrs. Jones asked. "Surely you'll want compensation."

"We've taken a share from Rockley's money," Simon answered. "For operating expenses. But we won't accept any from you."

The members of the Jones family made sounds of

protest, but no one would be swayed. At last, seeing that this was an argument he couldn't win, Miss Jones's father said to her, "Come, my dear. It's time for us to take our first steps in our new lives." Trepidation edged his voice, and Miss Jones looked daunted by the prospect of the unknown that lay ahead of her, but she attempted a brave smile.

Before the Joneses left, there were handshakes all around, and Mrs. Jones wept delicately into a handkerchief, murmuring over and over her gratitude. And then they were gone. But a minute hadn't passed before Ockham himself came into the back room, bearing a little muslin-wrapped parcel.

"I was to give you this," he said, handing it to Eva.

She opened the parcel, revealing a few one-pound notes. Judging by their crumpled appearance, they'd come from Miss Jones's own pocketbook. A scrap of paper read, *For additional operating expenses.*

After a moment, Simon handed each member of Nemesis a banknote. Including one to Jack.

"The hell is this for?" Jack demanded.

"Everyone on the team is paid equally." Simon met his gaze levelly. "That includes you."

Briefly, Jack appeared as if he'd argue, but then, with a shrug, he tucked the money into the back pocket of his trousers. "Nobility ain't for the likes of me. Besides, I'll need this for when I start over, too."

Eva smiled, but fractures spread through her heart. The clock had already begun to tick. Toward the hour when Jack would have to leave, and she would discover what it truly meant to be alone.

CHAPTER EIGHTEEN

Jack stared at the envelope. It seemed like an ordinary piece of paper, but he knew that inside, it held an entire life. His new life. Sitting on a table in the Nemesis headquarters parlor.

"It's all there," Simon explained. "Fifty pounds. Train ticket to Liverpool, and a ticket for one berth on the steamship *Catalonia,* which docks in Boston. The train leaves from Euston Station tomorrow at twelve-thirty. Oh, and Marco's provided you with a passport."

"You're now Mr. John Dutton," Marco added, "born May 18, 1854."

Jack opened the envelope and studied the passport, including the made-up birthday. "Never knew the actual day I was born."

"Now you've got something to celebrate," said Lazarus, puffing on his pipe.

Jack stared at Eva, standing on the other side of the room with her arms wrapped around herself. Her face had a far-off look, as if she was walking complicated paths in her mind. She hadn't spoken a word since they'd left the public house, not even the entire way back to headquarters, when she'd sat opposite him in the growler. As if she was already getting used to him being gone.

"Guess I do," he said, distracted.

"Vengeance, for one thing," Harriet noted. "Rockley's not only dead, but disgraced. That's got to give you satisfaction."

At one point, Jack would've wanted that more than anything. Now . . .

"America, eh?" Lazarus said. "Never been there, myself. They say it's nothing but Puritans and rowdies."

"Got the rowdy part down," Jack said. "So maybe I'll fit in."

"You could become one of those cowboys I've read about." Harriet's eyes lit up with excitement. "A Stetson on your head and a six-shooter on your hip."

Jack snorted. "Had enough of guns, and I ain't wearing that stupid hat."

"What *are* your plans?" Eva broke from her reverie to stare at him intently.

Jack stood quickly, his chair tipping back and falling to the ground with a loud clatter. "I don't bloody know." He threw the money, passport, and tickets onto the table.

Silence. Everyone looked back and forth between him and Eva. Her face was a tight mask, clear of any expression.

Finally, she pushed away from the wall, walked past him, then up the stairs leading to the next floor.

Jack left the parlor, aware of all the Nemesis folk watching him. For all that he was bone weary, he took the steps two at a time.

Eva waited beside the window in his room. As he entered, he shut the door behind him. The walls in this damn building were made of paper and excuses, so anyone would be able to hear whatever he and Eva said, but he didn't want to help out the eavesdroppers.

"We knew this was coming," she said.

"Doesn't make it easier."

"No," she said quietly, "it doesn't."

He'd taken more than his share of hits. Hell, he couldn't even remember the first time he'd felt a punch. They were just part of his life. He'd even lived with the agony of Edith's death.

So he knew what pain was. But thinking of not having her beside him, not hearing her voice, not feeling her hands on him or knowing all her sharp, clever thoughts . . . it was like someone had come along and torn him open and everything inside was shredded and bleeding. The way she looked at him now, she felt the same pain.

No—they couldn't suffer like this.

"We *can* make it easy, though," he said.

She looked baffled. "How?"

He gripped her shoulders. "We stay together, you and me."

"What?"

"Come with me. To America. Or wherever you want to go." The more he talked, the more sense it made, the more excited he got. "Canada. Australia. Hell, I'd go to Nigeria if that's what you want."

She said, so quietly he barely heard, "I don't want to go to Nigeria."

"Anyplace. Just name it." He spoke quickly, urgently. *God, why didn't I think of this sooner?* "We make a good team, you and me. In every way. It don't matter that you're an educated lady and I'm just Bethnal Green trash—"

"You're *not*," she insisted, angry on his behalf. "You're one of the finest men I know, and if you or anyone else calls you trash again, I'll punch them right in the face."

He grinned. "There, see? Brandishing your fists like a born fighter. We're meant to be together." His mind churned. "I can start a boxing school. You can tutor, and . . ." It came to him then, and the moment he thought of if, he felt a rightness he'd never known. "We'll be married."

Her face went white, and she twisted out of his grip. One hand pressed to her stomach, she said, "Stop. God, stop. No talk of leaving England, or marriage."

"So I ain't good enough for you." He spat the words like acid.

Her cheeks turned an angry red. "Damn it, that's not what I meant!"

"Tell me what you *do* mean."

She pressed the heels of her hands into her eyes and drew a shaky breath. Collecting herself. "What you're offering me—it's so tempting."

"Then give in to it."

Taking her hands from her eyes, she spread them open at her sides. "Nothing's that simple, Jack."

"Never said it would be simple."

"And my work here, with Nemesis?" she demanded. "I'm supposed to just walk away from it?"

"I . . . don't know." He hated saying these words, but he had no answer, no solution.

"But you want me to choose. Nemesis or you."

He swallowed hard. "Maybe I do."

She shut her eyes, said nothing for a long while, and in those moments, fresh and unfamiliar hope broke apart into nothing.

The raw pain in her face cut him deep. She held everything inside, kept herself shielded, but not now. In this room, with him alone, she was exposed. Suffering. Her pain rang through him, metal against bone.

When she opened her eyes, they gleamed wetly. "It's got to be Nemesis, Jack. It always has to be Nemesis. I've dedicated everything to our work. That's my choice. I'm staying here."

There was a strange rushing sound in his ears. Someone had wrapped metal bands around his ribs, because he couldn't breathe. He turned away from her and stared out the window, but all he saw was emptiness.

"And now you hate me," she said, sounding far away.

"Can't do that." He looked back at her, but the sunlight had bleached his eyes, and she was a ghost in the middle of the room. "But you need to do something for me now."

"Anything," she answered at once.

"Tomorrow, when I leave, I bet you're going to go somewhere, someplace that's your favorite, the place that always cheers you up."

She thought about it, then gave a small smile. "The British Museum."

"Take me there now."

"Been quite tight-lipped about your interest in museums."

"Never gone to one. But when I think of you tomorrow, and the days after that, I want to be able to see you. Want to picture you where you're happiest."

Her smile faded away.

Then she took his hand, and together they left his room. No one in the parlor said anything as Jack and Eva came downstairs. They kept quiet, too, when he and Eva left headquarters.

Instead of taking a cab, Jack and Eva walked to Bloomsbury. He'd passed the huge building on Great Russell Street before, but hadn't ever had an interest in going inside. Now, with Eva beside him, he climbed the stairs and walked between the big columns out front. It was an odd place, full of people but surprisingly quiet. Eva seemed to know exactly where to go.

She led him through a maze of rooms, each one stuffed full of old things, chipped statues, and big slabs of carved stone. Part of him wanted to linger. He didn't have much experience with things that were old but also valuable. Someone had gone to a lot of trouble to dig all this out of the dirt, drag it across mountains and over the water so that people like Jack could get the smallest look at what it meant to be alive thousands of years ago.

But he barely looked at the objects and stones in the different rooms. It was her that interested him, the way her gaze moved over everything, how he could see her thoughts forming.

"It's always so peaceful here," she said softly as they walked. "So orderly."

"Not like it is outside."

She smiled at that. "When I see these Assyrian friezes," she murmured, "or Egyptian sarcophagi or Roman statues, it makes me think that, for all the transience of our lives, there's something of us that's eternal. Something remains, even when we are turned to dust."

He stared up at a very tall statue of a man wearing a strange wrap on his head, with a long, pointy beard, and stone eyes that saw nothing. "The bloke who carved that," he said quietly, "nobody made a statue of him. But a thousand years later, here we are, looking at something he made. So he ain't really gone."

"So long as we have this," she said, looking at him, "we can remember."

They spent several hours at the museum, going slowly from gallery to gallery. Neither spoke much. But she didn't want words, and he didn't, either. It was enough to be in the museum with him. He'd be with her, even when she came back alone.

When they left the museum, a cold evening drizzle blurred the streets. They took a cab back to headquarters, and found it empty. Silently, she and Jack ascended the stairs and went into his room. They helped each other out of their clothes and got into bed. With his arms warm and solid around her, his heartbeat beneath her ear, she fell asleep and dreamt of kingdoms disappearing beneath oceans of sand.

When she woke, cold sunlight filled the empty room. She was alone. She had a memory from earlier that morning of Jack getting out of bed, saying he was heading downstairs to use the privy. She must have dozed after that. But the space beside her was still empty.

His minimal possessions were likewise absent. She threw on her clothing, forgoing her corset, shoved her feet into her boots and hurried downstairs.

Simon sat at the parlor table. Newspapers and documents were spread out, and he lifted his head from studying them as she clattered into the room.

"He left," Simon said.

She glanced at the clock. "It's only eleven-thirty. The train leaves in an hour."

"Think he was determined not to miss it. I offered to take him to the station, but he wanted to go on his own. Left this for you." He dug into the pocket of his waistcoat, then held something out to her.

A tiny, sparkling bead. Picking it up between her fingers, she examined it. A moment later, she realized where it came from. Her gown. The one she'd worn to the ball she and Jack had attended. At some point in the evening, the bead must have come off her dress— most likely when she and Jack had kissed in the carriage—and he'd kept it. As if it were something precious.

But he'd given it back. The only thing he left behind. She sank down into a crouch, her head in her hands. Distantly, she heard Simon push back his chair and walk to her. Everything came from a great distance now, including his voice when he said, "Come with me."

Numbness stiffened her limbs as she rose. She followed him up the stairs, down the hallway, through another door, and up a narrow set of steps. Then they were on the roof, with the neighborhood spread around them and the bustle of quotidian life. Everything resembled a child's set of toys, as consequential as dolls.

"I never really come up to this place." Simon turned, taking in the view from all directions. "Shame, that. Gives one perspective." He gazed at her. "What are you doing here?"

"You brought me up here," she answered. Pushing words out of her mouth took tremendous effort. Far easier to simply collapse into silence, never to speak again.

"Not on the roof," he said. "Why aren't you with Dalton? He asked you to go with him, and you declined."

Of course Simon had heard every word. All of Nemesis had to have listened to the conversation between her and Jack. Yet instead of feeling the burn of shame because her colleagues knew about her private life, all she could muster was a cold emptiness.

"I couldn't do that," she finally answered Simon.

"Why?"

She stared at him. "My life's work is *here*. I have a job, responsibilities. I can't dedicate years of my life to helping right wrongs and then simply toss that aside for a man. I was the one who ensured that button factory with the appalling conditions was closed down, and the children working there were properly fed and clothed. I helped break the ring trafficking in Chinese boys. I can't leave Nemesis."

"You're one of our most valuable operatives," Simon agreed.

"Then you see how I can't chuck everything away," she countered, "just because . . . because . . ." She swallowed the words that wanted to come.

"Because you love him," Simon filled in.

She forgot how to breathe. Or think. Or do anything at all except stare, aghast, at Simon. There it was. The hidden self she'd kept carefully locked away—even from herself. Now it was out in the open, in the bitter chill of a London morning, naked and shivering.

"Yes," she said at last. "I do. I do love him." The words newly spoken stunned her with their truth. She thought she'd reject the idea, find some way to dismiss it. Jack and she hadn't known each other for very long. And yet . . . it was exactly right.

But it didn't matter.

She said, "There are sacrifices that have to be made—"

"Oh, bollocks," Simon answered. "Naught gets in your way when you're doing a job for Nemesis. Dalton's the one that you want, you should let nothing stop you."

"So speaks the man with a different paramour every fortnight."

Simon's expression shuttered. "I don't play an instrument, but I know when a melody's out of tune." He stepped closer to her. "It isn't your dedication to Nemesis that's keeping you and Dalton apart."

She planted her hands on her hips. "Oh, it isn't?"

"You fear the unknown."

"I was in a pitched gun battle not two days ago. Didn't scream, didn't faint. Not even when Rockley had a spike digging into my jugular." She glared at him. "I think that proves that I'm not afraid."

"Of bullets and bullies, no." Softly, he asked, "What of your heart?"

He may as well have stabbed her, for she felt his words pierce her. God, did he speak the truth?

Images flooded her mind. An endless succession of days—colorless, flat. Fighting battles, escaping danger, but forever anesthetized. Dining continually upon the bitter ashes of self-made heartbreak. Jack had roared into her life, an unstoppable force, and helped break her from the prison she'd constructed. And now he was gone.

She'd pushed him away. She thought it was because her work demanded that she remain in England. But Simon was right. She *had* been frightened. Protecting herself came at a devastating cost—the only man she'd ever loved.

"How can you claim to fight for anyone else," Simon said, "when you refuse to stand up for yourself?"

The unknown beckoned. And she would willingly embrace it.

Eva rushed toward the door leading back down to the house.

Simon was right behind her. When they reached the parlor, he said, "Wait."

"There isn't time." It was almost noon. Only thirty minutes until Jack's train left.

He took her hand and pressed a coin into it. "Cab fare."

She was on the street and waving down a hansom seconds later. The driver looked dubious as she climbed into the cab—a respectable woman on her own in broad daylight would never take a hansom—but he was more than amenable when she waved money at him.

"Euston Station," she commanded. "Fast as you can."

With a snap of the ribbons, the cab pulled out. The driver kept to her instructions, speeding the hansom around pedestrians and slower-moving vehicles. People cursed after them as they raced through the streets. She braced her hand on the cab's front panel. Her heart pounded, but not from the speed. The timepiece in her pocket revealed the hour to be twenty minutes past twelve. Passengers were likely boarding the train.

The cab lurched to a stop, then crawled forward as traffic around the station thickened. Everywhere were carriages, coaches, wagons, people.

"There has to be a way around," she called up to the driver.

"Sorry, miss," he answered. "It gets like this round the height of the day. Nothing to do for it but wait it out."

She banged her fist against the side of the cab in frustration. There wasn't much time.

"I'll walk the rest of the way." She threw Simon's coin at the driver, then jumped down from the cab. Weaving her way quickly through the traffic, she saw the soaring Doric columns that marked the entrance of Euston Station up ahead. The moment she could, she broke from the snarl of people and vehicles and ran full-out toward the station.

She dashed beneath the massive portico and into the station's Great Hall, heedless of the curious looks she received from travelers. For a moment, she stood beneath the hall's soaring ceiling, trying to get her bearings.

A uniformed porter passed by, and stared at her with surprise when she grabbed his arm. "The twelve-thirty to Liverpool," she demanded. "What platform?"

"Platform five, miss. But—"

She shoved a coin into his hand and sprinted off. The crowds were thick, passengers and luggage thronging the platforms, and she ducked and twisted through the mob as she made her way toward platform 5.

Please please please don't let me be too late.

There. Just ahead. Tearing free from the crowd, she ran to the platform.

Just in time to see the train pulling out.

She sprinted after it, calling Jack's name—though she knew he'd never hear her above the shrill whistle or sound of the engine. The train left the station in a cloud of steam. She trotted to a stop, watching the last carriage grow smaller, then disappear as the track curved. It felt like the disappearance of hope itself.

No—this wasn't failure. As Simon had revealed to her, she'd fought for others, now she would fight for herself and for Jack. There were other trains to Liverpool. And if his ship sailed before she could reach it, there were other ships that voyaged to Boston. Whatever it took, for however long, she'd find him.

Intending to head straight to the ticket office, she turned.

Jack stood right behind her.

Neither of them seemed capable of movement or speech for several moments. They simply stared at each other. He looked as stunned as she felt.

Hand shaking, she reached into her pocket and pulled out the bead from her gown. "Forgot this."

"I've got another." He plucked the tiny piece of glass from his coat's breast pocket. It looked like the smallest bit of punctuation between his thick fingers. Then he tucked it away, right beside his heart.

They spoke at the same time. "You came." "You stayed."

She shook her head. "Let me . . ." Stepping closer, her heart pounding in her throat, she said, "My work is important—but there are people who need justice all over the world. There's only one you. I . . ." Her mouth went dry, but she pressed on. "I love you, Jack."

He closed his eyes, and a tremor ran through him. It

stunned her, to see such a large, strong man so shaken. Doubt crept poisonously into her mind. Had he changed his mind? Did he no longer want her? She couldn't truly blame him if he turned away, but if he did, she'd do whatever she must to get him back.

"I was afraid," she continued.

"Afraid?" He opened his eyes, looking angry that she might even suggest such a thing. "I've seen you storm a brothel crawling with bullies. You marched through the roughest neighborhood in London. Frightened women don't do things like that."

"Being with you," she said, "seeing who I could become—it all taught me something about courage. It's more than staring down the barrel of a gun. It means running through Euston Station like a madwoman, hoping that it's not too late to share my life with you." Her voice lowered to a whisper. "Please tell me it isn't too late."

To the shock and scandal of everyone on platform 5, he pulled Eva tight against him and kissed her. She ignored the gasps of outrage, aware only of him, his mouth, his unguarded need. For her.

It was as though all the meaningless nonsense in the world arranged itself into a poem of aching beauty and clarity.

He pulled back just enough to growl, "Goddamn, I love you. From the first time I saw you, pointing a gun at me, I knew you'd be either my death or my salvation."

"Not death," she said. "Not salvation. We are each other's future."

EPILOGUE

"It's a jab, a straight right, then a left hook." Jack demonstrated the combination for the crowd of boys gathered around him. "Got that?"

"Yes, sir," the boys chorused.

"Not *sir*," he corrected. "Either call me Jack or Mr. Dutton, but I'm nobody's *sir*."

Shyly, the boys nodded.

"All right," he said, clapping his hands, "I want to see everyone practice the combination. And if you've got any questions, be sure to ask me."

The boys broke from their ring surrounding him and began to go over the moves. He walked up and down, making necessary adjustments, offering encouragement. One thing these lads didn't get enough of outside the school—praise. But when they came to Dutton's Boxing and Academic Training, he made sure that their mistakes were corrected but their efforts were cheered.

The place had a fancy name, but there wasn't anything fancy about it. The warehouse he and Eva had converted had a leaky roof, the boxing ring wasn't more than ropes tied to posts he'd hammered into the ground, and the desks Eva used for tutoring children were mismatched, usually broken castoffs.

But he felt a strange thing when he stood as he did now, watching the rows of boys practicing their boxing combinations and hearing Eva in the next room taking a dozen girls and boys through their mathematics—pride.

They'd made this, him and Eva. It took hard work, and they weren't living a plush life, but it was theirs.

They'd debated for a while where they would settle. With a new name, a new identity, he could go anywhere. Jack honestly hadn't cared about where he went, so long as he was with her. So they ultimately decided on Manchester. Less worry that he might run into someone who'd recognize him as Diamond Jack Dalton, but close enough that if the London branch of Nemesis needed them, they were easily reached by telegram and train.

"All right," he called out after several minutes, "that's enough for today. Anyone who wants to stay and take lessons with Mrs. Dutton is welcome to."

It never failed to surprise and please him how many of the boys chose to stick around and work on their learning. It also never failed to fill him with heat and pleasure to call Eva missus. They'd been married almost a year ago in a little, out-of-the-way church, with the Nemesis operatives as witnesses, and he'd never felt bigger or stronger than he had when she'd said, *I do thee wed*.

He now ambled over to the partition that served to divide the warehouse—boxing studio on one side, school on the other. Leaning against the door he'd cut into the partition, he watched Eva walking up and down the rows of desks. Just as he'd done with the boxing practice, she stopped here and there to help one of her students with a knotty mathematics problem, or give a pat on the head and praise to the children.

Not all of the children made it out of the grip of poverty. Sometimes the students dropped out to work longer hours at the factories, and he and Eva never saw them again. Sometimes the students just disappeared. But some of the children found a way out, and that was the best he and Eva could hope for.

She caught him watching and smiled, before returning to her work. More warmth spread through him. He'd lie awake at night, half afraid to fall asleep in case he might wake up to find himself back in Dunmoor, and everything had been a dream. But every morning, he was still in the bed he shared with Eva, and she'd snuggle her sleek, naked body against him—and he forgot everything about fear.

He and Eva had new identities, but some things from the past stayed with them. He still had a scar around his ankle from his shackles. Just as her hand was scarred from the nail that had stabbed her.

Battle scars, she called them. They'd have them forever.

He felt a tug on his sleeve and turned. A young girl in a threadbare dress and ragged shoes stood there, her eyes wide and pleading.

"Please," she whispered, "I've got nowhere else to turn. They said I was to find you and your missus." She trembled.

He placed a reassuring hand on her thin shoulder. "You did the right thing, my dear. Go and wait in the kitchen, and fix yourself a cup of tea. Me and my wife'll be along in just a minute."

Tears gleamed in her eyes. Gratitude. "Thank you, sir." She hurried off to the little kitchen that was right beside the boxing area.

He and Eva had picked Manchester for a reason. A city like this never had a shortage of people who needed justice, who needed someone to listen and to help. Though he and Eva worked for justice, they never pulled their punches going after it. Ruthless as Nemesis, they were. They had to be.

When a situation got too rough for only Jack and Eva to handle, other Nemesis operatives would come up from London to lend a hand. And a few times, he and Eva had been called down to the city. They were all Nemesis now, no matter what part of the country served as home.

Eva had written to her parents, telling them of her marriage and the school she'd established in Manchester. To her utter shock, they seemed to approve—of both ventures. Though she never said it aloud, he knew their approval made her happy, which was all he ever wanted.

Entering the classroom, he walked up to Eva. The pleasure in her face at his approach faded when she saw his frown.

"We've got another little bird," he murmured.

She understood at once. Turning to one of the older students she said, "Clara, you're in charge. There's something important I have to do."

"Yes, missus," Clara said.

Together, he and Eva left the classroom and headed to the kitchen.

"What do we know?" she asked in a low voice.

"Nothing, yet. But the girl seems desperate."

"They always are," Eva said. Yet she sounded determined. Unshakable.

Jack stopped walking and took her in his arms. He kissed her—not a chaste little peck, but a deep kiss, full of heat.

"Not that I'm objecting," she said when they broke apart, "but what was that for?"

"Because you're the toughest woman I know," he answered. "And because I love you."

She gave him that look, the one that promised a long and busy night. "I love you, too."

He could hear those words a thousand times and never tire of them. "Come on," he said, linking their hands and leading her to the kitchen, "it's time for us to deal out some vengeance."

Read on for an excerpt from Zoë Archer's next book

DANGEROUS SEDUCTION

Coming soon from St. Martin's Paperbacks

For several minutes, Simon simply watched her. Every so often, he'd lift the cigarette to his lips and take a drag, then slowly exhale smoke. He held the end between his index finger and thumb, which mysteriously fascinated her. All the chaps in Trewyn wedged their cigarettes between their index and middle fingers, but he made this ordinary action exotic. She tried not to watch him, focusing instead on her task, yet from the corner of her eye she caught small details: the shape of his lips as he drew on the end, the way he let his arm casually drop after each inhalation, how his fingers curled around the cigarette itself to keep it protected from the slight breeze. How smoke drifted up from his mouth in a way that was almost. . . . sensuous.

Alyce had seen dozens, maybe hundreds, of men smoking. But only he made it look like a rough seduction.

"You can't smoke on the dressing floor," she said without looking at him. It felt vitally important to act indifferent to him—a kind of balm after the fear that had twisted through her earlier.

He immediately knocked off the cigarette's smoldering end and pinched it shut, then tucked it in his pocket. "Still learning the rules."

"Is that why Constable Tippet came to see you?"

One of his eyebrows rose. "Five other men work in the engine house. Tippet could've been talking with any of them."

She swung her hammer again, splitting apart another hunk of rock. "Abel, Bill, and the others, they know their place. The rules. Not you. There's something about you that warrants keeping an eye on."

"I'm harmless as eiderdown," he answered, sticking his hands in his pockets.

She laughed at that. "Don't forget, I saw *everything* last night." Lifting her hammer once more, she said, "You're anything but harmless." She swung again and smashed apart more hunks of ore.

He eyed the pieces of rock. "I could say the same about you. My arms ache just watching."

"Can't get paid if I don't keep swinging. Besides," she added, "I've been spalling nearly seven years now, ever since I got big and strong enough to wield the hammer. Before that, I was carting away deads." She nodded toward a group of girls carrying barrows heaped with the discards and rubbish that remained after the ore had been cleaned and sorted. "That's not light work, either."

Lifting her arm, she flexed. "This isn't a fine lady's arm. Not a bit soft."

She almost jumped when he reached out and gently squeezed her bicep. It was a quick, impersonal touch, but it made her heart leap like a miner catching his first sight of daylight.

"It's a powerful arm," he said. "Much better than a limb that's yielding and weak."

Was he having her on? From what he'd said about himself, he'd been around working women for years, so he wouldn't be shocked by a female with muscles. But, outside of mines and factories, women were supposed to be supple, delicate creatures. She'd seen a few fashion journals—though they'd been at least two years out of date. All the ladies in those magazines had smooth, white arms. One could hardly think they had bones, let alone muscles.

Proud as Alyce was of her strength, she knew she wasn't the height of femininity. Dainty women didn't put bread on the table. Men did have their fantasies about what women were supposed to be, and that didn't necessarily mean a woman who could wield a bucking iron.

Yet she thought she saw real admiration in Simon's gaze, and his voice was low and earnest.

He *liked* that she was strong. Just as much as she did. A quick, swift pleasure coursed through her.

The constant thump and clatter of the dressing floor stopped. All of the bal-maidens and the other workers stared at her and Simon with open fascination. Women normally didn't go about flexing their arms and men didn't squeeze their biceps. Especially not a man and a woman who'd met just the day before.

Damn, there'll be talk all over the village.

"You'd best be getting back to manning the pump engine. We can't have our lads swimming down there."

"That we can't." He started to turn from her, then stopped. "Does Tippet report to anyone?"

"Why? Do you want to lodge a complaint against him?" The very idea made her laugh.

He shrugged. "Just wondering if he's the final word here."

"It's the managers who run the circus," she answered.

"Not the owners?"

She snorted. "They're snug and oblivious in Plymouth. So long as their profits keep coming, they don't give a parson's belch what happens at Wheal Prosperity." Her eyes narrowed. "That's why you came out here, to ask me about Tippet and the fat-bellied owners?"

It was his turn to chuckle. "I'm just a machinist. As the good constable phrased it, I'm only a cog in the engine. If I'm desperate enough to take this job, I wouldn't do a bloody thing to make me lose it."

She had to admit, that made sense. Still she pressed, "Then why'd you come out here?"

He grinned, and she thought she heard some of the other women sigh. "Maybe I find a nice bit of sunshine in your company."

He tipped his cap at her, and then at the other balmaidens, before strolling back to the engine house. He didn't look back.

Once he'd gone, Alyce felt dozens of eyes on her. She stared them all down, until everyone returned to their hammering, shoveling, and carting. She, too, got back to work, but the arm he'd touched continued to pulse with the echo of sensation, and she turned the words over and over, like pretty, smooth stones.

Much better than yielding and weak. I find a nice bit of sunshine in your company.

Careful, she warned herself. *He's still just a stranger.* A flirtatious stranger, but unknown, just the same. And if the eyes of the law were on him, she needed to keep a protective distance. She couldn't make a difference at the mine if the managers and constabulary watched her every move. Better to keep away from Simon—the bright blue of his eyes and his warm grins and the way he matched her, thought for thought, the way no other man in the village had ever been able to.

It was the right choice to hold him off. Yet when she swung her hammer again, it felt a little heavier, as if the pull of gravity had grown stronger.